The Journning Plague

by

Shaune Lafferty Webb

THE JOURNING PLAGUE

The moral rights of Shaune Lafferty Webb to be identified as the author of this work have been asserted.

Copyright 2024
Hague Publishing
PO Box 451
Bassendean, Western AUSTRALIA 6934
Email: contact@haguepublishing.com
Web: www.haguepublishing.com

ISBN 978-1-922984-03-6

Cover artwork and design by Jade Zivanovic, SteamPower-Studios.com. Other images used under license from Shutter-stock.com.

Acknowledgement

Despite its release post-Pandemic, *The Journing Plague* was lying at the bottom of a box of partially-written manuscripts for some decades. I'd like to thank Andrew Harvey of Hague Publishing for helping me bring a fresh adaptation of the original story into the daylight. My thanks also to Jade Zivanovic for providing The *Journing Plague* its visual finishing touch with the cover.

THE PLAYERS

Journer Ward Minor

The Pilots

- Kai Astada – pilot intern
- Anan Astada – Kai's father and crew member on The Nether
- Usha Kaidador – Kai's mother and former Sub pilot

- Jak Inopo – former Continental pilot and Kai Astada's early mentor
- Ino Paollu – Jak's daughter and instructor at the Lycea
- Paol Inopo – Ino's fraternal twin and instructor at the Lycea

- Gannin Tewel – pilot intern and Kai Astada's closest friend
- Arlin Tewel – Gannin's older brother and crew member on The Nether
- Eff Ganninarl – Gannin and Arlin's mother

- Henneh Sek – pilot intern and Kai Astada's friend
- Rei Sek – Henneh's mother and crew member on The Nether
- Astorl Penn – pilot intern and Kai Astada's friend

The Young Ones
- Asta Kaidador – Kai Astada's sister
- Mig Sek – Henneh Sek's sister

The Raiders
- Ceilu Daibor – the leader
- Doon Gaed'owin – the rebel
- Gaed Doo'naib – Doon Gaed'owin's brother

Ularon City
- Saera/Registrar Brawse – Registrar of the Repository
- Gove – Saera's informant
- Eine Vidamore – Director of the Lycea
- Veeda – the messenger
- Bes Gannaline-ro – distinguished Continental pilot

Quarantine Station Two
- Julyen Koale – Doser-in-charge of the station
- Madgel Swar – Scrubber

CHAPTER 1

Year 1574 of the Modern Wheel

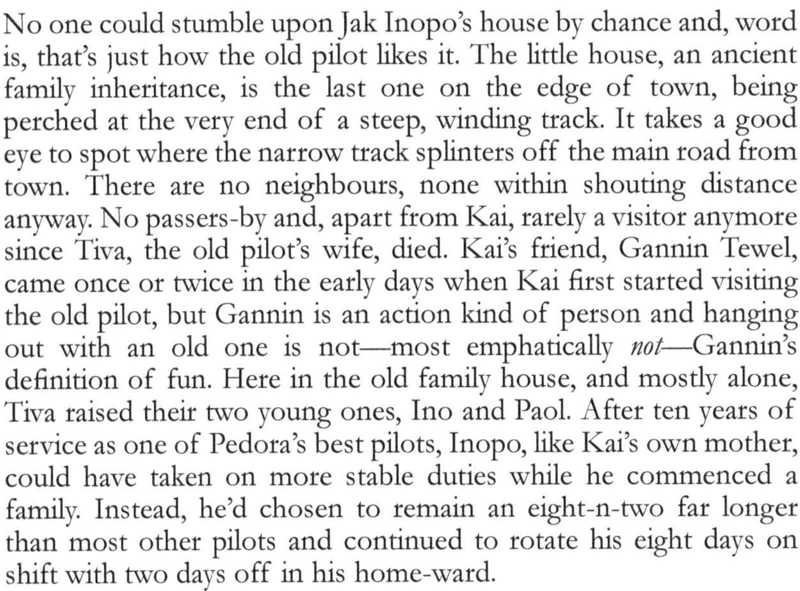

No one could stumble upon Jak Inopo's house by chance and, word is, that's just how the old pilot likes it. The little house, an ancient family inheritance, is the last one on the edge of town, being perched at the very end of a steep, winding track. It takes a good eye to spot where the narrow track splinters off the main road from town. There are no neighbours, none within shouting distance anyway. No passers-by and, apart from Kai, rarely a visitor anymore since Tiva, the old pilot's wife, died. Kai's friend, Gannin Tewel, came once or twice in the early days when Kai first started visiting the old pilot, but Gannin is an action kind of person and hanging out with an old one is not—most emphatically *not*—Gannin's definition of fun. Here in the old family house, and mostly alone, Tiva raised their two young ones, Ino and Paol. After ten years of service as one of Pedora's best pilots, Inopo, like Kai's own mother, could have taken on more stable duties while he commenced a family. Instead, he'd chosen to remain an eight-n-two far longer than most other pilots and continued to rotate his eight days on shift with two days off in his home-ward.

Kai is tall for his age but, at only seven, his game attempt to steady the ladder while Pilot Jak ascends to the roof of the little house is largely token. Since the house is so remote, Jak can usually get away with scaling the ladder to the roof unobserved but if Ino found out her father was up the ladder again, she'd be livid. Clearly the old pilot is taking advantage of her absence. Ino and her twin brother Paol are instructors at the Lycea and they're far away now in Ularon City. Paol's temperament is a little cooler than his sister's, although Kai doesn't doubt for one moment that he wouldn't be any happier to see his skinny old father clambering his way up to the rooftop. As he waits for Jak to reach the top of the ladder, Kai becomes acutely aware of the silence, and it suddenly occurs to him how lonely Ino and Paol must have been every time their father went away. Kai is no stranger to the emptiness left behind when someone goes away—it seems his own father is home barely any time at all before he leaves again.

It's Kai's turn to climb the ladder and his ascent is no easier, the distance between the rungs a challenge for his legs. This business of climbing up onto Jak's roof has become something of a pastime for the recently retired pilot and his protégé. From the roof of Jak's little house, it's possible to see all the way across the wardland and sometimes, on a good day, past the Phane village in Plaited Bay. Pilot Jak has an antique proximer and Kai likes to look through it to watch the Phanes out and about on the water. Kai's view through the proximer is a bit shaky but that's all right; he'll get better with practice. The old pilot says the hul-reed antans the Phanes sail are something to see up-close, so brightly coloured and madly decorated in all kinds of strange designs. The old pilot knows a lot. The old pilot has seen a lot. Someday Kai will see those antans for himself. Someday Kai will see just as much as Jak has seen. Maybe more. But he'll have to become a Continental pilot, like Jak, to do that. Only a Continental pilot has permission to journ among Pedora's hundred odd islands or transit between its two continents. Jak claims that the Phanes sometimes sail beyond Pedoran borders as far as their lightweight antans can safely take them. Kai thinks Jak is just teasing him. *No one* ignores Pedoran borders. Everyone knows that.

"So, young pilot," Jak says, reaching down to haul Kai up and over the last rung of the ladder, "what shall we look at today?"

It's hot up there on the stone-slab roof. Hot and glaringly bright under the searing midday sun. But it's one of those good days for gazing far out to sea. One of those days when Kai won't just content himself with looking at the inlet and listening while the old pilot explains how, a very, very long time ago, a spike of the Karish Sea punched landward, piercing what would become the eastern perimeter of their village.

Jak's eyes have become so sensitive, sometimes he brings his U-visor up to the roof. In most wards, prolonged and unprotected exposure to their sun's harsh rays causes inoperable blindness, but here, inside Journer Ward Minor where the light is kinder, they can usually survive without the protection of a U-visor until old age. Since Kai has never been outside his own ward, he doesn't have a U-visor yet. Still, either Jak forgot to bring his visor today or he decided to go without. He's squinting as he makes for the larger of two wooden chairs that have become a permanent fixture on the scorching rooftop. Kai knows not to sit on the slab roof or touch the surface with his bare hands. Rather, having made that mistake once, he knows *now*. He didn't confess to his mother how he got the blister on his hand, but she guessed. Must have, because since the day he came home with that blister, she's been lecturing him not to go bothering the old pilot. It's no use trying to tell her that Jak Inopo *wants* Kai to bother him. It's no use trying to tell Usha Kaidador *anything*.

Kai follows the old pilot's shadow across the rooftop and settles into the second chair. The chairs can't be seen from the ground. Just as well. If Ino knew they were there, she'd have scaled the ladder long ago and launched them over the side.

"Antans," Kai replies, answering Jak's question, and reaches for the proximer he knows the old pilot has inside his pocket. "I want to see the antans."

"Again?" The wrinkles in the old pilot's sun-hardened face crease into a smile.

Kai wonders if he'll ever get to be as old as Jak. His friends say that Jak Inopo is the oldest living pilot in their ward. Kai asked his father once if that was true, but his father only said it wasn't polite to go around asking questions about an old one's age and that Kai and his friends should know better. Kai couldn't understand why it was impolite, but he accepted his father's word. Like Pilot Jak, Kai's father knows things. He knows what is right and what is wrong, and Kai always tries to take notice of whatever his father tells him. His father is a Continental pilot, too. Not a famous one like Jak Inopo, of course, but then Anan Astada isn't near as old as Jak. He's chosen to follow Jak's example though and has signed on for another ten years as an eight-n-two. Kai can think of only one reason why his father would do that—to distance himself from Ush.

"You should ask your mother to take you out to the bay," Jak says, producing the proximer from his pocket. "Then you can see all the antans you want."

Kai's eyes lock with surprise on the pilot.

Is he joking? Usha Kaidador was born in the northeastern province of Journer Ward Minor, about as close to Plaited Bay as you could get without stepping in it. She spent the first two years of her life there, but Kai has never once heard her express any interest in seeing her birthplace again. If she won't go for herself, it's a sure bet she won't take Kai there just to satisfy what she'd dismiss as a silly whim.

Pilot Jak can't know his mother very well, Kai decides as he takes the proximer from the old one's wrinkled hand and raises it to his eyes. He struggles to focus over the untidy jumble of dun-coloured roofs and ragged hills of his ward. It takes a few tries but finally he brings the blue of the bay sharply into view. Sunlight is leaping in brilliant sparks off the surface of the Karish Sea and the intense glare starts Kai's eyes watering. He blinks once, twice in rapid succession but can still see ghosts of the brilliant shimmer even with his eyes closed. Eventually his vision clears.

It doesn't happen very often but every now and then he's been able to spot an antan outside the waterwall and each time he sees one of those crazy little crafts, it starts him wondering if Jak isn't simply teasing him with those stories about Phanes traveling outside Pedora. There are an unusual number of antans about today, but they're all moored inside the enveloping arc of the high waterwall, close to the gentle shoreline. Kai adjusts the focus of Jak's proximer and scans the village instead, hoping to spy a Phane. The villagers are as difficult to sight as an antan out to sea. Rumour has it that Phanes mostly sleep during the day, screened away inside little houses constructed of the same yellowish hul-reed that's used to build their thick floating islands. Just once Kai would like to spend a day inside a Phane home. Not to sleep. To watch. Three, sometimes four times a day, an Urban en route from one part of Pedora's larger continent to another hurtles along the tracks atop the waterwall. He guesses the Phanes must be accustomed to the wailing. He guesses that, in some ways, the Phanes are lucky. Still, despite the drawback of having Usha Kaidador for a mother, Kai wouldn't want to be of orphan stock like a Phane, no matter how frequent the opportunity to see an Urban. Better to stomach a few years with someone like Ush than to never have the chance to actually pilot an Urban. To actually pilot an Urban has got to be a hundred—no a thousand—times more exciting than simply hearing one scream past.

"Who's that?" Jak barks, snatching Kai's attention with an unexpected nudge that knocks the proximer painfully against his cheek and almost catapults it out of his hands.

That's all he needs, Kai groans inwardly, massaging his battered cheek, a new bruise to try to explain to Ush.

"Down there." The old pilot is pointing toward someone wending their way up the steep track to his door. "Give me that," he says, wrenching the proximer out of Kai's hand.

Kai hopes Jak hasn't spotted Ino. They'll both be in trouble then.

"Just our luck," the old pilot grumps, lowering the proximer. "Duck!" With a bony hand to the shoulder, he pushes Kai down hard in his chair. "If he sees us, he'll be up that ladder in no time."

Kai is left struggling to stay in his chair, backside slipping along the seat. Very soon he'll be out of it, rear planted on the scorching surface of the roof. Beside him, Jak is bent over at the waist, head pulled down past his knees. He's pretty agile for an old one.

"Who's down there?" Kai asks in little above a whisper, figuring Jak wouldn't want whoever is below to hear them, either. He always tries to think through every situation, 'to gather the facts' the way his father says all good pilots do.

"I thought he was still journing. Keep low! Low! Low!" Jak warns faintly but firmly when Kai attempts to scoot back up in his chair.

Kai's backside has slipped closer to the rooftop and he can't see a thing now but the cloudless sky overhead. With a bit of a roll and flip, he gets himself back on the seat. He's leaning a little askew, but at least he's no longer in any danger of falling off. A bruise to his cheek is one thing but how could he possibly suffer and conceal the discomfort of a painful blister on his rear.

"Who is it?" Kai asks again. He's trying to get a better look but can't without straightening in his chair.

"Dinan Kin," the old pilot whispers in exasperation. "Don't let him see you."

That was kind of an unnecessary thing to say, Kai feels. By word and action, Jak has already made that wish abundantly clear and his dogged attempt at evasion puzzles Kai. He has known Journer Kin since he was very little. He couldn't count very well then, but thinking back, Kai reckons there were maybe twenty or so Journers who used to visit his parents on a regular basis. There was Kin, of course. And Jak. Who else? His friend Gannin's parents. Henneh's parents, too. Others whose names and faces he can't now recall. Kai never got to participate in those parties. He was always sent off to bed but he did enjoy the sense of anticipation that preceded them: his father, moving about the house, collecting every chair they owned to set about the table; his mother at the back of the house, shuffling things around in the little room she always kept locked, and then, just before everyone arrived, in the kitchen, preparing more food than they'd eat in a week by themselves. Better food, too. At least Kai surmised so. He never got to participate in the eating, either. But after the second or third such gathering, it became obvious to him that his parents' guests were more interested in talk and the odd game they played than food. Such a shame. Sometimes Kai could hear their talk from his room, although he was never able to make out exactly what was said. It was more of a drone of different voices really—one, then another. He never asked what the game was about, but overhearing the words 'Journers' Leap' now and again, assumed that was its name. He and Gannin sometimes grow tired of the same games and maybe it's that way for old ones, too, because after a while, the visitors just stopped coming. Kai misses that old sense of anticipation but it's nice to know that in the years ahead there'll still be time for games.

So, unless something went terribly wrong in the game and someone got hurt, he can't imagine why Jak doesn't want to see Kin now when they were obviously such good friends in the past.

"What's he doing here?"

Kai's sure Jak is only talking to himself but since he happens to know the answer...

"His mother died," Kai tells the old pilot. "I heard my mother telling Eff Ganninarl."

"Did you?" Jak's tone has mellowed. "Still," he adds with a flip of his hand and a snappy return of demeanour, "that's no excuse to go around disturbing someone."

The old pilot's house being so out of the way, it certainly seems that Kin's intention *is* to disturb Jak Inopo.

And so they wait in silence, listening. First to the hollow-sounding rap on the front door below. Then to Kin's voice, lifting to the rooftop as he calls the old pilot's name.

Jak raises a finger to his lips.

Kai already knows to be quiet and he's starting to get a little annoyed at Jak, who seems to think he hasn't got sense enough to do what an old one tells him.

"I think he might be leaving," Kai whispers eventually. He can hear the crunch of footsteps now and Dinan Kin muttering to himself.

Still, it's a long time before Jak straightens. Kai takes the cue to perch himself more comfortably in his seat. Below them, Dinan Kin has started down the steep meandering track toward town.

"I wonder what he wanted," Jak says dreamily.

Old ones! There was an easy way to find out what Dinan Kin wanted but Jak did everything possible to avoid it! Why is it that old ones *never* do what any kyne a fraction of their age could tell them is the *easiest* thing to do? Old ones sure know how to make big problems out of the littlest things. Young ones have a lot to learn. He'll admit that. Like how to read and write and, for the young ones in his caste, how to journ. But honestly, old ones could learn a few things as well. But Jak's not as bad as most, so Kai decides to forgive him this one small lapse. He didn't particularly want to have his fun disturbed by Dinan Kin, either.

Jak and Kai spend the rest of the afternoon taking turns with the antique proximer. The view doesn't change much. Even so, Kai can't imagine ever becoming bored looking at the Karish Sea. Maybe someday he will go out to the bay like Jak suggested. It won't be with Ush—Gannin maybe. Since they'll actually be *doing* something as opposed to *watching* nothing at all, as Gannin would have it, he might be able to talk his friend into making the long trek.

When Jak declares it's time to come down off the roof, the sun is already resting low on a streaky mauve horizon behind them. Kai would like to stay longer but he isn't prepared to risk having the old pilot fall down the ladder in the dark or to weather his mother's anger for getting home too late. All right, he's already late, but 'late' and 'late after dark' are different. At least they seem to be to Ush.

His walk home is brisker than he'd like and even before he reaches the front door, he can hear his mother moving about in the kitchen. By habit, he tries to sense the atmosphere inside before he steps through the open door. That's another of those things he can't yet understand; how he can sense the depth of trouble he's in simply from the 'feel' of the house. Today his skin doesn't crawl. There's no empty hole in the pit of his stomach. Ush can't be too angry.

"Where have you been all day?" she asks, turning on him.

"Out," Kai replies from the kitchen doorway. He knows better than to go to his room before Ush is finished with him.

"With Jak Inopo, I suppose?"

Kai nods. What's the point of lying? Ush can always tell.

"I've told you repeatedly not to bother that old pilot." Reaching into a little drawer in her workbench, she withdraws a woven bag. It's threadbare and a little dirty. She dumps it on the table.

Kai knows what that means. He steps forward and picks up the bag.

Ush brings her hands to her hips, plants them there. She's staring him down in that challenging way only Ush has. "And three parchis, not two! Are you going to remember this time?"

Again Kai nods as he turns, heading back toward the front door.

So he made a little mistake!

"Make it quick," Ush calls after him. "The market will be closing soon and I want you home before dark."

Sure! Sure! What's so bad about the dark, he'd like to know. Especially this time of year when the nights are two-moon? It's tight confined spaces that are bad, like the tight confined spaces in the market place. Everyone pushing and shoving. Air someone else has already breathed. Produce that's been mauled and picked over by every passer-by. Now dark *and* tight spaces are another matter. But dark and open air? Kai couldn't care a parchi about that.

Three parchis! He's got to remember that!

It would be good, Kai reckons, if he had a brother or sister to share the responsibility of traipsing back and forth to the market. He dislikes having to deal with Vendors. Not that they're bad people or anything. He just doesn't feel comfortable around them. They're not Journers after all and it's not like Journers and Vendors ever associate outside the marketplace. There's only as many Vendors in any ward as necessary, just like there's only so many Preservers to maintain the wards. Enough to get the job done. He actually knows as little about those castes as he does about the Phanes who, so Jak maintains, come wardland to carry out the other menial tasks real Journers simply won't do or don't have to do since the Phanes do it for them. And that's about the extent of Kai's knowledge. Vendors vend their wares. Preservers preserve the towns and cities. And Phanes do everything else.

All things considered, he's glad he was born a Journer. Better if he had been born a Journer to someone other than Usha Kaidador but this world only makes so many offers and only a fool would snub one. Well, that's what the old ones say anyway....

CHAPTER 2

Year 1583 of the Modern Wheel

"But why won't you come?"

Back turned, his mother continues peeling bauma over the sink.

"Well?" Kai presses, shoulder propped against the flaking paint of the kitchen doorway.

Still his mother does not answer. Instead, she goes on expertly twisting the large yellow gourd in her hand. Peeling. Peeling.

There's a pervasive hum of chatter on the street outside, and every now and then, the quick rap-rap-rap of footsteps as someone hurries past. All the same, Kai can hear the 'thunk' every time a long curl of heavy rind hits the bottom of the earthen sink. And his mother hears *him*. Ush never fails to use her slight hearing loss to best advantage.

"You'll have to answer me some time," he says patiently.

If he didn't know better, he'd swear his mother was a Cross. She has the stubborn demeanour of a Crafter, but none of the skills. Besides, he knew his maternal grandparents very well and both were Journers through and through.

"Go then," Ush replies. She could be talking to the gourd. "I can't stop you. You'll be at the Lycea soon anyway and I won't be there to hold your hand."

Kai can't readily recall a time when Ush *was* there to hold his hand.

"Fine," he says, spinning on his heels. "I'll be sure to tell father you wish him well."

He won't get the chance and his mother knows that as well as he does. If he's exceptionally lucky, he may get a distant glimpse of his father. Nothing more. And his father won't even be aware that he's looking.

He speeds toward the door. When Asta makes to intercept him, he executes a deft little manoeuvre and darts past her.

"Where you going?" she demands, limply trailing a ragged and dirty doll behind her.

"To see *The Nether* leave," Kai tells her as he reaches for the door knob.

Lunging forward, Asta pulls his arm away before he can get a hand to it.

"You can't. Mother says so."

Kai shrugs off her tiny hand. Asta, round face tilted up, is glaring at him disapprovingly, black eyes punched like two symmetrical holes in a pale ball that someone has comically dressed with an untidy wig of hul-coloured curls. She's eight years younger than him and eight times whinier that he ever was at her age. For brother and sister, they couldn't look or be any less alike.

"She just said I could."

Asta's focus shifts briefly toward the kitchen. She doesn't believe him. She won't confirm it with Mother though. Asta might be young but even she knows there are some questions you simply don't bother to ask Mother.

"Then I'm going with you," she announces, hefting the doll up from the floor to tuck it securely under her arm.

"No," Kai snaps as he wrenches the front door open and steps outside. "It's too far for you to walk. We won't get halfway before you start whining for me to carry you. Besides, Mother didn't say *you* could go and little kynes aren't allowed."

"Big kynes aren't allowed on the dock, either."

"I'm only going to the concourse."

He slams the door shut, cutting off further opportunity for Asta to argue. But it's true. Young ones aren't allowed on the dock or even the concourse. Kai isn't sure how far he'll get, considering the attention the launch has garnered. He's never been to the concourse before, at least not during a launch. Once when a common U-Class Continental was being launched, Henneh and

Gannin tried. They even had it in mind to attempt to make it all the way to the dock. Of course, they got caught very quickly and never saw a blessed thing. Although that's not quite how Gannin tells it, claiming the pilot even talked to him for some time before he climbed onboard. A daring lie considering Henneh was there the whole time. They didn't even get as far as the concourse, Henneh confided to Kai afterward. She's never challenged Gannin with the truth though despite the frequency with which he tells the story and the escalation of his heroics with each retelling. Instead, Henneh just rolls her pretty brown eyes and smiles. She'll make an outstanding Journer. She has the patience, tact and composure that every good Journer needs—good Journers like Anan Astada, Kai's father. Kai aspires but doubts he's inherited those same essential qualities. At least he's not like Ush; he's confident about that much. Asta, though, is another matter.

"Hey, wait up!"

Kai spins around. He's barely two houses from home and while the streets aren't too crowded yet, he doesn't want to run the risk of missing a possible spot on the concourse.

But it's only Gannin, sprinting full-pelt down the street, heedless of a small group of fellow sightseers directly in his path. He almost sends Jak Inopo sprawling and probably would have if the old pilot didn't still possess some of his ancient reflexes. Kai knows for a fact that, in his day, the old pilot piloted more T-Class Continentals than any other Journer in their ward and his father has always maintained that Inopo was one of the best.

Gannin pulls up in a shower of loose stones. Nothing in their ward is very grand. Not the largely identical one-storey cottages the wardlanders live in and certainly not the narrow little streets that wind haphazardly between the modest cottages, which are regime designed and built of course, like the majority of housing provided for the castes under the broad umbrella of the Pedorate, Pedora's governing caste. At least that's Kai's understanding. He's still never been outside his ward to know for sure. Still never seen the Phane district in his own ward up-close, either. Once he and Gannin defied their curfews and hiked to the high ridge above Plaited Bay. It took them a good three days there and back to do it, but they didn't see much more than Kai had already seen through Jak Inopo's proximer when he was young. And Ush, true to form, exacted a hefty price for the wasted effort when they got back.

"Pilot Jak's still got a lot of influence," Kai reminds his friend. "You're not doing yourself any favours."

Although they're the same age, Gannin stands a good head shorter than Kai. Being shorter and of a stockier frame, Kai is only too aware that Gannin looks every bit more the pilot than he does.

"I'm set for a T-Class Continental," Gannin says, dismissing Kai's warning with a brisk wave of his hand. "Nothing Pilot Jak can do about it."

Set for a T-Class Continental! Not likely! But Kai isn't about to tell him. His own sights aren't set so high. A T-Class Urban would suit him just fine.

Gannin glances over his shoulder. "The old gleat shearer couldn't tell the business end of a T-Class Continental from the backside of a U-Class Urban these days."

"Wouldn't be so sure," Kai replies as he sets off once again down the street.

Gannin shrugs and falls into step beside him. "Heading for the concourse?"

That's Gannin—always asking the obvious.

Kai simply nods.

"Ush said you could?"

"Ush doesn't care."

Gannin's pace falters but he says nothing more about it. Instead, he claps a hand over Kai's shoulder. "Here comes Henneh."

Kai glances left, spots Henneh rushing through the door of her parents' cottage.

At the gate that guards a small and well-tended patch of vegetation from the less delicate world beyond, Henneh stops to let two of her neighbours pass, then raises her hand to wave.

She wants them to wait for her. Happy to, Kai says to himself.

"What?" Gannin asks, rolling his attention back to Kai.

As Henneh turns to shut the gate, Kai notices what looks like a pack on her back.

"Didn't say anything," Kai replies. "Watch out." He drags Gannin aside to let Jak Inopo pass. The old pilot spares a nod for Kai but shoots Gannin the dagger of a glance as he shuffles by. Ino Paollu, Inopo's daughter, is walking beside him. At least Kai thinks it's Ino. She's so easy to confuse with her twin, not that Kai has ever tried too hard to tell them apart. Since both have the reputation for coolly decking a Lycea intern at the slightest provocation and both are also towering giants with the overdeveloped musculature to back up said reputation, Kai concluded long ago that it was best to keep his curiosity to himself. Jak's daughter has one arm locked through the old pilot's crooked elbow as though he requires her assistance to steady him. Kai isn't fooled.

"What's that you've brought us? Lunch?" Gannin asks with a smile when Henneh joins them. He's noticed the straps over her shoulder.

"Hardly," she says, swinging around to display what's inside the pack.

Gannin's smile dissolves. "What did you bring *her* for?"

He's talking about Henneh's little sister, who is currently packed inside the sling-type arrangement securely harnessed to Henneh's back.

"What did you expect me to do with her? Leave her alone in the house?" Her gaze darts briefly toward Kai. "She's no trouble. Anyway, what's it got to do with you?" she challenges Gannin.

"How can we sneak onto the dock with her?" Gannin grumbles. "She could start crying at any moment and give us away."

"She's not going to cry," Henneh snaps back. "And I have no delusions about getting as far as the dock." She starts off ahead of them down the street. "And, judging on past performances, nor should you."

Kai hurries to catch up, leaving Gannin licking his invisible wounds a pace or two behind.

"Why *did* you bring her?" Kai asks matter-of-factly.

"There's no one else to look after her," Henneh replies, glancing sidelong at Kai. "Father has to work." She nods into the distance, "Mother is … leaving," then shrugs. "Mig is my responsibility now."

"Forever?" Kai asks, shocked.

He and Henneh are the same age and just like him, two days from now, she's supposed to start the training that will lead her in her parents' journing footsteps.

"Of course not." She executes a little jump, settling Mig more comfortably on her back.

The little one giggles, drawing Kai's attention. She's a miniature version of Henneh, red-haired, brown-eyed and, in his admittedly limited experience with the young one, always quick to smile.

"Father promised me," Henneh adds.

She knows what he's thinking and he wasn't imaging the trace of uncertainty when she spoke. With her mother leaving, what does that mean for Mig? Will she be sent away? When he was three, perhaps four years old, the young ones who lived next door to him were sent away. Kai has barely given a thought to that fair-haired kyne and her brother over the intervening years. Why would he? The kyne was maybe... what?... three or four years older than him and her brother perhaps six or more years older than that. Kai hardly remembers him at all. Orphans and sometimes those with a single parent too busy or disinterested to take care of them often find themselves sent off to live with the Phanes. It's what Phanes are anyway—generation upon generation bred of ancient orphan stock. Perhaps being orphaned of both parents might have made it inevitable for those kynes next door. However, although Henneh's father is a sought-after Journer and sometimes still travels far from home, he is *not*, by any means, a disinterested parent.

Kai's glance drifts in the direction of Plaited Bay, but he'd have to be right on top of 'Headcracker Hill' to even get a glimpse of it in the distance. That kyne and her brother are probably out there now, living with the Phanes. As he sees it, there are only two possible outcomes for Mig and Henneh. Either Mig's future will be forfeited to the Phanes, which doesn't seem at all likely to him, or Henneh will not be going with them to the Lycea. For his friend's sake, Kai decides to speak no more about it.

By the time they reach the base of 'Headcracker Hill', Gannin has caught up. The gates are open and the residents of Journer Ward Minor are finally at liberty to pass into what has been restricted territory for the duration of work on *The Nether*. By Kai's reckoning, he's been watching the construction crews routinely come and go through the swinging gates in the high wire fence for a very long time.

"I hate this walk to the docks," Gannin says as he passes through the open gates and begins the uphill trudge. "Someday they're going to put a Sub under the southern sector and then we'll be able to ride all the way to the concourse."

Both Kai and Henneh smile.

Gannin thinks he knows everything and has never been one to withhold any alleged intelligence. But there are *castes* even within castes and the corresponding favours that come with the division. The most privileged of the Journer caste don't live in Journer Ward Minor and especially not in its southern sector like Kai and his friends, who must rely on their own two sturdy feet and enough stamina to get them anywhere they need to go inside their ward.

"If they do put in a Sub, you'll be first choice for pilot," Henneh observes.

She's offended Gannin well and truly now. It's common ground for them.

"Only if you've Crossed by then," Gannin snaps back.

Kai has never really gazed too far into the future, blindly assuming that, by and large, every new graduate will be given the posts of their choice. But the matter of Mig's future has him thinking. There are no guarantees. Whatever made him think there would be? All he ever had to do was look at his own mother to know that. Both Ush's father and mother were given the command of Continentals at some point during their careers. What has Ush ever commanded but a Sub? A Sub! For the first time in his life, Kai tries, *really* tries, to visualise piloting a Sub through the narrow, pitch black tunnels. The mere prospect makes him shudder. Tight spaces and darkness, his worst fear. How did Ush face it? Time and time again! In that at least, perhaps he's sold his mother too short.

Behind him, someone laughs, distracting Kai from his bleak thoughts. He turns around to find a group of young ones hurtling directly for them. The crest isn't too far away and once on the summit, momentum will fling them downhill at an unstoppable speed. It's a time-honoured young ones' game. They've all played it on 'Headcracker Hill', but the hill has been off limits for a long time now and likely these young kynes have never had the chance to make good on the tradition.

Kai nudges Henneh and Gannin off to the side.

"Young ones!" Gannin jeers, stumbling on an uneven patch of road, as the group rocket past, screaming and laughing.

Kai's ears begin to ring. Then he remembers Jak Inopo. The old pilot is just ahead of them, out of sight, ambling arm-in-arm with Ino down the far side of the hill.

"Hey, you kynes," he shouts. "Look out for..."

Too late. They're up and over the summit already. Kai holds his breath, waiting.

"What's the matter?" Henneh asks, breathing a little heavily.

Kai looks down and discovers that he's subconsciously grasped her arm. He still has a soft spot for that old pilot.

He shakes his head and releases Henneh when all he hears is a medley of excited laughter bubble over the summit. By luck rather than good planning, Jak must have been spared a head-over-heels tumble to the bottom of the hill.

Gannin is first to reach the top where he stops to point.

"There she is! *The Nether Supercontinental.* And she's a beauty." He turns to encourage Kai and Henneh upward with an enthusiastic wave. His face is flushed, beaming with pride, and filmed in sweat from the strenuous climb.

Arlin Tewel, Gannin's older brother, is already somewhere on *The Nether.* So, too, is Rei Sek, Henneh's mother, Anan Astada, Kai's father, as well as forty or so other Journers from their ward and Journer Ward Major plus a moderate number of support crew from some of the undercastes. There's not a single Journer onboard from any of the remote Journer wards. Journers from those wards aren't called marginals for nothing. Few progress beyond Subs and none expect anything different. *The Nether* will be gone a long time. Perhaps even long enough for Gannin, Henneh and Kai to graduate. No one really knows.

Kai comes to the top of the hill and, reaching out a hand, helps Henneh the rest of the way up. Perhaps he should have offered to take Mig, but Henneh only would have refused.

Henneh gasps.

At first, Kai thinks she's winded but he's mistaken.

"Oh, she *is* beautiful," Henneh cries. "The best ship ever."

Maybe. Maybe not. After all, it's only the second Supercontinental to ever be launched and the first from Journer Ward Minor. Henneh hardly has adequate means for comparison. But Kai has to admit, whether *The Nether* is the best ship ever or not, she certainly is imposing, all silver and shiny silhouetted against the still grey water of the slender inlet behind her. If anything, the haphazard array of large workshops and assembly buildings in the foreground only make her look more colossal.

Henneh is beaming a smile broader than Gannin's.

"Come on," Gannin calls as he starts off with urgency down the hill. "We still might be able to find a good spot on the concourse."

"What happened to making it to the dock?" Kai goads his friend with a downhill shout. Without waiting for a reply, he turns around and looks back the way they came, down 'Headcracker Hill'. Their neighbours are arriving in throngs now. "We're ahead of most of the crowd," he tells Henneh. "We *could* get a place on the concourse if we hurry."

Henneh shakes her head. "I'll watch the launch from here."

"Why?" Kai asks, then quickly glances over his shoulder to check on Gannin's progress. He's three-quarters of the way down the hill.

Henneh swings her shoulder around to remind Kai what she's carrying on her back.

"Oh," Kai mutters.

Kynes aren't allowed on the concourse!

Mig's tiny hand reaches out to Kai and, when he doesn't take it, she begins waving at each passer-by.

"What's holding you up?"

Kai turns to respond to Gannin's barely audible shout. He's almost reached the bottom of the hill, where he is stopped, waiting on them.

Kai makes a quick decision. "We're staying here," he calls down to Gannin.

His friend's arms shoot out from his sides, a gesture of either confusion or frustration. "Why!"

"Mig," Henneh hollers before Kai has a chance to respond.

"Told you not to bring her," Gannin fires back. "I hope you don't expect me to hang around up there with you."

Kai waves him off. "No one asked you to. Go on. It'll be easier for you to make it to the dock alone anyway." He feels a little slap against his back, but Henneh is laughing.

"You'll get him detained again," she says.

"He won't even try it," Kai replies, waving Gannin on once more.

"Suit yourself then," Gannin yells before resuming his sprint toward the concourse. Ahead of him are Jak and his daughter; they've already made it to the bottom of the hill.

"You should go with him," Henneh says, sobering.

Kai isn't really listening. He looks out, far past the striking bulk of *The Nether* to the sea, then allows his gaze to drift up. It's a fine morning for a launch. The water in the inlet is calm and, with little haze out to sea, visibility is at its prime. They'll be able to follow the ship's progress for a long time.

"What did you say?" he asks, shifting his focus to Henneh.

"I said there's no need for you to stay here with me. You can go with Gannin if you want to."

Kai just shrugs. "We'll be fine here. Better than being stuck down there in the crowd." He motions for Henneh to follow him into the grass beside the road. "Here's a good place," he says. "You can even let Mig down. We can watch her. She can't get into much trouble."

"She won't get into any trouble," Henneh assures Kai as she drops to her knees in the long grass and begins to loosen the straps from the sling that's cradling her little sister. Mig tries to help but only succeeds in lengthening the process of liberating herself. "There you go, Mig," Henneh finally says with a smile of indulgence. "You mind Kai and me now and, if you're a good one, maybe Kai will put you up on his shoulders to see the launch." She turns her little sister around and, resting her arm on Mig's shoulder, points. "Look there," she coaxes. "Mother is over there. On *The Nether*."

Mig nods solemnly. "Mother," she repeats a little awkwardly and swings her tiny face toward Henneh. "Home?"

Henneh takes a moment to answer. "Soon, I hope."

It's a hope Kai earnestly shares.

***

Morning breaks uncommonly crisp and cool but, in spite of the unusual chill, the sun is shining brightly. Kai's tiny room is cleaned and his bag is packed, admission papers securely stashed in the front pocket.

It's customary for new interns to take the long walk to the station alone but more than likely the other five interns scheduled to leave this morning are receiving a warm farewell right now. Still Kai didn't expect anything like that from Ush, so isn't surprised when her parting words are brief and cooler than the morning air. Asta is sitting ensconced on the couch, dirty and ever-present doll shoved carelessly under one arm, but she takes a moment to divert her attention from Kai's old school reader, which she has thrust in front of her eyes. *Emergence from Chaos*, the Pedorate Council's official primer for young ones, is the only book on the reader and it's obvious that she's merely pretending to read it. When he makes to say goodbye, she sticks her tongue out at him and returns to her sham study. Kai doesn't care. This is going to be the best day of his life. He is finally leaving Ush and Asta behind and if he never sees either one of them again, it will still be too soon. Whether he will ever return to his home-ward, Kai doesn't know. When, with deliberate gentleness, he closes the door and steps into the street, Kai carries only two misgivings with him. If he never returns to this place, then he may never see his father again. That's misgiving one. And although he's excited at the prospect of his first journ on an Urban, he's also apprehensive about it and principally because of the tunnel. That's his second misgiving. Journer Ward Minor is bounded to the east by water and to the north and west by the high peaks of a mountain system simply known as The Range. There are only two Urban routes in and out of the ward, one over the waterwall located in the northeast of the ward and the other by way of the long narrow tunnel punched through The Range. The direct route to Ularon City is through the tunnel. Kai knows he should be more concerned about what lies in wait for him beyond The Range but there'll be time for that later. In truth he'd rather trek The Range and make his way on foot to Ularon City, but that's impossible, not simply because of the distance, but due to the ruggedness of the mountains. The Range can't be traversed on foot.

Gannin is waiting for him on the street outside. He looks a little nervous and is shuffling from one foot to the other, crunching loose stones. His bag is much larger than Kai's. He has over-packed and it's a long walk to the station.

Kai glances past Gannin, looking for the four other interns who'll accompany them this day. Mikl Arannan and Sance Palador are making their way down the street, but there's no sign of Henneh or Astorl Penn. He hasn't seen Henneh since they watched the launch of *The Nether* together.

"Are the others coming?" Kai asks, turning to Gannin.

His friend bends to collect his bag, grunting with the effort. "Suppose," he says with little interest.

If, for whatever reason, Henneh and Astorl are staying behind then the likelihood of ever seeing either of them again is also in question. He isn't sure why the thought of that bothers him so much.

"Seen Henneh and Astorl this morning?" Kai calls to Mikl.

"Gone to the station already," Mikl sings out from across the street as he passes, side by side with Sance.

"Satisfied?" Gannin asks. He's looking at Kai strangely, a touch of impatience, maybe confusion, crinkling the skin around his light-coloured eyes.

Kai breathes a silent sigh although, again, he isn't quite sure why he should feel so relieved. He doesn't reply but sets off in pursuit of Mikl and Sance.

"It's a competition, you know," Gannin says, struggling after him. "We'll all have to look after our own interests from now on. I mean if you want to get the best posting, you've got to—"

"Can't a person be curious?" Kai snaps, cutting Gannin off. "Just asking. You always have to make a big issue out of everything." He puts some distance between himself and Gannin, who has no hope of catching up considering the load he's shouldering.

Kai's mood is darkening. And it had started out such a good morning! But he only has himself to blame. Gannin hadn't really said anything wrong. In fact, there *will* be no watching out for each other from now on. It's something else Kai neglected to consider and he isn't sure how he really feels about that. Perhaps it isn't just Gannin's overall physique that makes him *look* like he has the potential to make a better pilot; perhaps he actually has the mental disposition to *be* a better pilot. By the time he's completed the long walk to the station, Kai has almost come to terms with that possibility. What does it matter? If Gannin really is set for a Continental like he says, then Kai is happy for him. After all, he's only counting on a standard Urban. But there are good Urban runs like the T-Class, top-of-the-line as far as Urbans go, the modest

Urban runs like the U-Class they'll be taking this morning, and, at the base of the scale, the everyday D-Class. He just has to make sure that he's a worthy enough pilot to be assigned one of the better runs, that's all. How hard can that be? He *must* have inherited some talents from his father.

He spies Astorl and Henneh standing on the platform. Mikl and Sance arrived only moments ago and all four of them are chattering over each other. Gannin is still bringing up the rear somewhere. Kai doesn't bother to wait for him. Like Gannin said, it's everyone for themselves from now on. He tries to attract Henneh's attention, but it's Astorl who notices his wave.

And now that Gannin has got him thinking along the lines of their futures again, Kai begins to wonder how Astorl Penn with her sweet little gamine face and diminutive frame will fare during their time at the Lycea. She's smart. She's quick. But she's also a little shy and deferential. Perhaps the Lycea will knock that out of her, although it doesn't seem likely. Of all of them, if anyone is destined for a Sub run, it's Astorl Penn. And that would be a shame. Kai likes her—not as much as he likes Henneh who along with Gannin has been a constant companion almost since birth—but he does like Astorl and, to his way of thinking, she deserves better than a Sub run where she'll spend the good part of every day in the confining darkness, ubiquitous dust and incapacitating noise in a labyrinth of underground tunnels. She'll become deaf within a few years, unable to move around on the surface without the aid of thick protective glasses and she'll cough incessantly. Ush is the rare breed of Sub pilot who reached middle age. Many don't.

Astorl steps away from the others to greet him, although Kai gets the impression that those sparkling yellow-green eyes of hers are actually looking past him. Kai dumps his light bag at his feet anyway and opens his arms to embrace her. There are only the six of them on the platform. Urbans rarely stop at Journer Ward Minor and generally just whizz past on their way to somewhere more important. But this is a special run for new students of the Lycea and there are only three stops. The Urban will already have stopped at Journer Ward Major, where it picked up one group of interns before it journed southward and seaward, striding the long arc of the waterwall to its second stop in Kai's ward to collect the remainder of the interns. Its last and final stop will be at the Lycea in Ularon City, where all of its passengers will disembark. There are no marginal interns this year; at least that's been the rumour. Apart from the pilot, the interns from the Major and Minor Journer wards will be the only ones onboard. Their instructors, including Paol Inopo and Ino Paollu, are already at the Lycea, waiting on the arrival of this fresh batch of naive interns. That's good. It means that no one from the Lycea will be onboard to see him should he lose control inside the dark and narrow tunnel inside The Range.

"You made it," Astorl says with a smile, stepping out of his light hold.

Was there some doubt?

She seems a little nervous, too. They all do, but there's a kind of rush in her voice and her focus shifts jerkily from place to place. Or is she just anxious for Gannin to arrive? Without another word, she hurries past Kai to intercept Gannin who is now towing as opposed to shouldering his cumbersome load. Astorl is quick to take the straps from Gannin's hand and proceeds to drag the heavy bag across the platform toward the others. At least that settles Kai's question.

As he passes, Gannin tosses Kai a triumphant smile. Kai frowns. Poor Astorl. She has no clue what she's trying to get herself into. Gannin is his friend—his good friend—but Kai harbours no delusions about the many little flaws in his friend's character.

Finally Henneh sees him. Her face breaks into a broad smile and she hurries over to brush his cheek with a kiss. That's new! Kai doesn't miss the quick exchange of glances between Mikl and Sance up on the platform, but he plays like it's nothing out of the ordinary.

"We thought you four would never get here. The Urban is due any moment."

Gannin opens his mouth to speak but a high-pitched whine cuts him off. The Urban is drawing close. Although it will be Kai's first time on an Urban, for years he watched them from the roof of Jak Inopo's house. From up there, they appeared as little more than a blur swiftly passing on top of the waterwall, a chimera that, whenever he chanced to blink, was missed.

When Henneh bends to retrieve her modestly sized bag, Kai draws Gannin's attention and nods toward it. Gannin just curls a lip and reaches for his own oversized bag. He was probably hoping Astorl would carry it for him all the way but she has her own bag to worry about. Like Mikl's and Sance's, it is noticeably smaller than

Gannin's and, only now, Kai begins to wonder exactly what his friend might have in there.

The whine begins to downshift smoothly to a frequency that's less of an assault to the ear; a clear sign that the Urban is slowing down. When Kai looks over at Gannin, he's surprised to see his friend's face turning a little green.

"Cheer up, Gannin," he says, nudging him with a crooked elbow. "It's not like you have to pilot it yet."

"Very funny," Gannin mutters and drops his baggage. Latching hold of Kai's arm, he drags him out of earshot of the others.

"What?" Kai asks. The approaching Urban is spawning a noise reminiscent of the wind on a blustery day now.

Gannin casts a furtive glance around, evidently to assure himself that no one is listening. They're not. They're all stooping forward, eyes and ears attentive to the approaching Urban, each desperate to be the first to catch sight of it. Kai is anxious to join them.

"Have you ever been motion sick?" Gannin whispers hesitantly.

"Of course not."

Gannin punches his arm, visibly irritated. "Have you ever been in a situation to *get* motion sick?"

Kai thinks for a moment. "No," he admits.

"What if you end up throwing up all over yourself in there?" Gannin says, pointing down-track in the direction of the still invisible Urban.

Kai takes another moment. "You mean what if *you* do, don't you?"

Gannin's jaw drops, but Kai doesn't allow the discomfit to continue too long. He grasps his friend's arm and begins leading him back to the edge of the platform. "Look at it this way, Gannin," he says as he propels his friend forward, "what if it's one of the others instead?"

Gannin's face brightens. "Yeah. It could be one of them." He leans closer to Kai. "I'm betting on Sance. What do you think?"

Kai hopes not. Sance has a legendary appetite and the body mass to support the distinction. Nervous or not, Sance would still have downed a hearty breakfast.

"No one's going to get sick, Gannin," Kai says. He's becoming impatient with his friend. After all, the Urban is coming.

Astorl starts jumping up and down. "There she is," she cries, swinging her head around to alert her companions. "I see her."

So Astorl is not only smart and quick, but it seems she also has one other essential quality for a pilot—good eyesight, the best of them all. Kai looks sidelong at Gannin. He's squinting into the distance and Kai succumbs to a fleeting moment of pity. Gannin may *think* he's set for a Continental. He turns to a grinning Henneh.

"*It's so exciting!*" she says with a few little jumps, mirroring Astorl.

She's squealing in competition with the slowing Urban and it makes Kai laugh.

The snub nose of the U-Class Urban is clearly visible now, crouched low to the tracks. The cab sweeps up gently and majestically from the nose and, from what Kai can make of the trailing carriage, she's silver, sleek and almost entirely cylindrical in shape, nothing at all like he was expecting. There's a barely perceptible join where carriage meets cab but overall she's a smooth-surfaced, ergonomic-looking machine.

"Take a good long look," Gannin urges, prodding Henneh in the ribs, "she'll be yours someday."

"Wouldn't mind," Henneh replies evenly, leaning forward so far Kai worries she might tumble onto the rails. He pulls her back gently and she beams another of those sunny smiles at him.

The Urban seems to drop a little as she pushes closer to the station and, with a kind of combination clunk and hum, eases to a stop. Upfront and entirely out of view behind the heavily tinted backward-sweeping window in the nose, the pilot is sitting hooked-in and he or she will stay hooked-in for the duration of the journ. The Urban is their responsibility, day-in, day-out, year-in, year-out, and she will stay their responsibility, *completely*, until the pilot has their rank upgraded (unlikely), is found derelict in their duties (possible), completes their eight-n-two (feasible) or dies (unfortunate).

As the door to the carriage hisses open and Sance, who has pushed his way to the front, steps onboard, Kai wonders if the pilot is anyone they might know, someone from their home-ward maybe.

Henneh hangs back, waiting her turn. She and Kai will be the last to board. Gannin shoulders past Mikl to be the next, but he bangs his oversized bag in the narrow doorway and barely averts a tumble backward onto the platform.

Kai does his best not to laugh until he hears Henneh's infectious giggle.

"Hey," he says, suddenly remembering, "whatever happened with Mig? Last I heard..."

He stops talking when the happy expression on Henneh's face begins to fade.

"Didn't Ush tell you?" she asks.

"*Ush?*" Kai replies, confused. "What's Ush got to do with anything?"

"She's going to take Mig," Henneh answers hesitantly. "I thought she would have told you."

Henneh has really thrown him.

"No one else has the time," Henneh says soberly and then immediately begins to brighten. "But it'll work out fine." She touches Kai's arm. "Ush raised you and look how you turned out."

No. If he was raised by anyone, it was Anan Astada, despite his frequent absences. But Kai isn't about to tell Henneh that. She was so happy and excited until he brought up the subject of Mig. He forces a smile for her benefit.

"Of course it'll be fine," he says. "I was just surprised, that's all. Ush probably thought you'd told me," he lies.

"Probably," Henneh agrees, her smile edging back to the surface.

Kai isn't quite sure if she's fallen for it but decides it's best just to let things go. Instead, he leans in close to Henneh's ear and whispers as she is about to step onboard, "Gannin's afraid he might throw up."

"Ew," she replies, wincing. "Then I'll *definitely* be sitting next to you."

CHAPTER 3

Year 1587 of the Modern Wheel

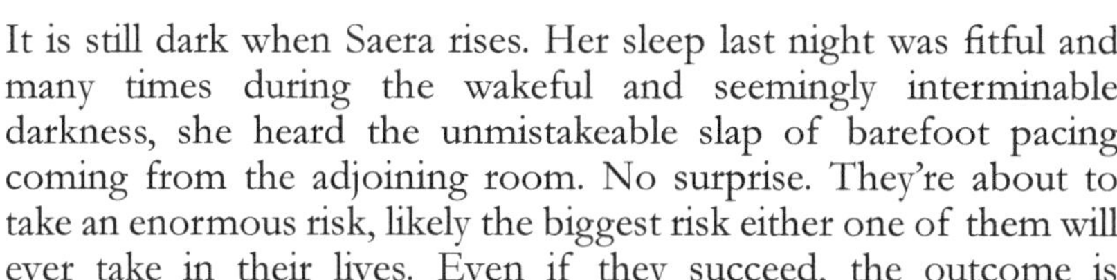

It is still dark when Saera rises. Her sleep last night was fitful and many times during the wakeful and seemingly interminable darkness, she heard the unmistakeable slap of barefoot pacing coming from the adjoining room. No surprise. They're about to take an enormous risk, likely the biggest risk either one of them will ever take in their lives. Even if they succeed, the outcome is uncertain.

Saera makes for the small kitchen in her cramped quarters and finds it already occupied. The old one is already dressed. Although Saera and the old one have known each other for a very long time, names are never used. The use of a name can become habit forming and Saera simply cannot afford to slip and accidently use the old one's name outside her quarters or intentionally use it even behind closed doors. The walls of her building are thin; someone passing by her door might hear. And so they always speak softly and only in the kitchen, the room furthest from the corridor.

This morning the old one is wearing the same clothes she had on the night she arrived. There's not much Saera can do about that. She's sacrificed some of her own precious few clothes but can buy no more. A sudden surge in spending on her clothes allowance might look suspicious. She's already increased her expenditure on food, but she has always been frugal, spending below her limit. Still, how much longer can it be before someone notices that she's chipping away at her credit?

The two lock eyes. They'll be thinking the same thing. So much rests upon today.

Saera wants to ask the old one if she is sure. She refrains. She's tired of repeating the same question and the old one is surely tired of countering with the same answer. They've spent two years doing just that.

Two years? Is that all it has been? To Saera, it feels like an eternity. Hiding and being hidden! It's a difficult feat to accomplish inside Pedora, one that would be even more difficult outside of the city. And it hasn't been painless. The things she has done. Any one of them could have finished her. And what will she do if the old one gets sick or injures herself somehow? Saera's healing knowledge is limited and the old one is of an age now when anything could happen.

Saera brings a chair to the simple table and sits down. She can't help herself; she has to ask this one last time but before she can get the first word out, the old one smiles at her across the room. The years in hiding, forever out of the light, have taken their toll, paled her skin and made her frail.

"This is the only way. It's taken too long already," she says.

Saera glances at the folder in front of her on the kitchen table. It's been lying there, waiting, since last night. Gove put himself at considerable risk to bring it to them. She wishes the old one had never sought her out. She wishes she'd never confided in Gove when the old one appeared at her door. But there was no one else to turn to. Why her? Why did the old one choose her?

Well, she knows the answer to that. She and Gove, they're not like everyone else and that's about the size of it. Keeping that little difference secret all these years will eventually take its toll on them, too. Has already. She's been watchful all her life. Suspicious. A cynic. Will she age before her time like the old one? Time! She may not have a lot of that left to worry about. Not if one of them gets caught. How long? she asks herself again. They've been lucky. Maybe too lucky. And there it is again. That same watchfulness. That same suspicion. Perhaps *they* are the ones being watched. How can they know there isn't a vis in her quarters? How can they know that every move they make isn't being monitored and logged? How can they know that the Pedorate isn't already aware of what Gove did?

It's no use. A person could go crazy thinking that way every moment of every day. Perhaps she already has.

Snatching up the folder, Saera returns to her small bedroom to dress.

***

Director Eine Vidamore can't keep still. He settles into his chair but soon finds himself aimlessly shuffling stacks of paper from one side of the desk to the other, papers he probably should have already flashed. Rising, he peers anxiously out the window. He's donned his formal robe and the weighty cloth of the sombre, floor-length gown is making him feel uncomfortably hot. After a clumsy fumble with the lock, he manages to fling the window open, but even the pre-dawn heat is too oppressive, and he quickly slams the window shut again.

It was foolishness, pure foolishness to have agreed to meet the Registrar. A junior Registrar at that. It simply is not done. Protocol has been entirely circumvented and he should have insisted that the junior Registrar communicate with him through the proper channels and enlist the services of a Talker. Even a junior Registrar can't be ignorant about such a fundamental procedure. Talkers are objective communicators—it's their profession—and they come straight to the point. The fact that she did not approach her superior to engage a Talker is what concerns him the most.

What does it mean?

His mind is running riot with possibilities and, again and again, his thoughts return to the three stacks of paper on his desk. Something is not right in the graduate postings. He saw it immediately, but the irregularity is surely nothing to draw the attention or interest of a junior Registrar. Even if the Registrar has noticed, she would be aware that he personally has no control over the postings. Besides, a graduate's posting is of no concern to a Registrar. She must want to see him about something else.

He is, by nature, a cautious person and, to his mind, it's a trait that has served him well, especially now as problems of a kind and magnitude unimagined before the return of *The Nether* continue to test him. But perhaps he hasn't been innovative enough and has somehow fallen short of expectation. Or has the Registrar found something amiss in the Lycea's records? Something she thinks she might be able to use to her own advantage? But what could possibly *be* amiss? And what could a junior Registrar possibly hope to gain by approaching him with some trivial infraction? And a trivial infraction is all it could possibly be. His reputation is impeccable and, although he'd have much preferred a posting more in line with his interests and inclination, he took up the position as senior administrator of the Lycea without question or complaint. When he came to the Lycea, he knew nothing about journing; twenty years on, he can recite the course requirements and graduate statistics off the top of his head, calculate expenditure at a moment's notice, although he can't say he's any more enlightened about the discipline. But still, as he reflects over the twenty years that have gone by, he can't recall a single noteworthy instance, even during the terrible challenges of the last years, that might occasion the notice, let alone interest, of a Registrar.

If not for the reckless act of a few Minor Journers, the challenges of the last years might not have been so terrible for him. Fools! What lunacy had prompted them to seek refuge outside their home-ward. Their ill-conceived flight into Journer Ward Major did immeasurable harm and spread the virus like wildfire, triggering the Major ward to suffer the same fate as her lesser sister. Although he, personally, has never seen a case of the plague, as rumour has it, the sickness starts with a gradual yellowing of the sclera; then comes the rash, insignificant at first, that develops into open welts and a relentless, screaming neuralgia; next the vital organs slowly begin to fail—kidneys, lungs, heart—until the ultimate crash and, mercifully, you are dead.

While the killer plague might have hit the Journer wards the hardest, its repercussions were felt in the cities and, naturally, touched the Lycea the most negatively of all Pedoran institutions. Still, thanks to his insistence that scruters be installed at every entrance to the Lycea, supplementing those already installed at every Sub and Urban station, there hasn't been a single incidence of plague recorded inside his institution. Of course, with the principal Journer wards in lockdown and only interns arriving from the marginal wards this and last year, it might be argued that he has been overcautious and wasteful of resources. The Lycea hardly boasts the prestige it once did. Being a Journer now has almost become a stigma.

Is that it?

Has the Registrar been sent to inform him about the future of the Lycea? But isn't it too soon? There are still the marginals to train and the last of the pre-plague cohort has yet to complete their studies. Surely the quarantine will be lifted before then. Besides, if the Lycea is to be closed, a junior Registrar wouldn't be sent to deliver the news.

"No," Vidamore says aloud as he falls back into his chair, "it can't be that."

Mindlessly he begins shuffling the three stacks of paper again. He wishes the Registrar would hurry. Better to know now than to be left fretting in this terrible in-between. His attention drifts to his hands mechanically rearranging the papers, surprised to discover them trembling. Sweat is beginning to bead on his forehead, too. He can feel it trickling down into his eyebrows.

Why is it so abysmally hot and stale in his office today? He glances at the unobtrusive little panel underneath the rim of his desk. Nothing has changed in the temperature settings. Is it him that has changed then? He's not young anymore and he's spent many years sitting behind this same desk. Whenever he chances to catch a reflection of himself, even he has begun to notice that his spine is no longer as ramrod straight as it once was, that there are now as many white as gold strands in his hair. Nonsense. He's aged as well as anyone in Pedora. There's simply something wrong with the climate control in his office. Tomorrow he'll arrange to have the entire building checked.

In an uncharacteristic fit of frustration, he sweeps aside the papers littering his desk. They land in a jumble on the floor. Now he'll have to sort them all once again. Not that he really needs to. He has the odd collection of postings already memorised. Bending, he gathers the papers but instead of organising them again immediately, shoots back his chair and returns to the window. Again, he's obliged to fumble with the lock to get the window open.

Dawn is more than just a promise on the horizon now. He shades his eyes against the overbright early morning light and squints at the flag poles that stand in the broad plaza beneath his office window. There should be two flags proudly flying, the Pedoran state flag and lower down, the standard of the Lycea. Both are hanging limp, draped about their respective poles. It's odd to see the plaza so empty of chairs and dais. There's to be no official graduation ceremony again today. Instead, graduates will be individually informed of their postings. Today, for the second time since the inception of the Lycea, no visiting family will come from the Journer wards to witness their sons and daughters, their brothers and sisters graduate and the plaza will serve its routine function as a simple thoroughfare for students and staff to transit from one building to another.

"Hot. It's always so hot in this city," Vidamore grumbles and, slamming the window shut again, looks away from the depressing emptiness. Little black specks dance before his eyes as though he's looking through a collection of tiny holes. He finds his chair again largely by feel and habit. Being posted out of his discipline was bad enough, but why had the Pedorate Council seen fit to post him to a place with such a hideous climate where the glare, even at dawn, is unbearable?

He wishes the Registrar would hurry. The early risers will be arriving soon. What if she is seen? What excuse could he possibly make for the presence of an unaccompanied junior Registrar on his campus? Perhaps she's been stopped by a scruter and he won't be obliged to invent some sort of explanation.

A gentle rap sounds at his closed door and Vidamore almost knocks his chair to the floor as he bolts to his feet.

She has come!

But how did she cross the plaza without him seeing her? There's a back way, of course, but no Registrar, even a junior, would travel on a Sub. Subs are for Preservers, Pedora's manual workforce.

Noticing the papers, he opens his desk drawer and sweeps the jumble out of sight before he sets off across the floor, smoothing the cloth of his maroon-coloured gown as he goes. He's dressed appropriately for this meeting, expecting the junior Registrar to have done the same, but is surprised when he opens the door. Her trousers are dark brown and simple, her waist length jacket buttoned down. She looks every bit a Registrar but she's younger than he expected. Still a genuine Thika graduate though, if a relatively recent one, otherwise she couldn't have known how to contact him. She's still wearing her U-visor. It's scratched up a little along the sides, much like his own. She's local.

He ushers the young Registrar into his office and waves her toward a chair.

The Registrar's visor is off now. She moves with stealth, Vidamore notes. He didn't see her hand go anywhere near her face. Her face. It's not to Vidamore's taste. It seems too angular, an impression only accentuated by the way her almost white hair is swept back severely from her forehead. Her face is too thin. Too closed. And those eyes. He wishes now that she'd kept her visor on. Such a strange colour violet. He doesn't think he's ever seen eyes quite that colour before.

He takes the opportunity to rid himself of his gown, bumping a hip painfully against the corner of his desk. Before slipping into his seat, he drapes the gown over the back of the chair. The Registrar doesn't seem to notice or care.

"You'll appreciate," Vidamore begins, "that I'm curious why you asked for this meeting."

"Of course," the Registrar replies with a barely perceptible nod. "I'd have concerns if you weren't."

She'd have concerns!

"It's highly irregular," he adds, suppressing an overwhelming desire to grump at the young Registrar's arrogance.

"Highly," she concurs. "And, in light of that, it's encouraging that you did agree to see me. It reassures me I've been sent to the right person."

Vidamore leans forward. "Sent?"

The young Registrar's lips part in a gentle smile, smoothing out the angularity that Vidamore found so unappealing at first.

"You don't, for one moment believe, that I came here of my own account."

Vidamore's hand goes out automatically. He's reaching for the stack of papers, but they're gone, so draws his hand back down into his lap.

"No," he says, gathering nerve.

She's not going to waste words, this one.

Vidamore watches, intrigued, as she begins to undo the top three buttons of her jacket. Slipping her hand between jacket and blouse, she withdraws a folder, which she then places on his desk.

Vidamore looks down at the folder. She's brought him a sheath of papers. Very odd. He, himself, only resorts to the use of paper for matters of an extremely sensitive nature. Cyphered data is so easily breached.

"You'll find all your answers in there," she says.

At the periphery of his vision, he notices the young Registrar begin to rise.

"Wait!" he barks, then reaches out and snatches up the folder. "You can't just drop this on my desk and then leave without a word of explanation."

"I can," the Registrar replies, although she has settled back down into the chair. "I think the sooner I leave, the better, don't you? It's still early. If I leave now, I suspect no one will know I've been here. And I can assure you that is to both our benefit." She nods toward the folder in his hand. "Besides, I can't tell you any more than what is in there already."

"You can tell me who sent you."

"Very well," the Registrar answers evenly. "I *won't* tell you any more."

Vidamore shoots the folder across the desk. "Clearly you're not here in any official capacity and I have the right to know who *did* send you."

"We all have rights, Director Vidamore."

Sweat isn't just trickling, it's running down his forehead now in what feels like sheets. It's dripping into his eyes, blurring his vision. What with the insufferable heat, his physical discomfort and the insolence of the young Registrar sitting in front of him, he's barely able to restrain himself from shouting.

"Meaning?" he demands.

"That I'm exercising my right not to answer."

It's Vidamore's turn to smile. "Young Registrar," he says, "I believe that is a right you have assumed, not one that is automatically granted."

The Registrar shrugs at him from her chair. "All rights are *assumed*, aren't they, Director?"

If he didn't know better, Vidamore would swear his arteries were about to burst and splatter the Registrar with blood. His fist slams the desk top. "Not in this office."

"I'm a Registrar," she reminds him casually from her chair. "Not one of your students. You have no authority over me."

"I have the authority to have you removed from the Lycea. With force if necessary."

"Indeed you do," the Registrar replies. "And I believe that I stated my desire to leave only moments ago." She rises to her feet. "Force will not be necessary, Director."

"Stop right there!" Vidamore shouts as she starts for the door. "You take this with you. Whatever it is, I don't want it."

To his surprise, the Registrar stops before she reaches the door and turns around.

"Nor did I," she replies, making for the door once more.

Snatching up the folder, he rushes across the room to intercept her. With inappropriate familiarity, he grabs a hold of her hand and thrusts the folder into it.

"*Nor did you*! What's that supposed to mean?"

He expects her to push the folder back at him, but she doesn't. Instead, she falters for a moment, looking down at the folder in her hand, before she levels those strange violet eyes on him. She's quite tall. He didn't notice that before.

"I was told," she says deliberately as her free hand delves inside the pocket of her jacket to remove her U-visor, "that you were a person of integrity."

She slips the visor over her eyes and reaches for the doorknob.

"I was told," she continues, "that if you knew what is inside this folder, you would want to help us."

"Us?" Vidamore's having a hard time now not shoving her out the door. "If you, Registrar, were likewise a person of integrity, then you would have gone through the proper channels and enlisted the service of a Talker to speak with me."

"Yes, a Talker," the Registrar replies. "The title says it all really, doesn't it?" Her glance flicks briefly again toward the folder in her hand before she looks back at Vidamore. "Perhaps we've been misled. Perhaps you're not the person we believed you to be." She pauses then adds with a smile as she opens the door, "but then again, since you refuse to even look at what I've brought you, I suppose we'll never know."

Vidamore's mouth drops open and he doesn't have the wits to close it until the brazen young Registrar is on the other side of his office door. His hands are shaking again, only now for an entirely different reason. He struts away from the door, bypassing his desk in favour of the window, shoots it open once again to stand in front of it, fuming. Raising a hand, he runs his fingers around the collar of his shirt, stretching it out from his damp neck. He'd like to return to his quarters and change into a fresh set of clothes, but his schedule won't permit it. This morning, he has to personally meet with each member of the graduating class and inform them of their postings. It's a task he was dreading even before the young Registrar, if she *is* a Registrar, stepped into his office, and now the unsettling encounter has made him doubt his usually dependable memory. He'll have to consult the papers again.

Reseated behind his desk, he opens the drawer and removes the stack of now disordered papers. As he glances across his desk, his attention is drawn to something lying on the floor just inside the closed door.

The folder!

While his back was turned, the Registrar had slipped the folder under his door.

Vidamore hurries from his desk, snatches up the folder and wrenches his door open. Holding the doorjamb with his free hand, he leans out to scan the corridor. Save for two of his students, there's no one else there.

Both students stop walking and the taller, who Vidamore recognises immediately as Kai Astada, one of the deaders, steps forward.

"Are you looking for someone, Director Vidamore?" he asks.

The shorter, stockier student, also a deader, has his head cocked to one side, looking a little confused. It's a pose Vidamore has seen many times. Gannin Tewel is not the sharpest of Lycea students and seeing him standing that way prompts Vidamore to think about the papers sitting on his desk. The posting for many of this year's graduates may have momentarily slipped his mind, but the posting for Gannin Tewel has not.

Papers!

Suddenly he remembers the folder clutched to his chest and, as casually as he can, brings the hand holding the folder down to his side.

"No," he says, focusing his attention on the dead son, Astada, "I thought someone knocked on my door."

"I didn't see anyone," Astada replies.

"I did," Tewel offers, righting his head. "She was turning the corner at the other end of the corridor when you opened the door, Director."

"Can't have been her then," he lies, inching the folder behind his back. "Must have been a grendel," he says and forces a smile. He wishes the Registrar *had* been a figment of his imagination. Considering the pressure he's been under these last two years, even the most well-adjusted person could be excused for surrendering to a little hallucination. But his visitor was real all right. The unwanted folder behind his back is proof of that. "You both have appointments with me today," he reminds them, desperate to change the subject.

"Yes, sir," Astada agrees.

"I believe I'm first, Director," Gannin interjects, speaking over the top of his companion.

"If you'll excuse me then," Vidamore says, backing slowly into his office while, at the same time, shutting the door. "I'll require a few moments to prepare."

Vidamore returns to his desk and, placing the folder to one side, sets about ordering the jumble of papers. He has a particular purpose in mind now and it isn't just to remind himself of each graduate's posting. It was seeing Gannin Tewel that did it; caused the suspicion that earlier was only a niggling embryo of a thing to mature into something much more troubling.

- Sub.

- Urban.

- Continental.

He makes three stacks and begins to sort the papers accordingly. There are twenty-four postings in all, nineteen for those graduates who came to the Lycea from Journer Ward Major and five for the graduates from the minor ward, one intern from each ward having been dismissed; no marginals whatsoever. As he sorts, Vidamore's attention keeps flicking toward the folder by his elbow. It's too coincidental, a junior Registrar coming to see him without proper authorisation and outside official channels, today of all days.

He's tempted to confirm that he is right even though he remains entirely ignorant about the exact contents of the folder. But he's a trained administrator, schooled not to make judgements without first verifying all the facts, and so he forces himself to methodically complete the process.

Once all twenty-four posting are placed into their corresponding piles, Vidamore draws the stack of Sub postings closer and begins to separate the postings that struck him as irregular from the outset. There are three and he places these together on his desk just above the stack of remaining Sub postings. Next, he gathers the stack of Urban postings and repeats the same procedure, finding two irregular postings, the same number he finds in the Continental stack.

He looks at each in turn, unsurprised now by what is there. Why didn't he see it before? It's so obvious. There are two dead sons in the Lycea, three dead daughters and two dead brothers. In all, seven *deaders*—seven students who'll carry that wretched label for life simply because they were ill-fated enough to have had a family member aboard *The Nether*. And each of those misfortunates— those deaders—has been assigned what in his professional opinion is an irregular posting. A very few, two in fact, have been assigned posts with requirements far above their tested skills; the rest have been assigned posts far below.

His focus drifts toward the Registrar's unopened folder. A moment ago, he was almost anxious to look inside. Now he's hesitant again. Exceptionally hesitant. Postings aren't his business. He's never known the criteria used to determine where each of his graduating students will go once they leave the Lycea, but he has a sickening feeling in the pit of his stomach that he's about to find out.

He pulls the folder forward, opens it and, after a brief glance at the topmost page, slams it shut.

Pautune, he swears silently. No wonder the young Registrar was so eager to offload the folder!

Taking a deep breath, he opens the folder again. He's shaking as he begins to read and with each turn of a page another little bead of sweat drops onto the paper. There isn't a lot of time. Gannin Tewel will be knocking on his door at any moment.

He's standing in front of the flash box, an inconspicuous-looking rectangular slot located to one side of the window in the back wall of his office, when he hears the rap on his door. Dropping the last sheet inside, he watches for the tiny flash of blue light to confirm that the page has been destroyed. Returning to his desk, he slips the empty folder into the drawer and looks around. Nothing. Nothing looks amiss in his office. Briefly he considers putting his heavy gown back on. It's still lying where he discarded it, draped over the back of his chair. On any other graduation day, he'd be standing on the dais in the plaza, dressed in his official attire, in front of a moderately sized gathering of family members, distributing postings to each graduate as they file past. But today isn't any other graduation day and it still feels so uncommonly hot inside his office. Electing to forgo the gown, he steps away from his desk, crosses to the door and reluctantly admits Gannin Tewel. It will be the first of seven unusual meetings today. Two of those meetings, including young Tewel's, will end well, at least for the graduate concerned. Vidamore harbours some serious concerns about how the remaining five graduates will respond to their less favourable news.

CHAPTER 4
Year 1588 of the Modern Wheel

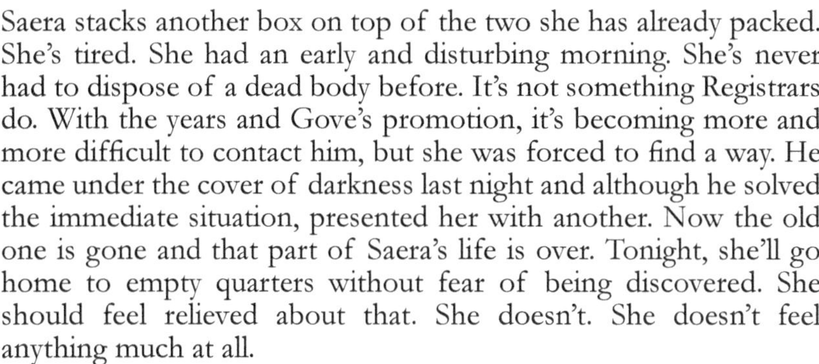

Saera stacks another box on top of the two she has already packed. She's tired. She had an early and disturbing morning. She's never had to dispose of a dead body before. It's not something Registrars do. With the years and Gove's promotion, it's becoming more and more difficult to contact him, but she was forced to find a way. He came under the cover of darkness last night and although he solved the immediate situation, presented her with another. Now the old one is gone and that part of Saera's life is over. Tonight, she'll go home to empty quarters without fear of being discovered. She should feel relieved about that. She doesn't. She doesn't feel anything much at all.

Packing up the last of the Repository this morning served as a welcome distraction but now that work, too, is done. There are boxes stacked all over the floor. Even the furniture has been broken down and laid flat in preparation for its relocation to the new Repository. So many changes so fast. Too fast. As much, perhaps more than she's going to miss company in her home she's going to miss this place. Located high up on the only hill worth calling a hill in Ularon City, it's one of the few spots that catches a breeze. More significantly, it's the only place she's actually felt safe in the last few years. But as long as she keeps Gove's latest intelligence to herself, her quarters should be safe now, too.

It will be as hot as pautune down in the valley. She's been assured it will be airier and an altogether more comfortable location for her to work. Better for the preservation of the old documents, too, the Registrar Prime keeps telling her—through the proper channels.

Proper channels!

She offers up a humourless chuckle and is immediately obliged to spit packing dust.

She'd like to know how it's going to be a more comfortable location. It's not like she and all her papers are being shifted into a new purpose-built building. She's only been permitted to view the place twice. Once to confirm it was of an adequate size. How generous of Arramur! She's often wondered what he would have done if she'd determined that it wasn't. And the second time she was permitted on the premises was to decide on the layout of 'the shed'. The shed. That's how she's starting to think of Arramur's *grand* facility, which she suspects had some prior association with Ularon City's sewage treatment system.

The Registrar Prime doesn't give a quinet's hoot about old documents. They take up too much room. *They* smell. What he really wants is to get them, *and her*, out of the way. Hoarding physical documents is wasting space and keeping a fully qualified Registrar on staff to maintain them is wasting resources. Sooner or later Arramur will get his way with the Pedorate Council and every last shred of paper will be flashed.

The realisation that Locan Arramur wouldn't be averse to having her flashed along with them almost brings a smile to her lips. She's gotten *her* way for now, largely because the Council has more important things to worry about than the storage of old papers. It would be a different story if they knew what else, in addition to her official duties, she's been doing these last few years. Last night, the chances of discovery were greatly reduced, but even so, she won't get her way with the Repository forever; she knows that and the budding smile slips away. With a sigh, Saera steadies the last box she's packed and returns to her empty office. It was only a small office but it was *her* office, a refuge away from the constant vulnerability of her home. In the new Repository, she'll be sitting out among all the shelving.

In a rare instance of magnanimity, Register Prime Arramur has allowed her an assistant for the next two weeks. Strange. Perhaps he was the victim of an extraordinary attack of pity. Lula Praedem, her young helper, is a student at the Thika and Saera has little doubt that Lula's unusual assignment represents penance for some infraction. But even with Lula's help it will be a long time before she'll have any real order restored to the archives. Then again, she may not have the chance to complete the work.

She takes her last look around. Leaving. For her, it always has been about leaving. If someone isn't leaving her, she's leaving someone or some place. She closes the door to her office and heads back to the large open storeroom filled with boxes and collapsed furniture, resigned that it's probably always going to be that way.

Donning her U-visor she steps out into the open where Lula is waiting on the arrival of the transport vehicles.

"Shouldn't be long now," Lula says, eyes trained on the valley below.

"I hope there's more than one," Saera replies without enthusiasm.

There's no station up on the hill. What doesn't find its way onto the hill by foot, the method Saera herself uses every morning, has to be powered up by one of the few free-progression vehicles still in operation in Ularon City. It's going to take more than one of those old coughing, spluttering freep vehicles to transport everything. If Arramur has only approved one—Saera wasn't privy to that information—then it's going to require multiple trips. With luck, the Registrar Prime is of a mind to get the whole business over and done with in a hurry. She's not fond of lengthy farewells. Whether she likes it or not, whether she had a say in it or not, this place is finished for her now. Once the freeps are loaded, she and Lula will hitch a ride to the new Repository where yet another new life will begin.

Abandoning Lula to her vigil, Saera makes her way to her favourite spot on the hill to wait. On her first day at the Repository, she stumbled on a nice long log hidden in the dry dead grass just outside the entrance. Grounds maintenance and irrigation, she quickly discovered, were not major priorities at the Repository, doubtless something that will change now that Arramur has his sights set on the place. It was while she was sitting on the log that Saera first experienced the coolish little breeze that she'll sorely miss down in the valley. Even now she can remember how surprised she had been that the breeze had actually been strong enough to cool her face and restore her confidence that she alone could manage the extensive archive. It seemed such a daunting task on that first day. Little did she know then that no one, Registrar Prime Arramur least of all, really cared if the archives were maintained. She was only a stooge, posted to the Repository to make Arramur look good. When she realised the truth, and that was very quickly, she feared that her Cross status had been discovered. But that wasn't it at all. They hadn't even bothered to investigate her file. She was simply the next in line.

The old reliable breeze starts to dry the droplets of sweat from her face but fails to lift her spirits. She feels sticky. Dirty and sticky and, despite Lula's welcome presence, very much alone. Below, the bright white buildings and thin ribbons of now largely unused road stretch out for as far as she can see. Ularon is by and large a treeless city—stark, ugly and heartless. She longs to go home. To her real home. A place she's essentially forgotten and can now only imagine. A place where crisp clean air rolls inland from the sea, alleviating the heat. A place where the grass isn't perennially brown. A place where, should she walk down the street, then chances are, even for someone like her, somewhere along the way, she'd encounter a friendly face. But a Cross never gets to go home. In every way that counts, a Cross has no home.

Lula's call severs her pointless daydreaming. Slowly she comes to her feet, only now aware of the low rumbling sound she'd been too distracted to even notice before. A freep is making its way up the hill in a cloud of dust and there are another two freeps behind it, billowing more dust in their wake. She can hear the crunch of wheel on loose gravel.

No, they hadn't even bothered to question her file. Strange how some things change, she thinks, stepping away from the log, and some things never do. It's that very hope she's been clinging to these last years. Without hope, she simply couldn't and *wouldn't* have persevered. She'll wait a little longer. Think a little harder about what she should do, if anything, with the new intelligence Gove just brought her.

***

Lula is a good worker. She's quiet, dedicated, and just genial enough to suit Saera's current mood. By the end of the first week, they have the shelving in place and all the boxes stacked, if not unpacked, into rows. If Lula works as diligently in the second week, they'll make some progress in setting the Repository in order before Saera loses her services. Today has been an exceptionally tiring day; the boxes were large and heavy, the distance to haul them long and winding. Saera releases Lula early. She's thinking about the intern's neglected studies. She's also thinking about the big old mutz they discovered skulking around the back doors of the Repository some days ago. Every time she sees the animal, Lula shoos it away, but whenever the intern isn't looking, Saera lures back what has to be the biggest, dirtiest, shaggiest and snarliest mutz in all of Ularon City. She calls and when the animal fails to appear, leaves a bowl of water just outside the rear doors along with some scraps of food. Securing the heavy doors, she starts for home.

The recent long hard hours have been a blessing. She's usually too tired to notice or care how empty her quarters have become and retires early. Tonight, she's interrupted. The com at her door is buzzing. Saera consults the shadowy image on the screen; there's a grey-clad Preserver standing outside her building, seeking admittance. It seems something's amiss with the power grid in her quarters and immediate repairs have been ordered.

Saera sighs and admits the Preserver. She's waiting by her open door when the Preserver emerges from the riser. Her appearance is mildly surprising. She's young, small, thin. Hardly good genetic material there! On turning around after closing the door, Saera is even more surprised to discover the Preserver making herself at home on her couch.

"What—"

"Registrar Brawse," the Preserver says, interrupting her, "a year ago, you took some documents to Director Vidamore at the Lycea."

Saera makes no reply. She can't. Her heart is pounding inside her chest. Her mouth's gone dry and her mind's an absolute blank. She's shaking. Enough for it to be noticed? She should be. This is *no* Preserver sitting on her couch.

"I'm not Pedorate," the young imposter says with a smile, reading Saera's fears.

Saera's mind clears enough to reply. "We're all Pedorate. And I'd thank you to get out."

The imposter shakes a finger at her. "We're all *Pedoran*," she observes. "We're not all *Pedorate*."

"I fail to see the difference." Saera is bluffing, hoping to put the imposter off-guard enough to get her to leave. "What?" she says when the imposter immediately fires off a string of numbers.

"That's my ident. You're a Registrar. You have the authority to confirm that."

Saera hurries to her cypher, nested discretely into the wall outside her kitchen, and does just that. She's had to turn her back on the imposter to do it, and when she turns around, shocked by what she's found, sees the imposter with her boots propped up on the small table in front of her couch.

"You'd think an Administrator would know better than to put their boots on someone else's furniture."

"You'd think so, wouldn't you?" Veeda replies, unmoving.

Veeda. That's her name. Her *real* name, as Saera has just discovered.

"Why are you here?" Saera asks. She's feeling a little calmer now, although she has no legitimate reason to. Administrators, more so than many castes, have the reputation, and the incentive, to spy for the Pedorate Council.

"Was it you, or was it not you, who took those documents to Director Vidamore?" Veeda asks. Tipping forward, she drops her boots to the floor.

"And if it was?"

"If it was," Veeda says, rising, "the Director would like you to provide the same material again."

Saera glances toward her cypher. Veeda is who she claims to be; Saera has no doubts about that. And she once believed that Vidamore could be trusted. But he's stayed silent for almost a year. Nothing positive came of her visit. But nothing negative came of it, either. No, whether she can or cannot trust Vidamore and this unwelcome visitor, evidently his envoy, it is too late. The Director has acted too late. Saera's gaze drifts toward the corridor leading to her small bedroom. Or has he?

"I can't," Saera says, deciding. "I no longer have access to that kind of information."

"No?" Veeda asks. She sounds suspicious.

"I'm telling you the truth," Saera protests. "Why would I lie now? I've just taken an incredible risk admitting it was me who went to see Director Vidamore."

Saera can actually *feel* Veeda study her. Young, small, thin; doesn't make a shred of difference. This Administrator is formidable, regardless of size.

"No risk as far as I'm concerned," the Administrator says at last, relaxing her gaze. "I don't suppose you'd be willing to explain why you no longer have access?"

Saera's jaw stiffens. "I wouldn't."

"Understood," the Administrator responds with a shrug. "But that's a great pity, because Director Vidamore fears the same irregularity is about to be repeated."

Saera always expected that the first incidence wouldn't be the last. Otherwise, she'd never have gone to Vidamore. Why hadn't he acted *then*? Had he been too scared? Only a stupid person wouldn't be scared. But ridding herself of the new documents Gove just brought her might be a wise thing to do and since the unexpected arrival of this young Administrator is offering her that very opportunity with the added bonus of not implicating him...

"Perhaps I can still help you."

Veeda can't uncover anything she isn't already aware of in her quarters so Saera feels comfortable enough to leave the Administrator alone while she goes to her bedroom.

"Here," she says, returning with the sheath of papers, bundled together in a folder. "It's not what you asked for, but I think Director Vidamore will find it even more interesting."

Veeda is slow to take the folder. She appears wary or, perhaps, confused.

Of course! Saera realises then why Veeda has baulked.

"Paper," the Administrator says, gingerly taking the folder. "I've heard that Registrars have an unnatural attachment for this kind of thing."

"As well for you," Saera fires back. "*And* Director Vidamore."

"We'll see," Veeda replies indifferently and, opening the front of her bland uniform, proceeds to secret the folder. "I suspect," she continues, looking up, "you're not going to tell me where you got this from, either."

"You suspect correctly," Saera replies, pointing toward the doorway. "Now I think it best you leave."

"Certainly," Veeda agrees and starts for the door. One step shy she stops to glance over her shoulder. "By the way, there really is a power surge coming from your quarters. I'd get that seen to if I were you."

CHAPTER 5

Year 1589 of the Modern Wheel

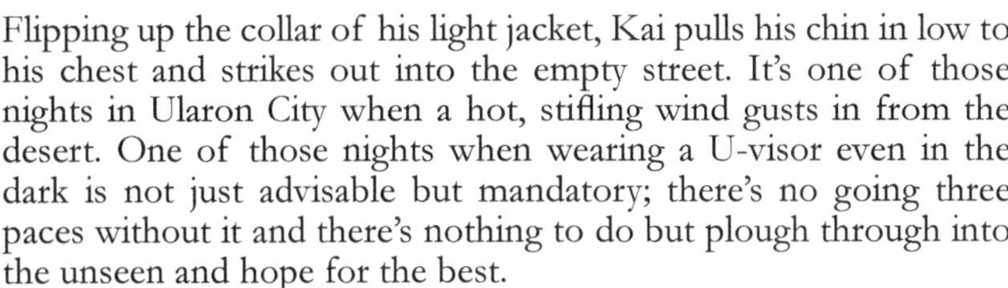

Flipping up the collar of his light jacket, Kai pulls his chin in low to his chest and strikes out into the empty street. It's one of those nights in Ularon City when a hot, stifling wind gusts in from the desert. One of those nights when wearing a U-visor even in the dark is not just advisable but mandatory; there's no going three paces without it and there's nothing to do but plough through into the unseen and hope for the best.

He's dressed plainly. There are no insignia, nothing to reveal his caste to anyone he passes. It's a precaution he probably need not have taken. He's alone. At least he seems to be. Even if there are Guardians out on the street tonight, how in pautune could they see him?

He goes over the instructions he was given, still of half a mind to believe the place doesn't really exist. He's heard about the club ever since his early days at the Lycea. Every Journer has heard about the Duck Down Club but Kai has never come across a Journer yet who believes it to be anything but a myth. The Lycea is full of legends and myths, most told to alarm new interns. Like the one about neural fry-out. Kai was only of half a mind to believe that piece of folklore, too, but the first time he stepped into the simulator, his whole body was shaking. He can still hear Gannin laughing at him. Gannin wasn't laughing so loud when his turn came. Neural fry-out! No such thing. If your brain lacks the inherent capacity to integrate, then the result is immediate dismissal from the Lycea—brain intact, though formally recorded as deficient—and you're Crossed. There were only two Crosses in Kai's class. One a native of Journer Ward Major and word was he crossed to Preserver. The last time anyone saw him, he was silently packing his belongings under the supervision of Ino Paollu. The other was Astorl Penn from Kai's home-ward; no one knew what happened to Astorl. But that day marked the beginning of a long sober period at the Lycea with the remainder of Kai's class wondering and worrying who was going to be next. In the end, Astorl and the unfortunate young Journer from Major were the only ones obliged to leave.

As for the Duck Down Club, Kai always suspected that myth was spawned a long time ago in higher places than the upper student cohort and, more than likely, at the very top rank of the Lycea itself. No up-and-coming Journer would risk frequenting such an infamous place as the Duck Down Club and any Journer foolish enough to attempt it wouldn't maintain their posting very long. It was just a threat, a device to keep the recent graduates in line. There are a lot of temptations for new graduates, ample opportunities to make mistakes. And with no Journer knowing for certain what exactly the Duck Down Club is supposed to be, where it is located, or if it even exists, any youthful inclination to stray outside established norms and investigate the authenticity of the myriad claims is essentially programmed out.

But now he's received a request from Henneh Sek to come to this fabled place and, since he can't believe that Henneh is lying to him, the Duck Down Club must exist. He and Henneh have drifted so far apart since they entered the Lycea together, he feels like he barely knows her anymore. What possible reason could she have for wanting to see him after so many years? And at the Duck Down Club of all places? Whatever it is, he hopes she's quick about it; he's anxious about leaving his Urban for too long. Like all Journers, Kai has established a psychological bond with his machine and he feels almost naked this far away from it. If word gets out he's visited the Duck Down Club, he may not *have* his Urban to go back to.

Kai thought he was religiously following the instructions he received, but on turning into this narrow laneway, he's confronted by a dead end. The windstorm has made it hard going; he must have taken a wrong turn somewhere. He's just about to abandon the whole idiotic business when he notices something amiss in the otherwise solid brick wall ahead of him.

Kai pulls off his visor to get a better look. The wind isn't gusting so savagely in the laneway and he can see—he thinks he can see—an old wooden door. But he's only relying on the ambient light seeping into the laneway from the street beyond. The door, or whatever it is, is small. The top of it may reach as high as his shoulder. If this is the Duck Down Club, then the door lends a whole new meaning to its name. He'd always assumed the Club's title alluded more to its clientele than its access. Kai makes his way to the door. Finding no handle, he raps, feeling more than a little foolish.

This can't possibly be the entrance to any club, fictitious or otherwise. Gannin must be back in Ularon City. His old friend is playing a trick on him. It even reeks of Gannin's warped sense of play. Kai fails to see the humour.

The door looks like it hasn't been used in a hundred years. The paint is all chipped and flaking. It's got to be the door to a storage room or something. Kai is at the point of turning away when the door opens, spilling bright white light into the laneway. He's met by the last thing he expected to find behind the door to the Duck Down Club, an old one so short in stature that her head manages to fall far short of the top of the open doorway. She's dressed in a set of faded non-descript coveralls. Her grey hair is cropped short in keeping with Sub style. But this one was no Sub. She's lasted too long. The cracks and creases that sculpt her face are natural, not the ugly product of a life spent in stale and filthy tunnels underground.

Her eyes commence a slow scan of Kai from the bottom of his feet to the top of his head. When she finishes, she settles her gaze on his face, but says nothing.

He was told to use Henneh's name, so that's just what he does. It seems to have the desired effect. The old one doesn't smile but there's a subtle shift in the set of her thin lips that tells Kai he's going to be admitted. He kind of hoped she'd slam the door in his face, so he could walk away with his conscious clear and tell himself he tried.

The old Journer steps to one side and, with an exaggerated sweep of her hand, invites Kai in. It's all a bit too theatrical for his liking. Still, he ducks his head and steps through the open doorway. The door is shut quickly behind him. It's a sound that makes Kai's heart skip a beat.

"So, you're Kai Astada," the old one says, surprising him with the crispness and clarity of her voice. He'd almost concluded her mute. "My. My. You're a tall one, aren't you?"

Kai ignores her to take in his surroundings, a narrow little corridor that doesn't tell him very much. But he can stand up straight now and won't be obliged to keep his head tucked into his chest the whole time he's inside the club.

The old one's sturdy grasp on his arm further startles him.

"This way," she says, taking the lead. "Just down those steps over there. See?"

Kai sees. The light is so bright in the empty corridor, it's hard to miss them. There's a wall at the base of the stairs; it's bare like the walls in the corridor.

"You haven't asked my name," she says, stopping at the head of the stairs, compelling Kai to stop with her.

"I wasn't sure it was allowed?"

The old Journer laughs. The sound is bell-like, almost beautiful.

"Allowed? This is the Duck Down Club, young Journer. There's virtually nothing that isn't allowed in here."

So, the place *is* real. No myth created by a long-forgotten cohort of upper students or the top rank of administrators at the Lycea, either. Actually real! Now Kai is seriously beginning to worry. Should he turn around and run? Undignified. Should he see it through? Imprudent.

He's turned on his heel before he knows it. But the old one is deceptively strong. She's not about to let him go so easily. He could shake her off, of course, knock her down.

Stay or go?

"Don't waste another thought on that, young Journer," the old one says calmly. "You made the decision to come here and that took courage. Such a shame to back out now before you know why you were summoned."

Summoned? Only the Pedorate Council has the power to summon someone, but Kai can't conceive that the Council would summon anyone to a place like this. Since the Duck Down Club appears to be real, then he's obviously been mistaken all along. Could be this place isn't sanctioned by the Lycea, but by the Pedorate itself for some purpose he has no hope of understanding—yet, anyway. Even so, why summon *him*, a simple Urban pilot? That doesn't seem right, either. This is no closet Pedorate facility, just like it's no prank of Gannin's.

The old pilot releases his arm and ushers him ahead of her down the steps.

Stay. Somehow the decision is made for him.

"Why do I get the feeling that you're not going to explain that?"

"Because you are a very smart young Journer," she says, following. "Henneh said you were."

He has serious doubts about that. No smart young Journer walks willingly into the Duck Down Club.

"My name is Bes Gannaline-ro, just in case you're interested."

Kai stumbles and almost falls down the last of the steps. He rights himself and spins around.

"You can't be!" he snaps at the old one. "Bes Gannaline-ro is dead."

"So I hear," she replies evenly and nudges Kai aside. "And there's no need to yell. I'm old. Not deaf." She rounds the corner to her left. "This way."

Kai glances behind him. There's another corridor winding right, but he can't see beyond it.

"What's that way?" he asks.

"Can't see it matters to you, Kai Astada."

The left corridor ends at a very solid-looking door. How did they know he was standing outside in the laneway? It's not like they could have heard or seen him. Has to be a concealed vis somewhere.

With her fingertips, the old Journer begins to tap on a little panel recessed into the wall beside the door. The panel is so small Kai could easily have missed it.

They're particular who gets in. Are they just as particular about who gets out? It was stupid to have come here. He knew better.

The door is as tight as the security. Ro uses her shoulder to nudge the door open. Either the door is out of square or the floor on the other side is uneven because the door jambs halfway. This time Kai doesn't have to duck, instead he is obliged to turn side-on to follow his guide through the opening. The first thing that strikes him is how gloomy it is on the other side of the door. If the rumours are right, the patrons of the Duck Down Club are mostly Subs. They've grown accustomed to the darkness of the tunnels underground. Their eyes are sensitive. It makes sense that the club

                         Shaune Lafferty Webb

is a dark and dingy place. It's also a relatively quiet place. He'd always assumed Subs to be a rowdy, vice-prone lot. Seems he's mistaken there, too; that or word of his arrival preceded him.

As Kai's eyes begin to adapt, he's able to pick out more of his surroundings. It's crowded under the low dark ceiling beams and there's a pervasive smell in the air of something Kai assumes must be *taint*. He's never tasted the stuff and the sickly-sweet stench of it has convinced him he never wants to. The room is equipped with tables crammed so closely together, they take up most of the space, leaving little room for passage between. There are few chairs. Most of the club's patron are seated, shoulder to shoulder, on stiff-backed wooden benches drawn in tightly against the tables. Five, maybe six, patrons are milling about the room. There could be a long bar-type arrangement extending along one whole side of the room, but in the dim light, it's difficult for Kai to tell if it actually reaches all the way to the back. For some reason, he was expecting the place to be quite a bit smaller. And as he takes in the clientele, he's even more surprised to see pilots whose attire suggests they were once Urbans, who may no longer be active but are simply wearing the old uniforms of their former rank. Kai spots no black uniforms, faded or otherwise, in the crowd. He's less surprised by that; if a Continental were to frequent this place then, like Gannaline-ro, they'd be careful to conceal their rank.

"So?" Bes's strong voice jars with ambient noise baffled by the heavy low beams. "What do you think of the place? Not even fit for an Urban like you?" She offers him a shrug and then smiles. "Suits me just fine. These are my kind of people. Good people. Could be your kind of people, too, if you've a mind for them to be."

"Look, Pilot Ro, if that's who you really are, I have no interest in becoming a member of your eccentric little club. If this is part of some very strange recruitment drive, then you're wasting my time and yours." He makes to move away, but the old pilot snatches his arm again.

"Wasn't me who called you here." She sniffs. "Frankly I was against it. Voted against it if you must know. It was Henneh who said you were all right. Personally, I don't know if you're all right or not. You've got an attitude problem. And that's a mark against you straight away."

"He's young, Bes."

Kai snaps his head around, seeking the person who spoke.

"Here, Pilot."

Across the room, an old one, dressed in the olive drab uniform of a Sub, is getting to his feet. He's tall, even for a Sub. Kai can't see his eyes; he's wearing his U-visor. But his face is gaunt, cheekbones sticking through and with a jaw so sharp you could cut with it.

His companions at the table watch as he makes for Kai.

The old one thrusts out his hand. "Markel Gallia," he says.

Kai glances down at the proffered hand. It's even bonier than his face, although Kai would have thought that impossible. In the dim light, the skin looks tissue thin. He's frightened to touch the old relic for fear it might crumble to dust.

"Are you stupid or just plain rude?" Bes barks. "Shake Markel's hand. He's blind. He can't see that you're standing there with your mouth hanging open."

"I'm sorry," Kai says in a rush. He takes the old one's hand as cautiously as he would take the paw of an angry pageeti. Gently he begins to shake until the old one starts to squeeze harder and then harder still. By the time Kai's hand is released, his fingers have gone numb.

"Sub controls aren't as delicate as an Urban's, young one. Piloting a Sub is a task for the hands as well as the brain. A weak-handed pilot is a dead pilot underground."

"So I've just learned," Kai replies, slyly massaging his fingers.

Behind him, Ro sniggers. He hasn't been quite sly enough.

"I'll take over from here," Gallia says, head cocked loosely in Ro's direction. "This way."

With a quick glance over his shoulder, Kai starts after Gallia. Ro has already melted back into the crowd and is sitting at one of the long tables, talking spiritedly. She doesn't seem the least interested in him anymore.

Without a single misstep, the old pilot leads Kai past the untidy jumble of tables. A few of the patrons glance up as they pass. The sweet stench of *taint* is even stronger now. Overwhelmed, Kai finds himself wiping his eyes. The stuff is highly illegal, of course, but the presence of *taint* is something he more or less would expect in the Duck Down Club.

He follows Gallia to the far corner of the room and a recess that was obscured earlier by the many tables, benches and patrons in the way.

"I'll leave you here," Gallia says, stopping short of the opening. "Henneh is waiting for you inside."

With that, the blind old pilot turns. Nearby someone leaps up from a table that is wedged so tightly against the wall Kai thinks for a moment he's going to knock old Gallia down. Instead, the leaping patron executes a neat little sidestep to let him pass.

Kai shakes his head in wonder. These pilots' reactions are as finely tuned as any Urban or Continental pilot he has ever come across. Why is it they were overlooked for the better positions? Kai knows it isn't the Lycea that determines a graduate's posting, but he starts to wonder, and not for the first time, what criteria is being used by those who do make those decisions.

"You came."

The voice is familiar. Cautiously, Kai steps through the narrow opening, finds the table by sensing rather than actually seeing it. His eyes are still adjusting and he uses the few moments to locate the back of a single chair. By the time he is seated, he's able to pick out the face of the Journer sitting in the opposite chair. It's a face he should know well, but her eyes are all he recognises. The rest of her has radically aged. If he had to guess, he'd say she was at least ten years older than him, but he knows with certainty that they were born in the same year. She isn't thin exactly, not like the old Sub pilot Markel Gallia is thin. Not enough time has passed for that. It's more like the skin of her face has come loose, the muscles behind it slackened. And although in this inadequate light he can't be sure, her colouring looks kind of dead flesh greyish. Her red hair, now dulled a characterless brown, has been cropped, too, in the typical style of a Sub pilot. The short, spiky cut makes caring for it easier in the grit and grime of the underground.

The stark change in her appearance leaves Kai momentarily speechless.

"Stop trying to think of something polite to say. This is how all Subs look. Why do you seem so surprised?"

"I'm not... I mean..."

"You mean you didn't think of it happening to me." There's a trace of resigned amusement in her voice.

"No, I didn't." What's the point of lying? They had known each other too well for that.

"Don't worry. There's breath left in me yet. I've hardly been in the post two years yet. So tell me," she says openly. "How's life on an Urban?"

"It's fine," Kai replies with little interest. He's still struggling to adjust to the changes in Henneh, changes that aren't just in her appearance. When he first heard her speak, he thought her voice was the same. But now that she has said more, he's noticed that the timbre is slightly deeper. And her tone is different, too, as though she's just going through the motions to communicate. The enthusiasm, the excitement, the quickness that once used to colour her speech are gone.

When Henneh raises her hands to place them on the surface of the table, Kai is briefly tempted to reach out and touch them. But no gesture of compassion, sincere or feigned, would mean a thing. What could he possibly say to her? He can't apologise. He wasn't responsible for her posting. He can't sympathise and say he'd rather it had been him instead. He doesn't. He can't promise to help her. He has no influence. Everything he thinks of to say, he immediately dismisses, realising it might only make matters worse.

"I've been rude."

Kai is relieved when Henneh speaks again, freeing him of the obligation to say anything more about his own posting. He's even more relieved, and a little surprised, to hear a ghost of the old mischievousness in her voice.

"I haven't offered you a drink."

"*Taint?*" Kai asks, attempting a smile.

"What else?" Henneh's smile comes more easily. "It's as real as the club, Kai. But I'm sure we can chase up something else if *taint* isn't to your taste." A glass half-filled with an iridescent blue liquid is sitting in front of her on the table, a fraction away from her hand. Glancing down, she begins to twist it slowly—around and around. "I guess Urbans wouldn't dream of touching this stuff. It's not as bad as they'd have you believe," she says, looking up. "Just takes a bit of getting used to. And it's not addictive." She taps the glass with a fingernail. "Just a little numbing really."

"I'll try it," Kai agrees reluctantly.

Henneh waves her hand and, almost instantly, a filled glass appears by Kai's elbow. He turns to thank whoever brought it but they've already gone.

Henneh nods toward the glass. "It's clean," she says. "Don't worry. Despite appearances, Subs are very particular about their health."

A Sub. Henneh is a Sub. Kai had never really gotten his head around that and, despite seeing her this way, still can't fully come to terms with it. Right at the start, when their postings became known, he'd assumed that, through some administrative error, Henneh's and Gannin's postings had been mixed up. It wasn't so. Gannin had been legitimately given the command of a Continental and Henneh, a Sub. He hadn't questioned his own Urban posting; it was pretty much what he was expecting. And so the three of them were posted poles apart and Kai hasn't seen either of them since that last day at the Lycea when Gannin was grossly insensitive about broadcasting his good fortune while Henneh remained silent and stoic in acceptance of her bad.

"I'm guessing you didn't get in touch with me just to reminisce about old times," Kai says. He's still eyeing the lethal-looking liquid in the glass in front of him, unwilling as yet to risk it.

Henneh's message came to him through a rather odd channel— a few words economically delivered by a particularly evasive young Preserver who caught him by surprise on the platform after his last run.

"Right as always," Henneh replies. She lifts her glass, drains it, then raises it briefly in the air.

Another glass appears miraculously by Kai's elbow. He's just about to scoot it across the table when Henneh reaches over to claim it. Her other hand has slipped underneath the table. When she brings it up, there's a folder in it. She places the folder, thick and dull in colour, on the table.

"Read it here or take it with you," she says. "It's just a copy."

Kai eyes the folder with even more suspicion than he's just eyed the glass of *taint*. Lifting the outer cover his attention is immediately drawn to the seal dominating the left corner of the first page—a rhombus as purple as blood enclosing a stylised *nesicum* flower in the standard form of four yellow petals symmetrically offset over four green petals. The official Pedorate insignia. The device every Journer pilots under.

"What's in it?" he asks, slamming the cover closed.

"And how did I come by official Pedorate documents?"

She's asked the next obvious question.

Kai nods.

"Maybe I'll tell you that after you read it. Maybe I won't. After all," she shrugs, "we don't know whose side you're on, do we?"

"Side! Side of what?"

Kai doesn't like the sound of this. Even Urbans are supposed to be possessed of above-average intelligence. And he's a pretty good Urban. The smart thing to do now is get up from the table, leave the folder unread where it is, and quit the Duck Down Club as fast as he possibly can. That would be the *smart* thing to do.

Henneh taps the folder with the tip of her finger. "Read it."

"I'm sorry, Henneh. I haven't forgotten our friendship. It goes back a long way. But you've changed. And I don't just mean your appearance. I'm not sure that I even know you anymore. I don't know what's in that folder and, now that I've had a moment to think about it, I don't think I want to know what's in it or how you came by it."

To his surprise, Henneh begins to smile. "Don't you realise we've heard that same reply before." She lifts her glass and takes a long swallow of *taint*. "Some of the biggest and best have come around. You'll be no different."

"You're being too mysterious," Kai tells her.

"Hardly," Henneh replies, tapping the folder once more. "I could tell you everything right here, right now, but why should you believe me? It would just be the word of a Sub. What's in here says it all and says it better."

"I have no intention of walking out of this club carrying official Pedorate documents under my arm. Pilot Ro, if that's who she really is, claims you said I'm smart, so you've got to expect I'm smarter than to do something like that."

"You mean carrying a *copy* of official Pedorate documents, don't you?" she corrects him. "We'd hardly give away the originals. I walked in *with* them but I suppose that's beside the point. We did anticipate you'd feel that way and that's why we didn't approach you ourselves and, by way of protecting you, asked you to come to us instead. It seemed quite considerate to us."

"I'm afraid it doesn't to me," Kai replies and shoots the folder back across the table.

He's put a little too much effort into it and the folder slides off the table, pages fluttering to the floor by Henneh's feet. She doesn't stoop to pick them up, simply raises her glass once again.

"We anticipated that response, too," she says, lowering the glass, "and would like to offer you an alternative."

"Are you joking? Look, Henneh. I'm not interested in any of this. I thought I made myself clear. If you Subs have some sort of grievance, I suggest you take it to the Lycea. Director Vidamore will see you. I'm sure he will, if you go through the proper channels."

"Enlist a Talker, you mean?"

"Yes," Kai answers emphatically.

"Have you ever attempted to approach a Talker?"

"No, I've never—"

Henneh cuts him off. "See, there's another problem. We've considered all our options, Kai. And considered them very well."

"You're forcing me to say it again, Henneh. I'm sorry. But I don't see myself as one of your options. It appears that you *haven't* considered my refusal so well after all."

Henneh falls silent for a while, eyes downcast, looking at her half-empty glass. She stays in that pose so long, Kai's about to take it as an admission of defeat, her concession that their brief meeting is done. He makes to rise when Henneh's focus shifts. She's looking at him again.

"You haven't touched your drink."

He looks at his full glass, its contents so blue and, although he's loath to admit it, inviting. Could it be the *taint*? Has Henneh's thinking been distorted by the drug? Mindful of his last experience shooting something across the table, he carefully pushes the glass with its iridescent blue contents toward her. "It's yours. You paid for it."

"No one pays for drinks in the Duck Down Club," she says. "No one pays for anything here."

"That just makes it easier for me to leave then." He starts to get to his feet, but changes his mind. "I'm sorry I can't help you,

Henneh. I really am. My mother was a Sub, remember. I have an idea of what it's like and what it can do to someone."

"I remember your mother well. She's taking care of Mig. Have you forgotten?"

He hadn't forgotten. He just hasn't given it much thought. It must sorely pain Henneh to have her little sister locked inside a quarantined ward with no idea if she'll ever see her or her father again. Kai doesn't have such problems. His father, like Henneh's mother, is dead. And he has no abiding desire to see either his own mother or sister ever again.

"I'm sorry about Mig as well," he says. "I know how hard it must be for you... with the quarantine." He doesn't mention the obvious. How being raised by Ush would be an even greater hardship for Mig than the quarantine. "You know," he says in sudden thought, "Gannin Tewel might be able to help you. He's a Continental pilot after all. I'm just an Urban."

He's surprised when Henneh begins to laugh.

"Gannin! Now I have to ask if *you're* joking. Gannin wouldn't even set foot through the door."

No, he wouldn't. And Kai always thought himself to be smarter than Gannin. But Gannin would put self-interest above old affections, something he had not done.

"Perhaps you're right," he says half-heartedly.

"You're a deader like me, Kai. That's one of the reasons you got into the club so easily."

"And the other reason?"

"My assurance that you'd respect the privacy of this meeting."

Despite himself, Kai smiles. "Believe me, Henneh, I have no intention of talking about tonight with anyone."

"I believe you," she replies. "I always have."

Clever. Now she's attempting to appeal to his conscience.

"You play dirty, Henneh. I never realised that about you."

He's expecting her to be shocked, at least show some sign that he's offended her. But there is nothing. She just sits there, contemplating her glass.

"Playing dirty," she says at last, "would be to say nothing at all. To conceal everything that's in these pages," she toes a loose sheet by her chair, "and go on as though nothing is wrong."

Now it's Kai who feels offended. "So you're accusing *me* of playing dirty?"

"Only in ignorance," she says with a little shrug.

"Nice try," he says, completing his rise this time. "But it isn't going to work. I'm sorry, Henneh. I really am. I won't and I can't help you. I want nothing to do with this. Whatever you've got yourself into, I'd advise you to get out of it as fast as you possibly can." He spins around and collides immediately into Bes Gannaline-ro. Before he can manage to sidestep the old Journer, he feels a sharp stabbing sensation in his neck. His hand shoots to the spot where a welt is already beginning to form. *Taint.*

He turns on Henneh, tempted to leap across the table and take her by the neck.

"*What have you done?*" His whole body has begun to tremble. From the drug? From pure unadulterated anger?

"Calm down, young Kai Astada."

It's the old Journer who replies. Henneh isn't even looking; she's down on the floor, gathering the scattered sheets of papers.

"I bet you're thinking that's *taint*," Ro says with a little chuckle. "Now that *is* all myth. You can't inject *taint*. It would kill you. You've just been deregistered. That's all."

The place where the old Journer injected him is beginning to sting. "What do you mean deregistered?"

"You're dead," she says calmly. "To all intents and purposes anyway. Oh," she continues with a flip of her hand, "I don't just mean you're a deader. That's nothing but an unfortunate blot on your official record. Now your record shows that you're well and truly dead. Cold as a limp mantii washed up on the beach. That pid I just injected you with simply formalises it. You were actually dead the moment you walked in the door. Go look up your Journer file, if you don't believe me. You'll find you're quite deceased. You're a *non,* just like the rest of us. Oh, how stupid of me. You're dead. How can you look at your file?"

"Take it out," Kai orders between clenched teeth. "Or I'll take it out myself."

"Hmmm." Ro taps her chin with the sturdy little needle she's just used on him. "You could. But then where would you be? Your official record says you're dead but the birth-pid embedded under your sternum will then imply you're on active service to Pedora." She taps the needle again. "There's a problem. You're alive. You're dead. Then you're alive again. That means an investigation, of course."

"And that would be exactly what I want."

"Really?" Ro raises her thin grey eyebrows in mock surprise. "Considering your disreputable activities? I'd think that's something you'd want to keep from the attention of the authorities. Any investigation would certainly bring them to light."

"I see." Kai pulls out his chair and sits down. "You've slipped something into my records somehow. What is it?"

He turns to look directly at Henneh. She's back in her own chair now, the scattered papers gathered and returned to the folder in front of her.

"Sale and distribution of *taint*," she replies.

"Henneh," Ro chastises the young Sub from behind Kai. "Credit where credit is due. Young Kai here is the *biggest* distributer in all of Ularon City." She rounds the little table to stand behind Henneh. "Maybe all of Pedora," she adds, spreading her hands. "Only a full investigation could say for sure. Oh, and by the way," her scrawny hand comes down to rest on Henneh's shoulder, "that's how you died in case you're interested. You got a bit too greedy and your supplier took exception."

"Nice!" Kai says. "I hope the Ditcher gave me a nice funeral. So, how did you do it?"

"Falsify your file, you mean?" It's Henneh asking the question.

Kai nods.

"Connections," she says.

Kai waves a hand toward the outer room. "And I suppose everyone in this club is likewise dead and had some sort of fallacious charge slipped into their records."

"Dead. Yes." Ro answers with a shrug. "*Some* of us."

"You see," Henneh takes up, "most of us came to the club voluntarily."

"How happy a circumstance for you."

"No need to get sarcastic, young pilot," Ro says in a warning tone.

"And those of us who arrived under...hmm," Henneh continues, "some persuasion, shall we say, came to our way of thinking soon enough. Just like you will. They've had their records cleared. They're still dead, of course. But now they prefer it that way."

"Does that include you?" Kai asks. It would explain a lot.

"Me? No," Henneh replies with little interest. "I was a volunteer."

Not completely convinced, Kai turns to Ro. "But there is a way to get my record cleared?"

"As easily as it was to muddy it."

"Then I suggest you do that." He's done with the duplicitous talk.

"Or what?" the old Journer asks.

"Oh, I don't know," he says with a smile. "But I think my first stop should be with the Director of the Lycea."

"Ah yes. Director Vidamore." Ro nods her head solemnly. "Of course, he wasn't the Director when I studied at the Lycea. That was someone by the name of Marga Sebalt. Nasty." Ro crinkles her nose. "Nothing but a Pedorate sycophant. Everyone knew it."

"Are you telling me that Vidamore is a... what did you call it? A *non*?"

"I don't recall saying any such thing," Ro replies. "Besides, how could Eine Vidamore possibly be a *non*? He's still the Director of the Lycea, isn't he?" She looks to Henneh for confirmation.

"Last I knew. Such as the Lycea is these days."

"Well then, there you have it," Ro tells Kai, smiling. "Eine Vidamore is quite alive. Officially and otherwise. A *non*!" She turns to Henneh once again. "And you said he was such a clever young Journer."

"You have to give him time, Bes."

Henneh's actually starting to sound a little sympathetic. Kai could do with a little sympathy right now. If he's to get out of this mess, then it's obvious he's going to have to gain the cooperation of Gannaline-ro to do it.

"If you want me to help you in some way," he says, "then you're going to have to make me want to help you or, failing that, convince me that I have no other option."

Ro waves her hand in summons and another chair is immediately brought into the alcove. She waits until the young Sub who brought the chair is out of earshot.

"And what will that take?" she asks, settling in.

Kai's hand drifts once again toward his neck. The welt is growing larger by the moment. "You can start by explaining to me how this pid formalises that I'm dead. If the official record says I'm dead, then I'm dead, aren't I? Dead is dead. I can't see any need for this violation. If you take it out, I'll still sit here and listen to what you have to say, but after that I'm gone. And I won't say a word to anyone about what happened here."

"You won't say a word?"

"You have my promise."

"I don't know about that," the old pilot says. "If all it takes is a little prick in the neck to get you to listen, what might it take to get you to talk?" She clucks her tongue. "Besides, for a *taint* distributor, you don't seem to know a lot about the pid trade."

"You're taunting him, Bes," Henneh interrupts, turning to the old one. "He's agreed to listen."

"Very well," Ro concedes. "I was just having a little fun at your expense, young pilot. No offence intended."

"Offence taken," Kai replies. "So?"

"I'm sorry but the pid stays. And since Henneh seems to feel you deserve an explanation, I'll comply. Although it's more than we've done for anyone else. Birth-pids are a lucrative commodity. No one in the upper castes is going to trade or give theirs up willingly now, are they? And given where they're located in the body, the only way to get one is surgically before or after someone is dead. No reputable Doser is going to perform an operation like that. Which leaves only two options. Either you abduct someone and remove their pid, which is likely to result in the death of the unfortunate abductee if the procedure is performed by someone incompetent, leaving *the thief* in the equally unfortunate position of having to dispose of a body, or you wait until someone dies, naturally or by accident, and then remove their pid. So how do you control the trade?"

Kai shrugs impatiently.

"It's very simple. When someone dies, you make sure their birth-pid dies with them. Of course, that's simplifying it. That pid I injected you with... its signal has scrambled your birth-pid's signal. In short, your birth-pid has been deactivated. That's one of the first responsibilities of every Ditcher."

"Seems to me that opens up a lot of opportunity for corruption among Ditchers," Kai observes.

"Yes, it does and that's why they're so closely monitored and the distribution of the scrambler pids is so tightly controlled."

"Yet you still managed to get one of them." Kai hesitates, recalling all the people he passed coming in, some of whom he assumes weren't quite as eager as Henneh to volunteer for membership in the club. "Or should I say a supply of them."

"Now that's really our business, isn't it? You asked how the pid formalises your death. And now I've explained it."

"There's something you left out."

Ro glances briefly at Henneh before she replies. "What?"

"When I threatened to take the pid out myself, you said it would leave me alive again, so to speak, but recorded as dead in my file. If the pid you injected scrambles the signal from my birth-pid, then how is it unscrambled?"

The old pilot lowers her gaze and, reaching out, takes Kai's untouched glass for herself. It's Henneh who finally answers.

"Bes wasn't telling you the truth before," she says. "Not all of it anyway. Your record can be cleared, of course. That's easy. But I'm afraid even we can't make you 'undead.' We could change the records, make it look like the report of your death was all some big mistake, but we can't do anything about returning your birth-pid to active."

Kai feels himself sinking in the chair. He's diminishing, growing smaller and smaller, so small in fact that surely at any moment, he must simply disappear. Maybe he really is dead—in every sense of the word. What's happening here cannot possibly be real.

Someone touches his hand. He looks down to see one of Henneh's hands enclosed over his. He hears her say she's sorry. He hears her say it was the only way.

"Why me?" he asks, slipping his hand free.

"We've been watching you, young pilot," Ro replies. "From a distance, of course. You're one of the best pilots I've ever seen by the way."

"I'm sure there are any number of good pilots here, Gannaline. Why can't you use one of them for whatever you've got in mind?"

She shakes her head. "You're right, there *are* many good pilots here. Your pilot skills aren't what we need. You didn't let me finish."

Kai flips a hand. "Go on then," he says. He almost doesn't care now what she has to say. It's all kind of irrelevant really. He's dead. Technically. Why not be physically dead as well? His father's dead. His mother and his sister don't matter. And now he can never go back to his Urban. What's left?

"It's your connections we need."

In light of what he's just been thinking, her assertion sounds positively ludicrous.

"Pilot Ro, or *again*, whoever you are, I don't have any connections. You've mistaken me for someone else. Besides, aren't you the one with *connections*? Use your own."

"Unfortunately our influence doesn't extend quite so far as we'd like."

"Pity."

"Indeed," Ro agrees coolly.

His attempt at derision has fallen flat.

"But yours does," the old pilot adds.

Kai turns to Henneh. "I don't know what you've been telling them here, but clearly it's lies. I'm nothing but a common Urban pilot. One step above a Sub. I've got no *connections* and certainly no influence with anyone and you know it. At least you should. What's happened to you, Henneh?"

His attention drifts again to Henneh's glass. The *taint*. Does it all come back to the *taint*?

"Read it," Henneh says, slowly nudging the folder across the table. "You really don't have much of a choice now. I can't say you'll be glad you did, but you'll certainly understand some things a lot better."

Kai snatches up the folder. "I really doubt that. I haven't understood one damn thing since I walked in here."

He tries not to look at the Pedorate seal in the corner of the topmost page and begins to read. The first page is full of tightly spaced text, much of which smacks of standard Pedorate officiousness. He glances at Henneh under his eyebrows.

"You can skip that part until later if you want. It won't make a lot of sense to you until you read the rest."

Typical. Everything in Pedora works back to front and the logic of many things only makes any kind of sense once you look at it from the wrong end. Some things never seem to make sense, at least not to people in the undercastes and since the plague, Journers have been sliding steadily in that direction.

Kai flips to the second page. Ninety percent of it is filled with tables, graphs and indecipherable diagrams.

"And you think I can understand this any better?"

"I did," Henneh tells him with a wry smile.

"He isn't trying," the old pilot grumbles. "You said he was better than this."

"I told you before, Bes, you have to give him time."

The edginess in Henneh's tone surprises him. If the old pilot really is Bes Gannaline-ro, then she warrants some respect. Henneh doesn't seem overly inclined to give the old pilot her due under just any circumstances. It leads Kai to wonder just who *is* in charge here. He had assumed it was Ro, but maybe he's got that wrong, too. Maybe it isn't Ro's sympathy he needs, but Henneh's. Gaining sympathy from the Henneh of old was never exactly painless. It had to be earned even then. But Henneh is a fair-minded person. At least she used to be. Just because he sees the situation he's been placed in as unjust and untenable, doesn't mean that she does.

Kai turns back to the pages in front of him. The sooner he's done reading them, the sooner he can get to the real issue, the matter of his 'deceased' status and what, if anything, Henneh and Ro intend to do about it.

There's nothing in any of the pages that he can readily understand. He recognises the images, of course. Even a young one could recognise those, if not interpret them. Kai can't do that, either, but he's seen enough of them produced on his own brain during his time at the Lycea to know what he's looking at. In all, he counts forty-two separate sets of images and he's guessing that all the tabulated data somehow refers to other brain function and physical tests carried out on the forty-two different subjects. It's all Doser stuff to him. About all he can say is that the forty-two individual brains appear to be firing up very nicely in every slice. He can't interpret the findings, which he's guessing is what all the tabulated data is about. Reaching the last page, he absorbs what he can of it, then closes the folder and looks over at Henneh.

"All right," he says, "I've read it. And now I understand *less* than I did before."

"There's one more page," Henneh says and slides a single sheet across the table. She must have been holding it on her lap.

Kai takes the page. She's handed it to him wrong way around. He spins it and finds that the page she's given him consists of a single two-column table. The left column lists ident numbers; the right, the names corresponding to those ident numbers. The first name on the list immediately strikes Kai as familiar. He runs a finger down the right-hand column, stopping abruptly when he comes to the name Rei Sek. Henneh's mother!

He can feel Henneh watching him, so he forces himself to continue down the list. Forty-two names, just like there were forty-two separate reports on forty-two separate individuals gathered together inside the folder. He's already expecting to see the name Anan Astada on the list but, when he finds it about halfway down, isn't expecting to feel quite so hollow inside. Beneath his father's name, he sees the name of Gannin's brother. He doesn't bother scanning the rest of the names. Opening the folder, he places the single page atop the rest, closes the folder again, then takes a moment to gather his thoughts.

"I don't know why you felt it necessary to show me this, Henneh. They're just some old records of some of the Journers who were on *The Nether*. They're all dead now. Why can't you just let them rest?"

"They're records of every Journer who went on *The Nether*."

"All right. So they are. What difference does that make?"

"Look at the dates."

He skims the folder back across the table to Henneh. "My father is dead, Henneh. And so is your mother and every other Journer from that ship. Looking at a collection of images from a time when they were alive can't bring them back. It's pointless."

Henneh hasn't touched the folder and Ro stretches out one thin bony hand to retrieve it. She stands to lean in his direction. Kai literally jumps in his seat when the old pilot slams the folder down in front of him again.

"Look at the dates, then tell us it's pointless!" she shouts.

Her face is so close to Kai's that, even in the dim light, he can see the little specks of yellow that mar the irises of her brown eyes. Before he gets a chance to touch the folder, she flips the cover back, strips the sheet bearing the list of ident numbers and names from the top and lays it upside down on the inside cover of the folder, does likewise with the next page, the one rife with Pedorate officialdom, and then slams her hand onto the first page of the reports.

Kai brushes her hand aside and looks at the date as she demands.

"Look at all of them!"

Old Ro is still leaning over the table. Now Kai can smell the sickly-sweet scent of *taint* on her breath. The scent seems to be muddying his thoughts, threatening to make his head ache.

Kai begins to scan. By the time he reaches the third report, Ro has reclaimed her chair. At least he can breathe a little better now but it seems the heady perfume of *taint* is destined to permeate the air from now on.

Completing the task, he closes the folder once again. The dates all fall within three days of each other.

"Well?" Henneh asks him. Unlike Ro, she's been patient. He'll give her that.

"I don't know what you expect me to get from this."

"How can you *not* understand what we've just shown you?" There's colour in her face, the first Kai has seen.

"I understand that all those tests were undertaken within a three-day period. Is that what I'm supposed to be seeing? If that's it, then I'm afraid I'm missing the point." He nudges the folder back toward Henneh.

"Yes, that's right," Henneh agrees, leaning forward. "All within a three-day period. After the return of *The Nether.*"

"I noticed that."

"That means they were alive when they returned."

Of course, they were alive. If they hadn't been alive, then their brains wouldn't have been all lit up brighter than the night sky over Ularon City on Unification Day. It still means nothing to Kai.

"Henneh," he says, "we know that some of *The Nether* crew died shortly after they returned. Not everyone died in transit."

"Oh, I see," she says, clearly in mock understanding. "So everyone who wasn't a Journer died *in* transit while everyone who was a Journer died *later?*"

"What?"

She points at the folder. "All those names on the list. They're all Journers. And every one of them was alive at least for some days after their return."

Reaching out, Kai snatches up the folder. "That can't be right."

Out of the corner of his eye, he notices Ro's wrinkled face crease further into what might pass as a satisfied smile.

"Look again," Henneh suggests. "See for yourself."

Kai opens the folder and scans the list again.

"If I showed you the records for the support crew," Henneh continues as he reads, "you'd be seeing the same thing."

Kai shrugs. "So you're trying to tell me they were all alive when they returned. What of it? Maybe they all *did* die later."

"But that's not what we were told, is it?" Henneh asks.

No. He can't argue that. Still...

"What difference does it make when they died, Henneh? They all still died. And they all still died of the plague."

"Did they now?" Ro prompts.

Kai glowers at the old pilot. "Just what are you trying to say?"

"I'm not *trying* to say anything at all," Ro replies. "I'm telling you that every single person who travelled on *The Nether* returned. And not only did they return, but they returned hail and healthy. Oh," she raises a hand before Kai can interrupt, "we suspect they're all quite dead by now, of course. Officially and otherwise. Dead and flashed."

Kai didn't like to think about his father that way. Dead and flashed.

"Then what's your point? You just agreed they're dead. So the logical conclusion is that something killed them, isn't it? They all couldn't have died within such a short space of time by natural causes, could they?"

Neither the old pilot nor Henneh answer and the silence stretches out so long, Kai's frustration with the pair soars to a point just below its own flash point. When he first met the pilot and discovered who she was, at least who she claimed to be, he was actually inclined to admire her, revere her even, as a survivor from the past. Now he can't help but think of Ro as anything but an aggravating old troublemaker. A reject. Worse—perhaps even a manipulative subversive. A very persuasive subversive! He had it right from the start. Ro, not Henneh, is in charge here and she's swayed Henneh to her warped way of thinking. In his experience, Henneh was never one to be easily swayed.

"Go on then," he says. "Spit it out and get it over with. What do you think happened to them?"

"That, young pilot, is where you come in. We want you to find out."

Kai looks quickly from the old pilot to Henneh and back again. "From whom?"

"I'm afraid that's an impossible question for us to answer with certainty. If we could, then we'd already know and we wouldn't need you now, would we? We've been unable to get to them."

"I see," Kai says with a little nod. "I don't suppose you'd be able to answer why you think I'm the only one who can?"

Ro's smile is infuriating. "Now I never said you were the only one. Just the *best* one."

"Oh, you'll pardon my misunderstanding, Pilot Ro. Perhaps you could indulge me with a little explanation."

"You're an Urban."

"Granted."

"But you're an Urban who should have been a Continental."

"What?" It's the first he's heard of that.

"We know what's in your Lycea records. Trust me."

"So Director Vidamore—"

Henneh interrupts. "We were given that information by someone else."

"Who?" Kai demands, turning on his old friend.

She doesn't reply.

So, they're right back where they started. And for all he knows, those records, if they even have them, could be as false as the documents lying beside his elbow on the table top.

"Your father was on *The Nether*," Ro takes up.

Kai flips a hand in response. "Common knowledge. And so were many other Journers' family members."

"Yes, but being a dead son will be an advantage."

Kai hasn't found it so yet.

"You're uncompromising. You're intelligent. You're not prone to naivety... at least we hadn't thought so. But most importantly," she leans again across the table, "you have access to the person who we believe is concealing the evidence."

"And who might that be?" Kai asks coolly.

"Ah. That's where we have a little problem."

"I'm glad it's just a little one."

"We could have made a mistake."

"Really!"

"And if we have made a mistake and we send you to the wrong person, then it could tip our hand. Do you understand?"

"Not a thing."

"I'm sure you do." Ro settles back in her seat. "And that, I'm afraid, is why you're going to have to find out for yourself. It's our insurance. If you reach the same conclusion... well, then our position is confirmed. And the bonus, of course, will be that, should you be successful, you'll come away with the evidence we need."

"Let's assume for the moment that I believe all this nonsense and do follow through. What if I conclude it's someone else?"

"That could be a problem, too."

"Undoubtedly. And what if I do conclude it is the same person, but I fail to get the evidence you're looking for?"

"Another problem. Most especially for you, of course. Then *your* hand is tipped. If you see what I mean."

"Not really, no," Kai replies with a single shake of his head. "I'd simply implicate the Duck Down Club, wouldn't I?"

"But we don't exist, remember?" Ro counters. "You could send them here, of course, and they'll find nothing but an old abandoned cellar and maybe a few filthy fiweams crawling around."

"You're mad. Both of you." He shoots another quick glance at Henneh. "My father... your mother... everyone on that ship died of the plague."

"And what proof do you have of that, young pilot?"

He'd like to wipe the smile off Ro's face. Maybe permanently. "None. Just like you have no proof that they didn't."

Ro taps the top of the folder with a thin finger.

"That's not proof," Kai tells her. "All those records could be falsified." Now it's his turn to smile. "It's not like you're averse to a little record falsifying, is it?"

"It's a lot of effort to go to," Henneh says.

"I assume it took a fair bit of effort to make me 'dead'."

"Not as much as you might think," Ro mutters, largely to herself.

"Then you've just proved my point, haven't you?"

It's a moment before anyone speaks.

"We're not following you, Kai," Henneh says.

"If it's easy to make me 'dead', then it's easy to *make* these records."

Henneh glances briefly at Pilot Ro before replying. "But I told you before that we have connections. And we have every faith in those connections."

"Maybe you have faith, Henneh, but I'm afraid I don't." His glance, too, shifts to the old pilot. "And I'm also beginning to have some real suspicions about what you injected me with."

"I can assure you it wasn't *taint*."

Kai waves the old pilot's assertion aside. "Oh, I believe that. That's probably the only thing I have believed since I walked in the door. But it wasn't any *scrambler* pid, either, was it? There's no such thing. I don't know why you picked on me. And frankly, I don't really want to know anymore. Maybe it's all just some sort of twisted game you play down here in the club. Maybe I was just the next gullible victim. That makes a lot more sense than me having some sort of special access to someone somewhere. I wish I did. Trust me, I wish I did."

"Believe what you want right now, young pilot," Ro tells him with a shrug. "You'll soon change your mind when you walk out the door."

"Then I guess I'll just have to test that." He rises to his feet. He's of a mind to simply turn his back and leave, but he can't. Instead, he looks at Henneh. "I don't know what you've got yourself into here, Henneh, but I suggest you get out of it as fast as you can." His focus wanders toward the glass by her elbow. "Maybe it's the taint. Maybe it's something else. Like I said, I don't know. But I do care. I'd help you if I could." His gaze settles briefly on the old pilot. "And I don't mean the kind of help she's got in mind. Get out, Henneh. That's the best advice I can give you. And it's all I can do for you."

CHAPTER 6

They let him go. *They just let him go*! Kai wasn't fully expecting that, but it's not quite over yet. There's still a long walk ahead of him back to his quarters and, just his luck, he has to plod all the way in the rain. It's a phenomenon known to occur in Ularon City—one Kai has never experienced before—when a dry dust storm isn't just any old dry dust storm but the precursor of a deluge powering in from behind. The rain is driving sideways in sheets. He's drenched before he even makes it out of the laneway. At least the miserable weather will keep the Guardians off the streets for a little longer. It's some compensation, but too little. He's angry. He's bewildered. He's anxious to get that pid out from under his skin. It's as irritating as a sharp stone in his boot. And now he's also wet and walking blind, relying on the memory of how he got to the Duck Down Club to get him home. He should never have left his modest two-room quarters in The Devid.

He ploughs into the sheets of rain, cursing his stupidity. If it had been anyone but Henneh who summoned him, he wouldn't have gone. They knew it. They used her to get to him. He can't make any sense of it and is slowly coming to the realisation that maybe he shouldn't bother trying. Tomorrow, he'll start afresh, go on as though his visit to the Duck Down Club never happened. He feels guilty about Henneh. He wishes he could get her out of whatever bad business she's got herself into. With each step he takes, battling the gusting rain, he tells himself that Henneh is not his responsibility. By the time he reaches the forecourt of The Devid, he almost believes it.

At the entrance to the building, Kai steps onto the sensor pad and waits, subconsciously massaging his neck. The pad is soaking wet and nothing happens. He steps briefly off and then back onto the pad to the accompaniment of a squeaking, squelching sound from his boots. This time something does happen; the building begins to speak. That's different!

"I'm sorry. You are attempting to enter a restricted area without proper authorisation. Please review your coordinates."

Kai backs up onto the street, whips off his visor and, shielding his eyes, looks up through the heavy rain. Thick drops of water blur his vision. He's never in his quarters very long—only to sleep—but he's never become lost on his way home before. There's nothing remarkable about The Devid. It's little but a fifteen-storey grey box. The Preserver caretaker and his scant staff live on the ground floor, where there's also a small and rarely frequented kitchen-cum-dining room and an area where the electronics that keep the building functioning are housed. There are fifty-six quarters in all, four a floor, each with two small windows. Still Kai is satisfied that he's standing outside the right building. A weak light is shining through one of the windows on the sixth floor; another on the tenth. Kai can't see the back of the building. There may be more lights there but it doesn't really matter. He's never made friends with his fellow residents, doubts he or any one of them would recognise each other should they pass on the street. Lowering his head, Kai steps onto the pad one more time, knowing already that he's wasting his time.

He's dead!

And The Devid knows it, telling him so again in the same gallingly conciliatory terms.

For a brief moment, he considers waiting outside in the rain, in the hope that, before too long, one of his neighbours will hurry in from their shift. He might be able to convince someone to let him in.

Who's he kidding? He wouldn't let some stranger in.

He's dead!

Kai fingers the welt in his neck again. What's he supposed to do now? Make his way back to the Duck Down Club? Slipping his visor back on, Kai turns, resigned there's no other option. He's barely taken one step before he hears another voice.

"Locked out?"

Kai searches the damp and the darkness, but there's no one there.

"Over here," the voice calls again.

He knows that voice although he's only heard it once before. The voice belongs to the young Preserver who approached him on the platform to tell him that Henneh wanted to see him. He didn't know her name; never had the chance to ask because she delivered her message with incredible brevity and then, while he was left standing momentarily dumbfounded, dashed out of sight.

He finds the Preserver hunched on the ground, knees to chest, sheltering from the heavy rain leeside of The Devid.

"There's no need to look so alarmed," she says with a scornful little laugh. "I'm not a grendel."

Water is running in thick streams down Kai's visor and he's going to have to rip it off again if he wants to get a good look at her. There's not much protection where she's crouching, just enough to keep her visor dry. She has a hood pulled up tightly over her head and hair. It obscures every feature of her face save for that dry visor. It's the same Preserver though. Kai is sure of it, even if he can't see her face. It was an unremarkable face he remembers. Young. Very young. In fact, when she first approached him, he took her to be a lost Preserver kyne. But she's no kyne. Preserver young are accustomed to the streets. They know every building in Ularon City, every mean laneway, every crack in the pavement. But they don't wander around unaccompanied this late at night, inviting to be Crossed. There's only one caste lower than Preserver—Ditcher. And every Preserver young one knows it and none in their right mind tempts demotion to processing the dead.

"You'd be best off taking the Sub," she says, raising a shoulder to swipe at non-existent water droplets on her visor.

"Why a Sub?" he asks.

Kai is probably one of the few ordinary residents in Ularon City who has never travelled on a Sub. He can pilot one, of course; every Lycea student learns how to sim-pilot a Sub. And every moment in that chair inside the simulator is sheer pautune. The tightness! The darkness! Whoever programs the simulations does it a little too well for Kai's comfort. How he never overshot the capacity of the cardiac and neural sensors he doesn't know.

"It's the fastest way to the gabber quadrant."

The Talkers' quadrant! Why in pautune would he want to go there?

"Get off at Sub Station Six," she continues.

"Subs don't go to the gabber quadrant," he tells her, thinking to flex his status.

"I'm aware of that."

There's a mocking smile behind her words.

"Sub Station Six is on the edge of the Preserver quadrant, closest to the gabber quadrant. But I guess you know that." She rises. "You walk from there."

When he makes to grasp her arm, all he collects is wet sleeve, but it's enough to keep her from moving off.

"Who are you?"

"A friend," she replies.

"I have no Preserver friends."

She shrugs and water cascades from her shoulders. "Never said I'm a Preserver. You can stand out here all night if you like. Doesn't matter to me. But if you want to find somewhere dry, then I suggest you go where I'm telling you to go. It's a nice place." She jerks her head, indicating The Devid. "Better than this. And it *will* let you in."

That was no simple scrambler pid Ro injected!

"I'm guessing I have a new name to go with my new lodgings?"

"You guess right."

"Care to share it?" he asks, releasing her.

"Sayker Gerit."

Kai has never heard that name before, but then he isn't acquainted with any Talkers and has never had the need to request the services of one.

"How long have you been waiting here?"

"Too long."

There's no trace of the contemptuous tone now. In fact, she sounds downright annoyed.

"I've been here since you left for the club, waiting for you to come back. Ro figured you'd resist. But once your own building refused..." she shrugs again, "you wouldn't have a lot of choice. Unfortunately, no one counted on it raining. You've caused me a lot of trouble."

"I've caused you trouble! Listen, you little Preserver kyne—"

"If you don't mind, my name is Vee and I'd thank you to call me that."

"All right, Vee, then—"

"And I'm not a *kyne*. I'm older than you are, young pilot... oh sorry, Talker... and I'd appreciate a little respect, considering I've been standing out here all night getting wet on your account." She points over Kai's shoulder. "You take the Sub to Station Six and turn left once you get to the street. You keep walking, cross two intersections and then you turn right. That will take you into the gabber quadrant. Stay on that same road and you'll soon come to a white building about twice the size of this one here. You can't miss it. You go to the eighth floor where you will find your lodgings under the name of Sayker Gerit. Inside you will find all your belongings. At least those of your belongings that don't identify you as the dead Kai Astada. Tomorrow, you meet your new contact. You'll find them at the Repository. Give them your name. Your new name, that is. You say nothing more than that. Your name and that you have an appointment. That's all. Understand?"

"No. Frankly I don't. The Repository is a long way from here. Just how do you expect me to get up onto that hill?"

"That's the old Repository," Vee snaps. "It's moved. Do I have to tell you everything? You can reach the Repository on an Urban. That should please you. What sort of pilot were you anyway?" She cocks her head to one side. "Don't even know that."

"It's not my run," Kai fires back, disappointed to have revealed his anger.

"*Wasn't* your run," Vee corrects him.

"Fine," Kai replies, affecting acceptance. "I don't suppose you could give me the name of this person I'm supposed to meet?"

"Not my business."

"What happens if I refuse to go?"

"That also is not my business."

"Whose then? Ro's?"

"Don't know. Don't care. Just a word of advice for you, Sayker Gerit. If you want to stay safe in this world, you'd better start taking notice of what is and isn't *your* business. It'll go a whole lot better for you if you do."

"That's exactly what I *was* doing until you came along. Now all of a sudden, I've got a new name, a new caste about which I know absolutely nothing and my whole life is now at the mercy of you and your demented friends. You tell me which of us is not taking notice of their own business?"

"You know," Vee says after a small pause. "I think they picked the wrong person."

"That's exactly what I've been trying to tell everyone all night."

Vee waves a hand. "I mean they picked the wrong person in *me*. You're really starting to annoy me. I don't have the patience to deal with you much longer. You're too stubborn not to realise that you haven't been taking notice—*really* taking notice—of anything since the moment you were born. It's time to look around." She pokes him hard in the shoulder. "You're Sayker Gerit now. A Talker." She pokes him again for emphasis. "And like you say, you're not equipped to handle that job. You go to the Repository like I tell you and they'll take care of it. You don't go and... then you've got a really big problem, haven't you?" She brings her hand down and props it on her hip, challenging him. "It's up to you."

Kai's at a loss to reply.

"I see we're agreed," she says, lowering her hand. "So, if it's all the same to you, I'll be going now. I'm soaked to the skin thanks to you. The Sub station is that way."

She points once again. Sub Station Three is the closest Sub station to his quarters; he knows that much about the Sub lines.

"Take it and it'll be a pleasure never to cross paths with you again." She pivots on her heels. "You're someone else's problem now," she tosses in parting over her shoulder. "And not soon enough."

But for the rain, Kai might have attempted to follow her. Perhaps it's just as well the weather is against him. She's said all she intends to say. Kai has no doubts about that; nor that she'd quickly be able to lose him in the streets and lanes of Ularon City. Preserver or not, she clearly knows more about the city than he does and Kai is little but a newcomer having spent most of his time since his arrival inside the grounds of the Lycea. He's intimately familiar with the Urban routes and stations, of course, and would be able to navigate his way among the Subs if obliged to, but the pedestrian thoroughfares that weave in odd and unexpected directions through the city are foreign to him. He can get himself home at the end of every shift and that's about the extent of his familiarity with the crooked streets in Ularon City. Should he try to trail her, he'd likely never find his way back to his quarters again.

His quarters! All right, evidently they aren't his quarters anymore. If she's lying about everything else, she isn't lying about that. So, it's either stand out in the street for the rest of the night in the rain or do what she said to do. Of course, even if he does manage to find the white building, there's no guarantee it will let him in, either, despite Vee's claim. And if it doesn't? He'll just have to face that problem if and when it arises.

Turning, he starts off down the street, heading for Sub Station Three. A Sub! He's going to have to ride a Sub! He's an Urban pilot and no Urban pilot would be caught dead on a Sub. That's ironic! He *has* been caught dead. Yes, he's been a deader for some time now and learned to live with it, but now Kai Astada is *well and truly* dead. Gone! Finished! At least as far as most people who knew him will think. As far as the records will reflect. And that leaves him wondering about the body and how they are going to produce one. Perhaps they don't need to. He didn't notice any Ditchers among the patrons of the Duck Down Club but then, he hadn't looked for any, either. Falsify the records! Flash an empty casket! Why not!

He turns the corner, concluding it's better if he doesn't know, convinced now that some how, some way, he's going to get himself out of his present situation. But the first step is to get himself out of the rain and if that means he'll have to play along, *be* Sayker Gerit for one night, then so be it. If Vee isn't lying, then unlike Kai Astada, Sayker Gerit is a real person who has nice dry quarters where there'll be a change of clothes and a comfortable bed to sleep in. It's a beginning.

He spies the entrance to the Sub station and, stealing himself, darts across the water-soaked street. The Subs here will be running few and far between this time of night but it will be dry inside the station and, with any luck, empty. Luck has been in short supply for him lately.

Sub entrances aren't anything he's thought about since his days at the Lycea when a crueller fate could have seen him piloting a Sub. The entrance is meaner than he expected, little more than a narrow fenced-off hole in the ground with a steep set of stairs descending into a poorly lit yellow void. Still, entering gets him out of the rain.

Reluctantly Kai removes his visor and looks down. So far down. He takes his time on the stairs, loath to reach the deep bottom but anxious to silence the hollow echo of his footsteps. He's alone there in that sickly yellow void and, despite his earlier hope, wishes he wasn't. This long, dark and descending hole is the stuff of every young Journer's nightmares. Surely this isn't how Sub pilots are obliged to begin their shifts. If this is a hub—and Kai has seen no indication yet that it is—then there must be another way in. If not, then it's no wonder Henneh has become what she is. The walls to either side of him are too close, the base of the steps elusive. The descent seems endless. And it's abysmally hot. He's used to the heat of the city, but this is a different kind of heat, a tacky, suffocating kind of heat that immediately snatches at every breath he tries to take. By the time he reaches the base of the steps, he's almost desperate enough to bolt up the stairs again. At least up above he can breathe. They may have stolen his identity but they can't steal his freedom to breathe. Not unless he allows them to. And by coming down these stairs, isn't that just what he's done?

He swings around quickly to look toward the street above. What's up there for him beyond the rain that is sheeting so heavily now it veils the narrow little opening to the station? What's *really* up there? He's let age-old Journer prejudices get the better of him. There's nothing so terribly alarming about the Sub station. It's just a hole in the ground. Nothing but a hole in the ground. And Subs aren't all that bad. Just inferior versions of the Urban he pilots day-in, day-out. What's there to fear about one very short journ on a Sub? Three stations. That's all. He's sim-piloted Subs, so he'll just pretend like he's at the Lycea, only this time he's a passenger not a pilot in the simulator. How hard can that be? Preservers travel these tunnels every day of their lives.

Three Sub stations. That's what he needs to think about. Not the closeness of the walls. Not the heaviness of the dark and heated air. His footsteps echo in the long oppressive channel running in either direction at the base of the stairs. He knows, almost instinctively, to turn left. Sub Station Six is on the western side of the city. He's still alone in the channel; he can tell by that solitary echo of his steps. Perhaps the platform will be a more open place where he won't be quite so aware of the weight of the city pressing down on the ceiling overhead. The platform *is* broader—just. But the ceiling is no higher. And he's not alone anymore. There are two other passengers waiting on the platform. They're Preservers. Kai can tell from their dull and shabby attire. One has the light hood of a drab-coloured jacket pulled over their head and is looking down at their boots. The boots are dirty, caked in mud. Like him, this Preserver was caught in the rain.

A sharp whistling sound from far off down the tracks signals the imminent arrival of the Sub. Kai's body relaxes. His mind clears. It's an automatic response, one all good pilots experience. But he's not the pilot on this run, just an unwilling passenger en route to an uncertain destination. Perhaps he should talk to the pilot, explain his situation. Get help. But what pilot would believe him? Besides, how could he even make contact with the pilot? This doesn't appear to be a hub and Sub Station Six certainly isn't. The pilot won't be emerging from his cabin the way Kai, himself, did when Vee first approached him. And he wouldn't be granted access to the cabin; his pid has been altered. Maybe! Perhaps Vee just interfered with his access to The Devid's outer doors. Why didn't he think of that before? Stupid! If there is a pilots' entrance to the Sub station, he'd have an answer for sure. His Urban status would give him access. Kai glances toward the oncoming Sub. It's a dirty machine, nose scratched and battered. He can't see the pilot through the mucky forward shield.

Should he turn back? Take a chance that this station is a hub after all. As the dirty Sub eases to a stop, Kai faces the truth. There's no pilot access here. So he'll ride the Sub and he'll get off at Sub Station Six. Has to. He'll walk to the building Vee described. No other choice. If the building lets him in, no questions asked, then more than likely his pid has been universally altered. Unless, of course, the clever little Preserver, or whatever she is, managed to manipulate his access to that building as well. How can he know?

Kai waits for the two Preservers to select their carriage, then steps to the one behind, the last in line. The doors acknowledge his presence, sliding open. That's useful information; Ro hasn't wiped him completely out of existence. The carriage is grubby. Dank. Half-lit. The pilot of this Sub is derelict. Someone should report them. It won't be Kai.

***

Leaving the suffocating confinement of the Sub behind, Kai makes his way through the empty lanes in the outer rim of the Preserver quadrant, feeling an almost satisfying sense of relief. It's good to be in the open, even in the dark of night. The rain has stopped and Vee gave good directions.

Visorless now, Kai stands outside the building, looking up. He's nervous to test the doors, but it's possible Vee told more truths than lies. His quarters in the big white building show every promise of being superior to those he has—*had* —in The Devid. The building is new. In the daylight, it will shine bright white. The cladding on the dual wings that are angled slightly out from a central core looks flimsy. Kai knows it isn't. He counts thirty or so floors, most in darkness. Unlike Journers, Talkers keep respectable hours. The floors are stacked, one atop the other, like oval-shaped storage crates with their rims protruding. The only relief is provided by a central transparent column that rises from ground level to the very top of the building. The entrance itself is housed in the broad recess at the base of the transparent column.

Kai takes a deep breath. The air slides down damp and dirty. At the doors, he stops to glance around again. There are still no Guardians about and no one else, either, to witness if the doors don't admit him. Darkness! Anonymity! They're nothing he's ever sought before. Tonight he's grateful for both. His dress is wrong. He knows nothing about Talker customs and practice. And he doesn't understand what he's doing here.

He actually jumps back a step when the doors begin to speak. The doors in the The Devid never spoke to him, not until tonight anyway. But it's all right; the doors only voice a welcome in an overly familiar tone, calling him by name. At least by the name Vee told him would be his from now on.

Talkers! Perhaps they don't value silence quite the same way he does. He's accustomed to hearing his Urban's voice, but that is inside his head. Machinery talking out loud and with such familiarity is unnerving. Are the floors and walls inside his room going to speak to him? Every stick of furniture? Already he doesn't like it.

The foyer isn't large. It's as bright white as the building's facade. Featureless save for a set of doors marring the uniformity of the wall to his right and a niche in the equally plain wall to his left. The doors, Kai assumes, will open to a riser. He opts for the niche where he's hoping to find a set of stairs. An eight-floor climb. It's preferable to an eight-floor ascent in a riser with potential company. The building itself recognised him, but it's just a machine; no living, breathing occupant could possibly do the same. Best to take the stairs that he's relieved to discover nested inside the niche.

The stairs are brightly lit. He can't identify the source of the well's lighting but then doesn't put a lot of effort into trying. Good enough that he can see. He counts each floor as he goes. It's a monotonous climb. Reaching eight, he stops and looks back down the last jagging flight of the staircase. If it all turns sour, then he can get out as easily as he got in—at least, he assumes he can—and so steps through the unguarded opening onto the eighth floor. It's as unremarkable as the foyer and the stairwell that brought him to it, with walls the same ubiquitous white as the broad square tiles that swathe the floor.

Vee could have at least told him which way to turn instead of leaving him to roam the corridors. Kai choses the left wing, that way he can avoid passing through the open column which would leave him a little too exposed. He finds his name, his *new* name, stencilled behind a transparent plate on the first door he comes to. The door slides away immediately. It doesn't say a word. Relieved, Kai steps inside. The door slides closed and someone speaks to him from behind.

"Good evening, Talker Gerit. I trust you've had a pleasant evening."

Kai swings around, anxious, desperate to see who is in the room with him. There's no one there. It's the door! He almost laughs at his mistake but finds himself, fist raised, punching the door instead. His heart feels like it's on the outside of his chest and now he's gone and bruised his hand. He forces himself to breathe. Once. Twice. Then looks around his quarters. It's not a particularly big room. Predictably all white, but larger than the quarters he had in The Devid. There's a bed with an unfamiliar case resting on it; two sets of discrete doors; and a window, currently darkened. He investigates the doors first, encouraged when neither speak. One set opens onto a closet, the other a compact bathroom. The closet contains four Talker uniforms, the standard dark blue and his size no doubt, and the bathroom, per the norm for this building, is bland and white. Nothing surprising. Kai turns his attention to the case resting on the bed. Unlatching it, he finds nothing remarkable there, either. Just a small collection of his street clothes. He rummages through the stash just the same, finding as Vee promised, not a single item redolent of his life as a Journer.

Sweeping the case and its scattered contents to the floor, he drops onto the bed to think. He's still of a mind to try and remove the pid, but begins to wonder if that's such a smart thing to do. Without it, will the building, let alone this room, recognise him? He'll leave it. At least until tomorrow. He'll be able to think better tomorrow. And he'll have all day to do it because sure as pautune he won't be keeping that appointment at the Repository. But somehow he has to extricate himself from this mess. He has to find someone who might believe what has happened to him. Only one person comes to mind. Eine Vidamore knows him. Eine Vidamore will recognise him. Through no fault or intent of his own, he's become entangled in something that smacks of sedition. He's an innocent victim. Innocent *and* ignorant. Vidamore can't fail to see that.

Kai's thoughts continue to churn and the ramifications of approaching Vidamore slowly surface. Perhaps he can connive a meeting, but Vidamore has his own problems. Before the quarantine, the Lycea was a prestigious institution, large and costly to maintain. Now all Vidamore has to justify expenditure is a skeleton cohort of marginals. Besides, even if the Director did agree to see him, where would that leave Henneh? How deeply is she involved? Can he avoid revealing anything about Henneh's involvement in... well... *what?* Kai drops his head into his upraised hands.

That's the problem. Just what is Henneh involved in?

Not a single thing that has happened since he first encountered Vee makes any sense. Least of all why this group of dissidents— and that's all Kai can imagine they must be—had to conscript him. He's done nothing. He knows nothing. He *is* nothing.

No, that isn't quite true. He's still a Journer, despite what Ro has done to him. But the undercastes despise the Pedorate. Always have. Rightly or wrongly, they hold the Pedorate personally responsible for their circumstances. Kai has no love for the Pedorate. He has no hatred for it, either. It's a system. Unarguably not the best system. Not even the fairest system. But it works as well as need demands. Sure, it could be improved. Everything can be improved. Kai isn't so naive as to think he has the talent to do it; and the same goes for Ro and Henneh.

Ro's response when he threatened to talk to Vidamore bothers him. It didn't seem to concern her in the least.

Kai raises his head and his hands fall limp into his lap.

Vidamore! He can't be part of this. Not the Director of the Lycea. But Ro must have good reason to believe he'll reject anything Kai has to say. He is *dead*, of course. That's an inconvenience. But all Vidamore has to do is see Kai standing there in front of him. He'll have to believe his own eyes and then he, too, will be forced to question how Kai can be both dead and alive at the same time and believe at least some of what Kai tells him. But how can a dead pilot get to Vidamore? There has to be a way, especially for a Talker since ostensibly that's what he is now. He'd be a fool not to use that guise to *his* advantage.

Kai flops back onto the bed and the lights blink out, leaving him in utter darkness.

"Sleep well, Sayker Gerit."

Kai isn't sure where the irritating voice is coming from; he'd just like it to shut up.

Something about approaching the Lycea Director isn't sitting right with him but he's too tired, confused, and disoriented to realise what it is. He doesn't think well in the dark and he simply has to get some sleep.

CHAPTER 7

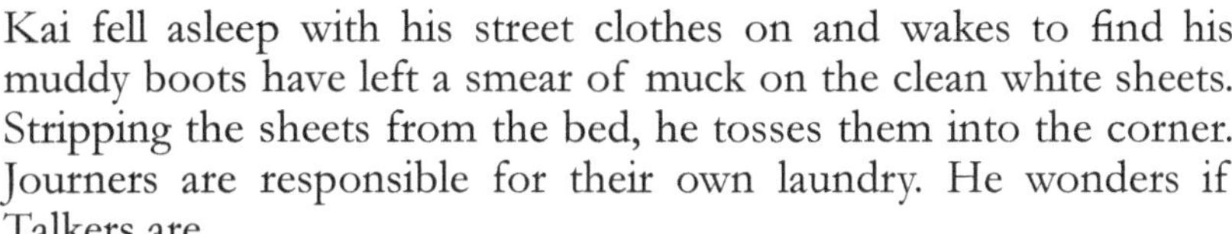

Kai fell asleep with his street clothes on and wakes to find his muddy boots have left a smear of muck on the clean white sheets. Stripping the sheets from the bed, he tosses them into the corner. Journers are responsible for their own laundry. He wonders if Talkers are.

"Good morning, Talker Gerit."

Kai's getting used to the monologue. He doesn't like it but he's learning to ignore it.

"Yeah. Yeah."

Going into the bathroom, he looks at his reflection in the mirror. The sight alarms him. His face is creased with lines and grooves that weren't there yesterday. His dark hair is sticking up at odd angles, still damp from last night's rain. Could Ro have changed his face? Aged him?

Kai pushes back the tangled strands of his hair and takes a closer look. He's tired. That's all. Tired and scared. As he lowers his eyes, he notices the mud tracked across the nice white tiles of the floor. Kicking off his boots, he pads back to the outer room and the closet that slides open the instant he touches it.

He waits, then sighs quietly in relief when the closet doesn't speak. Grabbing the closest set of clothes and boots, he heads back to the bathroom. He'll dress as a Talker, a decision he isn't even obliged to think about. It's his best option. During his fitful sleep, Kai's mind was well occupied. He's decided against seeing Vidamore. At least not straight away. He doesn't really suspect that the Director has anything to do with what is happening to him, but if these dissidents or subversives, or whatever they are, have gotten to Vidamore, too, then talking to him might actually play in their favour. He needs more evidence before he speaks to Vidamore and the first bit of evidence he needs is proof that *Kai Astada* is well and truly 'dead'. In the hard light of day, he's able to think more clearly. Just because one building denied him access and another granted it doesn't necessarily prove a thing.

The room speaks to him when he steps, fully dressed, from the bathroom.

"You're late, Sayker Gerit. You neglected to leave rise instructions."

Kai spreads his arms. "Late for what?"

"The dining room is closed. Breakfast is no longer being served."

"Oh, that."

He's forgotten all about food.

"Doesn't matter."

Snatching up his discarded visor, he makes for the door, but stops before he's halfway across to scan the room from wall-to-wall, floor-to-ceiling. It's no use. He can't locate the source of the voice, so poses his question to the air.

"I don't suppose you can tell me my agenda for the day?"

"I could," the voice replies. "But you have none."

"Really?" Kai's actually talking to himself, but the room replies.

"That is correct, Talker Gerit. You have no assignments today."

The response gives Kai an idea.

"What about yesterday?" he asks. "What assignment did I have yesterday?"

There's a pause before the room replies. "This is most unusual. I can't seem to locate that information."

"Imagine that." He strikes off once again for the door.

"My apologies, Talker Gerit, but I'm not programmed to imagine."

The doors slide open.

"Have a pleasant—"

Kai misses the rest of the room's parting words, courtesy of the swiftly closing doors.

Last night the chance of encountering a neighbour was slim. It's daylight now and his 'fellow' Talkers will be on the move but, so far, the hallway appears empty. Kai makes quickly for the stairwell. No sooner is his foot on the top step than he hears the whoosh of the riser doors. Someone is alighting on his floor. Kai sprints all the way down to the foyer, only to face the same problem.

Donning his visor, he starts for the outer door. He sees movement, veiled, through the left side of his visor, hopes it's just some Talker heading back to their quarters. He doesn't know where the dining room is and doesn't stop to find out. He just keeps moving.

Not too quickly; that could arouse suspicion. Not too slowly; that could invite interception.

He makes it to the outer doors unchallenged, cringing when the doors bid him, by name, a pleasant day as they slide open. He hurries onto the street. The pavement is still wet from last night's sudden rain. Steaming. He can feel the rising heat through the soles of his new, perfectly fitted boots. Oppressive heat; it's nothing new in Ularon City. He's facing a bigger problem. He won't return to Sub Station Six. He could ride a Sub from now to sundown and it won't advance him a step. Besides no gabber would be caught dead on a Sub. Talk about drawing attention!

Although there's Urban service to the Talker quadrant, no Urban runs directly between the Talker and Journer quadrants, but the Journer quadrant isn't the only place Kai might find some answers. Any Urban station will do, as long as it has pilot access. The stations in the southwestern quadrants aren't Urban hubs and he can't journ on an Urban to one that is without risking discovery; any gabbers journing with him are likely to strike up a conversation and will soon realise he isn't one of their own. The closest hub station will be in Ularon Arch and he'll have to make his way there on foot. Kai isn't used to walking anymore. Piloting an Urban has made him soft. But there's no option. He needs answers and an Urban station, one with pilot access, is the best place to start.

Pautune! It's the *only* place to start!

Talkers talk! Talkers don't walk! His new boots may be a perfect fit but they're anything but comfortable and the maker certainly hadn't taken walking in them for any distance into consideration. At least he only attracts scant attention as he pounds the streets. The patrolling Guardians are his major concern. As if to compensate for their absence from the streets last night, they're out in full force this morning. The citizens of Ularon have grown accustomed to the strident bark of their orders, the crisp snap their light brown uniforms make as they strut, generally in pairs, about the city. Even Kai has become accustomed to the sight and sound of them and usually pays them little attention. It's a different matter today. He's aware of every little move they make, every nuance of the expressions on their faces when they look everywhere and nowhere at once. Still, he makes it through to Ularon Arch without interference, although he's cursing under his breath by the time he gets there. But it should be smoother going for him from now on, at least as far as his chances of being intercepted by a Guardian are concerned. Talkers are a common sight inside Ularon Arch. That's where they do the bulk of their work since the Pedorate, more so than any other caste, engage Talkers to carry out the more menial of their communications and the skyline of Ularon Arch is dominated by Pedorate Council buildings.

Kai has never accessed his or any Urban through Ularon Arch. He's never even stepped onto the platform. He knows the location of all the Urban hubs, of course, but has never had cause to use any but his own before, so he's counting on all Urban hubs being configured alike.

His heart sinks when he spies what he guesses to be the station, looming at the heart of a vast, raised platform ahead of him. The station, too, is equally massive. A large hewn-stone edifice that looks like it dropped into Ularon Arch out of the city's distant past. Drawing closer, Kai hears a distinctive whine, then spies an Urban shooting out from the western side of the platform, speeding along tracks that, while level with the top of the platform, are elevated above the city beyond.

He should have anticipated that the Pedorate would have the biggest and the best of everything, including, unfortunately for him, lavish transport options. There appears to be only one entrance and that by way of the raised platform ringing the station. There are no stairs ascending to the platform, but a gentle incline of thick and well-tended grass, just another incongruous sight in the desert city of Ularon.

The platform is wide, paved in thick slabs of expensive-looking white stone that contrast with the yellow stone of the building at its heart, but the plaza in front of it is heavily treed and, as a consequence, unusually shady. Reaching it, Kai is able to get a better view of the station and what he sees offers little hope. Perhaps pilots using this hub know of an access other than the building's pillared front entrance, but Kai doesn't. The building, too, is like nothing Kai has ever seen before. At the centre and at each of its cardinal corners, domes sheathed in an unfamiliar greenish metal interrupt the standard Pedoran symmetry of what is an otherwise flat roof. The central dome is perhaps twice as large as those on the corners.

He hurries on, mingles with the throng of people walking in all directions through the plaza. He's never seen so many people wandering around or, for all intents and purposes, sitting aimlessly on benches artfully positioned to take best advantage of the shade beneath the trees. They're Pedorate for the most part, Kai can tell from their dress. All castes have their own style with generally something to set them just that little bit apart and differentiate the sexes. Something to say they're a person in their own right. For Journers, it's their visors. Each one is colour- or style-distinct. Kai's is deep, dark maroon. A fortunate choice under the circumstances; it's hard to distinguish from the Talkers' ubiquitous black. Talkers prefer to state their individuality by the way they wear their hair. There's no unifying style and he supposes the impression he's leaving as a Talker is a little plain. That's good. He's unmemorable. But Kai has never seen a Pedorate yet who he wouldn't describe as boring. Totally utterly boring. It takes a keen eye to identify one from another in that pure white costume they favour. Whether through conscious choice or genetics, it's rare to sight a Pedorate who couldn't have spilled from the one mould.

Kai spots three dark blue-uniformed Talkers making directly for the station ahead of him. He falls in behind, careful to stay far enough back not to be noticed by anyone, particularly the patrolling Guardians, whose numbers have understandably swollen since he has entered Ularon Arch. He can't afford to shadow the trio of Talkers too distantly though; to a casual observer it has to look like he's with them. Following at what he hopes is a satisfactory compromise, he wonders if anyone else is so keenly aware of the many Urbans scuttling along on the tracks far beneath their feet or if it's only him, because he's a pilot.

They've reached the large, broadly spaced stone pillars that frame the entrance and Kai feels uncomfortably dwarfed as he passes through, close but not too close on the heels of the three in front of him. The interior of the building is as anachronistic as its facade and Kai becomes enveloped in a swarm of activity. The three Talkers are of no further use to him, so he allows them to edge away. His goal is the pilots' entrance; every hub has one and this station is most *certainly* a hub.

The ceiling soars in shades of gold over Kai's head and, beneath it, sweeping in enormous ovals, the building's three mezzanine floors. The pierced railings that girdle each mezzanine appear to be made of the same green metal as the domes on the roof. There's a narrow walkway inside each railing and, beyond that, shop after shop running around the perimeter on every floor. On the entrance floor, where he is standing, flanking the diaphanous run-board, sprawl open-sided restaurants, loosely canopied in gold-coloured cloth above tables and chairs haphazardly arranged into circles and squares. All are occupied by lower ranking Pedorate and most the focus of loud and overstruck conversation.

This isn't just some station hub, it's also a merchant and meeting nexus.

Kai stands for a moment, pretending to consult the schedule flashing on the run-board in front of him. Every so often, the display is disrupted as someone passes through it, but the distortion is of no concern to Kai. He isn't really looking at the board. He's thinking, trying to get his bearings and compare the layout of this station with the ones he knows so well. It seems hopeless; this station-cum-mercantile fusion is simply too large, too complex.

When someone speaks too close to his ear, Kai inadvertently jumps.

"May I be of assistance?"

Turning, Kai finds a Journer in Lycea uniform standing beside him. The Journer is young, a cut below average in carriage and presentation. Kai marks him as a marginal. He's 'station stooping', Vidamore's favoured penalty for mediocre performance.

"No, thank you," Kai replies, hoping to deflect the intern's attention.

Instantly Kai realises his mistake. He should never have thanked the intern. No genuine gabber would.

The intern's brow creases. He's clearly taken aback but, to Kai's relief, says nothing further, simply nods and hurries off, seeking a better opportunity to work off his penance.

Kai pretends that he's still scanning the run-board but he's actually watching the intern. There's a chance the intern has made his amends and is now heading for the pilots' entrance. But the intern soon stops to speak to a low-ranking Pedorate. Seems the intern's punishment isn't *yet* complete. Too bad. But he has already delayed too long in front of the board. Even if no one else notices, that intern surely would have had he not found himself a mark. The close encounter is motivation enough.

Kai has zigged and zagged halfway across the eastern wing of the station before he spots a Journer walking briskly ahead of him. Darting past a dawdling traveller, Kai falls in behind the Journer. The Journer is older than him and no one he knows. Fortunate! He follows. It's easier now; the crowd is thinning. Fewer people have business in this part of the station. Of course, that also means that a Talker has little call to be there, either.

The Journer makes a sharp turn and Kai briefly loses sight of her, gaining it again in a narrow alcove. He hangs back to watch. He can't see all of her, just her head and shoulders. Then, in an instant, he can't see anything of her at all.

Hurrying up to the alcove, Kai is surprised to find a high ornamental gate barring his way. Beyond the gate, there's a descending spiral staircase. Looking down, he sees the top of the Journer's head before she rounds a turn. The sound of her footsteps lingers. She's got to be heading for the pilots' entrance. Kai shifts his attention to the gate. It's an old-style swinging-type affair, something that's usually only seen in the older quadrants. Tentatively Kai gives the gate a push. Nothing. Examining the outside, he finds no obvious latch, lock or handle. This can't be the pilots' entrance, not the actual entrance anyway or he would know it immediately and either be admitted if the stripping of his Journer status is a ruse or denied entrance if it isn't. The gate is high but the open mesh would make it possible to clamber over.

Not a good idea.

He looks around, satisfies himself that he is not being observed, then glides his hand through the mesh. There's a small old-style bolt on the opposite side of the gate. He slips it blindly but easily and then waits a moment, listening. He can't hear the Journer's footsteps any longer. The pilots' entrance has to be on the lower level beyond the base of the stairs. Kai takes a deep breath and gently pushes on the gate, which swings noiselessly open.

He's in and no one seems aware that he's there. Not yet anyway. But if the pilots' entrance in this station is anything like the pilots' entrance in his own, then there'll be a lot of activity when he reaches the base of the stairs. Some pilots going on shift; others coming off. And he'll be the standout Talker among them. If Ro, Vee and Henneh have lied to him, his Talker dress will take some explaining but that's a later concern.

Easing the gate closed again behind him, he starts down the steps. He'd like to run but can't risk making a noise in the narrow stairwell. By the time he's halfway down the stairs, he's becoming dizzy and disoriented. It's the combination of the too-white walls, the too-white steps and the closeness. Always the closeness! He's anxious to get out of the stairwell but there's no comfort when he reaches the bottom. The steps end hard up against a wall. That's it. They simply end. Steps can't just end and the Journer went somewhere! He has to forget about how things *look;* forget about the disorienting and absolute whiteness of the space. Slowly Kai steps up to the blank white wall. It doesn't speak, advise him he's in a restricted section of the station as he might have expected.

Could be it's a sim!

He looks back up the winding staircase. No one. Ripping off his visor, he moves in to inspect the wall, bringing his nose closer and closer until he can see the finest of lines running down the centre of the narrow panel. No. Not panel. Door! It's not a sim, but an entrance. A *silent* entrance. This is where the Journer went. And where he *can't.*

Kai doesn't bother to investigate the junction with his fingers. He knows he won't be able to feel it. Instead, he turns away and heads back up the winding staircase.

He's a Journer no longer!

No one witnessed his failed attempt to gain entry, but now he's got to make it back out again. He takes to the stairs and manages to sneak safely back through the ornate gate, closing it gently as before. Turning, he collides immediately into one of a pair of brown-uniformed Guardians. His visor clutters to the floor at his feet. There's a moment of sheer panic when the Guardian locks eyes with him. He's a Talker—ostensibly anyway. But what exactly would a genuine Talker do and say after blundering into a patrolling Guardian? Kai opens his mouth, at the point of admonishing the Guardian. He doesn't get the chance. The Guardian stoops to the ground to retrieve Kai's fallen visor. Out of the corner of his eye, Kai is aware of the Guardian's companion already starting away. Kai nods when the Guardian hands him the lost visor with one sharp word of apology. Seems Guardians are as anxious to avoid him as he is to avoid the Guardians and the Talker uniform he's wearing does come with its advantages. *Lucky*!

The hollowness of the thought grates. One lucky escape doesn't amount to much in the big scheme of things. There's a lifetime still ahead of him. What's lucky about having nowhere to live it? What's lucky about having no one to turn to? What's lucky about having no identity?

CHAPTER 8

Mechanically, Kai watches the scene outside the broad window of the Urban whizz past. He's been watching it all day; first as he travelled north and then, watching it unravel as he journed back south again. He's taking a chance but it's an unpopular run and there are only two other travellers in the carriage, minor Pedorates who embarked at the last station. Neither have shown any interest in him. Talkers tend to receive that sort of detached recognition. They're a caste apart and, right now, Kai will settle for that; after all, it served him well during his recent encounter with the Guardians back in Arch.

He's comfortable on the Urban and, for the moment, content with his placement in space if not time. Still, he'd prefer to be sitting in the pilot's seat. What Journer wouldn't? But riding as a passenger on something as innately fundamental to him as an Urban is the best he can do for now. The feeling of detachment from his own Urban has tested him, at times even mentally disoriented him. Perhaps there'll be an underlying sense of confusion that will never leave him.

Time and distance pass swiftly on an Urban and since he left Ularon Arch, he's covered a lot of territory, taking little notice of any of it. There isn't much to see, just a transient and tantalising hint of the world beyond the protective shield of his window. Kai is accustomed to the obscurity, although there have been times when, seated in his pilot's seat, he found himself wondering what it might be like to see the outside clearly. Not today. Today it is all just inconsequential 'noise'. His focus has been directed inward on the Duck Down Club, the locus of all his current troubles.

Sunset is already on the move, a hazy, ill-defined pinkish coloured stain stealing skyward on the western horizon. He urges the darkness to hurry. There's more cover for him in the darkness. And the temperature will be just that little bit cooler. He's been spoiled these past years, lived virtually every moment of every day in temperature-controlled environments. He's not looking forward to the trek in the open air back to the Duck Down Club, but not even Subs service that sector of Ularon City.

They've come to the outskirts of the city. The Urban's speed transforms the low-rise buildings into a single dun-coloured band that blots out the blushing horizon. Soon they'll be entering the heart of the city where there is no horizon. Kai feels himself plummeting back toward those same feelings of panic and foreboding he experienced when he found himself locked out of his own building. He's been safe. For most of the day, he's been safe. That time is drawing to a close.

Kai dons his visor; Ularon is a dirty, dusty city, immersed in grit and grime. He's the last to leave the carriage, stepping onto the platform behind one other passenger. The station is plain and utilitarian, inferior in size and quality to the station at Ularon Arch, with little attempt made to protect passengers from the whizz and whir of the departing and arriving Urbans. Nor is it a station with which Kai has any particular familiarity; it's off his run. But it's an Urban station and that in itself goes someway to heal Kai's splintered confidence. He's going to need some confidence when he enters the Duck Down Club to tackle his enemies.

His enemies.

That's how he's come to see them. It bothers him—sorely bothers him to the core—to see Henneh in that light. Perhaps, like him, Henneh is an innocent, ignorant of Ro's motives. He can't dwell on that. Henneh has harmed him and he has to look out for himself.

Kai trails a safe distance behind the minor Pedorate, forced to weave a circuitous path when they enter the congested concourse. The Pedorate seems familiar with the station and will know the most direct route out. It's a fine evening in Ularon City, as fine an evening as Ularon ever experiences. It's hot. It's always hot in Ularon. But there is no wind blowing tonight and, with luck, Kai will make good time. He should have thought to return to the Talkers' quarters to change into some of the street clothes they left him. But the Duck Down Club is in his sights and he'll have no distractions now. Besides, as he's been walking, with his mouth dry and his chest thumping and his focus tunnelled narrowly forward, he's successfully marched past every Guardian he encountered, courtesy of the Talker uniform.

Twice Kai loses his way during the long walk and is obliged to retrace his footsteps. He can't exactly stop and ask directions, so he falls back on his knowledge of the placement of the Urban stations throughout the city. There's a picture in his brain—a map of sorts—and he relies on that as a guide. At last, he comes on the narrow lane leading to the Duck Down Club, recognises the odd little wooden door dead centre of the brick wall at the end of it. The light creeping down the laneway from the street beyond glows brighter in the calmer night. Heading for the door, he raps on the chipped paint and waits. Perhaps it won't be Ro herself who comes to the door. He fully expects someone will, but his knock goes unanswered. Anticipating the door will be locked, he pushes on it anyway, surprised when it swings inward. Ducking his head low, he steps inside.

Just another stupid decision?

No one comes toward him out of the darkness. He straightens, recalling that the corridor is quite narrow and that, last night, it was brilliantly lit. So, there's lighting and if it isn't going to come on automatically, then somewhere there's a switch. He eases the door closed, careful not to latch it, and begins to feel along the walls, netting a splinter of wood for his trouble. It stings. Blind, Kai uses his teeth to extract it. He tastes blood. Just his luck for the door to lock on him, to be stuck in here and die a slow painful death from infection. The club, to his way of thinking, is a filthy place.

He reaches out again and this time, high on the wall to the left, feels something that could be an antiquated type of light switch. He's never used one. Never seen one. Only pictures. He thinks maybe you're supposed to punch the pad, so presses it forcefully with the knuckles of his left hand. The corridor is bathed in light so suddenly Kai's thankful his visor is still on. He heads for the same set of stairs Ro sent him down before, reaches the wall at the base, turns left and comes to the door that, last night, was solidly shut, but tonight is standing half open. It can't open fully on account of the uneven flooring on the other side of it. Turning side-on, Kai slips through the narrow opening into darkness once again. Sidling his way around the door, he feels once again for another of those antiquated light switches, finally finds and punches it, a little more gently this time. The light comes on. It's a dim light that offers little beyond confirmation that the place is deserted. There are no tables, no benches, no patrons. Nothing! Just the low dark ceiling beams overhead and a lingering aroma of *taint*. If it weren't for the stink of *taint*, Kai would suspect that maybe, just maybe, he'd come to the wrong place. But this is the club all right. At least it was last night.

He steps into the stripped room, heads for the alcove where he sat talking to Henneh and old Ro. Empty. But a flash of white on the floor catches Kai's eye. Stooping, he retrieves a scrap of paper. It's a small corner, torn off something, probably one of the pages Henneh showed him. Kai lets the scrap flutter back to the floor.

They've tricked him! No, that isn't entirely true. Ro warned him the Club could disappear just like that! He should have believed her. Perhaps he should start believing her about a lot things. But what, exactly, do they want from *him*? What does *he* have that they need so badly?

He'd like to get his hands around Ro's throat and squeeze; watch her eyes pop. He'd like to pin Henneh to the wall and pound the truth out of her.

Why him? He's nothing! Nothing at all!

***

No one came. They told her someone would come. And it has taken months and months already just to get *this* far.

If Saera knew who 'they' were, she might have been able to do something about it. She doesn't like this dependence on the unseen. There's too much uncertainty. It involves too many people. People without names. People without caste. Or people with too *many* castes.

Closing the door to her quarters, she collapses onto her small couch, regretting again that she'd ever passed those papers to Veeda. Now all she can do is wait for Veeda to contact her. Or find Veeda herself. But where would she even begin to look? Veeda could be anywhere, feign any caste.

She can't go back to Vidamore; he's out of it. At least, so 'they' say. Why is she doing what 'they' tell her to do anyway? Because she was stupid enough to hand over those papers, that's why. And Gove put himself at too much risk to get them just for her to wash her hands and walk away now. Still, she doesn't like dealing with these nameless, casteless people who won't come out in the open.

The irony doesn't escape her. She could be talking about herself.

***

Kai has dressed in Talker clothes. It's a Talker they'll be expecting at the Repository, right? So, he's one day late. What of it? Like every other member of every other caste, Talkers are regulated but, like the top echelon of the Pedorate, have a reputation for modifying their own schedules. Perhaps it's in the name. They can talk themselves into or out of any situation. He's never heard of a Talker who's been forced to Cross.

Kai finds the Repository, the new one, pinpointed quite clearly on the run-board in the nearest Urban station. Yesterday's successful masquerade has lent him confidence. Today, he'll risk riding from the gabber sector in Talker clothes. It's either that or another long walk in incredibly uncomfortable shoes when a short Urban journ and a brief walk at the end of it will get him there.

Still, he selects the least occupied of carriages and proceeds to mull over what he's going to say as he rides, allowing the familiar sense of calm he always experiences on an Urban to sweep through him. But the moment he steps out of the station and realises that the walk, though brief, is going to be unpleasant, the old dread resurfaces. This is a dead part of the city, only intermittently patrolled by Guardians. The straight broad street ahead of him is deserted; the massive, block-like buildings that line it on either side, crumbling. In places, large chunks of masonry and roof are lying across the footpath. If they could have chosen a less prodigious site for the new Pedoran Repository, Kai can't think where that might be. Seems to him that the old one up on the hill was located in a far better position. It's searingly hot down here in the valley, too. At the end of the ruined road, Kai spies a set of equally dreary gates. From a distance, they look misaligned, time-weary. The structure behind it doesn't look any better. Like the rest of the buildings in the area, it's a large flat-roofed square edifice, ringed at the very top with sets of barred windows. It looks dirty and a little bent.

Kai starts off for the gates as the delicate whine reaching out from the Urban station dies away. There's only the sound of his own steps now. It feels unnatural. He could be all alone in the world—the last living creature. An urgency to reach those old, crooked gates at the end of the ruined road overwhelms him. If only he could hear something other than the ring of his footsteps on the footpath. By the time he comes to the gates, his throat is raw, breath ragged from the heat and dry.

There doesn't seem to be any clear way in. Certainly, no obvious vis. All he can find is an old-looking lever-type arrangement, so he lifts it and opens the creaking gate.

This can't be right. He's come to the wrong place. Or Vee sent him somewhere other than the Repository; that wouldn't surprise him at all.

"Please identify yourself."

Kai jumps at the ghostly voice.

Either the building is talking to him or someone inside it is. He looks around once more, but still can't locate a vis.

"There's no vis on the gate," the voice tells him. "But I can see you."

Seems it's *someone*, not *something*, talking to him.

He gives his name—at least the name Vee told him to give— informing the voice that he has an appointment, exactly as Vee instructed. There may be no obvious vis on the gate but the entrance is definitely being monitored, because whoever is behind the voice hears him and immediately replies.

"I expected you yesterday."

Kai shrugs. Talkers don't explain themselves or offer excuses.

"Come up then," the voice tells him. "And be sure to shut the gate behind you."

Kai eyes the gate with sullen amusement, then shuts and latches it with exaggerated flair.

There's a broad expanse of concrete he must walk before he reaches the building. The concrete is cracked, stained, barren. Kai's grateful for his visor; the glare in the broad forecourt would be intolerable without it. Someone is waiting for him in a miserable sliver of shade at the very end of the forecourt. The owner of the voice? The Registrar is tall, fair almost white-haired, and maybe a year or two older than him. She's dressed in the standard rich, brown-coloured uniform of her caste. He takes a breath and prepares to launch into his rehearsed patter, although he's not altogether sure he can pull off the ruse with any degree of credibility.

"If you'd care to step inside, we can discuss the nature of your services," she says with a lack-lustre sweep of an arm, indicating the wide-open doorway behind her. "It's not good for my documents to be exposed to the open air too long. I'd like to shut the door as soon as possible."

So, she seems to be of the opinion that he actually *is* a Talker. Kai isn't sure if he was expecting that or not. In fact, he's consciously avoided making any decision in that regard until he actually spoke to his *contact*.

He's never made use of the Repository. He's never had the need. Everything he required to hone his skills as a pilot was provided for him at the Lycea. As he understands it, the Repository is a place dedicated to the outmoded storage of documents and reference materials that are long past their relevancy—archival stowage and such. In hindsight, his first impression of the building was fitting; it is little more than a warehouse. He notices the vis the Registrar must have been watching him on to the right side of the doorway, waits on her to slide the heavy doors closed before she begins to weave what gives every indication of being a long circuitous path around ceiling-high shelving crammed with old-style crates and boxes, many of which have obviously seen better days. Following, he starts to wonder how the Registrar can possibly be productively occupied just shuffling trivia around.

The warehouse—for that's how he sees it—is well lit. There's no risk of a stumble in the chaos. Lighting he supposes is of a paramount importance in a place like this. Just like Sub pilots, old Registrars develop poor eyesight, be it from very different causes. Although the shelving has been packed over-tightly, there's no indication that any of the boxes or crates have been carelessly stacked, leaving him unconcerned about a sudden collapse and an ensuing crack to his head.

The high shelving opens up in front of him to reveal a space outfitted with a single chair and a desk stacked so remarkably high with paper, Kai almost misses seeing the old-style cypher sitting on top of it. There's what he takes to be a large free-standing flash unit stationed to one side of the desk. He's never seen so much paper before or a free-standing flash unit for that matter; he's rarely seen paper or any flash unit really, only the one in Vidamore's office at the Lycea. The Registrar's unit smells a bit like an overcooked meal. Like the crates and boxes, it looks timeworn; the unit has seen a lot of use.

The Registrar makes directly for the chair behind her desk, then hesitates.

"Please take my chair," she says, brandishing her hand once again in that same liquid way she ushered Kai into the Repository. "I'm afraid my office isn't equipped for visitors."

He's worked that out already.

"No need," he says with a short, sharp headshake. "I don't anticipate you'll be keeping me very long."

It is an exceptionally good comment, he thinks, one in keeping with a Talker. Perhaps he is going to be better at this than he feared. Then, of course, he might be playing out this little charade for nothing. Vee hasn't been very forthcoming with information. The Registrar could be fully aware that he's not who he claims he is. If she is aware, she's playing out her part very well. Kai is struggling to read her. It seems unlikely that a Registrar would have any association with the Duck Down Club but then Kai would never have suspected that an esteemed pilot like Bes Gannaline-ro would have any connection with it, either.

"I assume I can speak freely," the Registrar asks, slipping, a little wearily Kai notes, into the chair he declined to take.

Kai offers a casual nod. Although Talkers' communication skills are universally acknowledged, it is just as widely acknowledged that the caste has a deserved reputation for discretion. His reaction is entirely appropriate.

The Registrar lays her hands upon the scattered contents of her desk. "I find myself in something of a difficult position."

Her unusually deep-blue eyes are looking right at him. For a moment, Kai thinks he sees something there. A hint of artifice? But it's just a flash and then it's gone. He doesn't really know what to make of her. Is she willingly playing the game or, like him, a hostage to it? There's something about the Registrar that's luring him into explaining every one of the nasty little circumstances that brought him to her and confessing that he's no Talker.

"Go on," he says instead.

"As you know, the Pedorate Council regularly monitors the status of the plague in the quarantine sectors."

He didn't know, but he assumed so.

"You'll also be aware that the Council relies upon me to regularly report the infection and fatality statistics from each of those sectors."

He wasn't aware of those little details, either, but it is only logical that someone must.

The Registrar lowers her eyes. For a moment, Kai becomes concerned that's all she's going to say and that somehow, as a Talker, he's expected to know what is required of him. He's left standing there in front of her for an uncomfortably long time, until she raises her eyes again and continues.

"Despite repeated attempts, I have been unable to obtain the latest report from one of the quarantine stations and," her shoulders lift slightly, "as a consequence, find myself in need of your particular services."

Surely she's not asking him to go to a quarantine sector! What can he say? What *should* he say? A Talker, *a real one*, would know the appropriate response. Instead Kai silently and nervously begins to weigh his options. Can a Talker refuse an assignment?

"I'm afraid it's beyond the scope of my duties to enter a plague sector, Registrar. At the very least, I will require the relevant authorisation and, unless you're about to offer that to me, then I can't assist you."

The Registrar simply stares at him. It's impossible for Kai to read what she's thinking behind those extraordinary blue eyes and the impassive expression on her face. When the corners of her mouth begin to lift in the vague semblance of a smile, Kai feels almost certain he's been unmasked.

"I do apologise. I'd just assumed... but I suppose Talkers may not know." She stands, lending her a certain air of authority that Kai finds immediately disconcerting. "My request involves you travelling to the quarantine station. I'm asking you to employ your influence to expedite the overdue report from the chief Doser there."

Kai knows such stations exist. Everyone does. But very few people have cause or permission to visit one and certainly even fewer leave. Could a Talker even visit a station? Evidently they could otherwise he wouldn't be here. But does a Talker have the authority to interfere with its procedures? Who ranks higher? A

Talker or a Doser? In the end he supposes it doesn't matter because the whole business isn't making a shred of sense. The Registrar's request sounds within the realms of reason to him. It probably could be undertaken by a legitimate Talker. So why set *him* up? Ro said something similar about his 'influence', although she couldn't have been referring to his influence with any Doser. Perhaps there's a vague connection here after all. The Registrar is in official need of some certain information and maybe, just maybe, it's the same information the Duck Down Club *wants*, although what good it could do them Kai can't imagine and doesn't care.

His head is threatening to ache and he's suddenly aware that the Registrar is looking at him strangely.

"Are you unwell?" she asks, sounding genuinely concerned. Her forehead is furrowed and there's hesitation in her voice.

"Mentally reviewing my schedule," he replies, a little pleased with himself for coming up with such a reasonable response.

But the furrow in the Registrar's brow doesn't go away; she's unconvinced.

"I see," she says nonetheless. "I'm afraid there's some urgency to this request. If you could see your way—"

"I'll take it," Kai interrupts, even surprising himself with the speed of his reply.

The Registrar nods and the little furrow in her brow disappears. "I've lodged all the required documents with your unit."

Although that piece of information confirms that Ro and her cohorts have legitimised him all the way up the Talker hierarchy, it is scant help otherwise. He has no idea about operations inside the Talker Unit. If it functions along similar lines to the Journer Unit, then there would already be a record of the Registrar's request and they'd be fully aware of her requirements. Does that also mean they've been informed of his failure to turn up yesterday? So! What does it matter? He isn't a Talker and has no intention of continuing the ruse for one moment longer than necessary. Perhaps if he does what Ro and Henneh ask and gets them the information they want, they might bring him back from the dead—as it were. If they could 'dead' him so easily, then they could 'undead' him just as easily.

The Registrar is making her way to the front of her desk. A signal he's about to be shown the door?

"The Doser in charge of the station is Julyen Koale," she tells him, raising her arm in invitation for him to precede her through the maze of shelving and boxes and crates.

Kai's thankful for his Journer legacy. At least he's saved the embarrassment of making a bad turn in the labyrinth of high shelving.

"I assume I'm expected?" he asks.

The Registrar offers him another of those strange half smiles. "Yes," she says. "And your permit for travel to Quarantine Station Two has been issued, of course."

Quarantine Station Two! That's the station in his *home*-ward, the seat of the plague.

"That station is in Journer Ward Minor, isn't it?" Kai asks, doing his very best to sound professional.

Unexpectedly the Registrar stops walking, prompting Kai to stop and turn around. Has he made a mistake? Perhaps a Talker should *know* the location of all the quarantine stations.

"Something wrong?" he asks, hoping the answer is going to be in the negative.

The Registrar takes a moment to reply. "I can count on your confidentiality?" she says at last. "I mean, I have made something of an accusation against the station. I wouldn't want it to go any—"

Kai raises his hand and smiles. *Do Talkers smile?*

"My mission at the station is to facilitate delivery of the information you require. I have no interest in either the content of the report or the station's level of efficiency."

No interest? Kai doesn't know if a Talker is even *permitted* to have any interest. Still, the Registrar does look reassured. She leaves him at the door and now he's baking under the merciless rays of the sun again, worrying over the Registrar's degree of implication, if any, with the Duck Down Club. He's halfway back to the Urban station, before he realises he forgot to get her name.

∗∗∗

Saera watches until she's satisfied the Talker is making his way to the Urban station.

A Talker! They sent an actual Talker! Of course, she knew to expect one but assumed all along it would be someone in the *guise* of a Talker. One of 'them'. How did they do it? Enlist a Talker? It doesn't seem possible. And it's far too daring.

Instead of experiencing a sense of relief that her part is over, she's even more anxious now. Did she play her part well enough? Did the Talker suspect anything? Notice her hand shake? Become aware of a catch in her voice? She isn't a good liar. Never has been.

What if the Talker discovers she lied about never receiving the report from the quarantine station? Could he even do that? If she knew why she'd just sent him there, perhaps that might calm her mind. But she doesn't even know the reason herself. And she's troubled about having to involve Gove again as well.

Saera heads back to her desk, weaving her way through the corridor on corridor of shelving. Oh, but she despises deception. She just isn't any good at it at all.

***

Anxiously Kai starts to count. Two. Three. Now four pairs of Guardians. It's too many. He'll have to pass them to get onto the platform. There's no alternative so, keeping his eyes trained directly ahead, he falls in with a small group of travellers making their way into the station. Most are Crafters. One, a diminutive young female about his age, is walking very quickly.

It's a sense all residents of Ularon City have only lately developed, but Kai can feel the Guardians on his heels as he makes his way from the entrance into the station concourse. He tries to maintain a measured pace, blend in. Perhaps this is the moment his Talker guise is going to undo him. The walk across the narrow concourse seems endless. He weaves through and around the crowd, endeavouring to appear casual. Still the Guardians are behind him, like an ill wind blowing steadily against his back.

They're onto him. Some how. Some way. They're onto him. He risks a subtle lengthening of his stride. The Guardians follow suit. He can see them now, reflected in a slick-tiled pillar just in front of him. The Crafters ahead of him splinter off, the young female cutting directly across his path as she makes for the nearest platform entrance. His is the next entrance, so he continues on behind the remaining Crafters. As acutely as he became aware of the Guardians trailing him, he's now just as acutely aware he's lost them. It's only when he steps onto his platform that he spots them again, patrolling the opposite platform. One of the Guardians appears to be equipped with a handheld scruter. Kai has never seen one up-close. But why would Guardians be patrolling the platform with a scruter? Like him, everyone who walked into the station passed through a concealed scruter.

Kai glances around, affecting indifference. No one looks sick. Others will be glancing around, too, and like him, hoping not to be noticed. He's got more cause than most. The sound of a scuffle on the opposite platform snatches his attention. The Guardians have converged while he was scoping his surroundings. Someone is on the ground. Looks to Kai like that young Crafter. Kai's desperate to look somewhere else but can't seem to drag his eyes away. There's little resistance when the Crafter is hauled onto her feet but a practiced and quiet retreat of those standing closest to her on the platform. The Guardians aren't obviously suited-up; the plague's got nothing to do with the Crafter's detainment. The scruter is nothing but staging, a show for the masses. Kai can't hear what the Crafter is pleading as she's towed away but it's a fair bet she's maintaining she isn't sick. She'll be wasting her time. She knows it, just like the rest of the passengers on the platform know it. Still, no one says a word, flinches a muscle, castes a further eye. This is Ularon City and everyone's relieved it isn't them. Kai leaps onto the Urban when it pulls in, oblivious to anyone boarding with him. There won't be too many going his way; it's an out-city run and few Ularons have business out-city anymore.

Kai pushes the memory of the hapless young Crafter aside as he makes a quick mental calculation. It's been six years and then some since he's taken this run. Of course, on that day, he was journing toward not away from Ularon City. He's returning home— as close to it as anyone can get now—and doesn't know how he feels about that. More importantly, he doesn't know why he's been sent. He's got no influence with anyone at the quarantine station and the task he's been sent to accomplish seems simple enough; for an *actual* Talker, that is. Why him? He probably won't even get close enough to gain an impression of what is happening inside his home-ward, let alone come across anyone he knows. It surprises him to realise that there isn't anyone he wants to come across. Unless it's Mig, Henneh's little sister, or Pilot Jak Inopo. But his mother may have already dulled Mig's light by now. And Pilot Jak

Inopo is more than likely dead, if not by the plague then by natural causes. The last time Kai saw him, the pilot was already very old.

The Urban tears through the ragged hem of the city, powering south into Ularon-Vicinal, the largest Gleaner ward in Pedora. So far, the ward is much as Kai remembers it. Broad fields with the same type of crops, showing the same deleterious effects of the sun and heat despite the thick canopies of woven hul that shield them; small towns where the residents still go about their day-to-day business, indifferent to the swift passage of just another Urban; settlements that consist of little more than the station where his Urban briefly stops. The quarantine hasn't changed any of that. It's only when they begin to near his old home that Kai notices the first real signs of change. The abandoned fields; the rotted canopies drooping over hard-baked and barren soil.

Desertion. Desolation. Silence.

The sight stirs nothing in Kai. No sorrow. No anger. No despair. His father is dead and, as a consequence, he's been forced to live these last years with the stigma of being branded a deader. What difference do a few sterile fields make?

There's a shunt veering west that didn't exist six years ago, but the Urban eschews it and continues along the original track toward Journer Ward Minor. Kai glances around the carriage, unsurprised to find himself alone now. The next stop will be the quarantine station and very few people have cause to travel there. The Urban won't stay long. Get in. Get out. And be quick about it. That's what he'd do. Without him onboard, the Urban would have taken the shunt instead. The pilot is probably cursing Talker Sayker Gerit. The presence of even semi-dignitaries on a run is a nuisance. For obvious reasons, Kai has kept his head low, but that won't matter to the pilot. It's enough that Kai has forced the pilot into the quarantine station.

The sight of the barren fields might not have unnerved him, but the prospect of what is to come does. Either the Registrar is in league with Duck Down Club or she genuinely took him for a Talker. Right now, Kai prefers to believe the latter. He'd rather enter the quarantine station under the delusion that his performance was convincing enough to fool someone. Believing that won't stop the pounding in his chest or fill the hollow pit at the bottom of his stomach though. But Kai's learning to live with that. Until his current situation is resolved, palpitations and queasiness are evidently going to be constant companions.

Kai expected Quarantine Station Two would lie outside his ward, north of the high mountain range abutting his home, but they're nearing the mountains now and the Urban is still powering on. He hadn't counted on them going *through* The Range. The carriage darkens abruptly and Kai holds his breath, willing the time of emptiness to pass swiftly. The whir of the Urban is louder inside the uneasy intimacy of the tunnel, the sound not wholly of the outside world. Pilots are trained to become one with a machine and, in the darkness, Kai has always experienced that unity most strongly. He breathes again when, as suddenly as it fled, light returns to the carriage. They're on the opposite side of The Range now. Inside his home-ward. Inside a plague sector. The last time he was here, he was paralysed with fear and struggling not to show it as he anticipated the imminent journ through the tunnel. Now he notices the foothills skirting out from the summit and, in the shallow valleys between the ridges, a few structures sprinkled among the tall and irregular grass. The Urban begins to slow. Looking out the broad window at his shoulder, Kai sees a scatter of short buildings and the high wire fence that envelopes them. The station is not what he was expecting, either. It's pedestrian, unimposing, easily overlooked. Then, he supposes, that's the point. And it appears he's going to have to hike halfway up a long low hill to get to it. He makes his way to the door, concluding that the Urban is simply going to come to a halt in the middle of nowhere, until the leading edge of a platform comes into sight. There's no one waiting on the platform to get on and there's no one standing beside him to get off. He's alone. It's a relatively new platform but a perfunctory one. A simple slab, unroofed, save for a small ancillary building at the very end of it. An amenity station and nothing more.

Kai steps onto the platform and looks around. The Urban has come to a standstill a short distance away from another high wire fence that crosses the tracks and arcs off into the distance, bumping over hill after hill until it dead-ends against The Range. The fence extends to both sides of the platform, forming a kind of semi-circular barrier penning the little platform and the cluster of buildings inside its own ring of tall fencing.

Kai's attention shifts to the horizon, but he's too far from the Karish Sea to glimpse it. It's sunny out on the platform, not sunny enough to require a U-visor though. No one wears a U-visor inside his home-ward. Kai slips off the visor and looks again toward the mean little cluster of buildings dotted midway up the hill. They're as low, snub, and unwelcoming as they appeared looking through the Urban's window. Signs are plastered all along the length of the wire fencing. Warnings, for sure. Still, Kai's surprised to find the station so lightly secured. Then again, who'd choose to come here?

Behind him, there's a click. The Urban's sophisticated gears have switched around as it prepares to start back toward the shunt. The pilot brings his machine up to speed too fast. Another time, another life, Kai would report the pilot. But he can understand the pilot's eagerness to put distance, and quickly, between themself and the station. He's of the same mind.

Kai heads for the small ancillary building at the end of the platform, assuming he's supposed to wait there for someone to come and get him. There's no door, so it appears the building isn't frequently used and there's nothing much inside it other than a low bench running the length of one wall. He scans the room—up and down, corner to corner—looking for a vis but can't find one, so takes a seat to wait. The bench is uncomfortable, little but ill-fitting lengths of hardwood capping a trough of hard and unforgiving aggregate of a type typically used to construct utility buildings. The walls and floor are made of the same ugly aggregate. Here and there, narrow cracks are visible in the aggregate, some crooked, others perfectly angular. There's a window at one end of the building facing the direction of any oncoming Urban. That's it.

Kai raises a hand to rub his eyes. He's tired, weary of the charade from the moment it began. As he sits, he listens. The Urban has long gone and the only sound is a kind of singing in the air, something Kai attributes to wind either fanning the spindly grass or whistling through the high wire fences. An eternity passes; at least it seems so. In reality, it can't have been very long before Kai realises no one is going to come for him. Rising, he steps outside.

At the end of the platform a short and narrow set of stairs leads down to the ground. There are no railings, a testament to the indifference with which this station was built. An uneven dirt track trends uphill from the base of the stairs toward the high wire fence. The climb is easier than he expected, and he reaches the high wire unchallenged. The fence doesn't look in the best of shape, bent and roughly patched in places. He's about to walk the perimeter in search of an entry when a voice booms down from above. Kai glances up. There's a small vis attached to the very top of the wire, angled down. Seems they've been watching him after all, probably since he stepped off the Urban.

"My name is Sayker Gerit," he says. He's stumbled a little over the foreign name and hopes no one on the other side of the fence noticed. "I understand I'm expected."

There's a pause and Kai holds his breath.

"We have your authorisation," the voice thunders back abruptly. "Please proceed to the southwest gate and someone will admit you."

Kai wavers. Which *is* the southwest gate? He's momentarily disoriented. Unforgiveable in a pilot. Turning, he starts following the narrow track that rings the perimeter fence. The gate is easily missed, like the gate at the Repository. He wonders if he's just supposed to push on it and walk in. No. He was told someone would admit him. As he stands outside the perimeter, waiting in the hot sun, he notices for the first time the little box-like arrangement attached to the fence on the other side of the gate. Had he pushed on the gate, he'd likely have been in for a shock—literally. Seems they do take security more seriously here than at the Repository. They have more cause to. But surely he's not risking infection. They wouldn't just permit anyone inside. He should have thought to ask the Registrar when he had the chance.

Someone emerged from the largest of buildings while his attention was on the box; she's walking toward him briskly. Kai is relieved to see her dressed only in the standard dusky green Doser uniform. There's no mask. No isolation suit. Still, he hopes the Registrar's request is met quickly. He'd like to get out of this place as fast as possible. They'll have to send an Urban back for him and that could take a little time, but he'll gladly pass that time on the open platform.

As the Doser draws closer, Kai notices that she's on the heavy side. A bad look for a Doser. Her uniform stretches tight across her stomach and chest, seems to be bulging at the seams across broad thighs. She's a lowly Scrubber. In the Doser caste, a Scrubber is about on par with a Sub among Journers.

"Just one moment, Talker Gerit," the Doser says, making for the little box beside the gate. "I just have to punch you in."

She's missed his nod, her attention directed toward her fingers, which are working at the little panel she's popped open on the box.

"That does it," she says with a smile, surprising him.

She's friendly enough. Kai was anticipating his arrival to be met with annoyance at best.

With a little click, the gate pivots inward and Kai steps through.

"If you could just wait there," the Scrubber says, pointing to a spot behind her. "I have to secure the gate again."

Kai steps behind her and turns away; it's poor form to watch what she's doing.

"I'm Madgel Swar," she says. "If you'd like to follow me, please." A sturdy arm swings out to guide him. "This way."

She's directing him down a paved path toward the largest of the squat buildings. The pavers are laid irregularly. These days the Pedorate has greater concerns than aesthetics, but the place also hints at a lack of activity and it could be that's the core of the Registrar's problem. This station seems undermanned. It would explain the quiet, the stillness, the overwhelming sense of emptiness. Nearing the building, Kai realises that the entrance itself is a sim. The Scrubber passes through, faintly disrupting the field and Kai passes through behind her. He's aware of a tingling in his hands and feet, the standard sensation when passing through a passive sim. Inside, the station is bright white with slick, unbroken flooring underfoot and rounded floor-to-ceiling joins. Kai would like to put his visor back on, but it's impolite. He's in some sort of outer room. There's nothing in it. No furniture. Not even a vis or scruter. Nothing but uninterrupted monotony and a little draft wafting toward the sim entrance behind him. Kai glances around, seeking the source of the draft that's keeping the inside air clean and confined. The snub and ordinary-looking building is a deception and perhaps more cleverly designed than he first thought.

"There's nothing to be concerned about," the Scrubber tells him.

She's picked up on his unease. Dosers are good at that; at least, they're supposed to be.

"We keep positive pressure in the building at all times." She points toward the sim. "We're inside the quarantine area. It's just a precaution. You understand?" she asks, peering into Kai's face, looking at his eyes a little too intently for comfort.

He's heard that's where it shows first. In the eyes. She's looking for early signs of infection. Habit? Kai hopes so. Like she said, they're inside the quarantine area.

"Certainly," Kai agrees, feigning composure. What if she does see something there? How fast does infection take hold? He's mingled with the dregs of the Journer caste in the Duck Down Club. Hadn't given a thought then to the possibility that one of them might be carrying the disease.

The Doser breaks off her stare. Should he call her on her boldness? A genuine Talker would.

"Where are your scruters?" he asks. "I'm surprised that you have the gall to visually assess me when your scruters should have told you everything you need to know."

To his surprise, the Scrubber's face crinkles once again into an unconcerned smile. "Call me old-fashioned," she says. "You did pass through a scruter when you entered through the sim. It's just our little joke." She shrugs and the smile fades away.

Kai sees nothing amusing about it.

"If you'd like to get into your suit now."

When Kai hesitates, unable to locate a suit or any receptacle to hold one, the Scrubber frowns.

"I'm afraid it's necessary."

"I'm quite prepared to wear an isolation suit," Kai replies. "In fact, I'd prefer to, but where exactly—"

"Oh, I do apologise," she says hurriedly. "We're not used to receiving visitors. Your suit will be automatically fitted the moment you step through the next sim. It's a field suit," she explains. "We have all the modern equipment here. I think you'll be quite impressed."

"I'm not here to be impressed. I'm simply here at the request of the Registrar of the Repository. I have no interest in your facilities."

The Scrubber eyes him for another long moment before responding. "Of course," she says and waves him ahead of her toward the opposite wall. "And we do regret the recent confusion. Perhaps you'll be kind enough to report that to Registrar Brawse when you see her."

"Brawse?" Kai falters over the name.

"Yes. Aralin Brawse. She is still in charge of the Repository, isn't she?" The Scrubber stops walking. "Oh, I hope this incident hasn't caused her any trouble."

Kai voices the first thing that comes to mind. "I'm sure the Registrar can cope."

The Scrubber seems to accept his response.

Aralin Brawse. So, he has the Registrar's name now. Not that it helps him any.

"Here we are then," she says, ushering him toward what, at first impression, looks to be a solid wall.

Kai's not so easily deceived now. A delicate shimmer in the white sameness of the wall gives it away as a sim. He steps through the illusion, this time experiencing significantly more than the usual tingle in his hands and feet. For a moment, he feels as though he's being suffocated. It's the field suit. Kai's never worn one before; has never had the need.

The Scrubber steps through behind him.

Kai is still trying to adjust to the stifling sensation, still gasping a little for breath when the Scrubber speaks again.

"This way please."

She says more but Kai isn't listening. He's examining his body, looking for any physical sign that he's adequately protected. He can't see a thing other than the Talker uniform he's wearing. Glancing toward Swar, he notices nothing different about her, either. She looks exactly the same; the green of her uniform is unchanged. Kai feels his face. Nothing. Nothing at first anyway. Then he notices it—a subtle, *very subtle*, difference in the elasticity of his skin.

All right! He's prepared to accept he's not being led unprotected into a plague-infected area. He isn't prepared to be led much further though. If someone other than this Scrubber doesn't appear soon, he'll abort and bolt back out through the sims. Whether he'll actually be able to do that is, of course, another matter. It may not be quite as easy to get *out* as it was to get *in*.

The Scrubber has brought him into a corridor. Directly in front of him is another blank wall—presumably—and, to the right and left, the outstretched arms of the corridor. Scrubber Swar starts down the left passage, Kai following. It's a short walk. She stops at a door, a real door this time, with no obvious security. She doesn't knock, simply steps inside. Kai steps in after her.

He's surprised to find such a large room. From the outside the building looked too small to house a functioning quarantine station. But what does he know of such places? Likely there are levels underground and he did see more than one auxiliary building. It's quiet in the room but not empty. Three rows of benches stretch from wall to wall, filling up nearly all the space. There's little scope to move around. The benches are manned by Dosers, heads bent in concentration. No one seems aware that he and the Scrubber have entered. Kai counts thirteen Dosers and, from what he can glean from the backs of their heads, they're all relatively young. The benches are equipped with cyphers popping with rapidly changing readouts and brightly coloured images that are unintelligible to Kai. He's guessing the Dosers are studying the infinitely small building blocks of the plague virus, trying to work out what makes the virus tick. He prefers *not* to understand the details.

The Scrubber ushers him to the second bench where a spare youngish Doser is seated. He, like the other Dosers in the room, seems unaware of Kai's presence. When Swar taps the Doser on the shoulder, his head snaps around. He looks annoyed.

"What is... oh," the Doser breaks off, noticing Kai. "You must be Registrar Brawse's representative. Yes, please..." He stands awkwardly, leaving Kai with the impression he's been sitting there in the one spot far too long. "I'm Julyen Koale," he says. "Doser-in-charge of this station. You're wanting our latest statistics, I understand." He's beginning to sound a little flustered. "I can't understand why the Registrar didn't receive our report. It was sent by courier as usual."

"I'm sure the Registrar would wish me to apologise for this inconvenience on her behalf." That sounded just Talker enough in Kai's view. Give them a little but not too much.

"Shall I attend to the Registrar's request for you?" Swar interjects.

Instead of sounding relieved, the offer appears to irritate Koale.

"No. I'll attend to it myself."

"Certainly," Swar replies, then turns to Kai. "It was a pleasure to meet you, Talker Gerit."

Somehow Kai doubts that.

"Come this way," Koale says, starting for the door. "This has never happened before. But then this quadrant is rather remote."

Remote? Kai has never thought of his birth-ward as remote exactly. Koale is a Ularon native. No doubt about it. For years now Kai might have made his home in Ularon City, but he's never come to like the place or its people. They're arrogant. Insular. Bigoted.

"And requiring all our reports to be submitted on *paper*," Koale continues. "It's a scarce commodity. Especially out here."

Kai can't argue with that.

"Please." Koale opens the door and invites Kai into the corridor. "I'm sure you're anxious to be on your way. You will assure the Registrar that we had every intention of resending the report?" The Doser heads off down the corridor, leading Kai deeper into the complex. "If I may ask you to do that," he says, aiming words over his shoulder. "Explain that everything is fine here at the station. We're just exceptionally busy."

Kai nods. Busy and *plagued* by the arrival of some Talker on a mundane errand from the Repository. Koale seems a little on edge. Sure, having a Talker arrive, brandishing their position in your face, should be unnerving. But Kai is no Talker. All he can do here is pressure the Dosers into supplying the report the Registrar wants and a routine report on plague statistics isn't of any obvious use to Ro and her associates. Evidence. That's what she sent him to find and by way of the person who is concealing it. She couldn't mean Doser Koale.

The Doser stops at another unassuming-looking door at the end of the bright corridor.

"This is my office," he explains, swinging the door wide open. "If you'd take a seat, I'll see about getting you that report. There's paper here somewhere."

Kai foregoes the seat and steps instead to an enormous window that takes up a large part of the rear wall of the Doser's office. Through it, he can look down to the floor below. Clearly it's a hospital ward, fitted out in two facing rows of beds. Twenty, no, twenty-two in all. Above each bed is a scruter, angled slightly downward. Not a single bed is occupied, each stripped uniformly bare. Not a single scruter is active. The ward is empty.

"Where are all your patients?" Kai asks over his shoulder.

Koale is on his hands and knees, shuffling through the contents of a long low cabinet. He looks up.

"I'm sorry?"

Kai points at the window. "Your hospital is empty."

The Doser flaps a hand, then returns to his searching. "Oh, that's just the emergency room. The isolation ward is on a lower level."

"You have no emergencies now?"

Koale is caught with his hand thrust inside the cabinet. "Ah, no. Not at this precise moment." He gets to his feet. "Talker Gerit, I was under the impression that you were sent here by Registrar Brawse and that your sole purpose is to obtain a replacement copy of our report. If you've come with the intention of inspecting our isolation facility, then I'm afraid I can't allow it. You don't have the proper authorisation for that."

He's gone too far. Made Koale suspicious.

"Just idle curiosity," Kai says, turning his back to the window.

He's probably just made the Doser even more suspicious. Are Talkers even *prone* to idle curiosity? Still, Koale appears to accept Kai's explanation. He shrugs, stoops and takes up his search for paper once again.

"If you'll just bear with me. I'll have to... please," he says, "do take a seat."

Acceding, Kai takes up the seat he was offered. It's the only empty chair in the room. The rest are strewn with discarded clothing and various bits and pieces of curious equipment. It looks as though Julyen Koale might actually be living in his office and the deep depression in the short garment-littered couch on the opposite side of the room just provides further evidence.

When the office door swings open, Kai looks over.

"Not now!" Koale snaps, firing a short dark glance toward the doorway.

The door closes again almost immediately, but Kai's had a brief moment to see the Preserver who opened the door. If she came to clean Koale's office, she'd have been busy. There was nothing remarkable about her appearance at the door or about the Preserver, herself, until Kai suddenly realises he's seen her before. Taken her for a Preserver before, too.

It was Vee! The cursed messenger who had sent him to the Duck Down Club in the first place and then ambushed him in the drenching rain outside his Journer quarters—his own private peddler of bad news.

Did Koale know?

He'd barely looked at her.

It is impossible to get into the station without clearance, so there is no way Vee could have passed through the gates and the vis without being stopped. Koale *has* to have recognised her, probably seen her many times before, even been disturbed by her vain attempts to put the clutter in his office into order.

More lies! Vee knew all along where Ro meant for him to go.

"No wait," Koale calls. Leaping up from the floor, he rushes to the door and opens it. "Come here," he shouts, leaning his head through the open doorway.

Vee's come back. Kai can't see her, but he can hear the Doser talking, catching only snatches of the conversation. Something about moving things around in his office.

"I do apologise," Koale says, returning to Kai. "The paper is being brought here now."

Perhaps a real Talker would complain, but Kai isn't concentrating on the charade right now. He's thinking through the greater implications of Vee's appearance.

The Doser betrays some discomfort as he first clears and then takes up the chair on the opposite side of his desk. He fidgets, can't seem to look Kai in the eye.

The door opens once again and Kai glances over. It's Vee, all right, and she enters the room, carrying a small lidded box.

"Put it here," Koale snaps.

Vee steps in front of Kai, bends and places the box before the Doser. As she turns, she looks at Kai. She's mouthing something at him very deliberately. One word.

Platform.

As he watches Koale fumble with the lid of the box, Kai is vaguely aware of the door closing behind him.

"Ah, here we are! Paper," Koale says, fanning fifty or so sheets of aged-looking paper.

Despite himself, Kai is almost fascinated with what Koale intends to do with it now. He's never seen a paper report produced. In the end it turns out to be a rather tedious process with Koale dashing to an odd kind of machine in the far corner of the room, where he stacks the paper, then dashing back to the cypher on his desk again. His fingers fly. Kai has never been that proficient with a cypher, not these types anyway.

There comes the laboured sound of clunking from the odd little machine in the far corner of the room and, one by one, the paper starts to move. Clunk! Whizz! It's a slow process to Kai's way of thinking, but eventually most of the fifty or so sheets have made their way to the other side of the machine.

The clunking stops and Koale jumps up from his desk to retrieve the neat stack of paper. The unused sheets he leaves.

"I'm afraid I can't allow you to see these," he says tentatively, fanning the sheets again. "I'm sorry but—"

Kai rises from his chair. "The content is of no concern to me."

It's a lie. The content is of *great* concern to him and maybe of even greater concern to Vee and Gannaline-ro. That business about using his influence with someone was all just some sort of sham. This has got to be what they're after and that means the Registrar isn't in on it or she could simply hand over the information and there'd be no need to involve him. He's disposable, that's all. If he gets caught, then there's nothing to link him back to the Duck Down Club.

Kai reaches for the stack of paper. "It's getting late. If I could have the report now, then..."

He stops talking when Koale's eyes widen.

"But..." the Doser stammers. "I thought you... it has to be sealed," he says, emphasising the last word.

Stupid! He's just been told he isn't permitted to see the report. He's too anxious to get out of the place, didn't stop to think.

"If you could just wait here a moment, I'll see to it."

"Quickly, if you don't mind," Kai snaps. "It's a long way back to Ularon City. Clearly you could have easily reproduced the report and the only obstacle was your disinterest."

Talker arrogance! He was back on track! If he can throw the Doser off-guard enough times, he'll be able to get out of the station with his authority unchallenged. Maybe he's better at fraud than he thought.

Koale hurries through the door and Kai is left alone in the room. He's wondering where Vee has gone. She won't be coming back into Koale's office. She wouldn't dare. She's just a Preserver or, at least, acting out the role as one. Pautune! Kai wishes he'd got more than 'platform' from her.

The door bangs open again and Koale rushes in.

"Here we are, Talker Gerit," the Doser says, offering Kai a small rectangular metal container. Inside must be the report. Kai doesn't spend any time examining the container, but at a quick glance, he can see no obvious seal. Brawse must have a particular way of opening it. But maybe there's something at the platform that will do it. Perhaps that's what Vee was trying to tell him.

"You will explain to Registrar Brawse that there is nothing at all out of the ordinary happening here at the station, won't you? And, of course, please accept my apology for bringing you out so far from Ularon City."

He's rushing his words as he directs Kai back the way they came, down the bright white corridor toward the entrance.

"Rest assured," Koale is saying, "you've suffered no exposure. Our suits are of the highest rating."

Kai almost doesn't care now if the suit he's wearing has protected him or not. When it comes down to it, what future has he got? The only thing he's thankful for is that he's managed to get himself out of the quarantine station. If he does succumb to the plague, then his last moments won't be spent languishing deep in the bowels of a place like this. He'll see to the solution himself—and quickly.

Kai, carrying the metal box, comes to the door of the large room where all the Dosers are working. The door is shut, just as it was before, and Kai can hear nothing of what's going on behind it. He passes on and makes to continue down the corridor until Julyen Koale calls him back.

"You've gone too far."

Kai turns to find Koale waiting for him some paces back.

"The sim is here," Koale explains.

It's a good sim. The best Kai has ever seen—or, rather, *never* seen.

"If you don't mind, I'll stay here." Koale gestures toward his clothes. "I'm suited," he says. "Once you pass through the sim, your suit is automatically removed. Just exit the way you came in. I'll alert the pilot that you're ready to leave and an Urban will return for you shortly. You can wait in the shelter at the platform."

Koale sounds uncertain, as though he's expecting Kai to object.

Kai nods instead.

"It won't be..."

The rest is lost as Kai steps through the sim. For an instant he thinks he sees a shift in Koale's demeanour as the Doser fades from sight. Relief at seeing the back of a Talker?

Emerging into the silence of the outer room, Kai feels the same tingling sensation in his hands and feet that he felt before but, this time, instead of experiencing a sense of suffocation, it's as though a constrictive band has been cut away from his chest and lungs. He's lost the suit and, without it, feels vulnerable. It's a fleeting panic. He wastes no further time inside and hastens to the gate.

"You may pass through," a voice pipes at him. It's Madgel Swar again. "The gate is unlocked and it will lock again once you're outside."

Kai doesn't bother to glance overhead as the gate swings open. He's done with this place. Tucking the small metal box under his arm, he passes out of the quarantine station, worrying on exactly what it is he's supposed to do at the platform. He hurries back to the shelter—not too fast in case someone from the quarantine station is watching him—and mounts the steps to the platform, listening for the sound of the Urban. Nothing yet. The last thing he expects to find inside the little shelter is Vee, sitting on that unforgiving bench, waiting for him.

"How did you get out of the station?"

"The Urban will be here soon," she says, rising. "We haven't got a lot of time."

It's only then Kai realises Vee is dressed in the uniform of a Talker.

She holds out her hand. "Give me the box."

Instinctively Kai grips the box tighter.

Vee shakes her outstretched hand at him. "Give it to me! I have to be carrying it to get on the Urban. You've already held us up a day. Do you intend to hold us up even longer?"

"I'm not giving you anything until you explain what's going on here. Who *are* you? You change castes like a karilli changes its skin."

"I haven't changed a thing," Vee replies, sounding exasperated. "I only *look* like I have. And what caste I really am is of no concern to you."

"No matter who or what you are, I'm not giving you this box. It's intended for the Registrar."

Vee waves her hand in dismissal. "What's inside that box is meaningless. I'm not interested, but I can't get on the Urban without it. The pilot knows a Talker came here to get something. We can't take the chance of him noticing that a Talker got back on the Urban empty-handed."

"You're going to substitute for *me*?" Kai asks, incredulous. "The pilot will never believe it. For one thing, you're too short to be me."

Vee shrugs. "That can't be helped. It'll be almost dark by the time the Urban gets here. I'll wait here until it arrives and then hurry on. A Talker got off without anything in his hands and a Talker will get back on carrying something. That's all the pilot will care about. It's a chance we have to take"

"It's not all *I'd* care about," Kai replies. "Or notice."

"Perhaps not." Vee points down-track. "But that pilot isn't you." She steps forward and taps Kai's forehead. "Think. They want off this run."

Kai can't fault her reasoning there.

"That pilot's not about to compromise a reassignment. Talker off. Talker on. End of their interest. Unless…" She lowers her hand tentatively. "You didn't talk to the pilot, did you? *Don't tell me you talked to the pilot?*"

"Of course, I didn't. I stayed as far away as possible."

Kai refrains from mentioning that the notion crossed his mind.

Vee relaxes. "That was the smart thing to do. But I never know with you. So," she continues, reaching out again, "just give me the box and we can both go our separate ways."

Kai hesitates, looks her up and down. It's all about impressions. Her hair is cropped short and it's about the same dark colour as his own. If she stays in the shelter until the Urban pulls up and then darts swiftly across the platform, the ploy might just work.

"Satisfied?" she asks.

"So, you get on the Urban," he says, handing over the box. "Where does that leave me?"

"Walking home," she replies. "You stay inside the shelter until it's completely dark and then head into Journer Ward Minor."

"Just like that? Walk down the track and climb over the perimeter fence?"

Vee cocks her head to one side. "Well, that *would* pose you some problems if you went that way. You're going to go through the tunnel."

"The *what?*"

"The tunnel. It's how I got out of the quarantine station without anyone seeing me. Those Dosers don't know it's here."

Before he can say anything, Vee shoves him out of her way and, drawing a very thin blade from her pocket, bends to her knees and begins to work on the aggregate flooring. "This," she explains, lifting the section of floor that had been directly under Kai's feet, "is the entrance to a Sub tunnel." Soundlessly she replaces the section of floor. She's smiling when she rises and hands him the blade. "You don't honestly think that quarantine station was purpose-built? The Pedorate wouldn't bother. It's just modified ventilator shafts and works shacks from the aborted Sub line."

So there *were* plans for a Sub line into Journer Ward Minor. All those years ago, Gannin had it right; he just didn't know that construction of the Sub was already underway.

"And beneath us," she stamps her foot, "is one of the maintenance tunnels."

"And they left this access open?"

That didn't seem likely.

"Of course not," she says, the smile surfacing once more. "We opened them up again. Those Dosers in there," she waves toward the quarantine station, "they have no idea they're working inside rejigged ventilator shafts or where the old access tunnels are located inside the complex."

Maybe not, but... "Then how do you know?"

"Can't see that's your business," Vee replies, turning serious. "Once you climb down there," she points to the closed hole in the floor, "you'll be in darkness, so you'll need these." She turns and, placing the box on the floor, bends to rip one of the lengths of hardwood from the top of the bench, then reaching inside, produces a pair of shine-sticks. At least Kai knows now where she was hiding the Talker uniform. "Replace the section of floor once you're inside the tunnel. There's only one way to go and that's toward the quarantine station. You'll come to a hatch at the end of the tunnel. Don't try it unless you want to end up inside the isolation room—"

"The access leads to the isolation room?"

"Eventually."

"And you've been coming and going *through* it?"

Vee shrugs. "My problem, not yours."

"I'd hardly say that since you're standing right in front..." Kai doesn't finish. Let her breathe on him. Touch him. What does it matter now?

"Go on," he says. He's just heard the promising whine of the Urban. He's attuned to the sound. Vee isn't, won't be aware that the Urban is closing in.

"Glad you've come to your senses," Vee observes with a nod. "Once you come to the hatch, turn left. If you've a mind to explore the other tunnels, don't bother. They'll just take you to ancillary buildings inside the station. The shine-sticks will last until you get to the exit. I can't say where you'll come out exactly because I understand the excavation was never finished, but it's your home-ward, you'll know where you are."

Kai opens his mouth to speak but Vee pre-empts him.

"I've never been there, to answer the question you're about to ask. What would have been the point? I can't do this."

"Do *what?*"

"You'll know when you get there. But you'll be able to do it a lot easier out of that Talker uniform you're wearing. You change into this," she says, wrenching a Guardian's uniform from its hiding place beneath the hardwood seat.

If she thinks he's about to pose as a Pedorate guard now, she's mad.

Vee stands, offering him the pale brown uniform.

He could knock her out. Maybe use the blade in his hand to dispose of her. Take the box and get back on the Urban himself. What's to stop him?

"Forget it," he says, slapping her hand away. The uniform falls to the floor.

He's surprised when Vee offers him another irritating smile.

"They said you'd say that."

"Then I'm glad we're all agreed on one thing. Now I suggest you return that box to me, then get back into your Preserver uniform and head back down that tunnel into the quarantine station before they realise you're missing."

"They'll never miss me," she tells him. "I'm just a Preserver. If they can't find me one place, they'll think I'm in another."

"Forever?"

"Doesn't need to be forever. Just long enough. And how long is up to you." Stooping, she gathers the Guardian's uniform from the floor. "You can't go in dressed as a Talker," she says, offering him the uniform once more. "Talkers never go into the quarantined areas."

"And Guardians do, I suppose."

"Some," she says. "Those who've been told they're inoculated."

Kai grabs her by the hand, heedless that she might be carrying the virus.

"Told? *Told!*"

She doesn't answer, just stands there, staring him down, holding out the uniform. When her focus darts over his shoulder, Kai realises she's heard the Urban.

"It's coming," she says with a trace of urgency and thrusts the uniform into his hand. "Maybe the pilot can't see inside here. But maybe they can. You don't have a lot of time. You do what I've told you to do or face the consequences. You want to be a pilot again, don't you? This is your only chance. Ro can do it." She points to her own uniform, then quickly at Kai's. "Who do you think did this?"

Ro! It always comes back to Ro! Always!

"So you're just like me after all. They made you dead, too," Kai says. "That scum in the Duck Down Club."

"Do you really think I want to be here? I thought I'd already seen the last of you. I just do what I'm told *when* I'm told. And I'd suggest you do the same if you ever want your life back."

"Give me that," Kai says, wrenching the uniform from her hand. "But you deceive me again, and I swear I'll spend every moment of the rest of my life hunting you down. You. Ro. And every last member of the Club."

"Fine. Fine," Vee replies. She's not looking at him now, but busily surveying her uniform, adjusting it.

Kai glances toward the window. It's dark out now. But like Vee said, maybe the pilot can still see inside the shelter. Urban pilots have good eyes. Dropping to the floor, he scrambles into position under the window. The Urban is beginning to howl and the floor beneath Kai is vibrating irregularly, a telling sign the machine needs maintenance. Whoever that pilot is, they're careless.

"When the Urban is gone," Vee says, glancing his way, "you change clothes and put your Talker uniform under the bench. Don't forget to replace the board." She starts for the open platform, turning briefly while she's still inside the shelter. "Oh, and good luck hunting us down, by the way. You couldn't seem to find us a couple of nights ago."

She's gone before Kai can respond.

CHAPTER 9

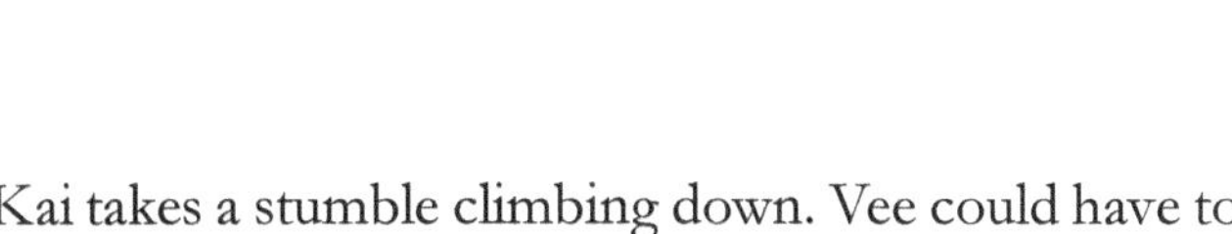

Kai takes a stumble climbing down. Vee could have told him there'd be a ladder. He should have had sense enough to know there would be. The shine-stick only shows him so much. With the hatch replaced, he can't even see the base of the ladder, so descends cautiously until there's solid ground beneath his feet and, save for the light of the shine-stick, darkness. There's only one direction he can go; Vee spoke the truth about that. The tunnel leads directly toward the quarantine station. There are no subsidiary tunnels that Kai can see; according to Vee, there will be. At least the floor is smooth and there's ample room overhead. Battling that same familiar fear of dark and confined spaces, Kai tries to imagine the way opening up in front of him.

He almost blunders into the hatch Vee warned him not to take, the one that leads into the station. He shines the light upon the hatch just the same. Just as Vee promised, the way divides. Kai glances north, swinging the light in that direction. There isn't much to see. Rock floor. Rock walls. Rock ceiling. It would be a long walk back to Ularon City. And what if that tunnel divides again? Kai's not sure he could find the way having nothing but a pair of shine-sticks of limited duration to guide him. If he's smart, he'll turn around, get topside and work out some other way to get back to Ularon City. Then again, if he *had* been smart he wouldn't have walked into the Duck Down Club in the first place.

Bypassing the hatch, he veers left and heads south down the tunnel Vee told him to take. It's straight if untried going. He won't be the first to go down this tunnel, but he'll probably be the first in a long time. Parts of these tunnels could have collapsed. Seems Ro and Vee, and whoever else is involved, never gave any thought to that. If his way is blocked, he'll have no choice but to turn back.

His mind's been wandering. He trips. Stops and bends to one knee. Using his shine-stick, he locates the obstacle in front of him. It's a pack of some kind. Old. Left here by the crew who built the tunnel? Kai flips it open. It's full of shine-sticks. Curious! Although it makes sense to have an emergency supply in the tunnel, why would the construction crew store sticks in an ordinary pack? Standing, Kai looks back the way he's just come. By a stroke of luck, he has enough shine-sticks now to get him to Ularon City. Maybe. Turn back or go on? Assuming he can walk all the way back to Ularon City, what will he have gained? Absolutely nothing. And if he continues on, tries to make it home, what will he gain? That's the big question, isn't it?

With a sense of stony resignation, Kai resumes his journey to the place he once called home. He's come this far. But the chance find of that cache of shine-sticks still troubles him. Why were they left behind? He worries on that for a while; it occupies his mind, draws his thoughts away from the intimacy of the walls and ceiling that have him entombed.

Kai falters over another irregularity in the floor. The deeper he advances through the tunnel, the more obstacles he's likely to encounter since excavation was abandoned before completion. Time to keep his wits about him, concentrate on his footing and not the cursed tightness around him.

Seeing a light dimly glowing in the darkness ahead, he pulls up. Surely he hasn't come far enough to have reached the end of the tunnel. A ceiling collapse that's channelling light from the surface? Can't be! It's night outside. Kai raises his shine-stick in an attempt to gauge the condition of the ceiling and the light ahead of him mimics the transit.

A reflection.

He walks on cautiously, swinging the shine-stick backward and forward, up and down, until bit by bit, piece by jagged piece, the enormous circular face of a machine becomes clear in the darkness. For a long while, Kai stands in front of the giant wheel, trying to comprehend what he's found. It can only be one of those mindless machines, manually operated by the subcaste of Preservers who bore the tunnels under Pedora. Kai's familiar with these hulking machines from the sims. If there's the potential for a Journer to be piloting a Sub in the tunnels, then a Journer better know how the tunnel got there. But seeing one for real is a very different experience.

It seems neither Ro nor Vee gave any thought to the possibility of an abandoned borer, either. The way ahead is blocked. There's no room above the machine and little to either side of it, certainly not enough for Kai to squeeze around. He's stuck this side of the borer. It's possible, just possible, he can find a way to climb through, stealing hand and foot holds on the teeth of the cutting head, squeezing a passage through the labyrinthine innards to the conveyor belt and then out onto the other side. It could be a long, a very long, crawl. And madness to try. On impulse, Kai rams the shine-stick between his teeth and jumps, managing to get his hand around one of the wheel's projecting teeth without ripping his skin. Scrambling, he gets his feet onto two of the teeth. It's a long way to the top but he only has to climb until he finds a way through into the machine. He starts to climb. Hand. Foot. Hand. Foot. The breach comes sooner than he expects. By pulling his shoulders in tightly and twisting the lower half of his body almost perpendicular to the upper, he squirms his way inside the big machine. It's a very tight fit. He can't even get a hand to any of his shine-sticks to look around. Keeping the one stick between his teeth, he squeezes forward. This way. That way. Around sharp angles and projecting sections of metal. Over small and large gaps in the tangle of parts, choking on the stench of stale machine oil that coats his hands and makes the going slippery. Perhaps it's imagination, but Kai senses a way opening up ahead of him. Still, he's surprised when his head breaks free into the open.

Someone has dismantled the machine. Parts of it anyway. There's no conveyor belt on the other side, just a drop onto the tunnel floor. Kai drags his trunk and legs through. He's hanging off his hands now, legs dangling. Climb down or jump? He opts for the latter and lands heavily, jars a knee, and almost bites through the shine-stick he's kept clenched between his teeth. But he's upright. More importantly, he's free. He hurries on, limping a little and passing as he goes, the separated hulk of the conveyor belt. His priority now is to get to the end of the tunnel; to reach open air. Time to worry about what he'll face on the other side when he gets there. He barely covers any distance at all before another light flashes in the darkness ahead.

Another borer?

Kai continues on, apprehensive. What if he can't find a way through the next machine?

But this time, it's not another borer that materialises in front of him, it's a little kyne and she's carrying a shine-stick of her own. Kai and the young one pull up sharply at the same moment. For a long time, they just stand there transfixed in the light radiating from their individual shine-sticks.

Finally, Kai hears something. Footsteps. More than one set! The young one isn't alone.

A hazy figure emerges out of the darkness behind the kyne.

"Get him!" it booms. "Kill him! He'll give us away!"

Kai is darting back the way he came before he realises it. The others are running, too, feet pounding close on his heels. He's tired. Hasn't slept properly for days. They'll wear him down for sure. For a moment, he considers tossing the shine-stick away, but that would leave him in darkness while those in pursuit can still see.

He makes it back to the borer just ahead of them. Climbing wildly, he frantically tries to remember the way through the twists and turns of contorted metal. Halfway up, he loses his grip and begins to slide, bumping painfully against jagged edges, the lost shine-stick catapulting end over end ahead of him all the way to the floor. He lands hard on one shoulder and someone is on him before he can right himself. The blue glow from other shine-sticks dances all about him and many hands drag him roughly onto his feet.

"My, my," someone says, close to his face. He can feel their breath on his skin, their grip on his upper arm, a stab of pain as someone else wrenches his other arm behind his back. There's a shine-stick being held directly in front of his eyes, blinding him to everything but the bright blue glow. He's lost his own shine-stick, not that it would be much use to him. He's still got the other shine-sticks. And he's still got the blade Vee gave him but can't get to it. What good would it do anyway? Kai's guessing there's about five or six of them. He's hoping they don't find the blade.

"Guardian!"

It's a different voice, higher-pitched, younger.

"What's a Guardian doing down here?" Another voice now.

"What they're always doing. Looking for one of us." That's the first voice again. And the owner sounds uneasy.

"Alone?" Voice four; more assured. "Don't be stupid!"

The shine-stick moves away from Kai's eyes, allowing him to see a little better. There are shine-sticks dancing all around him, illuminating faces, and there's his own shine-stick lying on the floor of the tunnel a short distance away.

His count was wrong. There are eight pursuers, most dressed in common, though shabby Journer clothes; one in a type of colourful knee-length tunic Kai has never seen before. They're all quite young save one who Kai guesses to be the owner of the self-assured voice he heard. She's older than the rest but not by much even though she stands a good head taller than anyone else. Her features are fine, almost delicate, in contrast to her hair which is standing up untidily, short-cropped and matted. Back-lit, it resembles a halo. The others in the party are hardly more than young ones. In fact, one is a little kyne. She's the one he came upon first. Standing a little back from the rest, her big round eyes are studying him intently. Kai's surprised when she is the next to speak.

"Ask him his name."

An older kyne, reedy as a hul shoot, turns to give her a rough shove. "Shut up, *fiweam*. That's the dumbest thing I ever heard. Why would we want to do a thing like that?"

The little kyne doesn't respond. She's just been likened to a fur-matted stinking sewer rodent, but it doesn't seem to bother her.

"Nice to know the name of your kills," the kyne in the strange tunic says, moving up into the light of a shine-stick.

"Why don't you all shut up," the older kyne barks.

Kai takes this older kyne to be the leader. These eight must have come from Journer Ward Minor. And they've all been exposed to the plague. And now so has he. So, it's done this time for sure! The nervousness. The fear. After all these years, it's over.

"Let me think," the older kyne says. She sounds calm. Deliberate. A little curious—well, she would be—but not panicked. "What *is* a Guardian doing down here alone?" She's talking to herself and, as she speaks, uses her shine-stick to study Kai's uniform before directing it straight on his face. "Got anything to say?"

Kai shakes his head. He's either going to die down here in the tunnels or die of plague on the surface. Let them think what they like. It's all the same to him. Whatever Ro sent him into the ward to do won't ever be completed. He can't say he's bothered by that, but he's going to die with the question of what it was unanswered.

So be it.

"Maybe he's a deserter," one of the kynes suggests, turning to another of the kynes who shrugs his disinterest.

"Then we can kill him and no one will ever notice." The same tunic-clad kyne again.

She's got a mean streak, that one. Courtesy of someone else's stick, Kai can finally see her face. It's thin, angular. Her hair must be very fair; in the light of the shine-stick, it's almost blue.

"That's real smart, Doon." The leader's head snaps around to confront her disagreeable companion. "Leave a dead body down here stinking up the place." She turns back to Kai. "You hurt? Break anything?"

"No," Kai replies.

"Then you can walk," she says. "Let him go."

She's talking over Kai's shoulder, giving orders to the kyne who has Kai's arm pinned behind his back.

"We take him back. Let someone else decide what to do with him."

"I say we kill him first."

Kai doesn't need to look to know who made that suggestion.

"You want him killed," the leader replies. She's down on one knee now, rummaging about in the pack she's slipped from her back. "You do it and you carry him back yourself." Rising, she instructs Kai to hold out his hands.

Kai looks down. She threading a length of twine or something through her fingers.

"Better if you cooperate," she says. "I'm going to tie you up or Doon there is going to kill you."

"Let her tie you up," the little kyne, the one the reedy kyne called *fiweam*, chimes in. "You'll get out of the tunnel a lot faster if you do." She steps forward and, stretching full height, stares up into Kai's face. She looks nothing like a spineless *fiweam*; she's lean and quick, sure, but that's where the similarity ends. "You don't like it down here, do you?" she asks. "I do. I like tight spaces and dark places. It's why they always take me along."

"Right, that's it!" one of the kynes snaps. Kai thinks it's the same one who gave her the shove earlier. He's walking across the tunnel, heading for Kai's lost shine-stick. "Couldn't be because you really are a *fiweam*?"

Kai holds out his hands and the leader starts working on his bonds.

"We shouldn't all go back," she's saying. "We'll split up." She glances toward the little kyne. "You have to go on. I'd better be the one to take him."

The reedy kyne steps out of the darkness, allowing Kai a good look at him. He's certainly a scrawny looking thing. Maybe plague-infected. Maybe just malnourished. Still, they all look a little on the thin side. They're wiry though; even if he hadn't fallen, there was a good chance they would have run him down anyway.

"By yourself?" the kyne asks.

"No," the leader replies. She's finishing up Kai's bonds. "You come with me. The rest of you go on. You know what you have to do. Joery," she says, singling out one of the kynes, "you take over. Get in. Get out. As fast as you can. No trouble."

No doubt that warning is directed at the nasty Doon who'd be pleased as pautune to finish Kai off.

"Take this," the leader says, handing over her pack, then glances toward the kyne holding Kai's shine-stick. "Give me his stick."

"I have four more," Kai says.

"Do you now?" she asks, turning again to Kai. "Stolen from our supplies I'm guessing."

Kai jerks his head, indicating the tunnel behind him. "If your supply was in an old pack back there, then yes."

"You Ularon people think you can just help yourself to anything you want, don't you?" She gives him a shove of encouragement.

"I'm not Ularon," Kai tells her.

She's having him take the lead and he has to rely on the shine-stick she's holding to see.

"I really don't care what you are," she says. "Go on, the rest of you," she calls back to her companions.

Kai glances over his shoulder, past the kyne the leader called Joery. The other young ones are still standing there, watching.

"You don't have all day," the leader barks.

It's the little kyne who starts them on their way. Kai catches her small hand rise in a sort of wave just before he looks away. But it's Doon who offers the parting words as they move off.

"Still say we should have killed him," she says in a sing-song voice.

She's scared, Kai decides all of a sudden. Scared of him? Scared of the mission they're on?

"Where are they going?" he asks, receiving another shove in reply.

"Can't see that's of any concern to you."

Kai shrugs. "The choices seem limited."

"Talkative, isn't it?" the reedy kyne says.

"City people," the leader observes. "But you'd think a Guardian would know when to shut up."

"I told you before I'm not from Ularon. And I'm not a Guardian, either."

"Sure look like one."

She gives Kai yet another shove and he stumbles, righting himself quickly.

"If you'd seen me this morning, you'd have taken me for a Talker."

"Really?" She's mocking him. "Let me guess. You're neither."

"That's right," Kai tells her. "In fact, I'm a Journer. Just like you."

The leader begins to laugh. "A Journer? You!"

"Yes, me! I studied at the Lycea and I've been a working pilot for almost two years." Kai aims another glance over his shoulder. "I guess you're too young to remember me. You and the others."

"That's got to be it," the leader agrees caustically. "Guardian this evening, Talker this morning and a Journer before that. Seems to me you're whatever caste suits you at the time."

"Funny you should say that. In some ways, you're right. Only I'm not whatever caste suits *me*. It's Gannaline-ro who's determining what caste I am on any given day."

The leader's laugh turns hearty. "Gannaline-ro? I'll give you this much. You know your Journers. Pity that one's dead, though."

"But she isn't! I mean I thought she was, too, until—"

The reedy kyne pokes him in the back with his shine-stick. "I'm sick of the sound of your voice. Are you going to keep this up all the way?"

"Depends," Kai replies. "On how long we're going to be in this tunnel."

"He's trying to talk his way free," the kyne warns his leader. "Thinks he's smart enough to do it."

"Maybe," she replies thoughtfully. "It would sure help us a lot if he told us what he's doing down here though. How he even knows about the place." She's talking to the kyne as though Kai isn't even there.

"I'm right here," Kai reminds her. "Unfortunately, I can't tell you what I'm doing here. I don't even know myself. Not yet. But it was Ro who sent me. I swear it's true. And it was someone going by the name Vee who showed me the tunnel."

"Never lets up," the reedy kyne mutters.

"Fine, then what do *you* think a Guardian is doing down here alone?"

Kai waits for a reply as he walks on. The tunnel is running straight again now and, if his feeling for direction is true, heading deep into his home-ward.

Finally, the leader speaks again. "It doesn't make sense. But then what has made any sense in the last couple of years? Not up to me to figure it out. If you're Journer like you say, then we'll know that soon enough. If you're not, then it's not up to me to figure out what to do with you, either."

"Why would I lie?"

He can hear amusement in the leader's voice. "It's what Pedorates do best."

"I keep telling you. I'm not Pedorate."

"Pedorate or the scum that serve them. Can't see it makes a lot of difference."

Kai is about to remind her that there isn't a single caste that doesn't serve the Pedorate, but immediately thinks better of it. This tack isn't getting him anywhere.

"What's your name?" he asks instead.

"Why do you want to know that?" She sounds suspicious.

"You tell me your name and I'll tell you your lineage."

There's a pause before the leader replies.

"Ceilu Daibor," she says. "So go on. Tell me all about myself."

Kai recognises the family. They're northeastern like his mother's family.

"Your mother's a Daibor," he says. "Your father's a Ceiluel. Don't know which one exactly."

"Anyone could know that," the reedy kyne interrupts.

"Let him finish," Ceilu snaps.

"The Ceiluel family were good Journers." Kai glances over his shoulder. "But I don't think it was your father who was on *The Nether*. It must have been your uncle. Brin Ceiluel. So you're not a deader yourself but your cousins would be. Except you don't have any, because Brin Ceiluel didn't have any young ones."

"You've done your research," Ceilu observes. "What else?"

"Do you want me to name every Journer on *The Nether*?" Kai asks, glancing over his shoulder again.

She snorts. "Proves nothing. Anyone can learn that."

"Then do you want me to name the Journer from my family on *The Nether*?"

"That could be amusing. Name?"

"Anan Astada," Kai replies quickly.

"Anan..." the reedy kyne stammers. "Anan Astada? What's he—"

"Just a moment."

Kai feels a rough hand on his shoulder. Ceilu is strong, spinning him around effortlessly.

"Are you trying to tell us you're Kai Astada?"

"That's exactly what I'm telling you," Kai replies, shrugging her off. "Kai Astada. Deader. Although now I'm really dead, thanks to Gannaline-ro."

"You don't believe that, do you?" The reedy kyne's shout echoes off the walls of the tunnel. "Kai Astada is dead."

So, they know he's supposed to be dead. In such a short space of time?

Ceilu delivers her young kyne companion a vicious elbow to the ribs. "Shut up. That's what he just said."

"I'm not going to shut up. What would Kai Astada be doing down here dressed like a Guardian?"

"I'd like an answer to that question myself," Kai interjects.

"You shut up, too," Ceilu shouts, running a hand through her cropped hair, dishevelling it further. "Let me think." She takes her time, looking Kai up and down. "All right," she says, settling her critical gaze on his face. "Let's suppose you're telling the truth. How did you get that uniform?"

"It was given to me. Just like the Talker uniform I had on before."

"You can't honestly expect us to believe that."

"It wasn't my idea," Kai tells her, aggrieved by the defensiveness he hears in his voice. "I didn't have any choice. It was Gannalinero's doing. Not mine. And it was Vee who gave me the uniforms."

"Don't know anyone named Vee," Ceilu snaps at him.

"Nor did I until a few days ago. But you *should*. She uses this tunnel same as you do."

"You mean that little Preserver? We saw her once, but she didn't see us. Anyway, she only came into the tunnel to sky on *taint*."

Vee? Drug herself on *taint*? It would explain a lot. But Kai's not sure he believes that. And if these Journers saw her, then she saw them, whether Ceilu thinks she did or not. So Vee must have realised there was a possibility he'd have company inside the tunnel and didn't warn him.

"Maybe that's what she wants you to think," he says, robbing Ceilu of the opportunity to say more. "How do you know I'm supposed to be dead? News doesn't travel well in and out of the quarantined wards."

Ceilu smiles. "Better than you think."

Perhaps she's right there. But the death of an insignificant Journer like him hardly seems newsworthy.

"But I'm nothing," Kai reminds her. "No one important. *Who* told you I was dead?"

"The death of the largest distributor of *taint* is big news. Kind of puts a dent in the trade."

Vee might not use *taint* but he wouldn't put it past her to be marketing it.

"Is that what you're doing in the tunnels? Procuring *taint* from Vee?"

"Never touch the stuff," Ceilu replies with a shrug. "Dulls the senses. Muddles the head." She taps his forehead with the tips of two fingers. Taps it hard. "Maybe that's your problem," she says, eyeing him up and down again. "Like I told you, we don't know that little Preserver. Just so happens—"

"Don't tell him," the reedy kyne interrupts, grabbing Ceilu by the arm.

She shrugs him off. "Can't see it matters," she says, then turns back to Kai. "We use the tunnels to get to the Dosers' warehouse. It's full of food. Food we need. We've been stealing it a little at a time."

"Oh, that's just brilliant, Ceilu!" The kyne spins on his heel, throwing the pack he's carrying to the floor. "Now *he* knows, *they'll* know."

"Don't be an idiot, Gaed. *He knew it already.* What do you think he's doing down here? They're on to us."

Kai does the best he can to back away. "Believe me. They're not on to you. Not as far as I'm aware anyway. I'm not Ularon and I'm not Pedorate. What have I got to do to convince you? I'm a Journer, just like you. At least I used to be. And I'd like to go back to being a Journer if it's all the same to you."

"Well, it's not all the same to me, *Kai Astada*! I don't know who or what you are. Although..." Ceilu hesitates a moment, "although... I am beginning to believe you're not a Pedorate Guardian. They *don't* send just one Guardian anywhere. Still Pedorate of some kind though. Sent to spy on us."

"In a Guardian's uniform?" Kai almost laughs. "If the Pedorate were going to send someone in to spy on you, I hardly think they'd have their spy dressed like this." He nods toward their surroundings. "Or send them down through this tunnel."

"No," Ceilu concedes. "Although they might send someone dressed like a Guardian but claiming that he isn't."

"That's just a little too convoluted, wouldn't you say?" Kai argues. "Who'd believe it? You don't."

Usha Kaidador! Why didn't he think of her earlier? Before today she was the last person he had any use for. "Take me to Usha Kaidador. She'll tell you I'm her son."

He's expecting Ceilu to immediately see the logic in his suggestion, but a furrow creases the skin of her forehead and her focus wavers. The prospect of taking him to Ush appears to trouble her. Not all that surprising; *he* always felt troubled anytime he was obliged to talk to Ush.

"We'll see," she says at last. "But right now, we've got to get out of the tunnel." She points past Kai into the darkness. "Start walking," she orders. "And no more talking." She turns to face her companion. "And that goes for you, too. The sooner we get out of here, the sooner he becomes someone else's problem." Pushing past Kai, she takes the lead. "And frankly I can't wait to be rid of him."

***

They emerge from the Sub tunnel underneath the dock where *The Nether* had been moored. At least that's what Ceilu claims and Kai takes her word for it. She's a long way from her home in the northeastern part of the ward and although Kai would like to know what brought her south, he doesn't question her further. It looks to him as though the Sub exit was never finished and, at some time during the plague years, opened up by the Journers. The station walls are jagged, rough, raw. How the Journers in his ward knew about the existence of the tunnel Ceilu doesn't or can't say. She makes Kai strip off his Guardian jacket but allows him to keep his visor.

The maze of snaking corridors, unmarked doors and overhanging catwalks crammed within the complex beneath the dock confound him. Alone, he doubts he could find his way to the surface. The lighting is random, unpredictable, leaving long stretches in darkness. Time and again Kai's shoulder collides with an unseen obstacle he takes to be a wall. The scramble up steep and crudely finished ramps is challenging enough with his hands tied but the series of usually open staircases that clang and bang and rattle as they ascend is worse. It's a zig-zag and disorienting route to the surface, but at last they emerge into the night through an unremarkable hatch at the head of a steeply pitched staircase. Likely the hatch marks the spot where the Sub entrance was intended to be. Kai stops a pace behind Ceilu to wait for Gaed, who, with a slam that echoes in the night, closes the hatch. The inlet is behind them, invisible in the darkness. Still, Kai can smell it, taste it, feel the wind from it buffet against him. Somewhere at his back rests *The Nether* and the vast complex that launched it into space. But he can't see any of that either, only an odd irregular patch of blackness where the stars on the horizon should be shining and overhead, distant worlds that twinkle and dance. It's a common enough sight in his ward, rare in Ularon City.

He's home.

Though both Ceilu and Gaed crack new shine-sticks, it's Ceilu who takes the lead like a little guiding light in the darkness.

Kai had grossly underestimated the effect the quarantine would have on his ward. His people, his *own* people, are living in wretched poverty. Some—many—have taken to living in the open fields. Sputtering lights from open fires outside shabby tents dot the landscape. His people look tired, worn out, broken but none, so far as Kai observes, bear any obvious mark of disease. No one who hasn't seen it knows exactly what the plague can do to the body. There are rumours, of course. There are always rumours. Death, it is said, is agonising and the slow progress toward it a demeaning and disfiguring journey. Perhaps everyone who is going to die in his home-ward has already died or been taken away. Or perhaps the plague is done—burned-out—maybe even eradicated by the Dosers. It's what the Pedorate has been working toward. Still, if so much progress has been made, then why hasn't Kai or anyone else heard about it? And why has the quarantine not been lifted?

As they begin the climb up 'Headcracker Hill', Kai can't tear his eyes away from the young ones lingering in the open doorways of poorly lighted tents along the road. For the most part, their clothes are torn and dirty. Just how often can a garment be washed before it becomes brittle? But it's their eyes, reflecting the sallow lights that disturb him the most—disinterested, expressionless orbs in the hollow sockets of gaunt and grimy faces.

He should have realised it would be this way. With the quarantine in place, how are necessities like food and clothing to be transported into the ward? The Pedorate is supposed to be seeing to it—promised they are—but the promises of the Pedorate aren't worth much. By the time they reach town, Kai is almost prepared for what he finds—but not quite. Without fresh supplies, the few

Preservers who were trapped inside when the barricades went up have no hope of maintaining the ward. Kai doesn't see a house, a public place, that isn't the casualty of ruin and darkness. Some look too dangerous to live in any longer. It explains the exodus of his people to the fields. Still there is the odd house where a fragile light shines from within. Kai doubts his home will be one of them. Ush may have tried to keep body and soul together for a little while, if only through dogged rigidity, but his mother isn't someone Kai would call adaptable or resourceful. He may have even passed by her mean little tent along the road. Has she managed to keep Asta and Mig alive as well? Has she even bothered to try?

Seems he's not going to get the opportunity to see his old house, which means he won't be able to check on Gannin's or Henneh's houses, either. Ceilu and Gaed are leading him in the opposite direction.

They pass through the centre of town and turn into a narrow street Kai has never ventured down before. Three young ones sprint toward them out of the darkness. They're barefooted, slapping unprotected skin on the sharp stone of the damaged roadway. Ceilu pulls up and, dropping to one knee, catches the first of the young ones in open arms.

"You're back! You're back!" a second young one cries from the rear as she struggles to edge her way forward.

Ceilu reaches over the head of the first and ruffles the matted curls of the little kyne.

"Didn't get to *go*," she says. "Have you seen Pilot Jak today?"

Does she mean Jak Inopo?

The kyne looks away from Ceilu to give Kai a brief and questioning look, but quickly turns to Ceilu's companion, Gaed, who still has a firm grasp on Kai's upper arm.

"You brought us a *person*?" she asks uncertainly. "That isn't any use."

"*Found* him," Gaed replies.

The kyne eyes Kai more keenly. "Where?"

"Living in a hole," Gaed answers gravely. "*With giant blood-sucking neegees*," he roars, lunging forward.

"Stop teasing them," Ceilu snaps. Rising, she instructs the kyne, "You go find Pilot Jak for us. Bring him to my place. Tell him we have a pilot here who claims to know him."

Kai never claimed such a thing, although he could have.

"I thought you were taking me to my mother."

"Never said that," Ceilu replies with a shrug. "If you're Anan Astada's son, Pilot Jak will know it. You two, as well," she says with a smile, turning to the other young ones. "Go with Tup and make it fast."

"You're talking about Jak Inopo." Out of the corner of his eye, Kai watches the young ones disappear into the night.

"Oh," she says, "don't try to impress me with your knowledge of our pilots again. Pilot Jak's as well known as Gannaline-ro. Just so happens that, unlike Gannaline-ro, Jak Inopo *is* still alive."

Gannaline-ro is still alive, too, even if there's nothing he can do to prove it. He could tell her where he came upon the old pilot, explain about the Duck Down Club, but Ceilu would probably refuse to believe the club is real. He had.

"Fine," Kai agrees. "You go get Pilot Jak and when he does confirm who I am, then what will you do with me?"

Ceilu gives him a shove forward. "We'll see."

Kai's getting pretty tired of hearing that.

"Where are we going?"

"My place."

"Is it far?"

Gaed jabs him in the back with his shine-stick. "If you're who you say you are, then you should already know the answer."

"Really!" Kai stumbles as he turns to confront his tormentor. "The Ceiluels and Daibors are northeastern families, but clearly Ceilu here isn't living in the northeast anymore unless she's bent on taking long treks just to get to and from the dock every time you go into the tunnel. So, if you won't answer me that then perhaps you can tell me where all the sick are?" He turns back to Ceilu. "I haven't seen a single sick person yet."

"They don't last long," she replies guardedly.

"But doesn't it take a long time to die? I mean... that's what we're told."

"Wouldn't know. Never seen anyone die of the plague."

"You mean they're taken immediately to the quarantine station?"

"Guess."

"How many?"

"How many what?" she asks, glancing sidelong at Kai.

"How many of our people have died?"

"*Our* people, is it?" She offers him a dry smile. "I really don't know," she adds, sobering. "That's not something they're inclined to tell us. Every so often a party of those Dosers from the station arrive in their fancy suits to test and counterject us with the *latest* dose of who knows what. Oh, they're quick enough with the promises to lift the quarantine if it works. But apparently it never does work because back they come again with the next test, the next counterjection but always with the same old promise. Some of us get taken away. Some don't. That's just how it is. No one gives us a count at the end of it. And no one ever tells us who died and who didn't."

"And once someone is taken away," Kai asks, "they never come back?"

Ceilu's slow to answer. "How is it you don't know that? You're from Ularon City, after all. You should know these things."

"Things like that? I'm afraid that's not something they're inclined to tell *us*."

"Huh," she says noncommittally.

She's hiding something.

"How do they do it?" Kai asks. "Test and counterject everyone in the ward?"

"They round us up, of course. How do you think?"

"What about the ones they miss?"

"What do you mean?" Ceilu pulls up abruptly. "You ask a lot of questions. What are you trying to get at?"

"Ro did send me here. That's the truth and the reason she sent me here was to find evidence that the Journers who returned on *The Nether* didn't die of any plague."

Gaed breaks out into a fit of laughter behind him. "Lies. All lies! Like I've said all along, he's no Journer. He's some sort of Pedorate spy sent here to check that we're all behaving. And you," he barks, stepping around Kai to confront Ceilu, "you've gone and told him too much."

"*I* didn't. But you just did!"

Kai can't see Gaed's face very well, but, if he could, he suspects he'd have seen it quite drained of blood.

That's right, Gaed, you did just tell me too much.

Not all the Journers here *are* behaving and it's Kai's guess that there are some who have managed to evade the roundups, some who have never been tested or counterjected and have never gotten sick.

"You're an idiot, Gaed. I should have sent you off with the rest. Besides, you're wrong!" she snarls, giving Gaed a shove. "I don't know what or who he is, but he's no spy. He's not *smart* enough to be a spy. And you're not smart enough to keep your mouth shut."

"So he knows," Gaed scoffs with lame bravado. "Who's he going to tell?"

***

Kai is growing anxious with the wait. Either the young ones can't find Jak Inopo or it's all been a sham. He simply can't believe that Inopo is still alive. Why, he'd have to be over a hundred now. Maybe more.

Ceilu's place is poorly furnished. There were no lights but the moment Ceilu fired up a couple of small oil lamps, bathing the room in a sombre yellow glow, Kai availed himself of one of the few chairs set either side of a mean rectangular table. Gaed opted for a seat on the floor by the door; he might have been the smart one. Any time now, Kai's expecting the chair to collapse beneath him. Ceilu is sitting in the chair opposite and, like Gaed, staring at him. Do they think he'll make a bolt for the door? Rush off blind into the night?

"Haven't you got some place else to be?" Kai asks, directing his words to the kyne on the floor.

Gaed simply smiles.

"So, whose place is this?" he asks, turning to Ceilu.

"Questions. Questions. Questions. You're just full of them, aren't you?"

Kai shrugs. "Clearly it's not your place," he replies evenly. "What are you doing here?"

"And another question," Ceilu says. "At the moment, I'm waiting for Jak Inopo."

"Aren't we all," Kai shoots back. He looks around, taking in what's left of the place. 'Stripped it clean, I see."

"I found it this way, if you must know," Ceilu tells him, sounding annoyed. "And I have no idea who used to live here. They left. I came. It was the best house around."

Maybe so. It did have a functioning door.

Kai's hands are beginning to go numb. He tries to flex his fingers but it doesn't help. "I don't suppose you could untie me now?"

"We'll untie you when, and if, Pilot Jak says so," Gaed responds.

Kai's request was directed at Ceilu, but her silence reveals she's of the same mind.

"Fine. But you're both going to look very stupid when Jak tells you who I am."

"We'll take that chance," Gaed says, breaking his study of Kai to glance through the open door. "You don't think something's happened to Pilot Jak, do you?"

"Pilot Jak's too sly to get taken. He'll be here." Ceilu's focus wavers briefly from Kai to respond. "You're pretty sure of yourself, *Pilot Astada*. I'll take those shine-sticks now if you don't mind." Rising, she steps to his chair and begins to untie his bonds.

"Hey," Gaed barks, leaping up from the floor. "What are you doing?"

"Where's he going to go, Gaed?"

"Thanks," Kai says. There's a momentary surge of pain as the blood begins to flow back into his hands. With numb fingers, he retrieves the shine-sticks from inside his clothes and hands them over to Ceilu. "Your friend is right. I was making my way here. Now that I am *here*, why would I run? I'm as anxious to see Jak Inopo as you are."

"Then you'll be pleased to know I've arrived."

Kai aims a look toward the doorway and the silhouette hanging bent and twisted inside it. He makes to stand but Ceilu quickly pushes on his shoulder, forcing him back down into his seat.

The figure approaches, silently, in a shuffling gait. Kai waits as the old one begins a wordless appraisal. He's brought his face close to Kai's, so close that the ridges and grooves of the ancient face blur in the sallow light until it's little more than a pale oval beneath a shock of pure white hair.

"So," the old one says, drawing back, "what brings Kai Astada home?"

Kai is obliquely aware of Ceilu gesturing toward her abandoned chair. The old pilot is slow to take up the offer.

"I thought," Kai begins, once Inopo is settled, "I thought—"

"I'd be dead by now," the old pilot says with a weak smile. "So did I." He glances at Gaed by the door. "You can stop your worrying, young one. This pilot is exactly who he says he is. The son of Anan Astada. A fine pilot in his own right so I understand."

Kai is taken aback. With the quarantine in place, no one inside his home-ward should know anything about him. Sometime during his early days at the Lycea either Ina Paollu or Paol Inopo must have talked about him to their father. If the siblings ever held him in such high regard, they never shared the view with him.

As they are talking, Ceilu returns from a brief absence in a back room; she's carrying another chair which she places beside the old pilot's.

"But you haven't answered my question," Inopo says. "What are you doing here?"

"I was sent," Kai replies, his focus on Ceilu as she seats herself comfortably in her chair. "By someone I met at the Duck Down Club. Someone who claims to be Bes Gannaline-Ro."

"*Claims* to be?" The old pilot leans forward.

"She says she is," Kai explains, "but like that one," he glances briefly over at Ceilu, "I thought Pilot Ro must surely be dead."

"Why?" Inopo asks. His tone is casual, unconcerned. "She's younger than I am." He waves dismissively. "Oh, not by much I concede, but I knew her at the Lycea. She was in the class behind mine."

Kai is startled. "You *knew* her? Then you'll agree that the person I met couldn't possibly be Gannaline-Ro. It has to be someone pretending to be Pilot Ro."

"Can't agree to any such thing," Inopo answers with another lazy wave of his hand. "Very likely the pilot you met was Ro. Can't think why she would have mellowed any through the years."

"Then what she told me could be true."

Kai was speaking softly to himself, but the old pilot's hearing hadn't failed too badly. He looks enquiringly at Ceilu before speaking.

"What could be true?"

Kai tells his story from his first encounter with Vee to the moment he came upon Ceilu in the Sub tunnel. Inopo and Ceilu listen without interruption but, every so often, Gaed sighs softly from the open doorway.

"How very strange."

It's not what Kai was expecting Inopo to say and, all things considered, a sizeable let-down.

"Why you?" Ceilu asks at last.

Indeed!

"They say I have a certain connection. Influence." He turns to old Jak Inopo. "Maybe they mean you."

"Me?" Inopo points a bent finger on himself. "It's not me, young pilot. I've been trapped inside this ward since long before the quarantine. I don't know what use you, or Ro for that matter, think I can be. It's not me," he says again. "Nor anyone else I can think of."

"Then I've been sent here on a wild waloo chase," Kai grumbles. "And to all intents and purposes, I'm dead outside this ward. Dead. And left with no possible way of coming back."

"No need to be so hasty," Inopo tells him calmly. "If Ro thinks you know something... or someone," he corrects himself, "then you very likely do."

"But I—"

"Just because we don't have any clue who that might be at this point doesn't mean Ro is wrong. Think, young Astada. Who here has any connection with the Pedorate?"

Kai smiles cynically. "Wouldn't *you* know that better than me?"

"You'd think, wouldn't you?" Inopo replies, turning his gaze on Ceilu.

"Don't look at me," she snaps. "I've never once set foot outside this ward. I didn't even get to start at the Lycea."

"Ro *is* mistaken."

All heads swing toward Gaed.

"Has to be," he continues. "Or your pilot friend here is lying. If you want my opinion—"

"We don't," Ceilu says, cutting him off.

"Let Gaed speak."

As Inopo waves the young Journer forward, Ceilu visibly shrinks into her seat.

"Well," Gaed begins, stepping up to the table, "it's like Ceilu said. Why him? He admits he knows nothing. Maybe he's guilty of some offence against the Pedorate and he's run to the only place he can think of."

Kai shrugs. "I've committed an offence all right. But it wasn't any of my doing. It was Ro and her cohorts inside the Duck Down Club who are to blame." Kai rises from his chair and looms over his accuser. "And if I was going to run somewhere, Gaed, do you really believe my first choice would be into a plague zone? And how in pautune do you think I could have gotten in so easily?"

"Sit down," Inopo insists. "If this problem's to be solved, it isn't going to be with shouting."

Kai lowers himself back down while Gaed glowers.

"It's possible Gaed is correct," Inopo continues. "I happen to think he isn't, but we can't just ignore what he says."

A poorly concealed smirk mars the smooth young skin of Ceilu's face. It's clear to Kai she's in the habit of ignoring most of what Gaed says.

"I'm sorry, Kai," Inopo says after a brief pause. "We aren't the ones who can help you."

"Maybe he can help us though," Ceilu suggests, straightening in her seat. "He's been inside Ularon City for a long time now," she adds in answer to Inopo's raised eyebrow. "He knows his way around. He's got contacts in the Duck Down Club. If he could get us to them, then maybe—"

"Maybe what?" Gaed breaks in. "Maybe *they* can do something about conditions here inside the ward? What's the chance?"

"He's right about that," Kai says, reluctantly agreeing with the young Journer. "They're relying on *me* after all and I'm afraid that doesn't give me a lot of confidence in their ability to do anything for the people in the wards. We're on our own."

"*We?*" Gaed barks. "Since when did *us* become *we?* You're a stranger here as far as I'm concerned."

"You're not much better than a stranger yourself, Gaed," Ceilu snaps back. "So, I wouldn't go making accusation like that too lightly."

Gaed? A stranger? He *looks* like a Journer.

"What are you talking about?" Kai asks.

"Gaed is Phane," Inopo explains before Ceilu has the chance to respond. "There are a lot of Phanes here now in the wardland. Their route to the Karish Sea is as effectively cut off as our route through The Range. The Pedorate has blockaded their sea lanes. No vessels can get in or out. Not even an antan. Haven't been able to for a long time now. Hardly anyone escaped that way."

"There were escapes? No one in Ularon City seems to know that."

"The Pedorate knows," Inopo replies.

A look Kai can't interpret passes between the old pilot and the young Phane.

"Tell him," Gaed says at last. "It won't make any difference now. The Pedorate already know. If he's Pedorate, then he knows, too. If not, then maybe it'll give him something to think about."

"All right," Inopo agrees. He turns to Kai. "Did you ever wonder what happened to the orphans we sent out to the Phanes?"

"Wonder? Well, no. I assumed they were integrated into the Phane community."

"Some are," Inopo concedes. "But the Phanes are old hands at relocation. They've been doing it for generations. Bartering the exchange of young orphans for... hmm, I guess there's no other way of putting it," Inopo says, running a hand through the spare white hair on his head, "for profit."

"What the—"

"Don't misunderstand now," Inopo hurries to say. "It's done very professionally and all for the mutual benefit of the orphan and the family he or she goes to. The Phanes are a very particular people."

"Particular!" Kai can barely get the word out. "That sounds an awful lot like slavery to me."

Gaed is still standing close behind him, but the young Phane seems content to have the old pilot do the explaining.

"Young Kai, do you think I'd get involved in something like that?"

"You? No! But then you never bargained for an orphan, did you? Unless you're trying to tell me that Ina and Paol aren't yours."

"Oh, they're mine all right. I wasn't referring to them. I was referring to Usha Kaidador."

"My mother!"

"Ush Kaidador is Phane," Inopo explains.

Kai swings his attention to Gaed. He's hoping for some reaction, but the young Phane simply shrugs and, sauntering away, reclaims his spot by the doorway.

Kai turns back to the old pilot. "I'm afraid there's only one way I'll believe that." He's recovered from the initial shock—mostly. "If she stands right here in front of me and tells me so."

"And *I'm* afraid that's not possible," Inopo says. "Your mother isn't here anymore."

"She's dead?" Kai asks. Inopo's news has jolted him, and he's surprised at his reaction. He has always assumed he'd feel little when informed of his mother's death. Instead, he feels what he can only describe as a deep sense of regret.

"Can't say for sure," Inopo tells him. "No one really knows. She's gone. Disappeared. Perhaps she was taken."

"Someone must know something," Kai insists. "People just don't disappear."

"They do around here," Ceilu interjects. She's taken to leaning back in her chair and, every so often, tipping it backward. "There's a story about where she went if you believe it." She lunges forward and the bottoms of the chair's forelegs smack hard against the floor. "She's supposed to have gone down into the Sub tunnel through an access inside the town."

"It's possible," Inopo says before Kai can voice his scepticism. "She knew the tunnel's location... access points and such."

"That can't be," Kai says, shaking his head. "No one knew a tunnel was being built. I mean, we heard rumours. But that was all. My mother couldn't have had any idea. Even if she did, she wouldn't have known where to enter the tunnel."

"You mean *you* wouldn't," Inopo corrects him. "I can assure you that Usha Kaidador knew very well where to go. It just never occurred to me that she might do it. And I'm still not so sure that she did."

"You knew about the tunnel, too?" Kai asks. The old pilot is just full of surprises. "Why the two of you and no one else?"

Inopo shrugs. "It was me they consulted about where to put it…"

Kai might concede that. Jak Inopo was one of the best. If anyone knew where to lay a Sub line in his home-ward, it was Jak Inopo.

"And," Inopo goes on, "it was me who recommended your mother as the pilot."

Kai is utterly dumbfounded. "Why would you do that?"

"Your mother was a good pilot, Kai, but instead of continuing as an eight-n-two like your father, she wanted to raise you and Asta."

She wanted to do that! Actually *wanted* to set aside her status! Kai is having a hard time swallowing that. But since Jak Inopo brought it up…

"Where's my sister? Where's Asta?"

"I took her to the Phanes." Inopo's head tilts toward Ceilu. "That's when I picked up Gaed and came across Ceilu. As far as I'm aware, your sister is still with them."

"Why there?" Kai asks.

"I thought she'd be safer with them. I thought they might be able to get her out." The old one's shoulders slump, aging him a decade. "But I left it too long. The blockade was already in place when I got there. Only a few managed to get out."

"Who?" Kai presses him. "Who got out?"

"Mostly northeastern Journers, those closest to the Phanes to start with."

"None from here?"

"Some," Inopo tells him. "Your friend Henneh's father was one."

"Mig, too?" Kai asks. "His daughter, Mig Sek?"

A snort sounds by the doorway. "The little fiweam! It's probably her fault they haven't come back yet. They've been gone too long," Gaed says, glancing at Ceilu.

"They're fine," she insists, dismissing him. "Mig knows what she's doing."

Only now, Kai takes Gaed's meaning. The young one who confronted him down in the tunnel is Henneh's little sister.

"I can't believe it." He's loosely aware of Gaed rising from the floor. "Mig's father just ran off and left her here!"

"He didn't. At least he didn't think that's what he was doing," Inopo tells Kai. "There was an arrangement for her to be sent on after he was settled." The old pilot shrugs. "He hadn't counted on the blockade."

"No one had," Gaed chimes in sourly, commencing a nervous march back and forth across the floor.

"Is there no way to get more out?" Kai asks of Gaed. "No way at all?"

Gaed shakes his head without slowing and Kai turns back to Inopo.

"Where was Mig's father sent?"

"Don't know," Inopo replies. "It's the usual way. In the past, young ones were mostly sent outside Pedora, a few to wards inside it, like your mother."

Like his mother! Kai is still of a mind not to believe the old pilot. But if he is telling the truth, then just who is Usha Kaidador? And what does that make him?

"She's Journer now," Inopo answers readily when Kai asks. "And a good pilot, born to it or not. I've always had a notion she was Reckoner. Could be I'm wrong and Ush's real parents were Journers from the northeast like Ceilu's here."

"Don't ask me," Ceilu says uninterestedly when Kai turns to her. "I don't know a thing about it. Don't care, either, frankly."

"Ah well, I can't really say for sure," Inopo continues. "Like I said, confidentiality was always part of the agreement. The Phanes had her at one point when she was very, very young. That's all I know with certainty."

"But aren't *all* Phanes really Journers anyway?" Kai asks.

"Natural born ones. But exchange also went the other way. Sometimes an orphan from outside the ward was brought in for the Phanes to raise. Either way, it's a stigma... being a Phane," he continues, glancing briefly toward the pacing Gaed, who appears to have lost all interest in everything but the empty lane beyond the doorway. "I was the only one who knew."

"Why you?" Kai prods the old pilot.

"Ush's adopted parents... the people you thought were your grandparents... were my friends when I was a student at the Lycea. I helped them relocate to the southern part of the ward where no one knew them. Thought it would be easier for them. And for Ush."

Kai isn't so sure about that. Usha Kaidador hadn't exactly thrived here in the south. She certainly never achieved her full potential if she truly was as good a pilot as Inopo claims. Kai's memory of his mother is of someone who was only ever present in any given moment in a superficial kind of way, someone who thoughtlessly followed the norm. The only time he ever saw a little of her spirit shine through was when he was very young and all those Journers used to visit their house.

"Does my mother know?" he asks.

"Of course, she knows," Inopo answers with a crooked smile. "Most Phanes know they're Phanes. It's no shame to them."

"Then why didn't she ever tell *me*?"

"I said being a Phane was no shame to *them*."

If the old pilot's intention is to make Kai feel small and petty, he's succeeded.

"Here they come."

Gaed's shout startles Kai so badly he almost jumps out of his seat. He glances past Gaed into a night spotted closely with the glow of three or more shine-sticks.

Ceilu rises and moves away from the table. When Inopo makes to follow, Kai reaches for his arm.

"Journers' Leap," he says, suddenly recalling the name of the odd little game the Journers played when they visited his parents' house all those years ago.

"What was that?" Inopo's wrinkles deepen in confusion.

"When I was little, there was a group of Journers who frequently came to my parents' house. You were one of them. You used to sit around the table half the night, playing a game called Journers' Leap. I've just now remembered it."

"I think you mean Journers' *League*, young pilot. Might be best if you forget all about it again."

"Why?" Kai asks half-heartedly.

Inopo is not of a mind to answer and Kai doesn't press it when the old pilot rises stiffly from the table.

Doon, the kyne who was so anxious to put a permanent end to Kai down in the tunnel, is the first to come through the door. She starts when she sees Kai sitting there, executes a little dance on the spot, clearly undecided about entering, before she marches into the room. The remaining four young ones come hard in behind her with Mig the last to arrive.

As each comes through the door, Ceilu collects their used shine-sticks, passing them to Gaed in what is obviously a well-practiced routine. Gaed is stacking the sticks into an old wooden crate by the door when Doon finds her voice.

"What's he doing here?"

She's still wearing that strange knee-length tunic that, in the better light, Kai decides isn't quite as gaudy as he first thought when he came across Doon down in the tunnel. Save for the identical red, green and orange geometric design on the panels either side, the tunic is the same boring olive drab of a Sub uniform. High up against her chest, Doon is cradling an intricately woven bag that, in contrast, is a muddle of crazy colour. The bag's overfilled, threatening to burst. Thumping it onto the table in front of Kai, she barely avoids toppling one of the oil lamps. The bag looks like it's made of hul, probably Phane. The rest of the raiding party are similarly laden except for Mig who carries only a large and rough-hewn wooden box. The box is almost half her size; clearly, it's been a struggle for her to carry it all the way from the station, but still she continues to hang on to it.

"Well?" Doon snarls. "Is no one going to answer me?" She plops down into Ceilu's vacated seat and fixes Kai with an unabashed stare. The others have gathered to one side of the room, seemingly unsure how to react.

It's left to Jak Inopo to reply. He's propped half-in, half-out of the door, as though waiting on someone else. "No need to worry," he says, back turned. "He's Kai Astada. A Journer just like he told Ceilu."

"So that's what he claims," Doon grumbles. "I still want to know what he was doing down in the tunnels," she says, darting a quick angry glance toward the door.

Ceilu spares the old pilot any obligation to respond. "Make yourself useful, Doon. And that goes for the rest of you. Start sorting these supplies. When we know why he was sent here, so will you."

Doon's eyes widen in surprise. "Sent! Then you believe him?"

Doon is thin, but she's feisty and unpredictable and Kai knows only too well that he's functioning at a level considerably below his best. He's grateful for Ceilu's intervention.

"For the moment," she answers. Returning to the table, she shoves the bag closer to Doon. "If Pilot Jak says he's Kai Astada, that's good enough for me. Sort!" she snaps, wrenching the young Journer's rigid attention from Kai.

One by one, the others approach. Doon goes to some lengths to keep on the opposite side of the table, furthest from Kai. The other kynes ignore him. Mig ignores him; she's more concerned with the wooden box she's brought. Her little hands are expertly working on the lid, ripping it, nails and all, free from the sides.

Ceilu turns to Kai. "I don't suppose you'd consider moving away from the table to give us some room?"

Kai's only too happy to oblige. He has a feeling that sooner, rather than later, he'd have been shoved aside anyway. The table is stacked high with items stolen from the quarantine station and hands are coming in all directions, making for the bags. Grabbing his chair, Kai carries it across the room to Jak Inopo.

"Here," he says, dumping the chair in the open doorway. "Looks to me like they're all back. Who are you waiting for?"

The old pilot smiles as he takes up the chair. "Once they have that all sorted, they'll distribute it. Figure, since I'm here, I could help keep things orderly."

Kai looks away from the dark and empty laneway toward the table. The young Journers don't appear to need a lot of help. Seems like they've done this same thing many times over already.

"How is it done?" Kai asks, turning back to the old pilot. "The distribution, I mean."

"Roster," Inopo replies evenly. "They elect a small group of people to come and collect it and after that it's up to them. They have a system of dividing it same as Ceilu has a system of collecting it."

Kai tries to imagine how that hungry horde of Journers he saw on his way from the dock could ever be coerced into conforming to any kind of order. Failing, he can't help but ask, "And they stick to it?"

"Mostly. If someone starts looking like they're about to get out of line," he shrugs, "there's always Doon, isn't there?"

Kai glances back toward the Journers, busy at the table. "How are they getting away with it? The Dosers aren't stupid," he says. "They've got to notice their supplies going missing over and over again."

Inopo offers up another shrug. "Inside help."

Kai wasn't prepared for yet another surprise. "You know that for a fact?"

"No," the old pilot replies. "But, like you, I can't see it happening any other way."

"Who would do that?" Kai asks, almost of himself. "Who inside the station would *possibly* do that?"

"Don't know. Don't want to know. Better for them. Better for us."

In the brief time he was at the quarantine station Kai only met two people. Could the Journers' silent benefactor be Madgel Swar? Kai doubts it. Too proper. Too Pedorate-proud. And it wouldn't be Julyen Koale, Doser-in-Charge; that would just be ridiculous.

"Vee!" Kai exclaims, garnering a puzzled look from Inopo. "I told you. Remember? The Preserver... or whatever she is... the one who sent me down into the tunnel."

"Oh yes." Inopo waves a hand. "Got to be someone with more pull than a Preserver."

Kai should have realised that without Inopo having to tell him.

"Doesn't matter who's helping us. No point in knowing. Like I said, better for them, better for us."

Even so, Kai's inclined to believe that Vee has a hand in it somewhere. Despite himself, he might just be starting to like Preserver Vee. But no matter who is facilitating or at least turning a blind eye to the pilfering, there can't be enough to go around, even if they raided the station every other day. Sure, the table where the young ones are busy sorting is full—overfull—but still…

"But what those young ones manage to take can't possibly be enough."

"Never is. But it's the medicines in that box the little one brought that are more important and Ceilu sees to that herself."

Yes, Ceilu would. Kai would, too, if he were in her position.

"How long has this been going on?" he asks.

"Almost as long as the Dosers have been at the station. We were on our own at the beginning. After *The Nether* first returned and it was only the dock that was isolated. But we really didn't need their help then. It was only after the Dosers died and—"

Kai's hand comes down hard to clamp the old pilot's bony shoulder. "What do you mean the Dosers died?"

"Go easy there, young pilot," Inopo protests with a grimace. "I'm not as young as I used to be."

Kai eases off and the old pilot continues. "The Dosers who autopsied the crew of *The Nether* all died. I thought that was common knowledge."

Kai shakes his head. "Not to anyone in Ularon City. No one that I know anyway."

Inopo simply shrugs. "Well, they did. Quick, too, so we were told. That's why they moved the quarantine station out to the border. Sealed us up tight after that. Nothing and no one coming in. Nothing and no one going out. Except on the new Dosers say so."

"And the original quarantine station was at the dock?"

Inopo nods.

"Then I went through it coming in?"

"Passed by it. Why?"

"And they..." Kai points to Ceilu's little band of raiders at the table, "... they pass it again and again going to and coming from the new quarantine station?"

"So?" Inopo remarks. "What are you getting at?"

"*That's* how Ro got those files." He comes down on one knee beside old Jak. "The ones I told you I saw inside the Duck Down Club, remember? That has to be where they came from. And someone here supplied them."

Inopo begins to laugh. He laughs so hard, he finally draws Ceilu's attention.

"What's going on?" she demands.

"Nothing," the old pilot replies, sobering. "Go back to your sorting. They'll be here soon. I can see them coming down the laneway."

Kai glances out through the open doorway. Some distance down the laneway, there's a light swinging to and fro in the darkness. Someone is carrying an oil lamp.

"You don't really think those files were just left behind, do you?" Inopo is saying. "Ro got them somewhere else. From someone else."

"Who?" Kai presses him.

"If I knew that, young Kai, then I'd know whether they're real or not, wouldn't I?" He rises, surprising Kai with a vice like grip on his shoulder. "We should get out of the doorway now. Let Ceilu do what she's best at."

Kai scrambles to his feet, wondering. Maybe the old pilot isn't as feeble as he makes out. Maybe the old pilot isn't even *what* he makes out.

CHAPTER 10

After watching Ceilu distribute the food to the six Journers who arrived, Kai is surprised to see Jak Inopo step up and take his place in line. Each in their turn, from oldest to youngest, the kynes, too, are given a share. Ceilu even goes so far as to offer a portion to Kai, but he simply can't bring himself to take it, not after seeing the gaunt and hollow faces of the wardlanders who passed through the door accept their share and then leave without thanks or comment, either heedless or uncaring of his presence. Instead, he picks up Inopo's vacated seat and carries it back to the table. The young ones go their separate ways, finding their own space in the shadows to sit and eat, while Kai and the old pilot take up their former places at the table.

There are no martyrs here in the ward, Kai concludes as he watches the young ones eat. No heroes, either. Only survivors. He turns again to the old pilot who has been slow to answer his last question.

"It's not me you were sent to find," Inopo says between mouthfuls of purloined food. "How many times do I have to tell you?"

"But you must have some—" Kai doesn't get to finish what he wants to say. Young Mig has crossed the room to stand in front of him.

"You don't look like Asta," she says matter-of-factly.

"No, I don't," Kai replies, hoping she's said her piece and will quickly wander off again.

"Pilot Jak says I look like Henneh." She cocks her head to one side. "Do I?"

Actually she does, at least how Henneh used to look, Kai realises, taking in all the subtle nuances of the little one's features for the first time: hair red as sunset; eyes quick and liquid brown.

"Yes, you do," Kai agrees, then turns again to Inopo. He barely gets his mouth open before Mig interrupts again.

"How?" she presses him. "I don't remember her very well."

Kai almost snaps at the young kyne to go away but reconsiders.

All right, so Jak Inopo can't tell him who he's supposed to contact in his home-ward, but maybe he can get some answers anyway. Answers to questions he didn't even know he had until he came home.

Bending, he brings his head level with Mig's.

"You lived with Ush and Asta Kaidador for quite a while, didn't you?"

Mig nods.

"Were you living with them the day Ush disappeared?"

After a quick, uneasy glance at Jak Inopo, who simply shrugs a shoulder, Mig replies.

"I *saw* her disappear."

The old pilot's interest seems mildly piqued now. He turns in his seat to look directly at Mig.

"Ush told me to stay at home," Mig explains, "but I didn't. She didn't know I was watching."

"First I've heard of that," Inopo says. "Asta told me she followed Ush, but she never said anything about Mig being there, too."

"Asta didn't know, either," Mig admits. Her voice grows smaller and she backs up a pace. "She thought I'd done what I was told."

No wonder Inopo has his suspicions about the exact circumstances of Ush's disappearance; he'd heard it from Asta. Given the source, Kai would have doubts, too. Now Mig on the other hand? That could be different. But Kai has no idea if she is reliable. Besides, she couldn't have been very old when she followed Ush and Asta that day. Assuming, of course, that she *had* followed them. She could easily be making the whole thing up.

"Are you sure you followed them? Really *sure*?" Kai presses the little kyne.

Again Mig nods, but he's beginning to make her anxious. She did something wrong—at least in her eyes—and it has taken courage to admit it. For that reason alone, Kai is inclined to believe her.

"Do you think you can tell us what happened to her?" He smiles. She's likely to shut down completely if he doesn't offer her some sort of incentive to continue.

Mig screws up her tiny face. "Of course, I can," she replies, seeming to take offence.

"I'm sorry," Kai says quickly. "*Will* you tell us? Please," he thinks to add before it's too late.

Again, the kyne glances at Inopo. She's seeking permission.

The old pilot gives her a nod.

"She walked a long way," Mig begins. "I'd never been there before. I don't think Asta had, either." She shrugs. "Or maybe she had. I don't know. But all of a sudden Ush stopped to look up and down the street... really quickly, you know... like she was about to do something she isn't supposed to and wanted to make sure no one was looking. And then... then she just wasn't there anymore."

It sounds like she's saying that Ush literally disappeared. But that isn't possible.

"Are you sure she didn't take a step or something?" Kai asks, trying to sound casual.

Mig hesitates. "Maybe," she says at last. "I couldn't see very well. Asta was closer." She turns to Jak Inopo. "You should have asked her. She tried to follow Ush, you know, but she couldn't."

"First I've heard of that, too," the old pilot says. "But it makes sense. Likely Ush stepped through a sim."

Kai nods. And the sim wouldn't let Asta pass. "Do you know where the sim is?" Kai asks Inopo.

"Sure I do," he replies, "but there's no point going there. Oh, maybe I could still get through but the tunnel only leads to the dock in one direction and the quarantine station in the other." He motions for Kai to follow as he rises and heads to the other side of the room, where Ceilu and her raiders are finishing their small meal.

"If you're thinking to find Ush's body down there," Inopo says once Mig is out of earshot, "forget it. You've already been there and

Ceilu and her friends here have been walking that tunnel for years. They would have found it."

Kai peers over his shoulder. Mig has lost interest in them; she's climbed onto one of the chairs. Her head's down on the old table, resting on crossed little arms. Kai's not sure why Inopo even bothered to lead him out of earshot. Likely Mig has heard more talk about the dead in her few short years than Kai ever expected to hear in an entire lifetime.

As Kai turns back to the old pilot, he spots Doon across the room. She's sitting alone half-in, half-out of the light cast by the oil lamps. She's finished with her scant meal and she's watching him. The skin on the back of Kai's neck begins to crawl; she's probably *been* watching him the whole time.

"What about past the quarantine station?" he asks Inopo. "Toward Ularon City?" He glanced that way when he was down in the tunnel but wasn't able to see much. He can't believe Ceilu and her raiders would be satisfied to leave the remainder of the tunnel unexplored and unexploited.

"Can't get through. It's blocked," Ceilu says, snatching Kai attention as she rises from the floor. "The roof has collapsed. No way around it. After we pulled enough of the borer apart to make a way through, we had an idea to do the same with the collapsed roof. Couldn't even make a dent in it. The tunnel could be blocked all the way back to Ularon City for all we know. Might as well be." She offers an indifferent shrug. "If you want my opinion, Usha Kaidador got taken. It happens. She got taken and she's dead. Whether she was in the tunnel like those young ones say or out of it." She levels her cool gaze on Kai as she passes. "You're just wasting your time thinking about it now."

"Ceilu talks good sense," Inopo says. "Who knows why your mother went into the tunnel. But knowing can't make any difference," he adds, ambling his way back to the table and a sleeping Mig.

Ceilu is probably right. Inopo, too. And he is wrong. There are no answers here. Not even to the *simplest* question. The fate of his mother will forever remain a mystery. And as far as his own fate is concerned, seems he might just be destined to follow the family tradition.

He finds Ceilu in the doorway, a black shape framed by the coming dawn.

"Waiting for someone?"

"Waiting for them to leave," she replies with a jerk of her head toward those gathered in the room behind her. "Feel free to be the first."

Kai just smiles. "And go where?"

"Your choice. There's a town's worth of houses to choose from out there. Take your pick."

"And do what?" Kai presses her.

She pushes off the door jamb to face him. "Do I look like I care? Go find whoever it is you're supposed to be looking for. Pilot Jak says you're Kai Astada and since you evidently *are* Kai Astada, you're free to run off and do that any time you like. In fact, I wish you would. You're taking up my space."

Her space? That is a matter of opinion.

"I have no idea where to look."

"Can't help you."

"Who I'm looking for."

"Like I said—"

"I know, you can't help me."

"Now we're communicating."

She makes to turn away, but Kai grabs her by the elbow.

"Look," he says, leading her outside. Already it's starting to heat up. Kai can feel the warmth of the sun on his skin through his shirt. Still the day won't burn as hotly here in his home-ward; *nowhere* do the days burn as hotly as they do in Ularon City. "I'm in desperate need of a friend right now," he tells her. "One who's on top of what's going on here. I mean *really* on top of it. And as far as I can see, that's you!"

"*You* look, pilot," Ceilu replies, wrenching her arm loose, "I said I believe you're Kai Astada and I'm afraid that's going to have to be good enough for you because that's all you're getting from me. I don't know who you're looking for and I don't have the time to waste trying to find out. Whatever you're doing here and whoever you're looking for is of absolutely no use to us. Maybe if you could tell me why Ro thinks this person is so important... then maybe I'd be able to help. But you really haven't given me much to go on, now, have you?"

"I've given you all Ro gave *me*."

"Then I'd suggest you go find yourself a nice empty house, sit yourself down and think it all through really carefully one more time. If you come up with something that might be useful to us here in this ward," she says, starting back toward the door, "maybe then, and *only* then, I can help you. Got it?" she says, disappearing inside.

A moment later, Doon steps out into the laneway.

"I heard what you said to Pilot Jak back there. But you didn't come here looking for Usha Kaidador, did you?"

"No," Kai agrees with some discomfort.

"So why *did* you come?"

He's already told them. Why is she asking him again? Oh, but Doon wasn't there when he explained about Gannaline-ro and the files she showed him in the Duck Down Club. Angry and loath to repeat it, he tells his story once more.

He's been brief about it but Doon seems to take enough of it in to ask the moment he finishes, "Did Gannaline-ro *really* show you those files?"

"Would I say she did if she didn't?"

"Maybe. If you really aren't who you say you are."

Kai suppresses a sigh. "I thought that was decided."

"It is," she replies quickly. "I can take you. Show you the rooms beneath the dock. Could be that's where you'll find what you're looking for."

"Why would you, of all people, do that?"

When she smiles at him, Kai finds it particularly unsettling.

"You interest me," she tells him. "Your story interests me. Ceilu thinks too small. She's only concerned about the next raid and then the one after that. Me," she says, jabbing a thumb to her chest, "I'm more concerned with making it so there doesn't have to *be* a next raid."

She's too hard on her Journer comrade. Sure, Kai might not be pleased about Ceilu dismissing him offhand, but as self-appointed minder of the ward, he can appreciate why she did it.

"And the way I see it," Doon is saying, "if you are telling the truth and Gannaline-ro is telling the truth, then there might just be something you can do about that."

Kai laughs and young Doon is quick enough to understand why.

"Not you personally, of course." She scans him from head to foot and smiles. It's a genuine smile this time. "You're not exactly a champion of justice now, are you? But you're all that's come along. Well?" she presses Kai when he doesn't immediately answer.

"All right," he agrees. "If I'm the best you've got, then it looks like you're the best I've got."

She delivers a hearty shove to his shoulder. "That's the spirit. Now let's go see what's down there."

She strides off into the morning light, leaving Kai hurrying to catch up.

"I thought you knew that already," he says as they begin to trek past silent and deserted houses.

Doon jerks one shoulder in a gesture that suggests long-standing frustration. "Ceilu won't let anyone go inside the actual quarantine area. She says it could still be contaminated, that we might all get infected and carry it back inside the ward."

"I'm guessing you don't think so."

Kai has never been in this part of the ward before but, like the more familiar parts of town, there was a time when this one, too, would have been busy, teeming with Journers going about their business. Kai still hasn't come to grips with the desolation, isn't sure he ever can. It looks far, far worse in the daylight.

"What difference does it make if we do infect the whole ward?" Doon asks. "We can't go on living like this. Besides, something doesn't add up for me. Never has."

Kai represses the urge to remind Doon that, at her age, she hasn't had much time for anything to add up.

"We're not sick," she continues, eyeing Kai sidelong. "*They*... the Dosers who come here say it's because the sick have been taken away and that stuff they keep pumping into us, those counterjections, are helping to stop things from getting worse. They say they're only still containing the disease and that's why the ward has to stay in lockdown."

"But Ceilu said some *were* taken away."

"Still are. Most went at the beginning though."

She stops walking, forcing Kai to pull up quickly in front of a particularly run-down house. He can hear something scurrying around somewhere inside and likely not the former resident.

"You know what I think?" Doon says. "I think they're trying to starve us out. Get rid of us... *all* of us."

She's floored him completely. "Cleanse an entire caste? But that's not possible."

"Isn't it? The quarantine only applies to Journer wards, doesn't it?"

"Yes, but that makes sense. It was a Journer ship that brought the plague."

She waves his argument aside and sets off again down the lane, kicking a fallen roof tile out of the way as she passes.

"Even so," Kai says, starting off after her, "even if they did manage to eliminate every Journer in both the prime wards, there's still Journers like me, the ones on duty outside the wards, not to mention the marginals."

Doon just snorts. "The marginals! Good for Sub runs, at best. How long do you think the rest will last? You're the exception. Most of you *can't* go home. Do you really believe that once everyone in the prime wards is gone, they'll allow the leavings like you to settle again somewhere else?"

"If worst comes to worst, they'll have no choice."

"Won't they now?" Doon counters.

They walk in silence for a while. Doon has said her piece and Kai is left trying to absorb it.

"You're not too fond of the Pedorate, are you?" he says at last.

"Are you?"

***

Kai is shaken by what he sees when they reach the crest of 'Headcracker Hill'. Although he's never witnessed a haze quite like it, he's been assuming that it was haze causing the shimmer in the sky over the dock until the view from the top of the hill tells him otherwise. The entire dock—launch *and* landing area—is sheathed in some kind of transparent dome that darkness concealed from him the night before.

"What *is* it?" he stammers.

Beside him, Doon smiles. "We call it The Cocoon. Impressive, don't you think?"

"Is it a sim?"

"Nah, solid," she replies.

"The Dosers built that?"

Her face crimples in scorn. "Of course the Dosers didn't build it. The Pedorate Council did! When they pulled all the Dosers back to the perimeter of the ward."

"Then we were actually inside it last night?" Kai asks, unable to turn his eyes away from the shimmering dome.

"Under it," Doon corrects him. "The very edge of it anyway. It seals off the dock completely."

"Then you've never been inside it? On the surface?"

"No. Only way in is through the Sub hatch and down into the tunnels. And the Sub hatch is outside The Cocoon. No one goes onto the dock."

"Ever?"

He's never given much thought to what might have happened to the dock or to *The Nether*. But it's understandable that the entire facility would be isolated. But isolated *this* way!

"Are you coming? Or do you intend to just stand there gawking all day?"

While he's been lost in thought, Doon has started down the hill. Kai stumbles as he takes off after her. Behind the dome, the clouds are building but they look all twisted and contorted as though he's looking at them through the bottom of a cheap piece of glass.

When he asks how the dome was built, Doon replies with an indifferent shrug.

"Don't know. We never saw it go up. It all went on behind the gates." She points back toward the old gates, not visible to them now on the other side of 'Headcracker Hill'. "This whole area was sealed off. Pilot Jak says it was sealed off the same way when they were constructing *The Nether*." She looks at Kai for confirmation.

"It was," he agrees. "No one was allowed inside then."

"Same straight after the quarantine," she tells him. "At least that's what everyone here says. I wouldn't know. I wasn't here then."

Kai is walking mechanically, his attention fixed on the dome and the way it distorts the horizon.

"Will you hurry up," Doon complains. She's stopped in the middle of a field where a light breeze is travelling through the scorched and withered grass in gentle waves.

Kai ploughs out through the calf-high grass toward the small, greyish-coloured slab where Doon is standing. In everything but size the slab is identical to the one at Quarantine Station Two, but here there is no ancillary building, just a square box-like protrusion at the centre of the pad. It's the hatch they came through last night, camouflaged now by the wavering grass.

"Watch your step," Doon says. She's bending over the hatch, hand poised to raise the cover. "There'll be no light until we get to the bottom of the stairs. Be sure to close the hatch after you," she adds, lifting the solid cover with surprising ease.

Easier said than done, Kai realises when he steps into the dark hole after Doon. He's got to keep both feet stable on a set of invisible steps and bring the hatch down directly over his head. He can hear her below him, tap-tap-tapping her way to the base of the steep staircase. He stumbles into her in the dark, reaching the base of the stairs before he expects. He hears rustling but can't see a thing until a flare of light momentarily blinds him.

Doon nudges his arm. "Shine-stick."

"I thought Ceilu was in charge of all the shine-sticks," Kai says, fingers closing around the stick she's just thrust into the palm of his hand.

Doon chuckles. "Ceilu's in charge of a lot of things in this ward, but she's not in charge of me." She gives him a little shove. "There'll be some light along the way, but a lot of dark patches like this one."

Doon leads off. At first, it's almost familiar going. Kai remembers something of the set upon set of stairwells and corridors. After all, it's barely a day since he's been here. But then Doon veers away from the mostly familiar, taking a route Kai can't recall. Ahead there's still little but darkness. And overhead? What? Are they still outside The Cocoon? Perhaps they're already well inside the perimeter of the dock, far below the dome.

"This isn't how we came before," he says, pulling up.

"Of course not," Doon agrees, stopping. "We're not going to the Sub station. But the lights have gone out in this sector since I was here last."

Kai sets off after her and immediately bumps his head. The ceiling's hanging lower now.

"How much of this place is in darkness?" Kai asks, feeling for a lump.

Their footsteps echo off the close walls and the light from Doon's shine-stick sweeps sideways as she spins around to answer him.

"Afraid of the dark?" she asks, sounding amused.

Afraid? No. Uncomfortable? Most definitely. And that whack to his head hurt.

When Kai doesn't reply, Doon begins to explain.

"It varies," she tells him. "At first, the lights were on in a lot of places. Now though, each time we come down here, there's fewer. Like this section. There was light last time Gaed and me were here."

If Doon has it in her head to abandon him, Kai has serious doubts he could find his way out again. She's enjoying his obvious discomfort; that he *doesn't* doubt.

"Are you sure you know where you're going?" he asks, still massaging the rising lump on his head.

"Stop worrying," Doon replies, swinging lithely around a door jammed half open in front of her. "I know exactly where I am. Gaed and me come here all the time."

"How many of these corridors have you explored?"

"All of them," she replies smugly. "Gaed and me have been everywhere."

"Are you a Phane like Gaed?" Kai asks. He would never have guessed Gaed to be Phane. The kyne looks and dresses just like any other Journer. Doon, on the other hand, doesn't.

"You know I'm glad I didn't kill you down in the tunnel." She's still walking slightly ahead of him. "You're funny. I kind of like you. Yes, I'm *just* like Gaed. More so than you might think. Gaed's my twin. Doon Gaed'owin at your service."

Sensing another beam overhead, Kai ducks. Twins! Like Jak Inopo's own son and daughter. That went some way to explain why the old pilot might have taken to Gaed and his surly sister.

"Are your parents dead?"

"No," Doon replies soberly.

"Then they came south as well?"

"No," Doon answers in the same grave tone.

Kai can't imagine any of his old friends being sent out into the world alone and so early. But then, the world isn't quite the same place anymore, is it?

"Weren't you and Gaed a little too young to be sent off by yourselves?"

"We're fifteen now," Doon replies defensively. "Anyway, we weren't sent off by ourselves. We went with Pilot Jak. It's a different life now in the Bay. Our parents thought it would be better for us here." She shrugs. "They weren't to know."

"You could go back."

"I'm more use here," Doon tells him. "And less of a bother. Gaed, too. We do all right."

"What's it like?"

Doon pulls up abruptly to confront him. "*Being a Phane?*"

"No," Kai rushes to explain. "I meant to live on those islands. Sleeping during the day. Sailing around the bay on an antan?"

"Oh." Doon starts off again, seemingly mollified. "I don't know. It's just... it's just... what we do. And we don't *all* sleep during the day. What's it like piloting an Urban?"

Doon, against his better judgement, is growing on him.

Around the next corner, directly ahead of them, is one of those areas where, for whatever reason, the lights still work. "This is it," Doon says, pausing in front of a closed, sturdy-looking door.

Kai stops just behind her. "The morgue is behind this *door?*"

One corner of Doon's mouth goes down, the other up. She's exasperated with him again.

"Of course, it's not the *morgue*," she says. "What use would that be? Useless!" She slams the palm of her hand hard against the closed door. "I don't know what the Dosers called it, but Gaed and me call it the Cypher Room."

The Cypher Room! Seems she's brought him to the right place. If he's to find anything here then it will be among all the cyphered data assuming, of course, any cyphered data remains to be found *and* they can get to it. But a plain door! Surely they'd have had sensitive data secured behind a sim.

"How would I know?" Doon replies when Kai voices his opinion. "Maybe they didn't have time. It's not like they expected the crew to return home with the plague after all."

No, they hadn't.

"How do we get in?"

Once *inside*, perhaps it will be clear why they hadn't bothered to erect a sim.

"Are you stupid?" Doon snaps at him. "You open the door."

"But isn't it locked or sealed or something?"

"Was once," Doon says brightly. "But Gaed saw to that. We Phanes don't just sail around in antans all day long you know. Who do you think fixed the things you wardlanders broke? If we can fix something, we can unfix it, too."

"You mean Gaed picked the lock?"

"Not exactly," Doon says with a smile. "He tried but it was an exceptionally *good* lock. So he blew it up."

Looking closer, Kai sees minor scorch marks around the circumference of the hole where a lock should have been. "How..." he begins to ask then decides he'd rather not know how a young one like Gaed got his hands on explosives. He'll satisfy himself that it must have been a *small* explosive and leave it at that.

"Have you ever tried to use any of the cyphers?" he asks instead as Doon makes to open the door.

She looks a little guilty.

"Um," she says at last. "We tried to turn one on."

"And?"

"Nothing happened."

So this long winding trek beneath the dock could be for nothing.

Doon's eyes begin to sparkle. "But we didn't try them all," she says, swinging the door wide open.

It's bright in the Cypher Room, the brightest of any place they've been in the complex. Luck! Sometimes it's with you; sometimes it isn't. Kai is reminded of the room at the quarantine station, the one Madgel Swar brought him to and where he met

Julyen Koale. Makes sense. The Dosers there are working on the same type of data the Dosers here must have worked on. But it also makes sense that they'd have stripped the cyphers clean before they left. And if they hadn't, then what could have happened to cause such an oversight? The plague itself? And the necessity to abandon the place in the same sort of hurry they had setting it up? Something else? The mistaken belief that no one would ever find the Cypher Room? Too simple! Too much of a stroke of good fortune for him!

"So, what are you looking for?" Doon asks as she begins a slow walk about the room, edging her way between tightly spaced desks and abandoned chairs. Everything looks orderly and it's beginning to appear that, against Kai's hopes, the Dosers' exit from here wasn't panicked.

"I wish I knew," he replies, following. "Try all the cyphers. See if any of them work."

Doon offers him a shrug and drops into the nearest seat. "Then what?"

Kai is barely listening, barely aware of the young Phane busying herself at the cypher. He doesn't know 'what'.

"Even if I can get one of these to work," Doon says, rising to shift to the next seat, "I don't know the code to get in. I'm good," she adds, glancing over at Kai, "but not that good. It could take me years to get past the security. You could help, you know," she says, vacating the seat she just took to move to the next. "Nothing," she mumbles to herself.

Kai finds a seat but his attempt, too, is a failure. It's the same with his second and third attempts. After his fourth try, Kai sighs and leans back in the seat. He looks over at Doon who is still working her way across the room.

"Aren't you frightened?" he asks. "Coming down here? It could still be contaminated."

"So?" Doon answers with a laugh. "What's the difference?" she says, turning in her seat to look at him. "Die now. Die later. But you'll notice I'm *not* dead. Gaed, either. What about you? Why aren't *you* frightened?"

"I was," Kai admits. "At first. But once I entered the ward... I figured what's done is done."

"There. You see? My point exactly," she says, rising to give the cypher a mighty thump. "This is a waste of time. These cyphers are just so much junk now. Even if I could get one to work, I'll bet they've been stripped."

"You're probably right." Disheartened, Kai gets to his feet, slamming his shin against the desk.

He glances about the room one more time, lost for all explanation. If Ro didn't get the files from here, then from *where?*

"Sorry," Doon says close by his ear. "I don't think you're going to find what you're looking for down here. Pity. I was kind of hoping you would. Come on."

***

"Huh!" Doon says, puzzled. "This isn't supposed to be here." She has stopped at the head of a long, dimly lit corridor. "No, it's all right. I know what I did wrong. It's the different lighting. Got me turned around for a moment." She points back the way they just came. "We have to go back and—"

"What's that?" Kai asks, interrupting her.

"What's what?"

He draws Doon's attention to a shimmering spot in the wall a little way down the corridor.

"I have no idea." Doon starts off immediately to investigate, Kai close on her heels.

"It's a sim," Kai announces.

The wall in front of him is flickering and there's an enormous hole in the middle of it as though someone had taken to a real wall with an axe. Through it, he can see into the still-lighted room beyond.

"Did you and Gaed do this?"

Doon shoots him an indignant look. "No," she grumps. "There's a room behind it," she tells him, stating the obvious. Without further word she steps through, a torso with guttering head and legs until she moves further inside the room. "Come on," she says, waving Kai on. "It's safe."

Kai resists the urge to lift his feet through the hole. He's never passed through a malfunctioning sim before but, as he steps through he's only aware of the usual vague tingling in his hands and feet.

"This must be it," Doon tells him. "Your morgue."

Kai looks around. Even in the semi-light it's easy to make out the row upon row of stripped beds, stacked three high down the length and breadth of the room. At the far end of the room, there's another chamber, smaller but by all appearances similarly outfitted.

"We never did find it. Now I know why. It was hidden before by the sim," Doon says as she begins a slow circuit of the newly discovered room. "So," she adds, matter-of-factly, "we've done it now. If there's still infection around, this is where it will be."

Maybe. But the rooms kind of remind Kai of the dormitory he slept in at the Lycea. Granted he shared his room with only five other interns and there are facilities here for many, many more people than that but these rooms just don't stack up to his notion of a morgue. Where are the autopsy tables? The cold chambers in which the bodies were stored?

"This isn't a morgue."

"No?" Doon replies, turning to him with hand on hip. "Then what do *you* think this place is?"

Kai starts toward her across the room. "It looks like a dormitory to me." He points to the smaller auxiliary chamber. "Higher ranks there. The rest of the crew here."

Doon screws up her face as she glances around. "No," she says half-heartedly. "Just how many morgues have you been in?"

"How many beds do you count?"

She shrugs. "I don't know. Fifty or so, I guess."

"Count them," Kai urges her, beginning his own tally.

"Sixty-two," Doon says, completing the count. "Including those in there." She's nodding toward the secondary chamber.

"That's my count, too. Now how many were on *The Nether*?"

"I'm guessing you're going to say sixty-two?"

"Sixty-two."

Doon's eyes scan the rooms more critically. She's thinking. She's thinking what he's thinking.

"So?" she says at last. "This is the morgue... like I said before."

She starts to edge away but Kai drags her back. "On beds?"

She doesn't reply.

"They kept the dead on ordinary *beds*?"

"All right," she says in a small voice. "It does seem unlikely." Moving away, she drops onto the corner of the nearest bed. "So what is this place then? The Dosers' sleeping quarters?"

"I might agree to that," Kai says, "if it weren't for the sim and the fact that there are sixty-two beds here and there were sixty-two Journers and support crew on *The Nether*."

Doon smiles at him from her perch. "Are you really trying to tell me that every one of them was alive when they returned from space?" She groans in ridicule. "That's simply not possible."

"Ro said it was," Kai reminds her.

"Pilot Ro doesn't know any better than you do." She glances around once more before turning back at Kai. "This place is something else. That's all."

"We need to get into *The Nether*," Kai says after a lengthy silence.

"*Impossible*," she tells him with a shake of her head. "It's sealed up tight inside The Cocoon. None of us have ever been there. And why would we try?" she asks, rising. "If anywhere is really contaminated, it's *there*."

"You come here and it was supposedly sealed up tight, wasn't it?"

"Oh," she says with a dismissive shrug. "That's just an accident. They must have thought no one but your mother knew about the Sub tunnel and they must have known she was dead."

"That's an interesting point. But they also must have known about Pilot Jak. He knew where the Sub entrance was inside the town and it was Pilot Jak who recommended my mother as the pilot on this run. Well, wasn't it?" he presses when she doesn't immediately answer.

Doon offers another shrug. "If he says so."

When he moves to seat himself by Doon, she shifts, putting distance between them.

"What aren't you telling me?"

"Nothing," she replies in an unconvincing little voice.

"You believe I'm Kai Astada, don't you?"

"Yes."

"That I'm only here because Ro sent me?"

"I don't know so much about that," she answers more confidently. "You *say* she did."

He'd like to reach out and shake her. "Why else would I be here?"

"All right," Doon agrees after a small pause. "But if Ceilu wants to know who told you, it wasn't me. You tell her Pilot Jak told you himself and he's forgotten. Agreed?"

"Agreed," Kai replies. As if Ceilu would believe him!

"Pilot Jak didn't just bring your sister to us. He brought himself. There were Dosers and Guardians swarming all over the ward here, questioning people, taking some away. And when he found out the Dosers were also looking for *him*... well, Pilot Jak figured the safest place for him to hide was with us."

"Did Pilot Jak say why they came for him?"

"Not specifically. But now that you've mentioned it..." she turns to face Kai full-on, "maybe it did have something to do with him knowing about the Sub entrance. Maybe it wasn't the Dosers' idea to take Pilot Jak. Maybe they were *sent* to get him."

"The Pedorate," Kai says softly, then realises something that makes Doon's story not fully hold together. "But Pilot Jak's not in your village now."

"Oh," she waves a hand, dismissing his concern. "That happened years ago. I told you... when Pilot Jak first brought Asta to us... right after your mother went missing. He stayed for a long time," she laces her hands, folds them palm down on her lap, "until they believed us when we told them he was dead. It was Ceilu's idea."

Who else?

"She said that someone went up to his house one day to check on him. That he'd fallen off the roof. He had a habit of climbing on to his roof, you know... or so they tell me."

"I know," Kai says.

"Anyway," she bends her elbows, shoots out her clasped hands to flex them, "they told the Dosers they buried him."

"Huh." Kai takes a moment to absorb what Doon has just told him. "I'm surprised they didn't want to see the body."

"Yes... um," Doon mumbles.

"They did, didn't they?" Kai grasps her clasped hands and begins to squeeze. "You're lying. They *had* no body."

"Oh, all right," Doon snaps back and wrenches her hands free. "But if Ceilu finds out you know, you swear you won't tell her it was me."

"I already did, didn't I?"

"They buried a Phane who'd died of natural causes," she says in a flurry of words.

"And that fooled them? What about the injuries Pilot Jak was supposed to have..." Kai stops talking when Doon just rolls her eyes. Fine, he's prepared not to hear all the details about *that* part of the plot. But there's still an unsurmountable problem. "What about his pid? They'd have checked his pid and realised that the body in the hole was not Jak Inopo."

"They would have," Doon replies shyly, "if the pid hadn't said that he was." She jumps up from the bed. "How do you think Phanes have been moving orphans all around Pedora all these years?"

Understanding drops on Kai like a rock from a mountain top. The Phanes know how to change pids! The Phanes could get him out of the mess Ro has put him in! Instead of saying something, Kai just sits there, staring up into the face of the liberator standing beside him.

"What?" Doon asks, sounding suspicious. Suddenly she bursts into a frenzied pacing in front of him. "I knew it. You tricked me! You are a Pedorate spy. Oh, Gaed is going to kill me. Forget about Gaed... Ceilu will..." Abruptly she stops talking and turns to Kai. "Unless..."

"I'm not a Pedorate spy," Kai assures her, rising. "And neither Gaed nor Ceilu will kill you. I won't kill you, either, if that's what you're worrying about. In fact," he says, smiling as he starts for the damaged sim, "I actually kind of like you."

"What?"

"I said I actually kind of like you, too." He turns to wave her on. "You're almost as funny as I am."

She gives him an exasperated look as she steps through the ragged translucent hole.

"Besides," he says stepping through after her, "who else can get me onto *The Nether*."

"Look," she snaps, swinging around to face him. "I've told you already I can't get you inside that ship. No one can."

Kai's smile surfaces once more. "So you *have* tried?"

"Of course, we tried. At least Gaed did. It isn't just food we need in this ward, in case you haven't noticed, Pilot Astada," she says, emphasising his journing title. "We're short on absolutely everything. I told you before, the Pedorate want to finish us and it's just a pity for them that people like Ceilu, Gaed and me refuse to go down without a fight."

Kai won't argue that they're resisting. But as for effectively resisting? That's something else. No matter how daring, a quick raid of the quarantine station doesn't amount to much. Still, who is he to judge? While living in Ularon City, he did absolutely nothing to alleviate the suffering inside his home-ward.

"We go that way," Doon says. "You better have that shine-stick ready."

Mechanically Kai draws his stick in readiness. As they walk toward the next staircase, he's thinking.

"Does The Cocoon encase the whole dock?" he asks as he follows Doon onto the first tread.

"You saw it," she answers disinterestedly. "What do you think? It's not like we can climb up the side to find out."

"What about underneath?" Kai asks, prompting Doon to pull up, foot shy of the next tread.

"What a stupid thing to ask. How in pautune do you expect us to know that?"

"We could be under it right now."

"Probably are," she says and starts up the stairs once more. "But how does that help? This complex is deep underground." She points upward. "And there's a lot of rock between us and the surface. You're going to ask why Gaed hasn't tried to blow up The Cocoon next," she says, voice dripping with sarcasm, then takes three more steps before she stops and turns around again. "You *were* going to ask that, weren't you?"

"No, I wasn't," Kai replies, "but now that you've brought it up. Why hasn't someone tried? I don't mean tried to blast a way through, but why hasn't anyone ever investigated if there *is* a way through from underneath?"

For the longest time, Doon remains standing, one step above him, fingers clasped loosely about her shine-stick. Her expression has turned kind of blank.

"Well?" Kai presses her.

Doon's mouth opens but it's some time before anything comes out. "I guess no one ever thought it was possible before."

***

"Maybe," Jak Inopo says a little groggily.

They returned directly to Ceilu's house from the dock on the chance that Pilot Jak would still be there. He was and lying sound asleep on some makeshift bedding in the far corner of the outer room. Ceilu was there, too, sifting through the box Mig brought earlier, but all of the young ones were gone.

"But the dock is enormous," Inopo goes on to say. "It covers a lot of ground." He waves his hands as if to express its scale.

Here it comes, Kai tells himself.

"Where would we even start to look?"

"That's what *I* said," Doon grumps. She's stationed herself at the table beside Ceilu. From the start, she wasn't enthusiastic about Kai's idea but she wasn't wholly dismissive, either.

Kai shifts position on the floor. He hasn't slept in a long time. His bones are aching. His head is aching. Even his teeth are aching. On their trek back from the dock, Doon went so far as to suggest that he might not be thinking straight. Maybe he isn't. Maybe it really is a stupid thing to even contemplate. But the old pilot speaks again.

"Still, if there was a way. Getting inside *The Nether* could tell us an awful lot."

Doon leans forward in her chair. "Like?"

"What really happened for one thing," he answers, glancing briefly at the young Phane.

"You believe Kai then?" Rising, she joins Inopo and Kai on the floor.

"I don't think Kai would lie. Intentionally anyway," Inopo says, "but if we could get inside the ship, then there's a good chance we would know for sure."

Doon's momentary enthusiasm begins to wane. "But how could we do it?" She shoots a quick look at Kai. "I'm not frightened but," her gaze drifts back to the old pilot, "unless you know a lot more about the dock than the rest of us, I don't see how it's possible. I mean..." she flips her hands in a quick gesture of frustration, "even if there *is* a way, we could stumble around looking for an access and still never find it."

"You need to find the bunker," Ceilu says without shifting focus from her sorting. "If there's a way in, it's there."

She hasn't said a word until now and Kai has been of the opinion that she wasn't listening.

"The safety bunker," she explains, glancing at Inopo.

"What's a safety bunker?" Doon asks of Inopo when Ceilu is slow to answer.

Either the old pilot is giving Ceilu's suggestion serious consideration or he's just as puzzled as Doon and Kai.

"That's a distinct possibility," he says at last. "If," he continues, raising a finger, "we knew where to find it."

Ceilu offers up a shrug. "I know where to find it. At least where it should be but we'd be taking a big chance. If the air inside The Cocoon is contaminated, then whoever goes in there can't be allowed to come out."

"Then what's the point of going in the first place?" Kai fires back.

"Exactly," Ceilu answers with another shrug. "Which is why I never suggested it before." She turns again to her sorting. "Waste of time."

Doon's face has visibly flushed. "Will someone *please* tell me what we're even talking about? *What* is a safety bunker?"

Ceilu continues with her sorting and the long silence is broken only by the gentle tink of bottles being stacked on the table.

"Fine," Doon shouts, leaping up from the floor. "I'll find it myself and Kai here will go with me. If you won't let us back into the ward, then so be it. We've been floundering around here too long just doing the same things and it's getting us nowhere. It isn't good enough."

The corners of Ceilu's mouth lift. Doon's little outburst has obviously amused her.

"You go then, Doon," she says calmly, "but you'll have to find the bunker first. And you don't even know what you're looking for."

"No!" Doon slams her fist on the table causing Ceilu's collection of bottles to dance. "Then you're just going to have to tell us, aren't you?"

When the old pilot begins to struggle onto his feet, Kai rises and lends a hand to his elbow.

"Calm down. There's a simple solution to this. Put it to a vote," Inopo says.

"A vote!" Ceilu's eyes look like they're about to pop out of her head.

"That's a great idea." It's Doon's turn to smile.

"Really?" Ceilu counters, hands on hips, as she challenges Doon with a confident stare. "And just who *gets* to vote? Everyone in the ward? I wouldn't call that simple." The last is aimed directly at the old pilot.

"No," Inopo grudgingly agrees.

"Then how about everyone who's ever risked capture in the tunnels," Kai suggests, "and Pilot Jak, of course," he adds in afterthought.

It's a gamble. He suspects most of the young ones will side with Ceilu. Still, it's the best—really the only—option.

"So," he presses the silent trio. "What do you say?"

CHAPTER 11

It's taking a long time for Ceilu and Doon to gather all the Journers who have taken part in the raids on the quarantine station. Kai puts the time to good use making himself and the old pilot something to eat. Pushing Ceilu's bottles of pilfered medicines to one side, he has Inopo sit at the table. Among Ceilu's supplies he finds some umiper leaves, a rare luxury even in Ularon City. All things considered, the Dosers at the quarantine station seem to live fairly well. He boils up some of the umiper and is sitting at the table by Jak, drinking it, when Ceilu and Doon return, leading a party of young Journers. Ceilu glances at Kai's cup, but says nothing.

Kai is surprised by the number of Journers who, at one time or other, have raided the station. It's a tight squeeze to get them all into Ceilu's small house. Some squat on the floor, others stand against the walls, a few are left filling the doorway. Even little Mig has come. Kai vacates his seat at the table but Jak remains where he is, nursing the cup of umiper. Courtesy of a few well-placed nudges, Kai scores a place by Doon at the back of the room. Gaed is sitting, knees to chest, on the floor beside her, with an enigmatic expression clouding his face.

Ceilu thumps the table and the buzz of hushed chatter trails to silence.

"We need numbers, Doon," she says, glancing at the young Phane beside Kai. "You take a count and so will I."

Doon gets to her feet and her eyes shift piecemeal over the room as she tallies.

"Thirty-seven," she calls to Ceilu.

"Same here," Ceilu confirms. "Excluding Kai and Pilot Jak that makes thirty-five."

"That's not fair," Doon protests.

"Too bad," Ceilu counters. "Kai doesn't get to vote. Only those who've risked capture in the tunnels. It was his own suggestion, remember."

Before Doon can say anything more, Kai speaks up. "I'll agree to that."

"I don't," Doon complains. "If Kai doesn't vote then I say Pilot Jak should."

"All right," Ceilu agrees at last. "But Pilot Jak only votes after everyone else. Otherwise he may influence the vote."

Reluctantly—because Ceilu's argument is probably sound—Doon agrees.

"Fine." Ceilu begins by pointing at Kai. "This pilot here is Kai Astada, son of Anan Astada and Usha Kaidador."

No one inside the room shows surprise. Save for Ceilu's voice, there isn't another sound.

"Some of you were with us when we found him in the tunnels. Others will have heard about it by now. He says he's Kai Astada and Pilot Jak confirms it. So there's no doubt about his identity. He says that Bes Gannaline-ro sent him here to uncover what really happened to the crew of *The Nether*. According to Kai there, Pilot Ro is of the opinion that every one of them was alive when they returned and the plague is nothing but a fabrication. And he claims Pilot Ro tricked him into coming here to find the evidence."

Now Kai hears the gasp he only half expected to hear before.

Ceilu raises her hand, warding off interruption. "I'm not so sure I believe it, either. But that's what he claims. So," she adds with a smile Kai has no difficulty interpreting, "his plan is to search *The Nether*. What we have to do now is decide if we're willing to let him and Doon try to go not just *inside* The Cocoon but all the way to the dock and, assuming they succeed, come back out again. If Ro is wrong or *he* is lying, then they could bring the plague back out with them and spread it through the ward."

"What if they're telling the truth?"

Kai tries but fails to spot who spoke.

"Then they'll have to prove it. And if they do, then it's the Pedorate Council who's been lying and we'll have something entirely different to discuss."

"Why Doon?"

Predictably the question comes from Gaed.

Doon pounces on her brother before Ceilu can get a word out. "Because I believe him. At least, I *want* to." She turns to Ceilu. "And I... we... *have* to know."

"Let him try then," Gaed says, coming to his feet. "Alone."

"Don't try to tell me what to do, Gaed," Doon shouts. "It's my choice, not yours." She looks around the room, challenging the gathered Journers with a menacing glower. "No one here has died of the plague in a very long time, have they?"

There's a restrained hum of accord in the room.

"And I, for one, am not so convinced that anyone ever did. Oh sure... sure," she hurries on before anyone can object, "some of us were taken away. But did anyone here ever *see* somebody infected with the plague?"

Someone on the other side of the room speaks up, an older kyne Kai doesn't recognise. "They were taken away before anything showed," he says, seeking support with a nervous glance about the room.

He is answered with another muffled buzz of accord. Doon simply snorts.

"That's enough talk," Ceilu interjects. "It's plain what Doon thinks. It comes down to a show of hands now. You'll wait?" she asks, glancing back at Jak Inopo.

"I'll wait," he agrees, setting his cup of umiper aside.

"Gaed," Ceilu says, waving him forward. "You take the count this time."

With an audible sigh, Gaed takes a place beside Ceilu.

"Those who agree to allow Pilot Kai and Doon inside The Cocoon, raise your hand."

Doon's hand shoots up. In the short time he's had, Kai has taken Doon's measure well enough to realise that, regardless of how the count comes down, she'll try it anyway.

Gaed reports the tally. "Twenty-three."

"Twenty-four," Inopo promptly corrects him.

Ceilu nods. "So we're going to permit an attempt. All right. But, if they do get inside, are we going to let them back out? Hands!"

Kai holds his breath and looks around the room. This is the vote that really counts. Left inside The Cocoon, he and Doon could surely devise a way to get word out of what they've found, but their fate will be sealed if Ro has misled them. Kai tries to take his own count but can't seem to keep the numbers straight.

"Nineteen," Gaed says.

"Twenty," Inopo tenders from the table.

With or without Jak Inopo, the vote would have come down the same. He and Doon are going in. And they'll be allowed to come back again once they're done.

"Then it's decided," Ceilu pronounces. "Doon and Pilot Kai will be permitted to attempt an entry and return from The Cocoon."

She sounds more complacent than Kai expected. He waits, anticipating that the real protest may come from the gathered Journers instead, but all he hears is a restrained and generally resigned grumble. They've accepted the results of the vote and he should have anticipated that better. Ceilu leads, old Jak mentors, and the rest of the young Journers follow. It's like Inopo told him earlier—the wardlanders have a new way of dealing with matters now and, for the most part, they conform to it.

Grabbing his elbow, Doon drags Kai to his feet. "You'd better be right," she whispers. "Or I'm going to seriously regret not having finished you off in the tunnel."

The young Journers begin to disperse in a haphazard ramble. Kai is the recipient of the odd sidelong glance but it's Doon who bears the brunt of the dissatisfaction, most particularly from Gaed. His anger is almost palpable as it leaches across the room. If anything happens to Doon, Kai knows full well he'll answer for it.

There's a tug on his arm and, looking down, he finds little Mig gazing up at him. He'd lost sight of her after she entered the house and wasn't aware how she voted or reacted once the vote was taken.

"I'm going with you."

"You can't," he replies, surprised by the little kyne's decision. "I don't think it would be a good idea and, anyway, I doubt Ceilu will let you."

She looks offended. "Ceilu lets me do almost anything I want."

Kai's about to explain that they don't need her but thinks better of it. She does have her uses and Ceilu does appear to be genuinely fond of her.

"The fewer of us who go inside The Cocoon, the better, don't you think?" he says instead.

"Not really, no," she replies, surprising Kai again. "There's nothing to be frightened of inside The Cocoon. It's the same on the inside as the outside."

"Yes, but you can't *see* infection. The air inside could be teeming with it."

She crosses her arms in defiance. "You don't think so." Freeing a hand, she points a little finger at Doon, who has been quietly listening to the exchange. "*She* doesn't think so."

"Now wait a minute," Doon rushes to say, "I never said that for sure. I'm counting on it but," she drops onto one knee to speak face to face with little Mig, "you don't have to. You're a lot younger than me."

Mig? A *lot* younger than Doon! Kai almost smiles.

"And if Kai is wrong," she casts him an upward glance, "then you could die."

"You, too," Mig counters with a shrug.

"I suppose," Doon answers after a little pause, "but that's a risk I'm willing to take."

"So am I," Mig hits back.

"But, Mig—"

Doon doesn't get the chance to say more; Ceilu has come striding up.

"Haven't you two done enough damage? Mig," she says, grabbing the young one by the arm, "you're not going and that's the end of it." She gives young Mig a healthy slap on the rear. "Get going. You'll be needed in the tunnel again soon."

Inopo catches Kai's eye, then turns to Ceilu. "So," he says, "now the little pleasantries are completed, perhaps you'll be kind enough to tell our two adventurers exactly where they're to begin their journey." His eyes remain on Ceilu as she settles herself into the opposite seat, stretches out her legs in front of her and casually folds her arms across her chest.

Gaed, no longer rooted to the spot, moves to stand behind her.

"The safety bunker is located on the far side of the complex, underground and close to the dock. The Sub and dock facilities are connected and if you—"

"So?" Doon interrupts. "We've been through all those tunnels and rooms. Are you saying you've already seen the bunker?"

Ceilu offers a little shrug. "No. But it's got to be there. We must have missed it. Or it's in another area that isn't connected to the Sub facility. But my bet is that if you get into one, you get into the other. It's never been a priority to find it. More than likely it's cut off. Caved-in maybe. Or sealed up."

Kai is looking at Doon. Her mouth has turned down at the corners.

"You're lying," she challenges Ceilu. "There's no such place. I don't know what game you're playing at, Ceilu... wasting all our time with that vote, but—"

"Fine," Ceilu replies with a flutter of one hand in the air. "Then we won't waste any more time on Pilot Kai's ridiculous idea, either." She makes to rise but the old pilot reaches out to stop her.

Kai is disappointed with himself for not seeing it before; a conflict has been brewing between these two young Journers for some time. He steps forward before Doon or Inopo have a chance to speak.

"I don't think you're lying about a bunker. It makes sense there'd be some sort of safety structure on the dock. Perhaps if you explain how you happen to know so much about it, it might give us some indication of where it is."

"If you insist," Ceilu replies uninterestedly. "When we met down in the Sub tunnel, you said that the only Journer from my family on *The Nether* was my uncle, Brin Ceiluel."

"That's right," Kai agrees, curious where she could be going with what seems to him like an unnecessary diversion.

"And that's true. My uncle was the only one. But my father could have been."

Kai looks to Inopo, seeking confirmation, but the old pilot has nothing to say.

"My father was an alternate. A backup crew member for *The Nether*."

"And that's supposed to help Pilot Kai and me how?" Doon challenges her.

"It helps *you*," Ceilu says, straightening in her chair, "because my father just happened to tell *me* about the safety bunker. I can't recall exactly everything he said. I was just a kyne then and, after a while, it all got a little bit boring."

She's taken Kai by surprise. Sure, there had to be alternates and there's no reason for Ceilu's father not to have been one of them. And Kai can easily empathise with a young one becoming bored with hearing all the little details. What surprises him is Ceilu's age. She can hardly be much older than Doon; no wonder the two vie for position.

"But if the bunker is still intact," Ceilu is saying, "and you can find it, then that's your best way in."

"How?" Doon presses her. "I can't see that finding just another room under the dock is going to be of any use at all."

"But it's not just any room. It's a room with a direct link to the dock above it." Realising that no one has understood, Ceilu goes on to explain. "*The Nether* is on the dock. The dock is inside The Cocoon. You find the room, crawl up the link and you're inside The Cocoon. How you actually get inside *The Nether* after that is your problem."

Kai hazards a glance at Doon. She looks as mortified as he feels.

"Crawl *up* the link! What do you mean crawl *up* it?" he demands. "Are you talking some sort of ladder?"

A smile creeps its way to Ceilu's lips. "No, it's not a ladder. It's a shoot. A slide," she raises her hand shoulder high, "from the dock here," then lowers it calf height, "to the bunker there."

"Oh, that's just about the most ridiculous thing I've ever heard."

Gaed has been so quiet, Kai had almost forgotten about him, standing sentinel-like behind Ceilu.

"Are you sure?" he asks, stepping around Ceilu's chair to question her. "I mean," he says, gesturing toward Kai and Doon, "they'll be going in on your word, Ceilu. And I know my sister well enough to assure you she intends to follow through on this. If this slide or shoot or whatever it is doesn't really exist, then they'll be climbing up every ventilation duct and ceiling crevasse they come across for absolutely no reason at all."

"The slide is real," Inopo says calmly from across the table. "I've heard of it but I don't know any details. Ceilu seems to know far more about it than I do."

"And that's precious little if you ask me," Gaed observes.

"Oh, shut up, Gaed," Doon barks, striding forward. "If Pilot Jak says it exists, then it does. So," she says, nudging her brother aside to question Ceilu herself, "where's the best place to start searching for this bunker? And what's this slide thing supposed to look like?"

"If it were me, I'd start looking where we've never looked before."

Kai tries to attract Doon's attention but her focus remains fixed on Ceilu. According to Doon, she and Gaed have combed absolutely everywhere inside the underground complex, so that leaves nowhere at all. The bunker and the slide that connect it to the dock *must* be myth. Or buried, as Ceilu suggested.

"It'll be deep," Ceilu warns her. "Keep that in mind, so don't waste your time on anything close to the surface." Glancing away, she reaches out and begins to tinker with one of the medicine bottles on the table. With the tip of one finger on the cap, she starts to spin it around and around. "The slide can't be too long or it wouldn't work as an evacuation route, but since it's going to be deep inside the complex, it's likely to be quite steep." Her focus drifts to the young Phane's feet, lingers there a while. "And it'll be slippery. You'll need better boots."

Kai looks toward Doon's feet. If she owns a pair of sturdy boots, she isn't wearing them. The ones on her feet are scuffed, dirty and worn down at the heels. Kai looks down at his own boots, wishing he'd worn his old Journer boots instead of these smart Talker excuses for a pair of decent walking boots. They'll have to suffice, unless he happens to find a good pair of Journer boots lying around somewhere. Not a likely prospect.

"I'll borrow Gaed's," Doon says at last.

Gaed opens his mouth to speak but Jak Inopo interjects.

"Then everything's settled," he says, rising. "I'd suggest you get a good night's rest now. Start fresh in the morning. That's exactly what I intend to do. Doon," he motions for the young Phane. "Time to go. You, too, Gaed. As I recall, you're cooking for me tonight."

Doon singles Kai out as she starts for the door ahead of Gaed. "First light tomorrow at the Sub entrance."

Kai nods and turns to Ceilu, at the point of asking where he's supposed to go now when Doon's head darts around the door. "And don't be late."

She's gone again in a flash.

"Proud of yourself?" Ceilu says, snatching Kai's attention from the empty doorway.

"I didn't ask her to go with me."

"You didn't tell her not to, either," Ceilu counters, rising. She walks to the back of the room and disappears around a corner.

"How do you expect me to tell Doon *anything?*" Kai calls after her. "She doesn't listen to me."

He's still shouting when Ceilu reappears, carrying a wad of bedding. "She listened well enough to want to go. Here." She dumps the bedding on the floor at his feet. "You can sleep out here tonight. I suppose you want something to eat now, too."

"Ceilu, I don't want to sleep here and I don't want your food!"

"That's just too bad," she says, "because you're not going underground with Doon tired and hungry. She'll have enough to do watching out for herself." She points to the table. "Sit!"

***

"You're late," Doon complains. She's seated on the edge of the platform, the hatch of the Sub station already open.

"I got lost," Kai explains. "It was dark when I started out and I don't know this part of town well."

"Then you should have brought a shine-stick," Doon replies, coming to her feet.

The only way he could have gotten a shine-stick was to steal one from Ceilu's stockpile and that didn't seem a good idea. He left before Ceilu was awake; at least, he didn't see her when he set out from her house some time before dawn. The streets were empty and no light spilled from any of the ruined cottages he passed along the way. Any wonder he became lost.

"If you're ready?" Doon says, hand cupped on the open cover of the hatch. "I'll go first."

Kai steps onto the top rung behind her and pulls the cover closed, plunging them into darkness. At the base of the stairs, he waits for the flare of Doon's shine-stick.

"Now, that's odd," she says playfully. Her face is glowing blue in the glare of the stick she holds up.

They're not alone; there's a glow at the end of the corridor and it's moving toward them. Gaed! It's Gaed. Kai can see his face now, glowing just like Doon's.

"Why is Gaed here?" he asks.

Doon thrusts two shine-sticks into Kai's hand, then pushes past him. "He asked to come. If Ceilu has it right," she says, addressing Gaed, "then we'll need to drive as deep into the complex as possible if we're going to find this bunker thing. I suggest—"

"Don't worry about it." The shine-stick wavers in Gaed's hands. "I know where to go," he says, starting out ahead of his sister, leaving Kai in a rush to catch up.

Gaed doesn't get far before Doon slaps a hand to his shoulder and spins him around.

"What do you mean 'you know'?"

"I've seen the bunker."

Judging by her wide-eyed response, that's the last thing Doon expected to hear.

"I didn't know it was a bunker but once Ceilu got talking about it, I realised what it was."

"Really!" Doon props a hand on her hip. "And just when were you going to tell *me*?"

Gaed shrugs. "There's a big hatch at both ends. I could open the one to get in but I couldn't budge the other one. I figured if you knew about the place, you'd just waste a lot of time trying to get the thing open. Didn't see the point."

Doon's shaking a fist at Gaed. "Then all that stuff you said to Ceilu was just to stop Kai and me from trying to get inside The Cocoon."

"I still don't see the point, Doon," Gaed says in his defence. "And it was the only way I could think of to stop you."

"How many times do I have to say it?" She's spitting out the words as she steps up to poke Gaed in the chest. "Don't try to tell me what to do. Now," she says, calming, "perhaps you can explain how the rest of us never saw this room before?"

"I think *I* can explain that."

Doon snaps her head around to glare at Kai.

"The power down here is failing intermittently," he tells them both, then turns directly to Doon. "I'm betting that *you* never saw the bunker because it was concealed behind a sim that had failed by the time Gaed stumbled on it."

She's still glaring at him, obviously unconvinced.

"We came across that failed sim yesterday, remember? And you'd never seen that room before, either."

"What failed sim?" Gaed asks.

"I'm not sure you need to know, Gaed," Doon counters. "Let's just both have our little secrets. Which way?" she barks, pushing past her brother.

"You're heading the right way for now," Gaed calls ahead, grasping Kai's arm when he makes to follow Doon. "What failed sim?"

"It's nothing to worry about, Gaed. Just a failed sim that was concealing what looked like a dormitory or something."

"A dormitory!"

Kai fixes Gaed with a smile. "Odd thing to find down here, wouldn't you agree? Makes you wonder if Ro isn't telling the truth after all, doesn't it?" Leaving Gaed with that thought, he starts after Doon once more.

Ceilu and Doon might be at a long-running standoff but it seems that, in their sparing, Doon is used to getting the better of Gaed. He turns silent, only giving the odd brief direction as Doon leads.

There should only be the three of them down in the tunnels, but every so often a little tingling sensation at the nape of his neck has Kai beginning to suspect they have company. He puts it down to a draft at first until he's finally forced to concede that, underground, there is no draft.

"Stop a moment," he whispers, pulling up. "Is it just me," he says when Gaed first, then Doon, turn around, "or do either of you get the feeling there's someone else down here?"

In the semi-darkness, he can see Gaed's head cock to one side like a mutz, listening. He motions Kai to draw closer, then gestures to a nearby recess.

"You two go into that corridor there. I'm going to go back and find out."

Before Doon can voice an objection, Kai grabs her arm and pushes her into the dark alcove.

"What did you do that for?"

"Gaed doesn't have permission to be down here. Better he gets sent back than us."

"You think it's a Guardian?" She sounds apprehensive.

"Maybe Ceilu had someone follow us."

"Don't be ridiculous. If we're being followed, I'd be more suspicious it's by one of *yours*."

"My *what*? If you're—"

Kai is interrupted by Gaed's call out of the darkness.

"Just look who I found."

Gaed emerges, ushering a small figure ahead of him.

"Stop shoving me," Mig whines, spinning around.

Gaed lets out a sharp shout. "The little fiweam just stomped on my foot."

"Then stop shoving me."

"Leave her be, Gaed," Doon orders.

"No." Gaed gives the little kyne a parting push forward. "She's not supposed to be here."

"Nor are you."

Kai can't see her face but he's willing to bet Doon is smiling.

"She's of no use here," Gaed objects.

"I *am*. You could come to a tight space. Then what are you going to do?"

Her argument sounds reasonable to Kai. He's about to say as much when Mig pivots around and points at him.

"And I've got the same right to be here as he has. My mother was on *The Nether*."

Another valid argument. If the Pedorate Council lied about the fate of his father, then they lied about the fate of Rei Sek as well.

"She can come," Kai finds himself saying.

"But she hasn't got permission," Gaed reminds him. "If Ceilu finds out she's been inside The Cocoon and come back out again, what do you think she'll do?"

"The same goes for you," Kai reminds him.

"Me?" Gaed jabs himself in the chest. "I'm not going *in*. I only came down here to get you two to the bunker. That's all."

"You're not coming with us?"

Doon reaches down to take Mig's hand. "Of course, he's not. Gaed's a big admirer of all your silly wardland laws. Thinks he *is* a wardlander. I heard Mig went off picking wild pimarines this morning," she says, leading the kyne away. "It's a long way to the pimarine glade. She couldn't possibly make it back before late afternoon."

"Well," Kai says, finally taking Doon's meaning. "I hope she brings some back for the rest of us."

***

"Unbelievable!" Doon gasps.

By Kai's count, it's the third time she's said that. Once they came to the failed sim, Gaed had no trouble at all opening the hatch that was once concealed behind it. The hatch was a spoked-wheel affair that spun to the right with barely a squeal despite the years since it had been routinely operated. Stepping through the hatch, they found themselves in the enormous room Gaed had identified as the bunker. Only Gaed and Mig seem comfortable. Gaed has been here before. But Mig? She is the pioneer among them after all. In their explorations, she's likely been the first to see a lot of strange things.

True to its name, the bunker is really just one large chamber. In the spare light from the shine-sticks, its walls and low-slung ceiling appear to be heavily reinforced and, at a guess, very thick. While the front of the bunker is washed in a sickly yellow glow spilling in from the corridor beyond the failed sim, the light from their shine-sticks reveals little about the far reaches of the bunker. All Kai can really see is row upon row of tightly packed seating.

"How far back is the other hatch?" he asks, turning to Gaed.

"Way back there," Gaed replies. "Tight going..." he starts to say and, then perhaps remembering Mig's insightful warning earlier, declines to finish.

"The place is full of chairs." Doon is standing a little way off, barely within reach of Kai's shine-stick. "What in pautune are all these chairs doing down here? Are you sure this is the bunker?" She strides back to confront Gaed. "You didn't stumble on a store room instead maybe."

"Yes, that's right, Doon," Gaed replies so coolly Kai actually feels a chill course down his spine. "It's a store room for chairs that are so valuable they have to be concealed behind a sim and bolted to the floor."

Kai reaches out, finds the closest chair and gives it a shake. The chairs *are* bolted to the floor.

"They're cushioned, too," Gaed tells Kai less caustically. "For protection from an explosion on the dock I guess."

Kai feels again for the chair, finds a thick layer of stiff padding lining the seat, back and sides. Little comfort, he'd think, for anyone trapped down here while the big engines of *The Nether* are exploding overhead.

"This must be it then," Kai says, finding Doon. "The bunker Ceilu was talking about."

"So, it's the bunker."

Even in the darkness, Kai can sense Doon's shrug of defeat.

"But I can't see how it could be very effective in an emergency. I mean how could they possibly get all those people down here in time?"

"Maybe they didn't care how well it worked. Maybe they only wanted to make it look like it would work."

It's the first thing Mig has said since they passed through the sim.

Save a few. Lose a few. There are always more Journers and Reckoners to replace them.

"That's a pleasant observation," Doon says as she starts threading her way between the packed rows of seating.

Kai follows, sweeping the light from his shine-stick from side to side. In what he takes to be the centre of the room, there's a clear area and, centre of that, a large cabinet or perhaps a small internal room. He can only guess what's inside. Safety equipment? Emergency supplies? Could be anything. It won't be the slide they're looking for. The slide wouldn't be located directly inside the bunker. It has to be on the other side of the far hatch. Even if they get the hatch open, there's still the climb up the slide to the dock. And then what? Additional hatches sealing off the slide?

"I think I've found it," Doon calls. "Get over here, Gaed."

Kai crawls onto one of the heavily padded seats to let Gaed pass.

"That's it," Gaed agrees as Kai, with Mig on his heel, joins them. He shines the light on what Doon has found, a hatch much like the one Gaed sprung to get them into the bunker.

"If we all grab hold and try to turn the wheel, maybe we can shift it," Gaed suggests. "Mig, you can't help with this."

Seems Mig is well aware where her use does and doesn't lie; without a word, she steps back out of the way.

Laying his shine-stick on the floor, Kai finds a place for his hands on the wheel beside Doon's and he starts to twist. The floor beneath his feet makes for good purchase but after three attempts, one small promising squeal and any number of grunts and curses, the wheel refuses to give.

"Stop! Stop!" Gaed calls. "We'll have to think of something else."

"Are you sure the hatch is meant to be opened from this side?" Doon asks.

"There's a wheel on it, isn't there? What do you think it's there for? Decoration?"

Doon slumps to the floor, knocking Kai's shine-stick askew. "All right. Just asking. Why don't you just blow it up?"

"Can't. The hatch is too thick. I don't have anything powerful enough." Gaed thumps a hand to the stubborn hatch.

For someone who is so opposed to going inside *The Cocoon*, Gaed is exhibiting an unexpected amount of aggravation at being thwarted.

"I think it's over, Gaed," Kai admits reluctantly. "We're not going to get through this."

Doon makes a grunting sound from the floor. "You're not a very determined sort, are you? Let's give it another try," she says, rising. "Only this time, why don't we try using a lever?"

"Got a lever on you?" Gaed quips.

"No, I don't." She gives her brother a shove. "So I'd suggest we all look around and try to find something that will do."

It's Mig who finds the broken length of a metal cylinder that's thin enough to slot through the spokes of the wheel and perhaps tough enough to withstand the torque.

"That's good, Mig," Doon tells the kyne encouragingly. "Now see if you can find us something to whack it with."

Gaed turns to Kai. "*Whack it?*" he says, then calls to Doon, who's scavenging the floor on hands and knees. "We don't want to wreck it completely, Doon."

"Forget it, Mig," Doon says, rising. "We'd better try it Gaed's way first or he'll just get all upset."

It takes three tries to budge the mechanism, Kai leaning heavily on the lever, Gaed and Doon wrenching with all their might on the wheel. By the end of it, Kai is exhausted, sweating, and he'd swear he's torn a muscle in his shoulder. Behind him, Mig is jumping up and down, clapping her hands and shouting 'you did it' over and over again.

Gaed shoves the hatch and the lever slips out of place, landing with a tinny echo on the floor of the black chamber beyond.

"No light," Gaed observes unnecessarily. "I'll go first."

Doon steps next and Kai ushers Mig in after her. Entering last, he's afforded the benefit of the trio's shine-sticks. They appear to have stepped into another tunnel. Gaed calls out, but his voice echoes off the tight walls and low ceiling, so Kai is obliged to sweep his stick around to find him.

"It looks like Ceilu knew what she was talking about," Gaed tells him. "This has got to be the slide."

Gaed is moving his shine-stick up and down, illuminating something that does look remarkably like a slide set hard against the wall in front of him.

Extending his arm, Kai uses his shine-stick to reveal what he can of the ceiling. The slide angles upwards and appears to pass through a squarish opening overhead.

Doon is hunched, hands to knees, beside him. "How are we supposed to get up that?" she asks, eyes tracking Kai's light. "We'll slip."

"No, we won't," Mig calls to them.

Kai shifts his stick to find her, just two big eyes gleaming back at him out of the darkness.

"I'm standing at the bottom of the slide and there's some sort of padding along both sides of it. It seems to go all the way up. If we grab a hold of the padding, we can pull ourselves along."

"I suppose it's possible," Doon says, testing the sturdy rubber-like padding for herself. "We can try. But Mig, you're not big enough to reach across the slide. You'll have to stay here."

"I don't need to reach *across* it, Doon. I can pull myself up along one side, wedge my boots between the edge of the slide and all that padding. It's my idea and I'm going."

Kai shifts his light to Doon, deferring to her decision. She knows the kyne's capabilities better than he does.

"If you say so," she agrees.

Kai swears he catches her winking before she turns to her brother. "Gaed, trade boots with me."

Without a word, Gaed drops to the floor. He's a little bigger than Doon and his boots won't be a perfect fit, but it's better she have some traction on the slippery surface than none at all.

"You'd better bring these back," Gaed warns his sister, rising to hand her the boots.

"I'll bring them back." She's on the floor now, making a loud performance of the boot exchange. "You just make sure you're still here when we do get back! So, who goes first?"

Kai's guessing the question is aimed at him. "Can't see it matters much but I think Mig should go in between us in case she slips."

Kai feels a tug on his arm. Mig.

"I am *not* going to slip," she tells him brusquely. "Gaed doesn't call me fiweam for nothing."

"Sorry," Kai mutters.

Flinging one leg over the edge, Kai pulls the rest of his body on to the slide, grabs a hold of the rubbery padding on either side. He's got his shine-stick wedged securely between his teeth but all he can see is the slide above him and the light from Mig's and Doon's shine-sticks shining up from below. He begins to pull. Left hand. Right. Left. Boots repeatedly fumbling for traction on the slippery surface of the slide. He's beginning to wonder if Mig, who can wedge her boots in as she goes, isn't having an easier time of it.

"This better be worth it," Doon grumbles in garbled tones close behind him.

They're keeping pace with him, even Mig. At less than half his size, she's doing better than just holding her own.

The longer he climbs, the colder the bed of the slide feels against his cheek. The more he grips the old padding, the more certain he grows that sooner or later it's going to rip. And the higher they go, the steeper the pitch becomes. The slide must surface but, as he hauls himself along, Kai is constantly battling with an irrational panic that it never will. And once they do get to the end of it, the hatch could be as difficult to budge as the one sealing off the chamber below. They could simply slide back down, of course—they were never in any danger of being stuck on the slide forever—but a pitiful retreat isn't compensation enough for the risk they're taking.

"Can you see anything yet?" Doon's garbled voice again.

"Nothing," Kai calls down to her between clenched teeth. "No, wait."

The light from his shine-stick is finally revealing something other than the endless slide and it appears to be just what he feared. Another hatch! A few more pulls on the padding and he's there. The hatch's wheel looms in front of him, taunting.

"Stop," he shouts, thinking Mig might blunder right into him and lose her grip. "Doon, make your way over Mig. You're going to have to stand on my shoulders and open the hatch."

"I'm going to have to *what?*" she shouts thickly at him from below.

"I can't turn the wheel *and* hold on," he explains, glancing down past Mig's head. "You can't take my weight, so it has to be you. Get up here. Don't drop your shine-stick," he says in afterthought and, quickly releasing his hold on one side of the slide, slips his own shine-stick inside his clothing.

"You fancy pilot types really do think Phanes are stupid, don't you?"

The light from Doon's shine-stick disappears but Kai can hear her making her way past Mig in the darkness. He's just positioned his hand back on the opposite side of the slide when he feels Doon grasping his calf.

"I think this could be a very bad idea," she mutters as her hands come about Kai's waist and she begins to crawl, hand over hand, up his back. "If you let me slide, I swear I'll kill you."

"I'm not going to let you slide." He can't look down so calls to Mig below. "Mig, lift your shine-stick closer to the wheel so Doon can see it."

The light from Mig's stick wavers about for a moment then fixes, sure and steady, on the centre of the hatch.

One of Doon's boots comes to rest on Kai's shoulder, followed quickly by her second boot on his other shoulder. He said he could hold her but once Doon's full weight is on him, he starts to wonder. It feels like the weight of a building being driven down on top of him. He's got both arms thrust sideways, clutching the padding to either side of the slide. That's the problem. But he can't afford to let go. The longer Doon stands there, the more it feels like he's about to be severed at the neck. The burning in his muscles is almost unbearable.

"Can you reach it?" he groans.

"No," Doon replies with a groan of her own. "I've got to turn around. Get my back against the slide."

"Why?" Kai's not sure how much longer he can last.

"Look here, pilots' elbows may bend backward, but Phanes' don't."

"Fine, then turn around. But make it quick."

Kai experiences a brief moment of relief when Doon lifts one of her boots off his shoulder. He can't raise his head, can't see her, but she's got to be swinging herself around, a guess confirmed when something, the heel of her boot most likely, collides with the side of his head, then settles onto his shoulder again.

"Sorry," Doon mumbles. "Gaed's boots are bigger than mine."

Kai resists an impulse to release one hand from the slide to massage his aching head.

"All right, I can reach it now. You hang on because I'm going to have to bend a little forward."

Kai braces himself. If his hands slip, they'll both go sliding and take out Mig in the process.

"I've got it," Doon says.

But it sounds to Kai like she's struggling. The soles of her boots twist on his shoulders and it feels like his skin is on fire. He'd dearly like to scream.

"Just have to get it to turn."

She's grunting, groaning and, in every way possible, convincing Kai that she can't possibly succeed in getting the hatch open. They'll have to give up, slide back down and abandon any hope of making it inside *The Nether.*

"It's giving!" Doon shouts with another wrenching twist of her boots on Kai's shoulders. "How you doing down there?

"Never mind me," Kai gasps. "Just get that hatch—"

An infusion of brilliant light blossoms over his head, ending what Kai intended to say.

"I can see sky. She's through," Mig calls from below as a loud reverberating crash sounds above.

"I'm going to step off you now. Pull myself out," Doon tells Kai as a weight is, literally, lifted from his shoulders.

His head still feels severed from his body. There's a sharp relentless pounding going on at the spot where Doon's boot collided with his temple. Every muscle in his neck and shoulders must have been stretched and shredded beyond all possible repair. And he's still got to haul himself up the rest of the way and crawl through the open hatchway.

"Kai?" Mig prompts meekly. "Is something wrong, Pilot Kai?"

"No." It's all he's got wind enough to say.

Slowly, painfully, he begins the short climb, hand after hand again, until his fingers close around the outer rim of the open hatch. His legs dangle and bang against the surface of the slide for a while before he finally manages to get the upper half of himself over the rim of the hatch. Immediately Doon starts pulling on his arms. With all his heart and soul, he wishes she wouldn't, but he's got absolutely no strength to object. She lets go and he rolls flat onto his back, arms like lead weights beside him.

He's aware of Doon striding off, sees her, in a kind of oblique way, dragging Mig out through the open hatch into sunlight.

"Who'd have thought it possible?" she purrs, dropping onto her rear. "We did it!" She's smiling as she turns to Kai.

Mig is standing, dusting off her little hands on the seat of her pants. "If I didn't think we could, *I* wouldn't have tried."

Doon's head snaps around to look at Mig. "Why, you little fiweam!" She leaps to her feet. "Gaed's right about you. You're nothing but a pain in the—"

"Please. Enough," Kai pleads, finally managing to lift his head. "We've only come so far. We've still got to get inside the ship." He tries to raise a hand to point at the hulking silhouette of *The Nether* below, but his arm doesn't feel like it's attached. A nod toward the distant strip where the ship is resting is the best he can do.

"Where are we?" Mig asks of Kai as he struggles on his feet.

Kai looks around. "Somewhere up on the launch structure," he says, assessing their surroundings.

They've emerged on a platform inside a cage-type arrangement high up inside a hatch-work tower of thick metal.

"We've got to get down onto the strip."

Mig is looking around, taking in the confounding complex of metal towers, randomly angled arms and the haphazard array of large buildings below. Doon's only interest appears to be the abandoned ship.

"See if you can find a way down," Kai says, glancing about. "There's got to be some way." He turns to the little kyne. "Mig, this is your territory."

Kai joins Mig in a search but Doon doesn't budge. He's about to demand her help when the young Phane turns around to speak.

"Something's not right."

"What?" Kai asks uninterestedly. He's focussed on finding a safe and easy way off the structure.

"*The Nether* isn't sitting in the centre of the strip," she says, cautiously making her way to him.

"So?" Kai replies after a quick glance. *The Nether* isn't sitting in the centre of the strip; in fact, it's far off to one side.

"If the ship was auto-piloted, shouldn't it have been brought in centred?"

Maybe it was moved. Kai looks toward the approach end of the strip. The start of the approach is outside The Cocoon, so his vision of it is distorted, like he's looking through watering eyes. Still, its terminus is pretty obvious. He's trying to work out how much of the strip *The Nether* would require to land. His knowledge is limited but, it seems to him that *The Nether* is sitting right about where it should be if it had come to a natural halt; that is, right where it should be but off-centre.

"What's she saying?" Mig calls.

"That *someone*, not something, landed *The Nether*. Come on." Kai spins Doon around with a hand to her shoulder, then waves Mig on toward the edge of the platform. "We've got to get down there."

"Then you're going the wrong way," Mig tells him. "Over there is better." She points toward the spot where they emerged from the hatch. "We can climb down inside the tower, use the struts as handholds. Easy," she says, striding off.

Doon is quick to follow; she's more accustomed to taking Mig's word on these sort of things. Kai hurries after them. As he swings inside the framework of the metal tower after Doon, he concludes that the little kyne has a very strange definition of 'easy'. Still, by not looking down too often and carefully gripping the supporting structure, they manage to make the base of the tower without incident. It's a long walk across the compound to reach *The Nether*, past that cluster of buildings they saw from above. Some of the buildings are squat, square and vast; others tall, cylindrical and unnerving.

The Lycea has completely abandoned its out-journing program but Kai has a rudimentary understanding. He can't fly a ship. And he doesn't know the purpose of all the buildings on the dock. But as long as they steer clear of those buildings, he's guessing they'll be safe—safe enough, anyway—unless *The Nether* truly is a plague ship.

The sun has fully risen and it's bright out in the open beneath The Cocoon. Bright, hot and exposed. Kai's annoyed he hadn't thought to bring his visor. Glancing back toward town, he can see 'Headcracker Hill' in the distance, its edges distorted through the fabric of The Cocoon. Years ago, when he sat on the summit of that hill with Henneh and Mig, watching *The Nether* depart, he would never have believed that a few years later, a subversive by default, he'd be trying to sneak onto it.

"So, what's Gaed's story?" he asks, turning to Doon striding out beside him. Mig is bringing up the rear, gawking unashamedly to right and left, tripping every so often on the deteriorating strip. "He was so opposed to us entering The Cocoon, I can't understand why he led us to the bunker."

"Oh, that. The thing you have to realise about Gaed is that he likes to be on the winning side. And right at the moment, he's not sure which side that is." The corners of Doon's mouth lift. "Come to think of it, nor am I." She shoots a glance over her shoulder to bark at Mig. "Hurry up, little *fiweam*. You're falling behind."

***

"That's something no one thought of," Doon grunts, looking up. She lowers her eyes to question Kai. "How are we supposed to get up there?"

"We got *here*," Mig observes, answering for him. She's pacing about the ship, studying its underbelly and heading for the nose. "And they got *down*."

"All right, fancy pilot," Doon says, thrusting both hands onto her hips. "You're supposed to know about things like this. *Where's the door?*"

"Over here," Mig calls, sparing Kai the need to admit that he doesn't have a clue. "It's over here." She's beaming as they walk toward her. "And it's open."

"That's handy," Doon observes, looking up at a rectangular hole in the side of *The Nether*. "What a pity we can't reach it."

"But we can," Mig tells her. "Look!" she says, pointing.

Kai looks and sees the front end of what appears to be a sort of mobile staircase—a very tall mobile staircase—sticking out from behind a nearby building.

Together, Doon and Kai begin to manoeuvre the stairs toward *The Nether*. It's tough going. The carriage and stairs are lightweight enough, Pedorate-engineered for efficiency, but never intended to be manhandled into place over ground that has degraded over the years. There are ruts and fissures in the strip now and the wheels on the staircase carriage frequently jam and lock. Mig can't help; she's far too small. Likely Kai could have piloted its hauler—had they found it. But if the machine is anywhere in the vicinity, it's inside the nearby building and Kai isn't willing to chance the building housing something less innocuous than a simple hauling machine. Again and again during the slow and tiring process of pushing, pulling and dragging, Kai wonders if he and Doon simply aren't strong enough to get the stairs into position.

Mig waits patiently by the nose of *The Nether* directly under the yawning hatch, periodically offering encouraging words that, under the circumstances, are having the opposite effect. Kai wants to tell her to shut up; would have if he had the breath to do it.

Finally, he and Doon succeed in getting the stairs close enough to the hatch. It's a long way up and they'll have to execute a little leap at the top because there's a rip-up on the strip right where the back wheels of the steps need to be to achieve a perfect fit. Mig is first up the stairs and she manages the leap with ease. Doon and Kai take their time. If she's fared as badly as he has, then Doon's legs and arms will be barely cooperating.

Mig's head pops out through the open hatch. "It's dark in here. Better get your shine-sticks."

Her head disappears again and Doon takes the leap ahead of Kai. He has his shine-stick ready, but the moment his feet make contact with the floor of *The Nether*, a brilliant white light blinds him. Disoriented, he shades his eyes.

"You could have given us some warning," Doon shouts.

Blundering into Doon, Kai lowers his hands from his eyes.

"I didn't do anything," Mig complains.

They're standing, single file, inside a narrow, low-ceiling corridor. Its floor, ceiling and walls are of a dull, non-reflective metal.

"Guess we won't be needing the shine-sticks then," Doon says. Stowing her stick, she gives Mig a push to get her moving.

The corridor ends abruptly and they enter an enormous room that vaguely reminds Kai of the bridge in his own Urban, only on a much, much larger scale.

"The bridge?" Doon asks, glancing at Kai.

Kai nods as he scans the row upon row of now dormant and enigmatic instruments.

"Should the lights just have come on like that?" Doon again.

"It must be auto," Mig suggests. She's wandering slowly about the bridge, stopping every so often to finger one of the panels.

"Don't touch that," Doon tells her. "It was probably you who switched the lights on."

Mig raises her hands in the air, "I never touched anything," then points directly at Kai. "They only came on when he stepped onboard."

"Yes, they did." Doon swings around to challenge Kai.

"I can't explain it. But I don't think it's anything to worry about."

"I guess not," Doon replies at last. "So where do we go from here? What should we be looking for?"

"Something... anything that can tell us if the crew was alive or dead when the ship returned."

Mig saunters up to join them. "That's easy. Look at the log."

Both Doon and Kai shake their heads.

"Assuming we could even access it, if the Pedorate Council is covering something up, don't you think they'd have stripped the log?" Kai explains.

"Oh." The kyne sounds crestfallen, but soon resumes what appears to be her aimless wander about the bridge.

Doon places a hand on Kai's forearm. "I suppose it's worth a try at least. Why don't you and Mig split up, search the rest of the ship? I'll see what I can do here."

"Doon, you can't be serious. Mig is just a kyne. She can't possibly know what to look for."

The Phane's eyes twinkle in amusement. "*You* don't know what to look for. Mig is a good observer. It's kind of..." she hesitates a moment, "I don't know... like everything she sees gets imprinted in her memory. The trick is to ask her the right questions to get it out."

"That's all well and good, but how do you know what questions to ask?"

Doon shrugs. "It's mostly a matter of luck."

"You mean you have to trick her?"

"Trick her! Pautune no! Mig would see right through that. You be honest with her. She's fully aware of her talents. Well?" she prompts. "Have you got a better idea?"

She has him there. "All right," Kai agrees half-heartedly. "You do what you can here. Mig," he calls to attract the kyne's attention, "you come with me. There'll be corridors all through this ship, leading off into different sections, and a lot of floors. We need to come up with a system to search them."

"All of them?" Mig asks.

"I hope not," Kai replies as he starts away from the bridge, leading Mig.

"How many floors?" she asks.

"Six," he tells her, ducking his head to step through an open inner hatch that will take them off the bridge. He thinks it's six, unsure if he's recalling something his father told him or one of the few things he was taught about Supercontinentals at the Lycea. Once off the bridge, he stops to glance around. There's an opening in the floor, not too far away. It's circled by a low metal railing with a narrow break and a set of stairs leading down. Around them are more instrument panels and sealed overhead compartments. Kai wishes he'd listened more closely to his father. He has no idea what the now silent instruments could have told him or what might possibly be of use to them behind the sealed compartments. "This is the fourth floor, I think."

"Then I'll take the three floors below and you can search the rest." Slipping her hand from Kai's, Mig makes for the stairs leading down.

"I don't suppose you could give me a hint what to look for?" she says, glancing back.

Kai can't think of a single thing.

"No," she says. "Then I'll just try to remember everything I see."

Suddenly she's gone down the hole and Kai feels very much alone. Alone and overwhelmed!

What *did* he hope to find here?

CHAPTER 12

"Well?" Doon says when Kai ducks his head back through the doorway. She's sitting at one of the cyphers that, to Kai, looks suspiciously dead.

"Not much." He's been dreading this, the moment he'll be obliged to admit to Doon that he's wasted her time and, if the Pedorate hasn't deceived them about the plague, quite possibly her life. He has searched his three floors and found only what he expected in a Supercontinental: more cryptic instruments and overhead compartments; more sealed wall panels, storage bays, food bins; a myriad of other odd paraphernalia.

"You?" he asks, stepping up behind her.

"Not a thing," she says, betraying frustration. "I can't get in. It's completely... what?" she asks, when Kai points to the cypher in front of her.

It has snapped to life, the logo of the Pedorate Council shining crisp and clean. Then, one by one, all the remaining cyphers come alive. There's three. Now five. Now ten Pedorate logos all glowing at once.

"It's you!" she says, launching herself out of the chair. "You're the reason the lights came on and you're the reason the cyphers have activated."

"Me!" Kai takes a step backward. There's a murderous look in the young Phane's eyes. "I didn't do anything," he says, echoing Mig's earlier plea of innocence.

"You didn't have to *do* anything," Doon says, advancing on him. "You just have to *be* here. This ship knows you."

Kai shakes his head, partly in confusion, partly in denial. "That's not possible."

Suddenly it starts to make a kind of sense; Ro tampered with his pid.

"No," he says disbelievingly and, swivelling the chair around, collapses into the seat. "It's not *me*. It's my *pid*."

Doon's eyes narrow. "Your pid? What's your pid got to do with anything?"

"It's not mine," Kai tells her. He's looking up, trying to read her eyes. "I told you. Ro did something. Changed it. And I'm willing to bet that for all intents and purposes I really *am* Sayker Gerit. And I'm also willing to bet there was a Sayker Gerit among the crew of *The Nether*."

"A Talker! Now I know that can't be true."

"Why not?" Kai presses her. "Do you really think the Pedorate would send *The Nether* out without someone onboard answering to them?"

Doon gives her head a shake and her short-cropped hair swings above her ears. "Maybe not. But then he's dead, too. So what's the point of turning you into him?"

"It got me onto the ship."

Doon smiles. "*Mig* and *I* got you onto the ship. Even Gaed."

"Fine! Fine!" Kai concedes. "It got me to the quarantine station which led to me getting onto the ship." He glances again at the ten now completely active cyphers. "And that means," he says, turning back to Doon, "that Aralin Brawse knew who I was from the very beginning."

"Aralin Brawse?" Doon asks, slipping into the seat beside his. "Who's that?"

"The Registrar. The one who sent me to the quarantine station."

"Oh, yes. You mentioned her before. But I don't see why she'd believe you were anything but who you said you were."

"How could she not?" Kai says with a satisfied smile. "She said she lodged all the required documents for my mission to the quarantine station with my unit. But she couldn't have. Because *my* unit would know that Sayker Gerit is dead."

"Who's dead?"

Kai's head snaps around. Unnoticed, Mig has walked back onto the bridge.

"He is," Doon tells her. "At least, in his guise as Sayer Gerit. So he says."

Mig stops walking, clearly puzzled.

"Don't worry about it." Doon waves Mig's impending question aside as she gets to her feet. "What did you see?"

Mig shoots Doon a pained look and says nothing.

"I thought you knew how to ask the right questions," Kai says from his seat.

"You want to try!"

"Maybe I should. I think you'd be more useful trying to get into that cypher. It might have recognised me as Sayker Gerit, but that's all it's done. It looks to me as though there's more levels of security on it. Let *me* talk to Mig."

Doon eyes him for a long moment, then points to the far end of the bridge. "All right," she says, "but go over there and do it. You're starting to annoy me again."

"Fine." Kai spreads his hands in surrender before leading Mig away.

Finding a vacant spot on the cramped floor, he invites Mig to sit.

"Let's start with how many floors you searched," he says when Mig settles in beside him.

"Three. Like you said there'd be."

"Anything special you can remember about any of them?"

"Like?" she prompts.

"Like..." Kai thinks a moment, trying to decide how best to phrase the question he has in mind. Be honest, Doon said. So he was. "Did you see any dead people for one?"

"What a stupid question. Why would they leave a dead body onboard?"

All right, so it *was* a stupid question. But it would be a terrible irony if he neglected to ask that one simple question because it seemed unlikely.

"Just checking."

Mig gives her head a shake. "You're not very good at this, are you?"

"I'm new. So, Mig, can you tell me what is on each floor?"

The kyne's eyes widen. "Everything?"

"No. No. I mean in general. What is each floor used for?"

"Oh, I see. So," Mig begins, "on the floor below this one there's a lot of instruments, cyphers... things like that. And more of those panel things we saw outside the bridge. On the floor below that a lot of rooms with beds in them. And the floor below that is mostly a big empty space."

"Just empty?"

Mig nods. "Except for all the cables running up the walls and this big platform type thing hanging over it."

That wasn't much to go on. Clearly there *is* a trick in questioning Mig effectively. Doon is already working on the cyphers and if she can't breach the ones on the bridge, it's unlikely she'll be able to breach any of the others. Empty spaces aren't going to tell them much. Kai decides to concentrate on the living quarters. It's there, or in the hospital, where any sick crew member would have spent the last days of their life.

"Did you see a room with more than a few beds in it? Maybe a room with medicines in it?"

"You mean a hospital? I think so. It's on the same floor as all the other rooms with beds." She points over her shoulder. "Down that end of the ship."

"What can you tell me about it?"

Mig shrugs. "I've never seen a hospital before. I don't know what one's supposed to look like. It had a lot of beds. They were lined up on either side of the room and there was something that looked like a vis maybe over each of the beds. A lot of cabinets and strange looking instruments everywhere."

That sounded like the hospital all right. It would probably be worth their while having Mig take them there. Three sets of eyes searching would certainly be more effective than one young one's.

"Pautune!" Doon curses and thumps the cypher in front of her. "I can't get past the logo."

"Maybe if you try a little longer," Kai suggests.

"Look," she grumbles, turning to face him. "I only know so many ways *to* try. Maybe Gaed could do it, but you won't get him inside *The Nether*."

"Then it's the hospital," Kai decides, rising. "Mig found the hospital. I think we should go there."

Doon swings around in her seat. "Not me. That's the one place I *will* not go. Sure! Sure!" she continues, fending off any protest from Kai. "I'm not convinced there ever was a plague. But what if there was? That's where they'll have taken the sick." She waves both hands in front of her. "I am not going to go anywhere near any beds they were lying on."

"Doon," Kai says with a smile. "The Dosers will have flashed all the bedding. There won't—" He's interrupted by a tug on his sleeve. "What?" he asks, glancing down impatiently at Mig.

"The Dosers didn't flash anything."

No! Could he have sent the little kyne into a contaminated room?

"What do you mean, Mig?" Bending onto one knee, he latches onto the young one's shoulders.

"It's all still there. All the coverings. All the pillows. Everything. Nothing's been moved."

"Well, that's just wonderful!" Doon bawls. "*Now* what do we do? We can't go back into the ward. We could infect *everyone*." Leaping from her seat, she turns on Kai, face flushed and menacing. "I should never have listened to you."

Mig isn't paying either one of them any attention. "I wish I could make a bed as tidy as those," she says, cutting off any reply Kai could have made.

His hands tighten on the kyne's shoulders. "What was that?"

Even Doon seems to have taken something from Mig's words. She's gone uncharacteristically silent.

"Ush was never happy with me. I always made such a mess making my bed. All the beds in the hospital were made just the way Ush likes them."

"What about the beds in the crew's quarters, the rooms where there weren't so many beds all in one place?" Kai asks.

"Oh, they were just the same. All made up neat like Ush's."

Releasing Mig's shoulder, Kai turns to Doon. She's looking down, blank-faced, at the little kyne.

"They were never sick," she says at last, eyes tracking Kai as he rises. "Not a single one of them."

***

"I don't know," Gaed says. He's sitting on the edge of the platform, relacing a boot, on the very spot where Doon had waited for Kai. Mig has wandered off, exploring, leaving Kai alone with Gaed and Doon.

"It's not much proof if you ask me," Gaed continues, then jerks his head at Kai. "Certainly not the type of proof he's supposed to have come here to find. Anyway, Mig could be making it all up."

Doon glares menacingly down at the top of her brother's head. "When has Mig *ever* made anything up? Everyone knows she tells us exactly what she sees. Perfectly made beds, Gaed! In the hospital *and* the crew's quarters! Don't try to tell me that after the Dosers flashed contaminated bedding, they brought in new bedding and made up the beds all nice and tidy for *no one*."

"One of you could have set it up that way," Gaed contends, rising. "*I'm* not saying that, but—"

"Yes, that's right. Kai and I sneaked into a bunker we never knew existed carrying a huge stack of bedding, then climbed up a ridiculously steep and slippery slide we also didn't know existed to make up a whole bunch of beds on the off-chance that Mig would be the one to stumble into those rooms and see them. I can see that. *Can't you?*"

Kai is caught by surprise, suddenly realising she's talking to him. "It's ridiculous. Mig saw what she said she saw and," he says, seeking out the young one in the open field, "I don't think she even understands the importance of what she saw."

"I don't think so, either," Doon agrees. "So, what do we do now? Tell Ceilu? The rest of them?"

"Is there some question about that?" Kai asks, glancing from Doon to Gaed.

"No," Doon replies hesitantly, "it's just that... like Gaed said... we haven't actually *proved* the crew was alive when they returned. I mean... you've proved it to me, but," she shrugs, "proving it to everyone else is going to be a different matter."

"That's an understatement," Gaed mutters. "I'm not sure you've proved it to me."

When Doon opens her mouth, Kai raises a hand to ward off further argument. "Gaed's right about some things, Doon. I sincerely doubt that what Ro sent me here to find are rooms full of made beds. There's someone here I'm supposed to approach, someone I can *influence*. Someone who *can* prove what happened here."

"Sorry, you're on your own there. I'm not even a wardlander. I wouldn't have any idea who that could be."

"I thought it must have been Pilot Jak but it isn't," Kai says. He's talking to himself, thinking things though aloud.

"There you are then," Doon replies nonetheless. "So, I suggest we assemble the same group again, those who voted to send us into The Cocoon, tell them what we found. Have them decide what to do now. Mig," she shouts, drawing the kyne's attention. "We're leaving." Grasping Gaed's arm, she starts them off for town. "I've been thinking about what you said earlier," she says to Kai. "If the Registrar at the Repository knew you really weren't Sayker Gerit, then someone at the quarantine station must have known, too."

Of course! Why hadn't he realised that himself? Someone must check the credentials of anyone coming into the station.

"Ro changed the official records somehow. She changed my pid." He's clutching at hul shoots and he knows it.

"But changing a pid would be a lot easier to do than changing an official record," Gaed reminds him, "especially the record of a Talker who was on *The Nether*."

"I'm missing something," Kai admits.

"You're missing a lot," Gaed says with a snort.

***

When Kai bypasses the direct route back to town and starts leading them up the long, winding track toward Jak Inopo's house, neither Gaed nor Doon question him. Kai trusts the old pilot and it's best that no one else knows what Mig has really been up to all morning. Mig manages the steep hill easily enough but by the time they reach the top, it's clear the day's exertions have taken their toll on her.

The old house looks exactly as Kai recollects; he could have last climbed down the ladder from the roof only yesterday. And Inopo doesn't seem all that surprised to see them. He shows them to some chairs arranged about the same old beaten-up table Kai remembers then, without interruption, allows Kai and Doon to tell him what they found.

"Ah," he says, smiling. "I wish I could have gone with you. But these old bones..." He slaps a knee and doesn't expound. "So, they probably weren't dead just like Ro thought. That leaves a problem, doesn't it?"

"Yes, it does," Kai agrees, leaning forward. "How to prove it conclusively."

"I was thinking something else, young pilot. I was thinking it leaves us with the problem of what *did* happen to them."

"The Pedorate killed them." Doon is seated next to the old pilot but across from Kai, so he's probably the only one to notice the full depth of bitterness in her eyes.

"Likely," Inopo agrees. "But why?"

"Yes, why." Kai's attention shifts to Mig. She's found a spot in the corner and appears to have fallen asleep. "You won't say anything about Mig?" he asks, turning back to Inopo.

The old pilot lifts a hand to scratch wearily at his head. "Got nothing *to* say." Rising, he stretches with an easiness Kai doesn't fail to notice and looks at Gaed. "I haven't eaten since this morning and, as I recall, it was Doon who did the cooking."

Gaed pushes up from his chair. "Long past time you learned to cook for yourself, old one," he grumps but, with the old pilot close behind him, makes for the sparse little kitchen.

Kai is surprised how well he recalls where everything is kept in Inopo's tiny kitchen when he goes to help Gaed. Doon passes behind him and, reaching into a cupboard overhead, starts to remove plates. One slips from her hands, shattering into a myriad of little pieces on the hard floor.

The noise wakes Mig.

"Sorry," Doon says self-consciously as, on hands and knees, she begins to gather the broken pieces.

Kai makes to help but Mig beats him to it.

"I'll do it," she says, jumping up.

"Time to eat now," Doon says with a light touch to Kai's arm.

Kai takes her message. Mig is a very reliable scout. She reports exactly what she sees *and* hears.

***

They leave Mig with Pilot Jak and continue into town. Not unexpectedly, Ceilu's greeting is cool and, although she's clearly surprised to see Gaed, says nothing. Instead, she takes up a chair for herself at the table. There's comfort in ignorance sometimes—even for someone like Ceilu. She sits back in her chair and, without interrupting, listens to Doon, who has taken it upon herself to be spokesperson.

Kai listens silently in admiration. Somehow, she manages to relate the entire story without once mentioning Mig's involvement.

"All right," Ceilu says the moment Doon finishes talking. "And just what do you want me to do?"

"That Registrar at the Repository knows more than she's telling and we need your help to get Kai back to Ularon City," Doon explains. She glances briefly in Kai's direction. "And I'm going with him."

First Kai has heard of it. But, all things considered, he won't mind the company. Doon is resourceful, trustworthy—now that she's stopped threatening to kill him.

Ceilu begins to laugh. "You can *try* to do whatever you want, Doon, but I can't get him to Ularon City. He *got* here. Let him figure out a way to get back."

"We know how to get back, Ceilu," Doon tells her.

She's pacing from place to place about the room. Watching her makes Kai's head spin.

"Through the Sub tunnel," she's saying. "But we need help to clear the tunnel where it's blocked on the other side of the quarantine station."

Ceilu just shakes her head. "Can't be done. We've tried in the past. It's blocked solid. Even Mig never managed to find a way through."

"But it can't have always been blocked," Kai objects. "Someone got those records through to Pilot Ro."

"Through the Sub tunnel?" Ceilu jeers. "It would take days. And they'd be in the dark the whole way."

"They might have had shine-sticks," Kai points out.

"And you're thinking it was Ush Kaidador," Ceilu replies with another shake of her head. "You're wrong. She died."

"What if they're not wrong?" Gaed breaks in.

Kai is surprised that it's Gaed who challenges Ceilu. Doon claims her brother likes to be on the winning side, but just when did Gaed decide that is Kai's side?

"Even if it wasn't my mother, someone escaped," Kai insists.

"The only *proof* you have of that is those records and who's to say they even exist," Ceilu fires back.

"But I *saw* them—"

"I believe they exist," Gaed says, cutting Kai off. "It's too elaborate a story to make up just to get him into the ward. He's nothing."

True. And Kai's of the same opinion, but he'd have preferred Gaed's observation to have been delivered with a little more tact.

Ceilu shrugs and turns to Doon. "If you're determined to do this, then I can let you have enough supplies to get the two of you to Ularon City. You can travel through the tunnel to the station and after that, you'll have to go overland."

"Overland," Doon snorts. "Just how do you expect us to get over The Range?"

"Go through it. Along the Urban line *he* rode to get in," Ceilu replies, glancing at Kai. "There's got to be a lineside path."

Abruptly Doon stops pacing to challenge Ceilu. "What if there is? We'll be seen!"

Stepping forward, Kai pulls Doon to his side. "We'll take it."

"But—" Doon begins with a stammer.

"We can travel by night. We'll need clothes," Kai tells Ceilu, casting an eye over Doon's colourful Phane attire, "for both of us."

"Something can be arranged," Ceilu agrees.

She's being too accommodating. Of course! His and Doon's departure provides the perfect solution to at least one of her problems. Just what do you do with two people who you're not quite sure you want walking around, potentially contaminating an entire town? She'll be left with Gaed if she discovers that he also ventured inside The Cocoon. But one potential plague carrier is better than three potential plague carriers any day.

"Then you'd better make the same arrangements for me," Gaed speaks up. "I'm going with them."

Make that no potential plague carriers...

***

"Would you call your mother a strong one?"

All three of them have been awake for some time now, sheltering among a scattering of large boulders on the bank of a small stream where they stopped at the first sign of light in the cloudless sky. They passed through the tunnel and emerged into the ancillary building on the platform outside the quarantine station just as night was descending, replaced the hatch so it fit as neatly and tidily as before and secreted Doon's small blade underneath the seat of the wooden bench. From there, it was a hard and fast walk through the night. For Kai, the worst part was the long slow trek lineside through the tunnel. In the darkness, it should have been easier to forget the crushing weight of rock overhead. Should have been!

"Why do you ask?" The afternoon sun is directing little sparks of light off the surface of the still water, intermittently blinding Kai in one eye.

For a while now Doon's been sitting and staring at him, only looking away occasionally to pull and drag at her unfamiliar clothes. True to her word, Ceilu found them more appropriate attire along with three worn but serviceable bags to carry the small quantity of rations she permitted. Although Kai feels more at home in Journer garb, even if his pid doesn't match it, it's clear Doon isn't taking to the restrictive clothing. She and Gaed look too young and scrawny but their Lycea uniforms should get them through if no one examines the wearers too closely.

"She's thinking this is too hard a walk for an old one like Ush Kaidador," Gaed says. Over the last day Gaed has taken to answering for his sister, a habit that's starting to grate on Kai's nerves. Gaed pitches another pebble into the stream. It lands with a little splash; save for their voices, it's the only sound around.

"She was strong enough. Besides," Kai says, "she may not have had to walk in the open. She could have had enough shine-sticks and supplies to have gone through the Sub tunnel."

"Blocked," Gaed says casually. "Ceilu is right about that."

"Now," Kai reminds him. "The roof could have collapsed or the Pedorate sealed it *after* she'd gone through."

Gaed simply shrugs.

"Then who did she get the sticks and supplies from?" Doon prods. There are leaves tangled up in her hair from this morning's brief spell of sleep on the rough ground.

Kai raises a hand to wipe a sticky film of sweat from his face. Despite the shade they've found, it's hot. Too hot for any sane Journer to be traipsing around in the open. And Doon's interrogation is making him feel even hotter.

"How do you expect me to know that?"

Gaed eases himself onto his feet. "Whether it was your mother or not, whoever made it to Ularon City had help. If we find them, we can ask."

"If?" Kai says, glancing up to question the young Phane.

Gaed pitches another pebble into the stream. "You don't know where they are."

"No," Kai agrees, catching Doon steal a look at her brother, "but Registrar Brawse knows *something*. So we go to the Repository."

"How?" Doon asks.

Kai frowns. "What do you mean 'how'?"

"Doon can't travel on an Urban," Gaed explains.

"Everyone can travel on an Urban."

Gaed bends to collect another stone. "Need a pid to travel, don't you?" He pitches the stone and it lands with a ping on a large boulder mid-stream, bounces off and sinks beneath the surface of the still water.

"Of course you do. Everyone's got a—"

"Not me," Doon says, interrupting. "I had it scrambled. Deactivated. Officially, I'm one dead Journer to the Pedorate."

"You, too?" Kai asks of Gaed, astonished.

This time Gaed doesn't get to answer ahead of his sister. "Don't be ridiculous," Doon says. "Gaed would never do a thing like that." She leans in close to whisper. "Remember what I told you about Gaed and the winning side?"

Kai has never heard of anyone doing such a thing before. "Why would you do that?"

"Because I could. I belong to me!" Doon pokes a slim finger into her slim chest. "I don't belong to the Pedorate."

"But—"

"I told her not to do it," Gaed says evenly. "She didn't listen. Never does. So," he continues, glancing down at Kai, "how are you going to get us to the Repository?"

"We'll walk." He looks into the distance. Toward Ularon City. Can't see it yet, of course. Even if they weren't hiding out in the little stream valley, it would still be impossible to see the buildings yet. They haven't gone far enough. Can they walk it all the way to the Repository? They are young. They have the stamina. But do they have the skills to evade detection?

He turns back to look at his two youthful companions. Phanes. In the end, worrying on their success or failure is pointless. The skills of these two brash Phanes are all he has to rely on.

"Why have you never left before?" he asks, almost casually. "If we can walk it, so could many others from the ward. You've known about the tunnel for a while. Seems to me you could have been getting people out to some place safe."

Abandoning his game with the stone, Gaed lowers himself to the ground beside Kai. "And just where might that safe place be, Pilot? Ularon City? Where could so many of us hide? The Gleaner ward between? Who there wouldn't turn us in, fearing we've brought the plague? Some other Pedoran sector?"

"How could we get there?" Doon chimes in. "Can't have us all ride an Urban or a Sub without getting discovered? Walk? Too far? And we did get some away until the Pedorate Council blockaded the bay. That fence back there," Doon says, pointing back the way they had come, "it's not the real barrier. The real barrier is our circumstances." She lowers her eyes and begins to pick at a patch of spindly grass by her feet. "I think Ceilu's wrong about a lot of things, but not about that. We can't all escape through the tunnel and we all have to stick together. That's why only a few of us know the location of the tunnel."

"I wouldn't call a rusty hatch in the middle of an open field well hidden," Kai observes.

"I wouldn't call a rusty hatch with a ring of guards around it well camouflaged." Rising, Doon slings her small bag of provisions over chest and shoulder. "It'll be dark again soon," she says. "Time to go."

***

They skirt the villages and cultivated fields of Ularon-Vicinal, but track as close to the Urban line as possible; it's their sure guide back to Ularon City. But tracking so close to the line poses a problem they hadn't allowed for; the chance sighting by pilot or passenger of three obviously handheld lights moving purposefully toward the city might just raise an alarm in Ularon City. What would the Pedorate Council make of a report like that? Gleaners inexplicably working their fields in the dead of night? Or a small band running the plague cordon? It was Kai's decision to forgo their sticks and now, with only the waning moon Caspilla to steer them, they stumble in the dark, obliged to periodically adjust direction when the streak of light and whizz of sound from a passing Urban tells them they've drifted off course.

It's going to be a long, long walk. They'll be exhausted, dusty and dirty, when they get to Ularon City. It would be madness to start wandering the streets in daylight looking like the trio of wayfarers they are. They'll have to rest, plan the best route and best time to make their way to the Repository. And that means they'll have to hole up somewhere for a while. Their best option would be the terminus of the Sub line from Ularon City to Journer Ward Minor; it's unused, likely unfinished. Unfortunately, its whereabouts is also unknown. Kai isn't intimately familiar with the fringes of Ularon City, but he knows the location if not the details of most of the functioning stations, even the Subs. And he knows how well they're monitored. There's a Sub station—a very small one—that's never been equipped with a scruter. Traffic there is light, but they'll be noticed by anyone who happens to arrive at the station. It's a risk they'll just have to take. Perhaps with darkness as a shield, they can slip into the station and find a place to hide before they're observed. They'll have to start out again before daylight though to arrive at the Repository around dawn to be sure to catch the Registrar alone. It'll be easier on Gaed and Doon that way, too; neither Ceilu nor Kai thought to try and equip them with U-visors.

"Lights," Doon calls.

She's spotted the glow of Ularon City in the distance. A thread of lights strung like a fine Pedoran necklace against the horizon.

From this far away, the city looks almost beautiful. But she's a deceiver. Up-close, she's something else.

Kai moves up to take the lead. His two Phane companions aren't patient types. Once they get to Ularon City, he's going to have a task ahead of him keeping them still and quiet until it's safe to start making their way to the Repository.

***

"Stop shushing me. There's no one here," Doon informs Gaed. "We're all alone." She turns to Kai and smiles.

He can see her teeth flash in the light of a bilious yellow glow.

"You did well. This is a great place to hide."

"You sound surprised!"

So is he. But better not to have his companions know that.

"It's a dump," Gaed declares. He kicks at a loose piece of trash littering the platform. "Filthy. Who uses this station?"

"We're in a Preserver sector."

They had descended to the platform through a small entrance Kai almost missed. The street, little more than a lane, was dark, deserted, neglected. The Preservers who live in this sector stir little during the day; they're night-workers, leaving home before dusk and returning just after dawn. The station, silent now, will be packed soon after daybreak and the Subs will be running nonstop for some time.

"The lights are barely working," Gaed observes. "And what in pautune is wrong with this?" He struts backward and forward in front of Kai, disrupting the twitching lines of a run-board. Each time he passes through, there's a sharp little crackle.

Doon comes wandering up. "Looks busted to me, Gaed," she says casually.

"Wonderful," Gaed snaps. "And *this* is a *Preserver* sector?"

Kai's just as surprised by the condition of the station but, all things considered, its raggedness plays in their favour. It's just the sort of place he was hoping to find.

"We won't stay long, Gaed. Just try to get some sleep."

"Good idea," Doon says, dropping to the floor to snare a patch, perhaps the only patch, of clean wall to rest against.

Kai nabs a place beside her and closes his eyes, hoping to dissuade Gaed's talk. The strategy seems successful because the next thing Kai knows he's waking with a start. For a moment he's concerned they've overslept but the station is as deserted as before.

"Come on," he says, nudging Doon, whose head is lolling against his shoulder. "Gaed?"

Doon's brother emerges around a dingy corner. "I hope you're going to tell me it's time to go."

"Your hopes are realised," Kai replies, easing himself up from the floor.

***

Saera is seated at her desk, lost in dark thought. She should be focusing on her work. She should be doing anything but aimlessly agonising. A drift of motion on the small vis by her desk catches her attention. She strains to focus with eyes that have already begun their slow decline.

Visitors. This early? Three of them. One a Journer Pilot; the others, two students from the Lycea. She doesn't know whether to be relieved or scared out of her wits. Has Veeda sent them or, despite the early hour, have they come on some harmless business of their own?

She rises from her chair, disturbing the sleeping mutz, to weave through the towering shelving. The mutz follows, its claws tapping directly behind her.

She'll have to let them in. It will look strange if she denies them even one of the minor functions of the Repository. Of course, if they fail to present the proper authorisation, she can send them on their way. But not *before*.

Tilting her head, she trains her eyes on the main vis just inside the entrance. "Please identify yourself." She's speaking officiously as anyone arriving without an appointment would expect.

"Registrar Brawse?"

The voice is short. Sharp. Familiar. She can't immediately place it until...

"We met some days ago, Registrar."

When Saera peers more closely into the vis, her legs threaten to buckle. She's all too aware of her heart—pounding—pounding.

Talker Gerit! *Talker Gerit in Journer uniform!* She's trapped. No, she was already trapped the moment she allowed Veeda into her quarters. Very likely she's been discovered. It's almost a relief. *Almost.* Ush is dead; they can't touch her. But Gove is still out there!

Even so, she'll have to let them in.

"Please enter," she says, falling again on standard patter. The sound she makes is thin, quavering. Did he notice? "And please close the gates behind you."

She stands in the blaring morning sun at the head of the forecourt, mutz at her heel, hand raised to shade her eyes, watching as the smallest of the Journers shuts the gates behind her. The pilot she already knows, so she focuses on the two yellow-haired Lycean students as they approach. They're thin, hollow-faced to the point of looking malnourished and appear almost too young to be students. More telling still, their bearing seems a little off, not to mention the state of their uniforms, dusty and noticeably worn. Like the pilot, both are shouldering small bags slung cross-wise over chest and shoulder but, unlike the pilot, neither are wearing U-visors; a rare sight, indeed, in Ularon City. Standing aside, she admits them into the Repository. No sooner does she close the doors, then the Talker removes his visor and begins to speak.

"This is Journer Doon Gaed'owin," he says, warily eyeing the mutz by Saera's feet, "and her brother, Journer Gaed Doo'naib. My name is Pilot Kai Astada."

She's as lost for thoughts as words. Kai Astada! Usha Kaidador's son!

The rays streaming in through the broad glass in the doorway are obscuring the pilot's face. Slowly, with effort, she walks around the pilot, obliging him to turn into shadow. Saera stares unapologetically into his face...at the dark eyes, the high cheekbones and the mouth that, by nature, curves slightly up at the corners. What she sees—and what she would have seen before had she been looking for it—is the face of Usha Kaidador. This pilot is not lying. Ush Kaidador was no Pedorate minion. But it isn't Ush Kaidador standing in front of her now.

"If you'll come this way," she says, starting out ahead of them on shaking legs. "I believe we'll be more comfortable in the reading room." The mutz begins to follow.

The reading room! Her fancy name for the narrowish rectangular room she set aside along one side of the Repository. She paid for its furnishing out of her own credit; scavenged plants and pots and non-reflective paint for the walls and had the glass of the large windows tinted to allow for just the right ingress of light. Her intent was to make visitors to the Repository feel more relaxed there. These three Journers will be the first to see it—and quite possibly the last.

"Please," she says, ushering her three visitors to a long, padded couch beneath the largest of the tinted windows. Ush's son opts for the middle of the couch and the two students settle on either side of him. She takes a seat for herself in a single chair, facing them over a low wooden table. The mutz settles down on the floor beside her. There are no cyphers in the reading room; no vis, either. Still, she allows Ush's pilot son a moment to complete his slow study of the room and the mutz, satisfying himself that they're not being watched or in any danger from the beast's lethally sharp teeth. She would have done the same.

"Kindly explain your presence here, Pilot Astada," she says at last, launching into the challenge that any loyal Pedorate would be expecting. "And, more importantly, why during your earlier visit, you represented yourself as a Talker."

"Registrar Brawse," Astada replies, turning his gaze on her as he rids himself of the small bag from his shoulder. "I think it's time we're honest with each other. You knew I wasn't a Talker. Sayker Gerit died on *The Nether*, so you couldn't possibly have lodged any documents formalising my visit to the quarantine station with the gabbers." He leans toward her. "I believe you're acquainted with a Preserver named Vee."

Confounded, Saera shakes her head. The first time she'd heard the name 'Sayker Gerit' was when Veeda told her that was who to expect. And she's never heard of a Talker, of any name, being on *The Nether*.

One of the Lycean students, the one Ush's son called Doon, speaks up. "You think we're Pedorate." She smiles. "And you couldn't be more wrong." Pointing to the student beside Astada, she then turns the finger to herself. "Him and me," she says, "we're what our friend Kai here calls Phanes."

Phanes! She should have seen it immediately. Yes, she did notice that they seemed too young and unpolished for the Lycea, but she hadn't looked closely for anything else. Now, as with Astada, she sees it. This time, she can't define exactly what 'it' is that allows her to acknowledge their 'Phaneness', but 'it' is there, lurking beneath the surface.

"Phanes are—"

"I know what Phanes are."

Astada's brief hesitation is replaced by a smile. The smile is warm, encouraging trust. "Of course, you do. You're the Registrar of the Repository."

Since the loss of Ush, she's become weary, so very weary. She had no idea how much she would miss Ush's company or just having someone near who knows the things she knows, someone with like hopes, like fears. If Kai Astada is not Pedorate, he's taken a grave risk in coming to her. She trusted Ush. She even trusted Veeda—to a point. How can she now not trust her own kind? It's a gamble but she decides to take it.

"More than that, Kai Astada. *I* am also Phane."

If he's Pedorate, she's not only condemned herself but Gove as well.

As one, the three Journers slump back into their seats. Doo'naib, the silent one, is sitting with his mouth open. Gaed'owin, the confident one, has latched her hand onto Pilot Astada's forearm, while Astada himself, seemingly oblivious to the pain the Phane must be inflicting, is staring at her, face devoid of all expression. If she just announced herself fresh from pautune, she'd have expected the same reaction.

"Seems we're all playing little games with identity," she says, glance skipping from Astada to each of the Phanes. "I was born Saera Govek. Perhaps you remember me?" Her eyes are on Ush's son now. The young Phanes would be too young to recall her time among them. "And now that I've had a moment to think about it, I believe I am acquainted with the Vee you mentioned. I know her as Veeda. Veeda Teimbo. The same," she says, anticipating the question Astada would have asked had he the self-possession to do it. "Eine Vidamore's daughter."

"The Duck Down Club," he says, blurting out the words like some sort of revelation.

"The *what?*" She has no idea what he's talking about.

"The Duck Down Club," he says again. "Vee is a member of the Duck Down Club. It's a... how can I put it?... a loose association of disgraced Journers." He twitches a shoulder, the gesture reminding Saera of someone shooing off a bothersome insect. "Supposedly."

"I'm afraid I've never heard of such a club."

"No, you wouldn't. Most Journers believe it's a myth, fabricated for the purpose of intimidation. *Measure* up or that's where you'll *end* up."

"Ah, yes, we have something similar at the Thika." Saera glances from one to the other of the young Phanes. "And how did you become associated with Pilot Astada?"

Ush's son pre-empts an answer. "You're the young one who used to live next door to me, aren't you? Osten Saerat's daughter? When I came to the Repository and saw you, something seemed... I don't know... familiar."

"You *know* her?" Journer Gaed'owin almost screeches. She hasn't let up on Astada's arm.

"I *knew* her," the pilot replies. "Her parents died when she was very young. I assumed she was sent to live with the Phanes. I never knew for sure. Never asked."

To Saera's ears, the admission sounds cold. Cold and entirely reasonable. "Why would you? Why would anyone?" She shrugs. "But you're correct. My brother and I were taken to the Phane village. Ush took us. You wouldn't remember that, I'm sure. But I do."

"No," Astada confesses, irritably shaking off Gaed'owin's persistent hold on his arm. "I don't have any memory of that at all. I do remember that my mother used to disappear a lot when I was young," he tells her. "I never thought much about it. That was just my mother."

Saera is of two minds if she should tell him the truth about his mother's own past. Seems though it's Astada, himself, who's called this the day for truths.

"There's something you should probably know about your mother, Pilot Astada."

To Saera's surprise, the pilot smiles. "If you're about to tell me that she's a Phane, don't bother. I just found that out for myself from Jak Inopo."

"Inopo?" Saera moves to the edge of her seat. "Jak Inopo is still alive?"

"Barely," the young Phane, Gaed'owin, volunteers. "Well, it's true," she says defensively when Astada's expression sours. "He's been around as long as The Range and he's twice as gnarly. The old gleat!"

A smile brushes Saera's lips and then is gone. Old Jak Inopo? Still alive!

"It was Inopo," Astada takes up, "who arranged for my mother's adoption."

"I wasn't aware of that," Saera says, lowering her eyes. "I only knew that she was Phane."

"Natural born?"

"I don't know," Saera replies, glancing up once more. "Confidentiality is—"

"Understood," Astada finishes for her.

"That's right. So, you see, it's entirely reasonable that when she escaped from the ward, she'd come to me."

"Well, I'll be! She *did* escape!"

Saera's gaze darts to the young male Phane.

"Some years ago, Journer Doo'naib," Saera tells him.

"How?" Astada asks. "I mean, how did she get out?"

"I assume you've come from the ward," Saera says, glance shifting from Doo'naib to his sister, "so the same way you did, I imagine. Through the Sub tunnel."

"It's blocked," the pilot tells her. "City-side of the quarantine station."

That's news to Saera. "It wasn't," she explains. "Not when Ush left the ward."

"We wondered about that," Astada replies. "But how did my mother know where to find you?"

Another small smile comes to Saera's lips. "There are ways to establish contact, Pilot. I don't know exactly how it works. Confidentially..." she says with a little shrug.

"Through that Duck Down Club you keep talking about," Journer Gaed'owin suggests, turning to Astada.

"Not them," Saera interjects. "If Ush had known they really existed, I'm sure she would have told me. Maybe they're part of it. Maybe not. They're certainly not all of it."

Journer Gaed'owin launches out of her seat, startling the mutz, and making it halfway to her feet before Astada pulls her back down by her sleeve.

"Look here, fancy pilot," she complains, tumbling back onto the couch. "People around here seem to be able to communicate with anyone they want but no one seems to know how it's done. I don't know about you, but that makes me feel a little uncomfortable." She points an accusing finger at Saera. "And so far, she's been pretty careful not to tell us much we didn't already know. Nothing much helpful anyway."

"She's told us who Vee is," Astada reminds her, "and we know that Vee's a member of the Duck Down Club. That means that the Director of the Lycea probably is, too."

"I never said that," Saera hurries to deny. "Just that Veeda is his daughter."

"See!" Journer Gaed'owin barks. "*More* evasion."

"As I see it," Doo'naib says, speaking up, "it's irrelevant if the Director is a member of this Duck Down Club or not. If he is, he's unlikely to admit it, isn't he? *Or* talk to us. So, *as I see it*," he repeats, directing a serious look at Saera, "it's up to you."

"I can only tell you so much," Saera explains. "Like you I suppose, I always believed what we were told about the fate of *The Nether*. Until Ush claimed otherwise. Oh, she had no proof of anything, not even that she'd actually been inside the quarantine station."

"Which station?" Astada asks.

"Which? Oh, yes. I mean the original station. The one on the dock."

"We've been there," Journer Gaed'owin tells her calmly.

"You've been *inside*?"

"Some days ago," Astada confirms. "We've been inside *The Nether* as well." He nods toward Gaed'owin. "She couldn't breach the cyphers."

"No," Saera agrees, "I expect she couldn't. What did you see there?"

"A tidy ship," Journer Gaed'owin snaps at her. "A *very* tidy ship and no sign whatsoever that anything bad had happened onboard."

"And that tells us something in itself."

"Yes, it does," Saera says, answering the pilot. "No one died of the plague on that ship. There *is* no plague. Never was."

"That's what he keeps saying." Journer Doo'naib once more. "And he's got *her* believing it now."

Her, Saera guesses, is his sister.

"That's what Ush came to tell me and I didn't believe it, either. Not at first. I felt she'd become confused somehow by what she'd seen or been told by someone inside the station. Then I began to start having doubts of my own. I knew Ush. I *trusted* her. So I decided to confide in someone who knew and trusted Ush as well as I did."

"Inopo?" Astada asks her.

"Jak Inopo! No, of course not. The ward was locked down. I couldn't contact anyone inside it." Looking down, Saera notices for the first time that her fingers are tightly interlaced on her lap. She's been wringing her hands. "I told my brother," she says, uncurling fingers that she hadn't even realised were numb.

The three Journers trade wary glances and Saera waits for the inevitable question, loath to hear it. Her answer will further implicate Gove. She's telling herself that she has to have faith in these three Journers, that they're on the *same* side.

"Gove Saerat," she explains.

"I barely remember Gove. But I can't see how—"

She cuts Astada off. "You know him as Julyen Koale."

"Doser Koale?" The pilot is shouting at her now. "The Doser in charge of the quarantine station?"

"Yes, but he wasn't at the station then. Before that, he was a consulting Doser to the Lycea."

Astada's dark eyes narrow. "Meaning?"

"Meaning he had access to all the imaging that was ever done on each of the graduating students and he started looking very closely into the records of all the students, particularly those students who had relatives on *The Nether*. Deaders like you, Pilot Astada."

"And?"

"And he began to notice that there were certain irregularities in the postings. Sometimes graduates with only Urban aptitudes were given postings to Continentals. Others with obvious Continental aptitudes were given postings to Urbans—"

"And some," Astada says, interrupting her, "with Urban or Continental aptitudes were given postings to a Sub?"

"That's right."

"And it only happened to the deaders?"

Saera nods, then is distracted as Journer Gaed'owin begins fluttering her hands in the air.

"Just a moment. I don't understand what that's got to do with anything."

"Nor do I," Journer Doo'naib agrees, sounding almost bored.

"Control," Saera replies. "Put those less inclined to think and *question* for themselves in the more prestigious positions and those who *are* inclined to think and question in positions where they're too busy or too remote to have the time and connections to do it. Understand?"

"If you say so," Gaed'owin mutters, stubbornly linking her arms over her chest.

"Well," Saera continues, "Gove gave a copy of that imaging to me and I took it to Director Vidamore. I suppose you could say I challenged him with it."

"The Director doesn't determine a Journer's posting," Astada tells her.

Saera shrugs. "No," she agrees. "Ush told us that."

"So what are you trying to say?" Journer Gaed'owin presses her. "That Kai should have been assigned to a Continental?"

"That's exactly what I'm saying."

"But he wasn't. So going to Vidamore did nothing."

"That's what I thought at first. But almost a year to the day after I turned over those records, Veeda came to my quarters, asking me to obtain the same records for the current class of graduates. I guess Vidamore *was* suspicious, after all." She lowers her gaze to the mutz; it has settled back down again, head resting heavily on her foot. "But I couldn't give her anything. Gove wasn't consulting for the Lycea anymore."

"He'd already been given the posting at the station?" Astada asks.

Saera smiles. "Given? Not exactly. He manoeuvred very hard to obtain it. It was there he found the proof Ush had been looking for."

"What proof?"

Saera turns to Doo'naib. "The Dosers' reports on everyone who was on *The Nether* taken *after* they returned well and truly alive."

Astada draws her attention. "I've seen those reports at the Duck Down Club."

"That's not possible. I turned them over to Veeda."

"And I told you Vee is a member of the Duck Down Club and the Duck Down Club sent me to *you*."

"I didn't know that. Our communications are—"

"Don't say it," Gaed'owin moans. "You know if you people actually talked to one another other, it could save a lot of time and effort."

"It's not the way it works."

"So I'm beginning to realise. Go on," Gaed'owin says, relaxing her crossed arms. "Then what?"

The young Phane must have her uses, otherwise Astada wouldn't have brought her, but she's sorely starting to get under Saera's skin.

"Some months after I turned over the reports," she continues, "Veeda contacted me again and asked me to devise a way to get someone, a Talker, into the quarantine station without going through official channels. When she asked me to do that, I thought they'd discovered it was Gove who'd given me the files—"

Astada interrupts. "The station itself wasn't important. I came across our friend Vee again, working at the quarantine station as a Preserver. It was Vee who showed me the Sub tunnel into the ward under the station."

"The tunnel is under the station?" Saera blurts out, looking to the Phanes for confirmation. "When Ush came through, there *was* no quarantine station there. I told Veeda nothing about Ush or the tunnel she came through. If Ush and I... and I'm guessing even Gove... didn't know the station is directly on top of the Sub tunnel, then how did she?"

"The Duck Down Club," Gaed'owin says with a loud sigh. "You said it was full of Sub pilots, didn't you?" she adds when Astada glares at her. "Maybe they spread the word about a new line going in." She switches her attention to her brother. "Before all this happened with *The Nether*, I mean."

Doo'naib simply shrugs. "Sounds as reasonable as anything so far."

"Seems to me, Registrar," Gaed'owin takes up, "that Vee and your brother have been working right under each other's noses unaware they're on the same side. Everyone is watching out for someone else, so no one talks to anyone! That's a fine system. Very efficient. Effective, too, judging by what I've seen."

"It's not the *best* system," Saera concedes, fixing the young Phane with a blunt gaze, "but it has kept us invisible. And I *am* talking to you now, Journer Gaed'owin. I didn't have to."

"Good point, Doon," her brother interjects. "So Vee has asked you to get a Talker into the station. Then what?"

"Then I contacted Gove. Like I told you, I was suspicious that Veeda knew the reports had come from him, so I asked him what I should do." She pauses for a moment. Talking about it has brought all the old fears she's battled so hard to repress perilously close to the surface. "I thought it was a bad idea, but agreed with his advice to go through with it. Then someone arrived like Veeda said they would. I thought she meant someone disguised as a Talker. I never expected a *real* Talker. And when I saw you," her focus shifts to Astada, "that's exactly what I thought you were."

"You didn't recognise the name Sayker Gerit?" Astada asks her.

"No. I've never heard there was a Talker on *The Nether*. And I only looked at the files once... the day Gove brought them. And the only names I paid any real attention to were Minor Journer... *our* people. A lot had happened that day and it never occurred to me that I *should* memorise any of the other names."

"And you never looked at those files again?"

Out of the corner of her eye, Saera is aware of Gaed'owin looking fitfully from her to Astada as they speak. "Never. I was frightened by what I saw, so I hid them. Veeda never told me the details of the plan. She never told me anything about the Talker they'd be sending. She just told me that I had to get a Talker to the quarantine station. Why Sayker Gerit, Pilot Astada? You knew who he was. Wasn't that a dangerous risk to take?"

To Saera's surprise, Astada smiles.

"I wasn't what you'd call a willing party to Veeda's plan. They wanted me because they said I had influence. What and with who, I don't know. And I'd never heard of Sayker Gerit, either. I—"

"But you saw the files. In the Duck Down Club. You just told me."

"I wasn't shown *all* the files. Just the *Journer* files."

"Only those? I don't understand. I gave Veeda the files for everyone who was on *The Nether*."

"Maybe so," Astada tells her, "but that's not what they showed me. But if I'd known I was using the pid of someone on *The Nether*, someone who supposedly died of the plague, then it's unlikely I'd have even tried. They'd know that. And Gerit's pid had its uses. It got us access to the cyphers on *The Nether*. But there was a layer of security they didn't seem to be counting on. The cyphers were useless to us. Still, that's how I realised Sayker Gerit must have been on *The Nether*. And that's what prompted me to suspect that *you* knew it, too."

Saera's gaze wanders from face to face. Astada looks... what?... hopeful perhaps; Gaed'owin, predictably still suspicious. And her brother? Of the three, he remains the most difficult for Saera to read.

"And so you came back here," she says at last, "hoping I could give you the answers you're looking for? I'm sorry," she says, edging back in her seat, "but I can't help you. I've told you everything I know."

"Not everything," Astada corrects her. "For one thing, you haven't explained how your brother got those files?"

No, she hasn't. What harm can it do now? She's already implicated Gove and the only other party involved is dead.

"Gove had a friend... a very good friend," she begins. "They'd even talked about marriage. Hetil was a Doser, too, and one of the first Dosers assigned to the quarantine station... the original station."

"Pilot Jak claims that every one of them contracted the plague and died," Astada tells her.

Saera nods. "Gove was consulting to the Lycea at the time and Ush had just gotten out of the ward. I don't know if it was Hetil's death or what he found in the Lycea records that gave Gove the idea to manoeuvre for the posting to the new quarantine station. That got him access to the ward and to the old station."

"We've been there, too," Journer Gaed'owin says.

There's an air of contempt in her voice that Saera's coming to expect.

"Unless he's better at bypassing cypher security than we are, he'd have been disappointed with what he found."

"You're right, Journer Gaed'owin. He couldn't breach the cypher security, either. But the security on the Dosers' quarters was far less sophisticated and he got into Hetil's quarters relatively easily."

"The *paper* files?" Astada prompts.

"The last thing Gove or *anyone* would expect to find." She looks toward Gaed'owin. "I'm sure you'd be happier if I could tell you what caused Hetil to become suspicious enough to keep paper records of her own, but I can't. Nor could Gove. But it seems that all those Dosers died the same way the crew of *The Nether* died. And it wasn't from any plague."

All three of her visitors turn quiet, even Journer Gaed'owin, who seems to have an opinion about everything.

It's Astada who finally breaks the silence. "If your brother knows with certainty that the crew of *The Nether* didn't die of any plague, then what are they working on at the station?"

Gaed'owin's recovered her composure and tacks on a question of her own. "And why?"

"The 'what' is hard to explain. Even Gove isn't really sure what they're looking at. He thinks it's an ancient virus of some sort. One that was contained long ago. One the Pedorate Council is hoping none of the Dosers recognise. So far, they haven't. And that's probably why all the Dosers sent to the station are young, relatively inexperienced."

Gaed'owin lurches to her feet, prompting the mutz to emit a throaty growl. The warning stills the Phane's advance, but it doesn't still her tongue.

"That's a fine story, Registrar," she says, wrenching up the sleeve of her uniform to expose bare skin. "But if your brother is working *with* us, then perhaps you can explain what he's been counterjecting us with these past years?"

Reaching out, Saera takes a hold of the young Phane's forearm to examine the speckling of healed prick marks near the crease of her inner elbow. "I can," she says, raising her eyes and releasing Gaed'owin's arm. "Supplements. Gove can't do much about the shortage of food in the ward, but he can try to keep you all alive. Unfortunately he's been unable to do anything for the Journers in Major. He has no authority there."

The young Phane says nothing and Astada pulls his companion back into her seat.

"You haven't answered Doon's earlier question," he says. "If the plague doesn't exist, then why have they gone to such trouble to cordon off the Journer wards?"

"It's just supposition," Saera replies. "We could be wrong. But Gove and I think... Ush, too... that the cordoning off of the Journer wards is just a ploy. A way to control the Journers—"

"I told you," Gaed'owin barks. "*The Pedorate want us dead.* Even she thinks so."

"I doubt they want us all dead, Journer Gaed'owin. *You* all dead," she says, conceding that these three Journers aren't likely to number her among their caste. "The Pedorate still need Journers."

"Subs and Urbans maybe," Doo'naib suggests, shrugging when his sister turns a surprised look at him behind Astada's back. "Perhaps a few Continentals from the marginals—"

"But why, Saera?" Astada asks, interrupting his young companion. "What have we done? Why are we such a threat to them?"

Saera shakes her head. "Seems that's what you were sent to find out."

"*Seems* they sent the wrong person," Gaed'owin quips. "Well, it does," she hurries to say when all eyes turn to her. "It's what we're all thinking."

"One last thing," Astada says, recapturing Saera's attention.

"All right." She's already anticipating what the pilot is about to ask, surprised really that it has taken this long.

"Where are you hiding my mother?"

And there it is.

Saera takes a brief moment to consider the best, the kindest way to tell him about Ush. "The night Gove brought those reports to me," she begins, "the ones he found in Hetil's quarters... remember I told you that a lot had happened that day? It was to do with Ush. She'd died earlier that night. I'm sorry... I..."

She doesn't finish, her thoughts disturbed by Journer Gaed'owin, who has gently placed her hand on the young pilot's forearm. Phanes! Saera shouldn't have allowed herself to be fooled.

"*I've* got something more to ask," Gaed'owin says after a moment.

Silently, Saera sighs. She thought Astada had put an end to the Phane's relentless questions.

"If there is no plague, then what happened to all the people your brother took from our ward?"

"I," Saera stammers, astonished, "I didn't know anyone *was* taken?"

"I have an idea," Astada interjects. "I suspect your brother hasn't told you everything, Saera. Not only is he keeping the Journers in the ward alive but, when he can, he's getting some of them out."

"That's something you'd better start thinking about yourself, Pilot Kai," Doo'naib says, speaking up. "How long do you think it's going to take for the Pedorate Council to discover that there's someone walking around using the name of a Talker who's supposed to have died on *The Nether*?"

"He's right," Saera agrees. "You've been lucky. Why in pautune did the Duck Down Club give you *that* name?"

Journer Gaed'owin answers with a dry little laugh. "Is everyone here stupid? They thought it would get him access to the cyphers like Kai said. But it's really more than that. By giving him Gerit's name, they have him cornered. If Kai ever wants to be a Journer again, then he's *got* to keep working for them. Have to admire that kind of thinking. It's brilliant."

***

The Registrar has been gone a long time and Kai is starting to worry. Ceilu only permitted them enough food and water to get to Ularon City; after that, she said, they'd have to fend for themselves. Now they need food and water to get back and the Registrar has promised to get it for them. Kai didn't ask how; he prefers not to know. She left them among the shelving-cum-office in the main section of the Repository. Her Lycea uniform concealed beneath dusty coveralls, it's Doon's job to deflect any unannounced visitors. She's a 'student from the Thika, helping out' and 'no, I'm sorry, the Registrar has stepped out on an errand, but if you'd care to return later the Registrar will attend to your request'. So far, Doon's skills at deception haven't been tested. She's sitting in the Registrar's chair, grubby boots flung across the Registrar's desk, looking pleased with her new, if short-lived, position.

"Do you think it's her you were sent to find?" Doon asks, turning to Kai. "Registrar Brawse? Saera whatever her name is?"

"Weren't you listening earlier?" Gaed snaps. While Doon's been fidgeting with the Registrar's cypher, ignoring every one of Kai's entreaties to stop, Gaed has passed the time pacing about among the shelves, pausing periodically to absently read a label. "Veeda's been in communication with the Registrar? How can it possibly be her?"

"Weren't *you* listening?" Doon fires back, "No one here is *communicating* with anyone. They just pop in and out, dispensing orders... or," she nods toward Kai, "in his case, threats. It's more likely to be her brother. He's the one who provided the evidence."

"I can't see it," Kai replies. He'd found himself a spot on the floor, propped his back against a large box behind the Registrar's desk with the smelly mutz settling in immediately beside him. Neither have moved since. The hulking beast, with its scraggy grey fur that reeks of mildew and its absurdly tiny pink eyes, seems to like him. "They said I was to find someone I have influence with. I only vaguely remember Saera. And I hardly remember her brother at all."

"Then it has to be your mother," Gaed suggests, staying his endless pacing. "As Doon is so fond of pointing out, they don't communicate with each other very well. They could have sent you into the ward, not realising she was already in Ularon City."

"Very likely," Kai agrees. "Seems I didn't know my mother as well as I thought I did."

"What makes you think it was any of them?" Doon interjects. "Just because they say it was someone you have influence with doesn't mean it's so." She shrugs. "Could be anyone. Or no one. Well? It's possible, isn't it? If you ask me what this outfit of theirs needs is a new leader. No, wait. I take that back." Her boots drop to the floor with a thud. "What this outfit needs is *a* leader... because I don't think they've got one."

"Volunteering?"

"Me?" Doon snorts at Gaed's goading. "Hardly. I'm more of a hands-on person, wouldn't you agree? I mean... all this sneaking around... passing documents backward and forward... people running here and there pretending to be something they're not. What's it got them?"

Kai eyes her attire top to toe.

"Yes, well..." she says, catching him. "Then you *do* see what I mean? If the Pedorate is ever to be overthrown, then someone... *anyone*... needs to take charge."

"Who said anything about overthrowing the Pedorate?" Kai asks.

"Pilot Astada, what do you think you've been doing these last few days? Picking bauma?"

"I..."

"Yes?" Doon prompts him, leaning forward, hands on knees.

"Pautune!" her brother mutters.

Rising, Doon walks to Gaed and gives him a rap on the head. "You never think things through! But I can confirm a couple of things for you, Pilot Kai. The Registrar told you at least one truth the day she sent you to the quarantine station. And I'm right about the Pedorate."

"What do you mean?" Kai asks, eyes following Doon back to the Registrar's desk.

"She *is* responsible for the plague statistics. There's a stack of them right here."

"Doon," Kai barks, jumping to his feet. "I told you to stop touching that cypher."

"Why? The Registrar put me in charge, didn't she?" Doon asks with a mischievous smile. "Don't tell me you're not curious. Come look. Read the numbers for yourself." She waves Kai forward.

"Since there's no plague, then what, if not the Pedorate itself, is killing us off?"

Despite his better judgement, Kai moves to lean in over Doon's shoulder, the mutz shambling behind. Even Gaed steps up to stand beside Kai and watch the long line of names and ident numbers scroll by.

"And this is just the latest list," Doon is saying.

"Wait! Go back," Kai orders, grasping her hand. "There."

Henneh! It's Henneh's name, he sees. Dead! But she *can't* be dead. Not of the plague.

"What's wrong?" Doon asks over her shoulder.

Kai isn't really listening. He's trying to make sense of what he's looking at. If Henneh is really dead, the plague wasn't responsible; it couldn't have taken her that quickly. Maybe she's still alive somewhere, pid scrambled just like his, living her life under an assumed name, an assumed caste. But more than likely Henneh was simply the next in line for an easy termination or she made some careless misstep that aroused the Pedorate's suspicion.

"I asked what's wrong?" Doon says again, more insistently this time.

"Nothing," he answers finally. Straightening, he catches motion on the vis by the Registrar's desk. "Someone's coming."

Doon glances sidelong toward the vis. "It's just Saera," she says, turning a puzzled look toward Kai. "She's back."

"Then you'd better get away from that cypher," Kai suggests.

He tries to follow the Registrar on the vis but loses track of her the moment she steps through the door. She soon emerges from the shelving. Tall and thin; the whiteness of her short hair set off by the deep maroon colour of her visor, which she hasn't yet thought to remove. It's a stroke of good fortune for her that not a trace of her Journer heritage shows.

"I couldn't bring much," she says, dropping a box onto the top of her desk. The box looks like any other box she might carry to or from the Repository. "But there should be enough food and water here to get you back to the ward. You'd better stay here until it's dark," she adds, only now slipping off her visor. "You can rest in the reading room. No one is scheduled to visit the Repository today so you shouldn't be disturbed. And you probably should take this there as well." She picks up the box once more. "Just in case."

Doon takes the box from Saera's hands with a muffled thanks, then leads the way back to the reading room, with her brother, Kai, and the big hairy mutz on her heels. She's quick to claim the couch for herself, leaving Kai to forfeit the chair to Gaed. Graciously, as much as Doon is capable of being gracious, she offers him two of the cushions from the couch. He finds a place on the floor and no sooner is he settled, then the mutz curls up beside him.

The last thing he sees when he closes his eyes is Henneh's face, not hovering and hollowed and aged past her years in the dreary anonymity of the Duck Down Club, but shinning bright with hopefulness under the sea-kissed sunshine of their home-ward the way it used to be.

When he wakes, it's to find the mutz gone and Saera standing over him. Looking around, he discovers the large window dark and his two Phane companions already up and moving around.

"It should be safe now," Saera says, offering her hand to hoist him onto his feet. "I can't stay here much longer. Someone might notice if I return home later than usual. This sector of Ularon City is relatively quiet at night, so there shouldn't be too many Guardians about and the Preservers will already have left their sector by the time you reach it."

Kai glances at Doon, seeking the box Saera gave them, and spies it open and emptied on the floor by her feet. Either she or Gaed has already stowed its contents into their small bags. He more or less expected the mutz to follow him to the entrance of the Repository and isn't disappointed. The lethally sharp claws of his massively padded feet tap loudly on the hard flooring behind him. It's only then he realises that the mutz probably hadn't befriended him the way he thought. The animal was guarding its mistress and, in error, judged Kai to be the more likely threat. It should have been shadowing Doon.

Sending the two Phanes out ahead of him, Kai lingers in the doorway.

"If we come across your brother in our travels, is there a message you'd like me to give him?"

"You intend to go through the station?" Saera asks him, sounding surprised and perhaps a touch apprehensive.

"Intend? No. But we'll have to use the access at the platform nearby. We've been lucky. But who's to say our luck will hold."

Saera levels her strange bluish eyes on him and smiles warmly. They're of a height.

"Then I'd suggest you be very careful. But should you get caught, tell Gove that I've shared everything I know with you. If he believes you're Kai Astada, he'll trust you."

"I don't think my identity will be what decides him." He nods toward the two Phanes who are waiting for him now by the gate. "It'll be them. They might not know him, but I think he might know them."

Saera's thin face crinkles into a frown.

"The wardlanders have been pilfering food from the station for some time now. Someone must have noticed... and overlooked it."

"I see what you mean."

She holds out her hand and, as Kai takes it, the mutz steps a little closer.

"You will be careful, Kai Astada."

"And you, Saera Govek." He looks her up and down. "Who'd have thought you'd grow so tall," he says and, dropping her hand, turns quickly away.

***

They backtrack the way they came, bypassing the Sub station where they took refuge, travelling by night, eluding the few roaming Guardians. Kai is anxious to return to the ward and confront Jak Inopo. But it's the quarantine station that poses their last challenge. Caught, he could relay Saera's message to her brother, but he'd prefer not to put Gove at further risk and so, as before, Kai has them sit out daylight under cover, bringing them to the tunnel only as the sun is beginning to set. They hurry through and, just shy of the exit, relinquish their shine-sticks to wait until the sliver edge of the sun dips fully beneath the horizon.

It's Doon who calls the moment, bolting into the open without warning. Kai and Gaed sprint after her. There's an instant of panic when a new light blooms over at the station but, running on, they reach the steps to the platform seemingly unseen. Kai finds Doon collapsed on the bench, chest heaving. Gaed's breathing just as heavily behind him. Dragging Doon to her feet, he wrenches the seat from the bench and retrieves the blade they left there. It's her blade, so he passes it to her. Thin and tough, she single-handedly manoeuvres the hatch up from the floor. The last to enter, Kai pulls the hatch down tightly after him. It's back to the shine-sticks now and a route that's becoming familiar all the way to the Sub entrance in the open field beyond The Cocoon.

When they finally emerge into the field, Kai starts them directly toward Pilot Jak's, climbing the steep hill slowly and cautious of footing in the darkness. Arriving, Doon barks a loud call to old Jak.

"You'll give the old one heart failure someday doing that," Gaed points out.

She pushes past her brother to open the door and a little figure materialises in the glow of a low-slung oil lamp. It's Mig and she's wiping at her eyes with her free hand.

Without Henneh, the young one will be all alone in the world now. No ...Kai stops to think again. Even if her sister really is dead, Mig is not as alone as it may seem. There's Ceilu, Doon and Gaed and, for as long as he may live, old Jak Inopo.

"Who's there?" she asks in a sleep-addled little voice. "Oh, it's you. What are you doing here? You woke us up."

"That was the idea," Doon snaps, making her way past Mig into Inopo's kitchen. "Now where's that old pilot?" she says, slinging her bag to the kitchen bench and helping herself to a lone bauma from a nearby basket all in one motion.

"Here I am, you disrespectful kyne. And I'll thank you to keep your hands off my food."

A shadowy figure inches forward from the back of the house. The old pilot is dressed in a sort of floor-length robe, but his feet are bare and they slap irregularly on the naked wooden floor.

"Where have you three been then?" he asks, collapsing into the sagging contours of a chair almost as ancient as he is. "And what possessed you to come visiting at this hour? Waking an old one like that. Disrespectful," he mutters, dragging the folds of the robe neatly over his legs.

Ceilu hasn't told him of their plans. Kai's a little surprised by that; he thought the old pilot was the one person she'd take into confidence on just about everything.

"Been to the big city," Doon says, jumping in ahead of Kai. She drops the mangled rind of the bauma loudly into the kitchen sink. "And you've got some explaining to do."

"Me?" He brings a gnarled finger up to his chest.

"You, Pilot Jak," Gaed says, making himself comfortable in the chair opposite Inopo. The chair is as old as its companion, mismatched, stuffing poking out in tuffs, white and crinkled, like the ruffled tuffs on the old pilot's head.

"You went to Ularon City *without* me?" Mig asks accusingly. She's fully awake now. She looks so much like Henneh, it stabs Kai's conscience to keep news of her sister from her.

"It was a long walk, Mig," he explains, dropping to one knee. "Out in the open. We had to move fast."

"You didn't miss much," Doon offers in consolation, rustling Mig's hair as she passes, bauma in hand, on the way to join her brother and the old pilot.

Rising, Kai leads Mig toward the others.

"Can't see I've got a thing to explain," Inopo maintains, eyeing Kai. "It's been a long time since I've been in Ularon City. Couldn't have offered you any advice in that regard."

Kai settles Mig, lamp in hand, on the floor by the old pilot's feet and steps over to join Doon; she's found herself a spot on the floor, back propped against the surrounds of an old hearth that looks like it hasn't had the benefit of use or cleaning in a long time. There's a big ancient pot hanging suspended from a horizontal beam above the dead fire. The pot has an enormous hole in one side. Kai seats himself on the chipped ledge of bricks framing the hearth.

"We weren't looking for advice, Pilot Jak," he says. "But you could have warned us that the Registrar of the Repository is an old friend of yours."

The light from Mig's lamp, angled up, lends the old pilot's wizened face an uncharacteristically sinister look.

"A friend of mine?" he asks nonplussed, then laughs. "I think you must be mistaken."

"She's Phane," Gaed says nonchalantly from the opposite chair.

"An orphan," Kai takes up. "An orphan *my mother* took to Plaited Bay. Her name was Saera Govek."

"Ah," Inopo breathes—long and low. "So that's what became of her. I knew your mother took them, of course. Her *and* her brother. But after that..." he spreads his hands, "at least it does clear up some things."

"Like?" Doon prompts.

"Where Ush Kaidador is."

"Was," Gaed corrects him. "Ush Kaidador is dead."

"That's right," Doon says. She has her legs crossed at the knee and is swinging the upper. "So you can stop trying to protect her now."

Kai is only half attentive to the others as they speak. His eyes are on little Mig. She's listening intently but if confirmation of Ush's death has affected her at all, she isn't prepared to show it.

The old pilot is slow to respond. "Dead!" Even in the dim light from Mig's single oil lamp, Kai can see that Inopo has noticeable paled.

"From natural causes," Kai explains before Inopo can rush to the wrong conclusion. "She *was* living with Saera Govek. And after she died, it was Saera's brother who saw to the necessary arrangements."

"Gove is in Ularon City, too?"

"Not any longer. But he *was*, and he's now living under the name of Julyen Koale."

"Koale..." Inopo rolls the name around between clenched teeth. "That name sounds familiar."

"It should, old one," Doon snaps at him from her retreat by the hearth. "It should sound *very* familiar." She discards the waste of the mangled bauma into the dead fire.

With Doon taking the lead, together they tell the old pilot all that Saera told them. Inopo's head is resting at a crooked angle against the back of the chair, looking for all the world as though he's asleep. Kai doesn't doubt for one moment that he's awake though. Awake and listening carefully.

"So, you see," Kai says at the end of the telling, "I was sent on a wild waloo chase after all. It seems the person they're looking for *is*... or rather *was*... my mother and she was right there under their noses."

"So *he* says," Doon objects. "*I* still say he's wrong."

Inopo's eyes ease open to focus on the young Phane.

"Why?" he presses her.

"How many times do I have to say it?" Doon fires back. "These people are too fond of intrigue. If they'd told Kai who to look for, then he might *actually* have found them by now."

"Perhaps, young one," Inopo agrees, surprising Kai.

Mig looks up inquiringly at the old pilot, red hair flaring in the glow of the oil lamp by her feet. Lowering his hand, Inopo begins to pat her head, the way someone might their pet.

"It all comes back to the Journers' League. Kai, here, remembers it. At least he thinks he does. But he's remembering it from a kyne's perspective. To all intents and purposes, it never existed and for a long time now," he says solemnly, "it hasn't. Oh, there's vestiges of it... like the Duck Down Club," he hurries to add just as Kai is about to suggest it, "but the Duck Down Club is a poor excuse for what we once were. It's all but toothless now."

Kai's not so sure about that. He hasn't found it so 'toothless'. He lets Inopo's observation slide because he, too, can see that a club, for want of a better description, that has garnered a bad reputation, real or imagined, is hardly an effective entity.

"Usha Kaidador was our leader."

Inopo's astonishing claim renders Kai speechless. All he can do is sit there, bolt upright, with his mouth hanging open while the old pilot continues his tale.

"There were members from both Journer wards," he is saying, "even one representative from the marginals, and the League was gathering power, moving from strength to strength. So much so that there was risk of exposure by its own members." His focus begins to drift as the past, like a physical presence beside him, seems to draw him back through the many years. "You can't always know who to trust and that's why we operated in isolation... small groups with only limited contact between. It was safer that way. No one in any one group knew who was in any other group. And we communicated through a liaison."

"Someone like a Talker?" Kai suggests, recovering a little from his shock.

"Loosely," Inopo agrees. "And that probably explains why Ro wasn't aware that Ush was in Ularon City."

And why he was sent on that wild waloo chase, Kai realises. No wonder the League failed. Too much intrigue and secrecy, just like Doon has been grumbling. And some day, maybe the Pedorate will fail for the same reasons, although Kai doubts he'll be around to see it.

"Some of us thought it was time to act," Inopo explains. "Time to move against the Pedorate. Just as many were opposed. We weren't ready. It wasn't enough just to have our caste onboard, we had to have the others, at least as many as we could feasibly gather. Besides there were rumours, credible rumours at the time, that the Pedorate Council was proceeding with plans for the construction of a Supercontinental. *The Nether.* We wanted that ship. And if we bided our time, we'd get it."

"Then it was all an act," Kai says, interrupting. "My mother was never opposed to my father leaving on *The Nether.*"

"Oh, she was opposed all right," Inopo replies. "She feared what *The Nether* might bring back."

"You mean she anticipated there could be a plague?" Doon asks, looking and sounding puzzled.

"A plague! Pautune, no, Doon! Ush wasn't scared of any plague. She was scared of what they might discover out there."

"Isn't that the point of going in the first place?" Gaed asks. His face is a mirror of his sister's. "Exploration and discovery?"

"Not for Ush. She was opposed as much to a pre-emptive move against the Pedorate as she was opposed to the Pedorate out-journing. The League wasn't ready to move on the Pedorate and the Pedorate wasn't ready to move off-planet." His shrug is barely discernible. "That's how Ush saw it. But your father, Kai, saw it differently."

"Huh!" Doon grumps. "And now the League is gone." There's a trace of disappointment in her voice.

"*Long* gone," Inopo confirms.

"Except for the Duck Down Club," Kai reminds him.

"Yes," the old pilot agrees. "But it's a travesty of the League's past. Exposed, if only by rumour. It surprised me when you said Gannaline-ro was part of it."

Kai smiles thinly. "I'd say she's the *head* of it."

"Hide in plain sight," Doon says so softly Kai almost misses it. "I think you're mistaken, Pilot Jak. I think the Duck Down Club might be more powerful and more far-reaching than the League *ever* was."

"Even if Doon is right," Kai interjects, "we're still left with the same question we started with. Whatever *The Nether* brought back, the Pedorate is desperate to conceal it."

"At our expense," Doon reminds them.

"So, if it wasn't a plague," Kai adds, nodding as he glances in turn at those gathered together in Inopo's little house, "then what was it?"

No one answers.

No one can.

CHAPTER 13

Abandoning Doon and Gaed to their latest argument, Kai and Mig—mostly Kai—push, pull and drag old Jak up the ladder onto the roof. He wants to see the sun rise. To Kai's surprise, the chairs are still there, looking more ancient, more battered, more weather- and time-weary for sure, but serviceable enough to keep their rears off the slowly heating surface of the roof. Mig takes it in her head to explore the rooftop, wandering close to the edge. There's only the narrow rim, ankle-high to corral her. But this is Mig, so Kai allows her to stroll the rooftop, confident she won't fall off.

"I've only got one option," Kai says to Inopo, whose gaze is trained on the far horizon as it slowly begins to lighten. "I can't go back to Ularon City as Sayker Gerit. The Phanes can give me a new identity and then I'll return to the city and forget any of this ever happened. Ro and the Duck Down Club can't touch me if they can't find me."

"You could have done that before," Inopo mutters from his chair.

"What did you say?"

"I said that you could have done that before," the old pilot replies, glancing at Kai. "When Doon first told you how the Phanes can manipulate pids. You didn't. And don't tell me the thought never crossed your mind. Ro and her followers have you obsessed."

"Not likely," Kai scoffs, shifting in his creaking chair. "Whatever else my mother knew, she took to the grave with her. Why? I don't know. Probably protecting someone, like Doon is so fond of pointing out. But I'm sure now that it was Ush who Ro sent me to find." He turns in his seat to face the old pilot.

"Probably so," Inopo agrees. "Ro was a member of the Journers' League. She knew your mother and her position in the League."

"I still don't understand why Ush didn't go to Ro with what she knew. Why Saera Govek?"

"I just told you. Ro knew your mother was opposed to moving against the Pedorate too fast. And Ro? Ro had her own opinions. By going to someone outside the Journer caste like the Director of the Lycea instead, I guess your mother was hoping to bring more of the castes on-side." He shrugs. "She couldn't have anticipated that Vidamore would enlist the aid of the Duck Down Club. Who would?" Inopo offers up a little chuckle. "Seems there's more to Eine Vidamore than any of us thought."

"Well, whatever Ush knew and whatever Vidamore does or doesn't intend to do about things now, I'm done with it. I'm sure I could eventually pilot *The Nether* and teach others to pilot it, too. And someday, maybe Gaed could figure out how to destroy The Cocoon. But then what? What do you do with a Supercontinental that's got nowhere to go? No, I'm going to make my way to the Phane village first and then I'm getting myself back to Ularon City. And I really don't care what caste they make me anymore."

"I heard that," Mig says, pinning Kai with a glance over her shoulder.

"So did I," another voice says.

Kai jerks his head around. Doon has come up the ladder. Her head and shoulders are visible, and she has her elbows looped over the short little wall ringing the roof.

"I'm going with you."

"Me, too," Mig says.

"I can't stop you from going home, Doon," Kai tells her indifferently.

"I mean to Ularon City," Doon says, clambering the rest of the way onto the roof. "I'll get myself a new pid and go with you."

"I'll argue against it," Kai warns.

Beside him, Inopo is staying mute.

"You can try." Doon's attention is on the horizon, not Kai. "Hey, I've never been up here before." She turns on him without warning. "The Phanes are *my* people. Who do you think they'll listen to?"

"Fine," Kai responds with a flip of his hand. "Do what you want. But you're not coming with me."

Doon smiles. "We'll see."

"What about me?" Mig says, rushing up. "You didn't take me last time. It's my turn."

Kai bends forward to reason with the young one. "I can't take care of you in Ularon City, Mig. And what would you do there? If you want to stay with the Phanes, then we can go there together. But you wouldn't like Ularon City. It's no place for you. Doon, either, but she's older than you are. She can make her own decisions."

He knows right away he's said the wrong thing.

"Ooo, now you've done it," Doon calls in a sing-song voice as she heads back to the ladder. "I'm going back down to tell Gaed. You can sort this one out for yourself."

Kai swears Inopo is laughing.

***

Seems Gaed has decided Kai's side, whatever that is now, isn't the winning side after all. He elects to stay behind and continue to take his chances with Ceilu. Kai, Doon and Mig will travel on to Plaited Bay. Kai has long given up arguing with either of them. Once the Phanes give him a new pid, he'll slip away from Doon and leave it to the Phanes to dissuade Mig. By all accounts, Asta will still be with the Phanes. That might be enough to convince Mig to stay. If she's still the same old Asta, it would convince Kai to do exactly the opposite. But they spent some years together under Ush's care and perhaps Mig managed to forge a relationship with Asta where he had failed.

The four take their leave of Jak Inopo in the late morning. It will be the last time Kai will ever see the old pilot. He's sure of that this time. Whatever happens, he will not be coming back. He knows Inopo is waving at them as they start off down the steep hill, but Kai can't make himself turn around. They have some history—he and Inopo—and those times he spent with the old pilot might just be the best times of his life.

Years ago, when he and Gannin attempted that impulsive trip to Plaited Bay, it took them a good day and a half to reach the ridge above the bay. But they were young then and ran a good part of the distance. Now Kai is reckoning on two full days at least just to reach the ridge and another half day perhaps coming down it into the bay. He's loath to see Ceilu again. Even more loath to beg supplies from her again, but there's no option. They have to eat and drink along the way. Before they come within sight of Ceilu's cottage, he's already concluded the negotiating is best left to Doon.

Ceilu is standing at the door when they arrive, almost as though she's expecting them.

"You're back."

It's noon and the sun is reflecting off the top of Ceilu's head like a beacon.

"Come inside," she says, waving them through. "I'm sure you've got a tale to tell me whether I want to hear it or not."

Kai follows the others inside, heads toward one of the chairs near the old table and sits down. As usual, it's Doon who's quick to tell the story and Kai is content to overlook the odd little error in the retelling. He's not concerned about Ceilu's opinion in any way. She'll believe or disbelieve at her pleasure. She certainly won't act on anything she learns. Doon does have her measure. There's cautious—like his mother, apparently. Then there's too cautious— like Ceilu. Still, he can't really fault her and it seems he should never have faulted his mother, either. He's hardly a shining example of someone who gets the job done efficiently.

Ceilu sits patiently in the chair opposite Kai while Doon speaks and paces, arms wheeling about. Mig, having heard it all already, looks bored. She wanders around Ceilu's cottage, snatching the odd morsel of food she finds. Gaed appears to be a little anxious, probably hoping Ceilu will talk Doon into staying. She won't.

"A fascinating tale," Ceilu says when Doon finally falls silent, fixing her with an expectant gaze. "And not a shred of proof to any of it. Oh," she adds, waving a hand, "some of it is probably true. I believe Pilot Astada here saw what he said he saw at that club and maybe it did come from that Doser at the quarantine station. But if it did and he is helping us here in the ward like you say, then I'm certainly not going to do anything to jeopardise that. So, all in all, none of your story does any of us much good." She turns to Kai. "Does it?"

"I'm sure Doon had no intention of persuading you, Ceilu," he says calmly. "You were told as a matter of courtesy."

"Courtesy! Pilot Astada," she snarls, thumping the table. "You try to sneak into this ward uninvited and then proceed to upset everyone you encounter. *And* you eat our food. What's courteous about that?"

"Yes, well," Kai replies, rising. "And we're about to ask you for more food. For Doon, Mig and me. Enough to get us to the Phane village."

Ceilu jumps to her feet, setting the table rocking. "Now just a minute. You and Doon can do whatever you want. In fact, I'm happy to see you go."

Kai bets she is.

"But you can't take Mig. No. That's out of the question."

"Actually," Doon says, stepping up to place her hands on Mig's shoulders, "we're not *taking* Mig. She wants to go."

If it were a matter of leaving Mig with Jak Inopo, Kai might side with Ceilu. But Inopo can't last much longer and, now that he's had a bit of time to think it through, it might be best for Mig to find a home among the Phanes. Asta will be there. Doon, too.

"Mig," Ceilu says, turning to the young kyne. "Is that true?" She sounds surprised.

Mig nods her head. She's got a piece of bauma shoved halfway into her mouth.

With a tap to the shoulder, Kai draws Ceilu's attention. "And there's something you've forgotten. Mig was under the care of my mother. And now that my mother is dead... well, you get the idea, I'm sure."

"You can't just *claim* someone, Pilot Astada," Ceilu protests. "I don't know how things work in the city, but that's not how we do things inside this ward."

Finally Kai is just frustrated enough to grab Ceilu's arm and drag her, protesting, through the open doorway.

Once outside, he says in a low voice, "I have no intention of taking Mig to Ularon City. It's no place for her. Pautune!" he curses, running a hand through his hair, "it's no place for me! But I have no choice. Let Mig grow up with the Phanes. She'll be safer there. If she stays here with you, sooner or later, she's going to get hurt. She's fearless. But fearless isn't the same as lucky. And she's been lucky so far… crawling through machinery for you… being the first to breach through tunnels and walls without getting hurt."

At first, Ceilu says nothing, just looks back into the dark cottage behind her.

"You promise to leave her with the Phanes?" she says at last.

"Ceilu, I'll be lucky if I can manage in the city myself now. I can't be responsible for a young one."

"And Doon?"

Kai pitches his voice even lower. "I'm planning to leave her behind in the village. Slip away without her knowing it."

"Are you now?" Ceilu says, glancing toward the ground. "I wish you luck with that, Kai Astada. But I won't argue with you any longer about Mig," she says, raising her eyes. "I'll get you the food and count *myself* lucky to see the back of you."

***

Mig is marching out ahead of them, leaving Doon and Kai to walk together. The Phane has said little since their departure from Ceilu's cottage. Her parting words to Gaed were cold and perhaps she's brooding on that.

Kai recognises little of the country around them. Doon is taking them on an unfamiliar route to the bay and during his journey with Gannin, he was more focussed on what he'd see when they got to the end of it rather than the terrain they passed on the way. There were few settlements between his home and the bay, Kai does recall that, and the settlements they pass now are abandoned. Doon is silent. The little houses they pass are silent. The only sound the occasional flap, flap, flap of a loose piece of sheeting on the wall or roof of a deserted house. The breeze against their skin blows hot and dry, light enough but unkind in other ways. While Mig and Doon, who changed back into her Phane clothes, walk unprotected, Kai has donned his visor.

"You know, even if my people alter your pid, you can't ever be a Journer again?" Doon says, breaking the silence.

"You mean the Phanes can't 'undead' Kai Astada?"

"No. I mean yes. But you have to understand, Kai." She glances at him sidelong. "It's usually young ones that are relocated. And the older ones that came to us after the quarantine were sent outside Pedora. Since the blockade of the bay, we can't do that anymore. We don't have access to the *right people* like Gannaline-Ro seems to have. The best that can be done is to make you a Preserver. Maybe a Ditcher. But, I don't know. You're still going to have trouble establishing yourself inside Ularon City again."

"*I'm* going to have trouble?" Kai trips on a loose piece of paving, rights himself. "What about you? Don't tell me you've changed your mind?"

Doon chuckles. "No. But I'm better at these sorts of things than you are. And I haven't been living the pampered life of a pilot all these years. I expect less."

Now the last simply didn't ring true for Kai at all. He smiles to himself.

But she's starting to have second thoughts and that's good. Maybe he can play on that, convince her it's a bad idea to even attempt to make it to Ularon City and save himself the effort of trying to give her the slip.

"Have you considered going to that Doser at the quarantine station?" she asks. "He might be able to get you out of Pedora. Looks like he's done it for others. If you turn around now—"

Kai doesn't let her get any further. "I considered it," he says. "But Koale... Saerat... he's already at enough risk. I know," he says, anticipating what Doon is about to say. "That's just another instance of someone watching out for someone else. But I think there's something you've failed to realise."

"Oh?" she says, frowning.

"*You've* been watching out for *me*."

"Really," she says, then calling ahead to Mig, sprints off to catch up with the young one.

At day's end, they take advantage of an old cottage in one of the abandoned villages. As Mig begins to distribute the food Ceilu gave them, Kai broaches a long-overdue matter with his travelling companions. He can trust Doon; she's quick and smart. Mig is quick and smart, too, but prone to impulsive honesty, a trait Doon is fortuitously lacking.

"Mig," he says, stilling the young one's hand. "We need to agree on what we're going to tell the Phanes."

Mig's gaze darts to Doon. "What do you mean? Tell the Phanes?"

"He means," Doon interjects, "that we can't tell them everything we know." She scoots forward on her knees along the dirty floor of the cottage, coming eye to eye with Mig. "It can't help anyone. We can't prove anything and it looks like we never will. It's like Kai said up on Pilot Jak's roof."

Doon had been listening longer than he realised.

"Whatever Ush might have known died with her and there's some people we just can't talk about. Like the Registrar. And the Doser at the quarantine station. If the Pedorate finds out what they've done, they could get in serious trouble."

The kyne's face crimples into a frown. "But the Phanes are our friends. They're not going to tell the Pedorate anything."

"That's right," Doon agrees. "We're friends... you and me... all the Phanes and all the wardlanders. But the Registrar and that Doser are our friends, too. You see, no Phane would intentionally betray them but the fewer people who know that they're our friends, the better. And it's safer for the Phanes as well. If they know nothing, then they can't talk about it by accident. Understand?"

"You mean like when I told Pilot Jak about Ush going through the tunnel?"

"Kind of like that, I guess," Doon agrees.

Mig inhales deeply and then slowly releases her breath. "But isn't that lying?"

Mig's question scrapes a raw nerve. Kai is lying, keeping what they've learned about Henneh from her. When the time is right, he *will* tell her, but his time with Mig is running short.

"In a way," Doon explains. "But, remember, the Phanes are *my* people and I wouldn't lie to them unless I really had to, would I?"

"All right, I'll try, but it's not going to be easy. Sometimes I talk without thinking."

"We all do," Kai says, interjecting. "And that's why we're all going to have to try really hard."

"The others, too?" she asks, looking at Kai. "Ceilu? Pilot Jak? And Gaed?"

"Them, too. And you're going to have to be especially careful around Asta," he warns her.

Mig lets out a giggle. "Asta! I *always* hid things from Asta. Otherwise she'd tell on me to Ush and get me in trouble. Oh," she says, brightening as she turns back to Doon. "*I* see what you mean."

Over the top of Mig's head, Kai gives the Phane a nod. She has a way with the young one but as they eat, largely in silence, it's clear to Kai that Doon is troubled. Only once Mig is settled in for the night, does she find Kai, propped against the far wall, to speak about it.

"So," she says in a whisper, "what *are* we going to tell my people? We have to have some excuse for you being there, asking for your pid to be altered."

"We could tell them I'm in trouble with the Pedorate," Kai says after a moment of thought.

That isn't far from the truth.

"That I need a new identity."

Doon shrugs. "That could work. Except for one small problem. Your pid identifies you as a Talker, not a Journer, and there'll be people in the village who recognise you. I suppose you could always say you got the Talker's pid from the Duck Down Club."

Kai shakes his head. "No. If we mention the Duck Down Club, then I'll have to explain what I was doing there. We'll say I got the pid from a Ditcher. A Ditcher who's become compromised."

"Ditchers do that?" Doon asks with some suspicion. "Trade in pids?"

"So I'm told."

"All right," she agrees with a shrug. "But then what's my excuse? My pid's scrambled. And then there's Mig as well. She'll need a new pid, too."

"Let me think about it." He can't exactly admit his intention to abandon them both in the village.

***

Kai is first to rise. Loath to wake the others, he treads carefully across the debris-strewn floor to the doorway. The sun hasn't risen high enough to make it too hot yet, so Kai takes a moment to revel in a moment of comfortable warmth. It's some time later before Doon finds him still seated on the broken boards of a little set of steps leading off the narrow porch.

"Mig is up," she says, dropping down beside him. "We can start off anytime you're ready."

Kai eases himself onto his feet, muscles stiff and sore from all the unaccustomed walking he's done over the last few days. His knee gives one ominous crack as he steps onto the porch.

"I can't understand how Jak Inopo ever made this journey," he says to Doon.

Doon doesn't stir from her spot on the step. "He didn't. There's more than one way to the bay. The one you took some years ago. This one." She lifts a hand to point. "That one. It's flatter, but it takes a lot longer."

Kai glances through the open doorway and sees Mig reorganising her little pack. "Maybe we should have gone that way, too," he says, twisting his neck to look at the back of Doon's head. "It might have been easier on Mig."

He's spoken too loudly. Mig's head snaps up from her sorting. Snatching up her pack, she struts toward him and the look she gives him as she passes speaks volumes.

"Never going to learn," Doon mumbles as she rises slowly to her feet, then steps past Kai to collect her own pack.

They trek steadily throughout the day, bypassing only one small, deserted village along the way. The night, as it comes, is two-moon and they spend it beneath a cluster of stars and tall trees on the steep lee side of the ridge above Plaited Bay. Doon starts them out just as the stars begin to fade and the first of the moons gives way behind them. By the time they reach the summit shortly after dawn, Kai has vowed he'll never misjudge Mig's abilities again. He and Doon are breathing heavily, while she's not even winded.

"Home," Doon declares with a board smile and exaggerated flourish.

Out in the bay, the Phane village looks unchanged from the day he and Gannin gazed down on it from a peak that, although further inland, was very similar to the one he's standing on now. Time seems to have stopped out on the bay. The sky is the same cloudless blue, sleek horizon merging water and air in an indeterminate haze. The hul islands, too, are much the same and the antans leisurely ambling between them could be the very same wildly coloured antans he and Gannin watched all those years ago. There's just one difference—the ring of black sea-going Pedorate vessels outside the waterwall. They're U-Class. Old. Reliable. A bit on the slow side by today's standards. Fast enough to stop an antan breaching the cordon though. And more than likely they're only skeleton-crewed. You'd think it would take a certain type of Journer to man a vessel that's cordoning off their home-ward. But Kai would have done it if he'd been ordered to. That's what Journers do. That's what everyone in Pedora does. Obeys orders.

Between the vessels and the waterwall, there's something else, a disturbance in the waters, something neither he nor Gannin had noticed on a day that was more blusterous than this one.

"I thought antans weren't permitted beyond the waterway," he says, turning to Doon.

"They're not," Doon replies, looking puzzled.

Kai points. "Then what's that?"

Immediately Kai knows he's about to be humiliated. Doon's beaming one of those 'how can you be so stupid?' smiles at him as she stoops to remove something from her pack.

Jak Inopo's old proximer! Kai hasn't seen it for years.

"That's the water turbines, you ignorant lander," she says, handing him the proximer. "What did you think we use for power? Felli oil and waste? *You did!*" she cackles then drives off into a breakneck descent off the peak.

Kai says nothing when Mig starts after her at speed. He takes a moment to gaze through the old proximer at a scene that is stubbornly shaky; he's no better at using the ancient instrument than he used to be. Stowing it inside his own pack, he sets off after his two young companions, taking the incline more cautiously. A slip, a slide, a shimmy down the rocky slope and he could break a leg.

Doon eventually slows down and Kai discovers why when he comes to a difficult stretch that demands some crafty negotiating up and over a field of large and slippery boulders and a crazed network of knee-deep crevices between. Mig is a born scrambler and even

Doon is doing better than he is, but then, he supposes, she's spent a good part of her life living on floating islands. Kai is in no position to take much notice of the shoreline but every time he looks up, it seems to be nudging closer.

Doon brings them to the base of the ridge unscathed. It's just a short trek now over a patch of soggy marshland to the shore where three antans are moored. The crafts are bobbing up, down, up, down in gentle waves. Kai can't see the Phane owners but they won't be far away. An antan means life itself to a Phane.

"We can take one of these antans," she says, beckoning Kai.

"We can't just *take* someone's property!" One of Kai's boots begins to sink into the soft marshy ground.

"Of course, we can," Doon tells him, snatching a hold of his arm. "It's family." She points at a splash of red, green and orange running from bow to stern. The pattern is a complex flurry of interlocked stripes, chevrons and triangles that match the panels on Doon's tunic.

She leaps aboard ahead of Mig and Kai carefully follows.

"Won't someone miss it?" he asks, struggling to steady himself on the stiff woven bottom of the antan. He trips over one of two long poles lying askew across the gunnel.

"It's not exactly hard to spot now, is it?" Doon says, grasping one of the poles. The pole wacks Kai in the shin as she rights it. "You *could* grab the other one."

Kai swings the second pole upright, careful to avoid Mig's head. The young one's enjoying the show, her attention flicking from Kai's inept handling of the pole to the brightly adorned smattering of islands out to sea.

"Push off now."

On Doon's instruction, Kai sinks the end of his pole into the soft bank.

"We're in the shallows." Doon's at the bow, leaving Kai to handle the stern. "Try not to swing us sideways. If we keep a straight heading, we won't have to resort to the oars."

Kai glances down, finds a short pair of paddles by Mig's feet.

"If you bring us off the sandbank, we'll have to row."

Row! Pautune! Kai has absolutely no idea *how* to row. He concentrates on the feel of the bottom as he plunges his pole down, pushes, lifts, then plunges down again. Seems they're going straight. They're making headway at least and Doon hasn't taken to yelling at him. Already Kai can feel his muscles strain while Doon manages her pole in comfort.

"You're doing well, Pilot Kai," Mig says encouragingly from the bottom of the antan.

Just what Kai needed! Appraisal from a young one.

"It's not far to the first island now." Mig comes to her knees. "Is that where we're going?"

Clearly she's asking Doon that question because Kai has absolutely no idea and, at this point, doesn't really care. He'll be happy if he manages not to overturn the antan and dump all three of them into the sea.

"Second," Doon answers, glancing over her shoulder. "That's my home. Mine and Gaed's. If you want, you can stay there."

Mig shakes her head. "I'm going on to the city with you and Pilot Kai."

Kai isn't in any frame of mind to argue just now.

Doon is laughing. "Come on, fancy pilot, put your back into it!"

They round the first island, but Kai has little time to notice much beyond the presence of a pair of Phanes on the shore and an unintelligible shout from one of them.

Doon returns the call in a dialect Kai cannot understand. He didn't know Phanes even *had* a dialect. Doon and Gaed haven't betrayed one.

Doon starts to swing the antan about, causing the sun to shine mercilessly into Kai's eyes and when they begin watering, there isn't a thing he can do about it for fear of losing his grip on the pole.

"Almost there," she tells Kai, sun gleaming off the top of her bright hair.

With a little jerk, she stills the antan, leaving Kai with the end of the pole still anchored into the sandbank aft of the stern.

"You can pull it up now," she tells him, wheeling her own pole over the top of Kai's and Mig's heads to lay it lengthwise across the gunnel. She leaps, landing expertly on the island-raft, a mooring rope in her hand. "Come ashore," she beckons, tying off the rope to a short mooring post projecting from the thickly matted bed of hul reeds that form the floor of the island.

Mig is already ashore before Kai has a foot overboard.

"A'yah," Doon begins calling, running across the island floor, heading for a conical-shaped... *house*, Kai supposes. The house is constructed from long lengths of hul tied off neatly and evenly along arched walls and there appear to be a number of other houses tightly crammed in behind it. The door at the narrow entrance also appears to be made of hul although the frame holding it together looks like wood. Seems the Phanes fell the odd tree up on the ridge. The door swings open and a Phane, perhaps a little older than Doon, emerges. She's wearing the same kind of tunic as Doon, be it considerably cleaner.

"This is my sister, Oona," Doon explains. She has a hold on the older Phane's arm and is leading her toward Kai and Mig, waiting by the antan.

Yes, she is. The closer they draw, her likeness to Doon is unmissable.

"Our parents aren't here." She points seaward. "They're felli trawling just inside the waterwall. They won't be back for some days. Oona says you're welcome to stay."

It seems Doon's sister has been struck temporarily mute by the arrival of two wardlanders at her home. Still, she does smile at them, a twist of lips and crinkle of eye that mirrors Doon's, and that's encouragement enough for Kai. He'd like to sit down somewhere before he falls down. He's just gained a whole new appreciation for the stamina of this remote subcaste of Journers who make their home on the waters of the bay.

***

They're seated on the floor under the arch of woven hul walls. Kai has finally mustered the courage to tell Mig about her sister and, as he is coming to expect, she accepts the ambiguous news with a stoicism and understanding beyond her years. There's a chance, a slim one in Kai's opinion, that Henneh is still alive with only her pid scrambled and he guesses the young one is clinging onto that. She's toying now with a broken shaft of hul she's found on the floor, splitting it lengthwise. Doon is half-sitting, half-lying beside Kai, back and head propped against one of the well-stuffed, gaudily coloured cushions that are scattered all over the floor. Oona is facing Kai, legs curled up gracefully beneath her.

He was mistaken earlier about the size of Oona's house. What he took to be smaller houses behind the fore-house turned out to be additional rooms all connected to the first house through many-arched openings. It's deceptively light inside the house. At regularly spaced intervals along the walls, the hul reeds have been gathered and bound to either side to form lozenge-shaped windows that allow the ingress of light. Every so often, Kai catches a glint of sunshine refracting through the transparent film that protects the interior from the elements and, although the seating is large simple cushions stuffed with what feels to Kai like tiny slivers of hul, there's a lot of furniture inside the house: tightly knit furniture made of hul, liberally painted; the odd lightweight wooden table; brightly coloured weavings distributed about the walls; and the biggest surprise of all, a cypher stationed discretely on a wooden bench contoured to fit neatly against the rear wall of the circular room.

True to her promise, Mig stays mute and Oona doesn't press for many details of their contrived story. Kai isn't the first wardlander refugee to come to the village seeking help. With the bay now blockaded, he'll likely be the last though.

"We haven't relocated anyone for a long time," Oona is saying in a voice that sounds just like Doon's. "But I'll introduce you to the elders. If you're determined to return to Ularon City, I'm sure they'll do what they can to help you." Her gaze drifts to Doon. "I don't know what good you think you're going to be able to do us in the city, Doon. You'll just get yourself into trouble. I can't stop you, but you know what the elders will say."

Doon expels a long breath between clenched lips.

It seems Doon is as much trouble at home as she is wardland. Kai's not surprised!

"Can we see more of the islands?" Mig says, looking up from her shredding. "And maybe find Asta now."

Asta! His sister! Kai completely forgot about her.

"Asta Kaidador?" Oona asks. "I can take you to Asta right now." Uncurling her legs to rise, she turns to Kai and smiles. "If you're up for another antan ride."

"As long as I don't have to steer," Kai answers, getting onto his feet.

Doon doesn't budge from the spot. "Not me. You three can go if you want."

Kai nudges her with his boot. "If you don't want to see your sister dumped overboard then you'd better get up."

Doon comes to her feet with a groan. "You could be stuck here, fancy pilot. There's no time like the present to learn to steer an antan."

"Not today," Kai tells her.

It's a tight squeeze on the little antan. Some of the other antans they pass and see along the way are quite a bit larger than the one Doon appropriated. Some, it appears, could seat as many as twenty; others look to be so small they might seat only a single occupant. Doon and Oona steer their family antan in well-practised unison, allowing Kai to take in every little nuance of their surroundings. He'd always assumed that living on the bay would have its advantages and disadvantages and that the latter would outweigh the former. But now the peace, the solitude, the cooler sea breezes inside the bay have him reconsidering. If it comes to it, perhaps it might not be so bad to pass the rest of his days here. If he can learn to pilot an Urban, he can learn to pilot an antan. For a brief moment, he finds himself wondering why Doon and Gaed ever took it in their heads to leave. But it is only a *brief* moment. What he sees on the bay is a temporary deception. The quarantine has also made inroads here. Their trade routes have been severed; there's no work for them wardland now, either. Nothing to supplement the living they make for themselves from the sea.

As they pass by each of the scattered islands, Doon lifts her hand to wave. None of the Phanes pay undue attention to Kai and Mig; likely they can't see them very well hunched down on the floor of the antan, avoiding a whack on the head from either Doon's or Oona's pole.

"There's a group of wardlanders living on the lee of that island over there," Oona says, pointing. "We call it Landers Island now. Asta is there. They trawl for felli like us but mostly keep to themselves."

"Asta trawls for felli?" Kai asks. For Oona to have recognised her name, she's clearly made her presence known. He's hoping it's in a good way but...

"*Sometimes,*" Oona agrees, smiling down on Kai.

Under the Phanes' direction, the little antan executes a gentle turn and Landers Island comes fully into view. It's a largish island, in fact one of the largest Kai has seen so far. As Doon pulls the antan to shore, Mig leaps overboard. She learns fast, reassuring Kai she'll do well here when he's gone.

"I can't find anything to tie it to," she says, darting from place to place in search of a mooring post.

"We have to pull it ashore, Mig," Oona explains. "There's no post here."

She jumps with measured practice, grabs a hold of the bow and once Doon and Kai are ashore, drags the little antan expertly out of the water. Kai lends a less expert hand and, with the antan safely resting on the dry floor of the island, he turns around to find a little group of the island's inhabitants standing behind them.

"A'yah," Oona says in greeting, marching forward. "We've brought you some visitors."

For the most part, the islanders are dressed in Phane attire, although one is still wearing standard wardlander clothes. A kyne, who looks to be roughly Doon's age, steps out from the small gathering.

Kai recognises her immediately. Eyes as dark as midnight; unruly hair the colour of the hul of the Phane houses behind her. Asta.

"Kai Astada," she says, stepping to the front of the group. "You're the last person I expected to see."

She's robbed of the chance to say more when Mig rushes past Kai and launches herself directly into Asta's arms.

Unsure of his words, Kai's grateful for the distraction. He and Asta... they were never exactly friends. He takes the plunge and moves forward, extending his hand. It's the least he can offer Ush's daughter, his own flesh and blood.

Asta frees herself from the cloying arms of little Mig, meeting Kai halfway. She takes his hand lightly, all the while eyeing him with obvious and understandable suspicion.

"What's this about?" she says, releasing his hand.

The question isn't directed at him, but Oona. That, too, he finds understandable.

"Your brother seems to have found himself in need of assistance," Oona says, wrapping an arm about Asta's shoulders.

Asta flicks another wary glance at Kai as someone else emerges from the small crowd gathered on the shore. Someone who, despite the Phane dress and the passage of years, Kai instantly recognises.

"Astorl," he says in a voice barely audible. "Astorl Penn." He's aware of the attention he's drawing from Mig and Asta.

Astorl's eyes, no longer that strong yellow-green colour he remembers, acknowledge him with a smile.

"I thought..." he begins as she steps up to take his hand. Actually, he didn't know what he thought. Astorl Penn was the only intern from his ward to be dismissed from the Lycea in the early days of their tenure there and Kai hasn't spared her a thought since the day she left. It was Gannin Tewel who'd said it right from the start—once at the Lycea, every Journer had to look out for themselves—but Kai hadn't fully grasped the gravity of his friend's words at the time.

"If you don't mind," Doon complains, giving Kai a gentle shove, "can we continue this reunion inside? It's bright out here." She struts off, uninvited, toward the clutch of houses, whipping Kai's visor away as she passes. "And some of us never got to own a U-visor. Not bad," she says, grinning back at Kai, visor donned.

Kai winces in the glare as the others are drawn along in Doon's wake, leaving him alone with Astorl.

"You assumed I'd been Crossed," Astorl says, finally offering Kai the smile her eyes had only promised.

"No. I thought you'd returned home," Kai tells her.

"I had," Astorl replies and, taking hold of his arm, begins to lead him after the others. "Or more precisely, I was sent home. And you?" she asks, tilting her head far back to look up at him. She hasn't grown any over the intervening years. "Did you make Continental Pilot like we expected?"

"What do you mean? I never—"

She waves his protest aside. "Oh, I know. *You* didn't expect it. But the rest of us did."

That, too, is news to Kai. "Maybe so," he says nonetheless, "but it didn't happen."

Astorl pulls up abruptly. "No?" She sounds genuinely surprised.

Kai looks down at her and returns his own long-overdue smile. "It's a long story."

She regards him quizzically for a while. "I have time," she replies at length, then starts him off again toward the house that, once inside, Kai discovers is no *house* at all.

"What is this place?" he says, glancing around the large empty space. There are cushions, much like the ones he saw in Oona's house, scattered all about the floor but nothing else.

"It's a meeting room, I guess you'd call it. We're mostly wardlanders here and this is where we have our meetings."

Mig has found herself a place in the corner with Asta. They've fallen into a huddle with Asta dominating the rapid talk. Kai scans the room to find Doon standing in the centre of the gathering, being bombarded with questions. Everyone has something to ask about her stay in the wardland. Some are probing for the latest news about the plague, others inquiring about the welfare of friends and family. A few even turn to Kai to ask about conditions in the city; he fobs them off with a simple assurance that no new outbreaks have been reported. Everyone is curious about something. Nearly everyone. Kai watches Astorl while, as fast as she can, Doon replies to each question that is fired at her. Astorl shows little interest, almost seeming removed from the excitement around her. She makes no inquiry about her own family, her neighbours, about her old friends from the Lycea. But something must have alerted her to Kai's observation because abruptly she turns to him to speak.

"You couldn't have chosen a better place to come to. The Phanes have been kind to us. I suppose it's really no place for a pilot. Still," she adds with a smile and a shrug, "we can't complain."

No, it's clear to Kai that Astorl complains about nothing and asks for nothing. She's changed—even more than Henneh had changed—so he's grateful when Mig comes running up.

"I'm going to stay here with Asta for a while, Pilot Kai. Tomorrow we're going to go felli trawling."

Felli trawling! Kai spots his sister waiting on Mig at the rear of the room. He just can't reconcile the Asta of his youth with an Asta who would go felli trawling on the bay.

"All right," he says. It would be easy for Mig to say too much— easy for any of them really—but sooner or later, he's going to have to trust her. He sends her back to Asta with a gentle touch to her back and, when he looks around to find Astorl, discovers her gone.

"Are you ready to go back now?"

Kai spins around with a start. Doon has come to collect him.

***

Kai spends the night in Oona's house in a little conical room at the back of the compound. He doesn't know what became of Doon during the night but finds her in the morning, stripping a felli carcass over a big bucket in front of the house. He slept poorly, unable to push Astorl's strange silence out of his head.

"Is it possible to take the antan again today?"

Doon looks up from her skinning. "I guess so. Where are you wanting to go?"

"Back to Landers Island."

Doon lifts a shoulder to swipe a trickle of sweat from her cheek. "To see Asta or Mig?"

"Neither," Kai confesses. "It's someone else."

"Oh?" Doon replies teasingly.

"No. Nothing like that. I met an old friend there yesterday. Something seems... I don't know... wrong with her. I wasn't *much* of a friend in the past. Maybe..." he says, then shrugs.

"You could be a better one now?"

"I suppose. I know I don't want to leave here wondering if she's all right."

Doon comes to her feet, the half-skinned felli dangling from her hand. "She's got the other wardlanders, Kai."

"I know." He's thinking as much about Henneh as Astorl. He walked off on Henneh back there in the Duck Down Club, thinking only about himself; he's not sure he'll ever forgive himself for that.

"Fine," Doon agrees, then glances down at the mangled, dripping felli in her hand. Looks like she's a bit out of practice. "Just let me finish this. I'll tell Oona we're taking the antan and meet you by the shore."

Doon takes her time and Kai is pleased to finally see her coming. The sooner he gets the antan to Landers Island, the happier he'll be. Never would he make a good sea-pilot. By the time they arrive, Kai feels like he's been the victim of multiple hits across the back from Doon's pole. She elects to stay by the antan, leaving Kai to seek out a wardlander who might know where Astorl is. After three attempts, he finds someone who informs him that she's casting nets on the other side of the island. He follows the wardlander's directions, spying few others along the way, and eventually comes upon Astorl, knee-deep in the water of the bay. She doesn't see him, so he watches for the moment it takes her to fling the net across the calm waters. When he finally calls her name, she turns around, a gentle wind blowing the loose dark strands of hair about her face.

She waves once before she begins the slow process of hauling the net into shore.

"Slow day," she says, coming up to Kai, dragging the sodden net behind her. "What brings you back so soon?"

"I didn't want to leave without telling you…asking you really…"

"You're leaving?" she says in surprise. It's the first evidence of emotion Kai has seen.

"Yes, but Mig is staying behind. At least," he says with a smile before sobering, "that's my intention. I didn't get the chance to tell you before. I think Henneh might be dead."

This time, he receives the emotional level of response he's coming to expect from Astorl—absolutely nothing. "The plague?"

Kai shakes his head. "Mig knows, but I only told her yesterday. So I wanted to ask you to watch out for her. Asta, too," he adds in afterthought although Asta seems to be managing just fine without him.

"Of course, I'll watch out for them, Kai. But where are *you* going?" She lowers herself to the hul floor of the shoreline and invites Kai to join her on the ground.

"I'm hoping the Phanes will help me get back to Ularon City."

"No," she exclaims so loudly it startles him. "I don't think you should go back there. It's safe here. You should stay."

"Astorl, it's not safe anywhere."

Her eyes hold him for a very long time before she speaks again, asking him with obvious suspicion, "What do you mean?"

"There's a lot Doon didn't tell you and it's better if you don't know."

He's come close to breaking his pledge to Doon and Mig. That was stupid. But instead of pressing him further, Astorl surprises him again. She begins to laugh mirthlessly.

"Astorl," Kai says, grasping her by the arm. "What's happened to you?"

"What's happened to *you*?" she counters. "Can't wait to get back to Ularon City and earn yourself a Continental posting? That sounds more like Gannin Tewel than the Kai Astada I used to know."

"Gannin's already a Continental pilot. Didn't you know?"

"No," she says. "I didn't know." She smiles quickly. "And I can't imagine how. So why such a hurry to get back to Ularon City then, Kai?" She waves a hand. "Yes, I know. I should be asking what brought you out of the city in the first place, but if it's all the same to you, I don't really care to know."

"Seems to me you don't really care to know much," Kai observes.

"Does it."

It's clear she's not seeking a reply.

Bringing the ends of the net onto her lap, she aimlessly starts to finger the fine knots. "Tell me, Kai, if you had to, what would you choose? To spend the rest of your life as a Preserver tidying up everyone else's messes or as a Phane," she lifts up the net to show him, "casting nets like these into the sea?"

"I thought you didn't care to know anything."

"Ah, you caught me. You always were the smartest of us."

Kai's smile is sombre. "If I were, I wouldn't have ended up here."

"Well," Astorl says, rising with the tail of the net still in her hand, "I certainly wasn't the smartest or I wouldn't have ended up here, either."

"Just how is it you came here, Astorl?"

"I was dismissed from the Lycea," she replies over her shoulder. "You know that."

Yes, he knew. And now he thinks he knows why. It wasn't Astorl's unsuitability as a pilot that had seen her dismissed. In fact, probably quite the opposite. That day on the platform, when the six of them had waited together for the Urban that would take them to the Lycea, Kai had noticed her instinctive mindfulness and the razor sharpness of her eyesight. She might just have made the best pilot of them all and, more than likely, the Pedorate had evidence that was so.

"And?" he presses her.

"And... I was recaste as a Preserver."

At least that explains her question about living as a Preserver or living Phane.

"Back home?"

"Yes and no."

She has answered in such a small voice and pauses for so long afterward, Kai starts to think that all she's prepared to tell him, until she speaks again. "Since *The Nether* had just come back and I had some knowledge of journing, I was sent to the quarantine station on the dock."

"But everyone who was there died. At least, that's what I was told."

"Most. Not all," she tells him casually.

It was a simple statement and not intended to be informative—wouldn't have been for someone not recently on a desperate hunt for a few missing pieces. He, like Ro and Henneh, had good reason to suspect it was Ush Kaidador who was holding those pieces. But perhaps they are all wrong.

"You escaped," Kai says, challenging her to deny it. "And you helped my mother escape, too."

"That's a strange thing to say," she replies at length.

"Listen to me, Astorl." He's about to break his pledge to Doon and Mig well and truly now because this time—*this time*—he's sure as pautune he's right. "Please," he says, "sit down again and listen to me." He motions for her to re-join him on the reeds.

When she lowers the net, clearly with some reluctance, and complies, Kai begins to explain.

"I was sent into the ward to find someone. Someone who was supposed to know what happened to the crew of *The Nether.*"

"That seems like an incredible waste of time under the circumstances."

"It was my mother," Kai continues, ignoring her. "But my mother was actually in Ularon City and by the time I discovered where she was, it was too late."

"Late," she says uninterestedly. "Late for what?"

"For both of us. She was already dead."

"Oh." The expression on his old friend's face begins to waver but it's only a flicker of change that comes and goes before Kai has a chance to interpret it.

"I'm sorry to hear that, Kai. I know you and Ush never really got on but..." she shrugs, "I'm just sorry I guess."

Kai inches closer across the matted hul. "I think she knew something, Astorl. More than she ever told anyone."

"And so, you're going back to Ularon City to find out what it was?"

"Now that would be a waste of time," he tells her. "I intended to return to Ularon City because there didn't seem to be anywhere else for me to go. When I discovered that Ush was dead, I was convinced that there was no one who could tell me what had really happened to the crew. But there are some people who aren't ever going to let it rest and they're never going to let me rest, either. As it turns out though, it wasn't my mother I should have been looking for after all."

"No?" Astorl looks down to finger the net once more. "Who then?"

"Guess."

"You think it's me," she says softly.

"I *know* it's you."

"I suppose it is me you were sent to find," she replies, lifting her gaze. "But I can't imagine who could have sent you."

"The Duck Down Club," Kai tells her.

"But they're... oh, I see... so they are real after all."

"Very real," Kai assures her. "Real enough to have stripped me of my identity and slipped me back into the ward right under the nose of the Pedorate."

"I'm sorry for that, Kai," she says, gaze drifting out to sea. "I'm sorry they've wasted your life that way."

"But you were at the quarantine station. You must have some idea what happened and the only chance I have of ever being a pilot again is to give the Duck Down Club what they're looking—"

"Knowing what happened won't change a thing," she says, interrupting him.

"Astorl, if my life truly has been wasted, then I think I deserve to know why."

"You can't hold me responsible for that, Kai. I never asked you to come here."

"You're asking me not to leave," he points out. "Give me a good reason why I shouldn't."

"All right, Kai," she concedes at last, turning to face him directly. "If that's what it takes to make you stay. It won't do much else for you. As you can see," she raises her hands, fanning them to indicate their surroundings, "it hasn't done much for me."

"I can't make that promise," Kai tells her.

"There'll be no need for promises once you hear what I have to say."

Her tone is too hollow for the Astorl he once knew.

"Like I told you," she begins with the same depth of indifference, "when I was dismissed from the Lycea, I was recaste as a Preserver and sent to the quarantine station. I didn't know why they chose me but one day I was assigned a very unusual task. A task that became mine for the rest of my time at the station. I'd always wondered why they'd taken such an incredible risk... having a Preserver attend to Eeo—"

"Who? Who are you talking about, Astorl?"

Kai couldn't recall anyone named Eeo on *The Nether*, but then he'd never learned the names of the twenty undercastes onboard.

"No, Kai, let me finish," she says, raising a hand, palm forward, to fend off interruption. "You asked for an explanation and now you're going to have to let me do it my way." She hesitates for a moment, almost as though she's waiting on Kai's assurance before she continues. "I wasn't aware what they had planned and that it really didn't make any difference who was assigned to Eeo. You see Eeo was held in a part of the station separate from the rest of the crew—"

"So the crew *were* alive?"

"I said to let me finish! Eeo was separated, as I explained, and there was no one but me to see to him. I thought I was taking care of him." She smiles. "Goes to show you, doesn't it? Anyway," she continues with a listless shrug, "one day when I was down in the supply room, I heard something. Someone really. It was Ush. She'd been hiding in the tunnels and corridors under the dock. Moving from place to place whenever she thought she was about to be discovered. She came out when she saw and recognised me. Gannin was right, Kai. They were building a Sub—"

"I know, Astorl. We've been there. Doon and me. We've seen the quarantine station."

"Then you probably saw the crew's quarters?"

Kai nods. "I think so."

"But you may not have found Eeo's. Not that it matters. I never told anyone about Ush," she says, taking up her story, "but I did tell Ush about the crew. I didn't tell her about Eeo though. I was never sure it was safe to. Not for Ush. Not for Eeo. It's probably not even safe to be telling you now but you're my friend, Kai, and I don't know of any other way to stop you from wasting the time you have left... the time we all have left... returning to Ularon City."

"Astorl, I don't understand."

"You said the Pedorate claim the crew of *The Nether* died. The crew, Eeo, the Dosers, the Preservers, anyone who was at the station."

"Yes, but—"

She cuts him off. "And that is true. Every last one of them, except for Ush and me. And I'm guessing that's the story Ush took with her to Ularon City. The story of their murder by the Pedorate."

"Astorl, you must be mistaken. It couldn't have happened that way."

"Were *you* there?" she challenges him, wringing the net in her hands. "I was. At first some of the crew just started getting sick. Then Eeo became ill. Finally, nearly everyone at the station was showing signs of the same sickness—"

"Then we've been wrong," Kai says, almost to himself. "They did bring back a plague."

"If there was a plague, Kai, then how do you explain that Ush and I *never* got sick?"

"Perhaps you're immune for some reason," Kai suggests, speaking up. "If there's even the possibility of immunity, then perhaps—"

"We weren't immune," Astorl snaps at him. "There was only one difference between Ush and me and everyone else at the station. We weren't eating food from the kitchen. I always ate with Ush and the food I brought her came directly from the storeroom."

"What are you trying to say?"

"Poison, Kai. They were poisoned. Everyone was fine until a new administrator came from Ularon City. None of the Dosers seemed to know who he was. I used to overhear them talking and it was only afterward I began to suspect that the Dosers who'd been there from the start probably weren't aware what was going on. One of the Dosers noticed I wasn't showing any symptoms. She became curious. Started asking me a lot of questions. What could I tell her? I didn't know then it was the food. If I had…" she leaves the rest unsaid.

"The food must have been contaminated."

"No, Kai. It was the Pedorate. I told Ush to go. She wanted me to come with her to Ularon City but I was scared. The Pedorate were in Ularon City and if I escaped, I knew they'd come looking for me. So Ush told me about the access to the ward, begged me to at least use that instead. And that's what I did. I found the access and, once out, I made my way here. It seemed the safest place to be. The best place to use the time we have left."

"Astorl, you keep saying that. What do you mean 'the time we have left'?"

"We can't win, Kai."

"Against the Pedorate?"

Astorl begins to laugh grimly. "The Pedorate!" she scoffs. "The Pedorate are nothing! We can't win the war with Eeo's people. They aren't *us*, Kai. Haven't you worked that out yet?"

All right, so he's been guilty of assuming it was a fellow Pedoran she was caring for, but it seems to him that Astorl is being too pessimistic about the outcome of any strike against the borders of Pedora.

"If someone from a territory outside Pedora was slipped onto *The Nether*," he objects, "then I think the Pedorate is well enough equipped to deal with any retribution for disposing of them."

Astorl is shaking her head. "Did you listen to me at all, Kai? You're still buying the lies the Pedorate is peddling. There was no plague. And Eeo was no spy from outside Pedora. Think, Kai! Think!" She taps her temple aggressively. "*The Nether* was out-journing. Eeo wasn't on the ship when they left. He *was* on the ship when they came back. Now how do you *explain* that?" she challenges him, glancing skyward.

When Kai himself glances skyward, her meaning suddenly hits home. His focus jerks back to Astorl as he weighs her outrageous claim.

"You don't expect me to believe that the crew of *The Nether* just captured a being from another world and brought him back?"

"I never said Eeo was *captured*," Astorl replies. "He came willingly. He was like a... ...a Talker, I suppose. And they *will* come looking for him," Astorl goes on, "and when they find out that he was killed, it's over for us. All of us. I doubt they'll care about the few friends Eeo had here. Pautune, if our positions were reversed, I think I'd kill us all, too."

Kai's head begins to shake. He can't seem to control it and isn't sure if it's due to simple disbelief or an inability to absorb what Astorl has been saying. If she's telling the truth, and he's never known Astorl to lie, then they most certainly have concerns. Serious concerns. Finally, he finds his tongue.

"But if there was no plague, then why was the crew even quarantined when they arrived? And why *kill* anyone? It doesn't make any sense."

"Oh, it makes a lot of sense, Kai," she answers with a sad, wry smile. "You're just not thinking it through."

From nowhere, an image pops into Kai's mind, an image of Doon, dressed in dusty coveralls, springing up from Saera Govek's desk in the Repository and making the same observation about her brother.

"Eeo's people are far more advanced than we are," Astorl is saying. "More advanced than you can ever imagine... and, unlike us, they're free. During the voyage, the crew taught him our language, so most of the time I spent with him, we talked. He told me things. His kind look a lot like us but inside... where it matters... they're very different. Eeo was harmless. Brilliant. But not brilliant enough to be wary. His people, when they come, will know better."

Kai places a gentle hand to Astorl's shoulder. "I can't believe that you're making this up intentionally," he says, "but I still don't see a reason for the Pedorate to have murdered anyone."

"I told you, Kai. Eeo's people are a lot like us. They look like us. They breathe the same kind of air. Use the same kind of resources. Eat similar food. Don't you get it?" she asks expectantly. "Our planet's as useful to them as it is to us. Try to think like the Pedorate. Consider how the Pedorate would react when confronted with the prospect of a race that's smarter... *and* casteless?"

His mother's concerns! They were sounder than even she had imagined.

"I think I'm finally beginning to see your point."

The Pedorate weren't ready to out-journ. Aren't still. Never will be. And now—like the proverbial ostel—they've stupidly stuck their head in the sand, as if that could make it go away just like they made all the witnesses go away and just like they're working to make anyone who has a stake in uncovering the truth go away.

"How long, Astorl?" Kai asks soberly.

She shrugs. "I don't know. A year. Two."

"Maybe they won't ever come," he suggests.

She's looking at him as indulgently as she would a naive young one. "They'll come. And now you understand why Ularon City would be the worst place to go. Here on the perimeter," she says, tapping the hul floor of Landers Island with her fingers, "we might have a little longer. And that's the best we can do."

"But Astorl, you're anticipating the worst," Kai insists. "If Eeo's people are as sophisticated as you say, then there's still hope."

"Not where the Pedorate is concerned."

They're interrupted by a call of 'A'yah'. Glancing up, Kai sees Doon making her way toward them.

"Rain's coming, Kai," she shouts, beckoning for him to come back. "We'd better get started or we'll be stuck here a while."

Kai looks to the horizon past the waterwall. A rain is indeed coming and judging by the mass of dark cloud tumbling in from the sea, it will be squally.

Should he tell Doon what Astorl has told him? That the time left for her, Mig, all of them is as limited as old Jak Inopo's.

"Why did you never tell anyone this before?" Kai asks, turning back to Astorl.

"How could I, Kai? I can't prove a word of it."

No, she couldn't. Even for him, it's a vast stretch to believe it. But he *knows* Astorl. He knows it *must* be true. His gaze drifts back to Doon, waiting for him on the shoreline. Of all of them, he thinks he might just feel the sorriest for her. With her unfaltering spirit, it seems she has the most to lose.

Kai rises, then reaches down to offer his hand to Astorl. Immediately he draws back when the weight of a small oversight he made earlier finally hits him—*not quite all the witnesses and champions have gone away*. There's still Astorl. His attention swings back to Doon. And there are still Journers, despite what appears to be the Pedorate's systematic attempt to cleanse the caste out of existence.

It's a crazy idea. Mad. Can't possibly succeed. But maybe. Just maybe...

"Astorl," he says, proffering his hand once more. "What if we offer Eeo's people an alternative to the Pedorate?"

"I don't understand what you mean," Astorl replies, taking his hand to rise.

"We still have a little time. We can prepare. Be ready for Eeo's people."

"Confront them? Kai, I told you—"

"No, Astorl, not confront them." He gives her hand a squeeze. "*Ally* with them."

"No," she says, shaking free. "We're too *few*."

"You think so?" he says. "Come on." Reclaiming her hand, he starts hurrying her away toward Doon. "There's more of us than you know."

When the first drops of rain begin to fall, Kai doesn't even notice. He's thinking of Gannaline-ro. Of Saera Govek and her brave brother. Of Veeda Teimbo and all the Crafters, Journers, Preservers, and Ditchers. Of every single member of every single caste in Pedora who's never been allowed a voice. He's even thinking of Ceilu. But it's the thought of Gaed that truly makes him smile. Gaed—and the oh so many others like him—who will go to whatever lengths it takes to be on the *winning* side. THE END

Thank you for reading THE JOURNING PLAGUE.
We hope you enjoyed it.

If you would like to be kept informed of further releases from
Hague Publishing, why not subscribe to our newsletter at:

www.HaguePublishing.com/subscribe.php

And if you loved the book and have a moment to spare we would
really appreciate a short review.
Your help in spreading the word is gratefully received.

About the Author

After obtaining a degree in geology, Shaune subsequently worked in geochemical laboratories, exploration companies, and a multinational scientific institute involved in exploration beneath the ocean floors.

Her short stories have appeared in AntipodeanSF, The Nautilus Engine, Blue Crow Magazine, and The Vandal and her novels, 'Bus Stop on a Strange Loop' and 'Balanced in An Angel's Eye', were released in 2011 and 2012, respectively.

'Cold Faith', the first book in The Safe Harbour Chronicle series, was released in May 2015 and, 'Faithless', the second in the trilogy, in April 2017, while the third and final volume, 'The Unforgotten', was released by Hague Publishing in November 2019.

'Once a Dog', which marked Shaune's venture into anthropomorphic story-telling, was ranked first runner-up in the 2018 Ursa Major Awards in the category of Best Novel.

Hague

Publishing

www.HaguePublishing.com

PO Box 451 Bassendean
Western Australia 6934